TREASURE TROVE

The trade journal of the publishing industry referred to the first volume of this anthology series as a "treasure trove." Truly it was, for it contained stories which have become the cornerstones of modern science fiction.

The discerning eyes of Isaac Asimov and Professor Greenberg (of the University of Wisconsin) keep up this high quality in this second in the series, representing the classic great stories of 1940, another year of the Golden Age of science fiction.

Once again this will prove to be a treasure trove to everyone who enjoys brilliant and "different" tales of the scientific and fantastic imagination. Here are real classics by such as Theodore Sturgeon, Jack Williamson, L. Sprague de Camp, Ross Rocklynne, and many more, including Asimov himself.

1940 in dating—but tomorrow in spirit!

Anthologies from DAW

ASIMOV PRESENTS THE GREAT SF STORIES: 1 (1939)

THE 1975 ANNUAL WORLD'S BEST SF
THE 1976 ANNUAL WORLD'S BEST SF
THE 1977 ANNUAL WORLD'S BEST SF
THE 1978 ANNUAL WORLD'S BEST SF
THE 1979 ANNUAL WORLD'S BEST SF

WOLLHEIM'S WORLD'S BEST SF: Vol. 1
WOLLHEIM'S WORLD'S BEST SF: Vol. 2

THE DAW SCIENCE FICTION READER

THE YEAR'S BEST HORROR STORIES: IV
THE YEAR'S BEST HORROR STORIES: V
THE YEAR'S BEST HORROR STORIES: VI
THE YEAR'S BEST HORROR STORIES: VII

THE YEAR'S BEST FANTASY STORIES: 1
THE YEAR'S BEST FANTASY STORIES: 2
THE YEAR'S BEST FANTASY STORIES: 3
THE YEAR'S BEST FANTASY STORIES: 4

THE BEST FROM THE REST OF THE WORLD

HEROIC FANTASY

ISAAC ASIMOV
Presents

THE GREAT SCIENCE FICTION STORIES

Volume 2, 1940

Edited by
Isaac Asimov and
Martin H. Greenberg

DAW BOOKS, INC.
DONALD A. WOLLHEIM, PUBLISHER
New York

COPYRIGHT ©, 1979, BY ISAAC ASIMOV
AND MARTIN H. GREENBERG.

All Rights Reserved.

Cover designed by Jack Gaughan.

Complete list of copyright acknowledgments for the contents will be found on the following pages.

FIRST PRINTING, AUGUST 1979

1 2 3 4 5 6 7 8 9

DAW TRADEMARK REGISTERED
U.S. PAT. OFF. MARCA
REGISTRADA, HECHO EN U.S.A.

PRINTED IN U.S.A.

ACKNOWLEDGMENTS

THE DWINDLING SPHERE by Willard Hawkins. Copyright 1940 by Street & Smith, Inc., 1968 © by Condé Nast Publications, Inc. By arrangement with the Scott Meredith Literary Agency, Inc.

THE AUTOMATIC PISTOL by Fritz Leiber. Copyright 1940, 1968, by Fritz Leiber. By permission of the author.

HINDSIGHT by Jack Williamson. Copyright 1940 by Street & Smith, Inc., 1968 © by Condé Nast Publications, Inc. By permission of the author.

POSTPAID TO PARADISE by Robert Arthur. Copyright © 1940 by Robert Arthur. Reprinted by permission of The Regents of the University of Michigan.

INTO THE DARKNESS by Ross Rocklynne. Copyright 1940 by Fictioneers, Inc.; published by permission of the author's agent, Forrest J. Ackerman.

DARK MISSION by Lester Del Rey. Copyright 1940 by Street & Smith, Inc., 1968 © by Condé Nast Publications, Inc. Reprinted by permission of the author and the author's agents, Scott Meredith Literary Agency, Inc.

IT by Theodore Sturgeon. Copyright 1940 by Street & Smith, Inc., 1968 © by Theodore Sturgeon. By permission of the author and his agents, Kirby McCauley, Ltd.

VAULT OF THE BEAST by A. E. van Vogt. Copyright 1940 by Street & Smith, Inc., 1968 © by Condé Nast Publications, Inc. By permission of the author and the author's agent, Forrest J Ackerman.

THE IMPOSSIBLE HIGHWAY by Oscar J. Friend. Copyright 1940 by Better Publications, Inc., 1951 by Random House, 1968 © by Oscar J. Friend. By permission of Kittie Friend West.

QUIETUS by Ross Rocklynne. Copyright 1940 by Street & Smith, Inc., 1968 © by Condé Nast Publications, Inc. By permission of the author's agent, Forrest J Ackerman.

STRANGE PLAYFELLOW by Isaac Asimov. Copyright 1940 by Fictioneers, Inc., 1968 © by Isaac Asimov. By permission of the author.

THE WARRIOR RACE by L. Sprague de Camp. Copyright 1940 by Street & Smith, Inc., 1968 © by L. Sprague de Camp. By permission of the author.

FAREWELL TO THE MASTER by Harry Bates. Copyright 1940 by Street & Smith, Inc., 1968 © by Condé Nast Publications, Inc. By permission of the author's agent, Forrest J Ackerman.

BUTYL AND THE BREATHER by Theodore Sturgeon. Copyright 1940 by Street & Smith, Inc., 1968 © by Theodore Sturgeon. By permission of the author and his agents, Kirby McCauley, Ltd.

THE EXALTED by L. Sprague de Camp. Copyright 1940 by Street & Smith, Inc., 1968 © by L. Sprague de Camp. By permission of the author.

OLD MAN MULLIGAN by P. Schuyler Miller. Copyright 1940 by Street & Smith, Inc., 1968 © by Condé Nast Publications, Inc. By permission of Mary E. Drake.

Table of Contents

Introduction	The Editors	9
THE DWINDLING SPHERE	Willard Hawkins	13
THE AUTOMATIC PISTOL	Fritz Leiber	30
HINDSIGHT	Jack Williamson	46
POSTPAID TO PARADISE	Robert Arthur	65
INTO THE DARKNESS	Ross Rocklynne	80
DARK MISSION	Lester Del Rey	108
IT	Theodore Sturgeon	125
VAULT OF THE BEAST	A. E. van Vogt	149
THE IMPOSSIBLE HIGHWAY	Oscar J. Friend	176
QUIETUS	Ross Rocklynne	191
STRANGE PLAYFELLOW	Isaac Asimov	206
THE WARRIOR RACE	L. Sprague De Camp	219
FAREWELL TO THE MASTER	Harry Bates	237
BUTYL AND THE BREATHER	Theodore Sturgeon	276
THE EXALTED	L. Sprague De Camp	297
OLD MAN MULLIGAN	P. Schuyler Miller	321

Introduction

In the world outside reality, it was another bad year. The war that had started in 1939 continued, and on April 9 Germany invaded Norway and Denmark. On May 10, under tremendous pressure, Neville Chamberlain took his umbrella and went home, dissolving the British government, which was replaced by one under the leadership of Winston S. Churchill. On the same day, Germany invaded Belgium and Holland. Within three days the Dutch army surrendered and Churchill, noting the despair now growing in many British hearts, responded with his famous "Blood, Tears, Toil and Sweat," speech. It had no effect on the fighting, as Belgium surrendered on the 28th, and the British Expeditionary Force was evacuated from the beaches of Dunkirk, barely escaping destruction at the hands of the advancing Germans.

On June 14, the Germans entered Paris and France formally capitulated on the 22nd. The Battle of Britain raged during the daylight hours through the month of August, reaching a peak the week of 11-18th, as the RAF fought to survive—and the Germans switched to city bombing on the night of the 23rd, initiating the Blitz on London. On September 3 the U.S. drew closer to the war as Roosevelt concluded a "Lend Lease" arrangement with the British that exchanged American destroyers for long-term leases on bases in Newfoundland and in the Caribbean.

On September 16, the Selective Training and Service Act went into effect in the United States, and the draft began. Few cards were burned.

On November 3 Franklin Delano Roosevelt defeated Wendell Wilkie and prepared to start his third term as President of the United States.

During 1940 Albert Einstein presented a paper in which he argued that there was no theory that could provide a logical basis for physics as it was presently formulated. Carl Jung published *The Interpretation of Personality*. Tom Harmon of the University of Michigan won the Heisman Trophy. Darius Milhaud composed *Medea*. Ernest Hemingway made a big splash with *For Whom the Bell Tolls*, while Minnesota captured the national college football championship. Charlie Chaplin directed and starred in *The Great Dictator* (Hitler was not amused). There were 32,400,000 private cars in the United States. The record for the mile run was *still* the 4:06:4 set in 1937 by Sydney Wooderson.

Construction of the first cyclotron began at the University of California. George Santayana published *The Realm of Spirit*. Whistler painted "Miss Laura Ridly." Alice Marble was still the best woman tennis player and Joe Louis was still heavyweight champion of the world. Igor Stravinsky wrote his *Symphony in C*. Eugene O'Neill's masterpiece, *Long Day's Journey into Night* was written, but would have to wait sixteen years to see production. Lawson Little won the U.S. Open Golf Championship, while the great Jimmy Demaret took the Masters.

Alfred Hitchcock's *Rebecca* and *Gaslight* were two of the top films of the year. Under the direction of Howard Florey, a team of researchers developed penicillin. The most widely sung song of the year was the German Army's "Lili Marlene." James Stewart and Ginger Rogers won Academy Awards. Johnny Mize led the majors in home runs with 43 (Hank Greenberg had 41), while somebody named Debs Garms took the batting title with a .355 average. There were 264,000 divorces in the United States. Death took Leon Trotsky (of an ice-pick in the brain) and Neville Chamberlain (of disillusionment as well as cancer).

Mel Brooks was still Melvin Kaminsky.

But in the real world it was another very good year.

In the real world the second World Science Fiction Convention (the Chicon) was held in faraway Chicago. In the real world nineteen-year-old Fred Pohl became editor (at $10 a week) of two new science fiction magazines—*Astonishing Stories* and *Super Science Stories*, while *three* more magazines, *Captain Future*, *Science Fiction Quarterly* and *Comet Stories* also saw the light of day for the first time.

In the real world, more important people made their maiden voyages into reality: in February—Leigh Brackett with *Martian Quest*, and H. B. Fyfe with *Locked Out*; in March—James Blish with *Emergency Refueling*; in April—

C. M. Kornbluth and Richard Wilson with *Stepsons of Mars*; and in July—Frederick Pohl with the co-authored *Before the Universe*.

More wonderous things happened in the real world: "Typewriter in the Sky" by L. Ron Hubbard and "Darker Than You Think" by Jack Williamson were published in *Unknown*. *Astounding Science Fiction* had three great serials—*If This Goes On* by Robert A. Heinlein, *Final Blackout* by L. Ron Hubbard (what a great one he could have been), and the immmortal *Slan* by A. E. van Vogt.

Death took fantasy writers E. F. Benson and Talbot Mundy as well as Farnsworth Wright, the great editor of the immortal *Weird Tales*.

But the distant wings were beating as Angela Carter, Thomas Disch, Peter Haining, Alexei Panshin, and Norman Spinrad were born.

Let us travel back to that honored year of 1940 and enjoy the best stories that the real world bequeathed to us.

EDITORIAL NOTE

The reader should note that three selections by Robert A. Heinlein are missing because arrangements for their use could not be made. We regret their absence and direct the reader to *The Past Through Tomorrow* (New York: Putnam, 1967, paperback edition by Berkley), which contains all three stories.

REQUIEM*

Astounding Science Fiction
January

by Robert A. Heinlein (1907-   )

1940 was to be the year of Robert Heinlein, and this story is the first of three in this book. "Requiem" is one of his most memorable stories, written at a time when the moon was a mystery and a fascination to most people. The struggle of the heroic Harriman to reach his objective left its mark on all who read the story.

Forget the faulty predictions and enjoy a tale that contains the elixir of science fiction—the sense of wonder.

(How much more exciting the thought of reaching the moon was *before* we reached it. We had the moon all to ourselves then. Bob's fascination with the moon weaved itself through many stories and reached a peak with the first adult science fiction movie, "Destination: Moon," which Bob, of course, wrote. I never forgave Bob, though, for introducing—or allowing the introduction of—a comic Brooklynite. It was such a silly stereotype and Bob *knew* I was from Brooklyn and would resent it. At least they might have obtained an actor who had lived in Brooklyn and spoke the language. The actor they did get, whom I have never seen before or since, must have been brought up in Montana for his Brooklyn accent was simply pitiful. I.A.)

* See note following end of Introduction.

THE DWINDLING SPHERE

Astounding Science Fiction
March

by Willard Hawkins

This fine story was rescued from oblivion by Laurence M. Janifer, who reprinted it in Master's Choice. *Although early science fiction had (and has) a reputation for accurate prediction and stories about "today's fiction, tomorrow's fact," there were some subjects that received relatively little attention. This was especially true of issues like resource consumption, with too many writers simply "inventing" new sources of energy or not dealing with the problem at all.*

Here is one of the early few that considered the consequences of this particular human activity.

(It's a lucky thing I have good old Marty around. I like to think I know every story that was published in the 1930s and 1940s but for some reason I missed this one completely and I don't know Willard Hawkins either then or now. Very upsetting, especially since this is one more story that discusses fission before Hiroshima. Of course, fission of elements less complex than iron involves an *input* of energy, but what the heck. No one's perfect. The important thing in the story is a certain element of satire.)

I.A.

EXTRACTS FROM THE DIARY OF
FRANK BAXTER, B.S., M.Sc.

June 23, 1945. I thought today I was on the track of something, but the results, while remarkable in their way, were disapppointing. The only thing of importance I can be said to have demonstrated is that, with my new technique of neutron bombardment, it is unnecessary to confine experiments to the heavier elements. This broadens the field of investigation enormously. Substituted a lump of common coal for uranium in today's experiment, and it was reduced to a small cinder. Probably oxidized, owing to a defect in the apparatus or in my procedure.

However, it seems remarkable that, despite the almost instantaneous nature of the combustion, there was no explosion. Nor, as far as I could detect, was any heat generated. In fact, I unthinkingly picked up the cinder—a small, smooth buttonlike object—and it was scarcely warm.

June 24, 1945. Repeated yesterday's experiment carefully checking each step, with results practically identical to yesterday's. Can it be that I am on the verge of success? But that is absurd. If—as might be assumed from the evidence—my neutron bombardment started a self-perpetuating reaction which continued until every atom in the mass had been subjected to fission, enormous energy would have been generated. In fact, I would no longer be here, all in one piece, to tell about it. Even the combustion of my lump of coal at such a practically instantaneous rate would be equivalent to exploding so much dynamite.

It is very puzzling, for the fact remains that the lump has been reduced to a fraction of its original weight and size. There is, after all, only one possible answer: the greater part of its mass must have been converted into energy. The question, then, is what became of the energy?

June 28, 1945. Have been continuing my experiments, checking and rechecking. I have evidently hit upon some new principle in the conversion of matter into energy. Here are some of the results thus far:

Tried the same experiment with a chuck of rock—identical result. Tried it with a lump of earth, a piece of wood, a brass doorknob. Only difference in results was the size and consistency of the resulting cinder. Have weighed the substance each time, then the residue after neutron bombardment. The original substance seems to be reduced to approximately one twentieth of its original mass, although this varies somewhat according to the strength of the magnetic field and various adjustments in the apparatus. These factors also seem to affect the composition of the cinder.

THE DWINDLING SPHERE

The essence of the problem, however, has thus far baffled me. Why is it that I cannot detect the force generated? What is its nature? Unless I can solve this problem, the whole discovery is pointless.

I have written to my old college roommate, Bernard Ogilvie, asking him to come and check my results. He is a capable engineer and I have faith in his honesty and common sense—even though he appears to have been lured away from scientific pursuits by commercialism.

July 15, 1945. Ogilvie has been here now for three days. He is greatly excited, but I am sorry that I sent for him. He has given me no help at all on my real problem—in fact, he seems more interested in the by-products than in the experiment itself. I had hoped he would help me to solve the mystery of what becomes of the energy generated by my process. Instead, he appears to be fascinated by those little chunks of residue—the cinders.

When I showed that it was possible, by certain adjustments in the apparatus, to control their texture and substance, he was beside himself with excitement. The result is that I have spent all my time since his arrival in making these cinders. We have produced them in consistency ranging all the way from hard little buttons to a mushy substance resembling cheese.

Analysis shows them to be composed of various elements, chiefly carbon and silica. Ogilvie appears to think there has been an actual transmutation of elements into this final result. I question it. The material is simply a form of ash—a residue.

We have enlarged the apparatus and installed a hopper, into which we shovel rock, debris—in fact, anything that comes handy, including garbage and other waste. If my experiment after all proves a failure, I shall at least have the ironic satisfaction of having produced an ideal incinerator. Ogilvie declares there is a fortune in that alone.

July 20, 1945. Bernard Ogilvie has gone. Now I can get down to actual work again. He took with him a quantity of samples and plans for the equipment. Before he left, he revealed what is on his mind. He thinks my process may revolutionize the plastics industry. What a waste of time to have called him in! A fine mind spoiled by commercialism. With an epochal discovery in sight, all he can think of is that here is an opportunity to convert raw material which costs practically nothing into commercial gadgets. He thinks the stuff can be molded and shaped—perhaps through a matrix principle incorporated right in the apparatus.

Partly, I must confess, to get rid of him, I signed the agreement he drew up. It authorizes him to patent the process in my name, and gives me a major interest in all subsidiary devices and patents that may be developed by his engineers. He himself is to have what he calls the promotion rights, but there is some sort of a clause whereby the control reverts wholly to me or to my heirs at his death. Ogilvie says it will mean millions to both of us.

He undoubtedly is carried away by his imagination. What could I do with such an absurd sum of money? However, a few thousand dollars might come in handy for improved equipment. I must find a means of capturing and controlling that energy.

EXTRACTS FROM THE DIARY OF QUENTIN BAXTER, PRESIDENT OF PLASTOSCENE PRODUCTS, INC.

August 3, 2065. I have made a discovery today which moved me profoundly—so profoundly that I have opened this journal so that my own thoughts and reactions may be likewise recorded for posterity. Diary-keeping has heretofore appeared to me as a rather foolish vanity—it now appears in an altogether different light.

The discovery which so altered my viewpoint was of a diary kept by my great-grandfather, Frank Baxter, the actual inventor of plastoscene.

I have often wondered what sort of a man this ancestor of mine could have been. History tells us almost nothing about him. I feel that I know him as intimately as I know my closest associates. And what a different picture this diary gives from the prevailing concept!

Most of us have no doubt thought of the discoverer of the plastoscene principle as a man who saw the need for a simple method of catering to humanity's needs—one which would supplant the many laborious makeshifts of his day—and painstakingly set out to evolve it.

Actually, the discovery appears to have been an accident. Frank Baxter took no interest in its development—regarded it as of little account. Think of it! An invention more revolutionary than the discovery of fire, yet its inventor failed entirely to grasp its importance! To the end of his days it was to him merely a by-product. He died considering himself a failure, because he was unable to attain the goal he sought—the creation of atomic power.

In a sense, much of the credit apparently belongs to his friend Bernard Ogilvie, who grasped the possibilities inherent in the new principle. Here again, what a different picture the diary gives from that found in our schoolbooks! The historians would have us regard Frank Baxter as a sort of master mind, Bernard Ogilvie as his humble disciple and Man Friday.

Actually, Ogilvie was a shrewd promoter who saw the possibilities of the discovery and exploited them—not especially to benefit humanity, but for personal gain. We must give him credit, however, for a scrupulous honesty which was amazing for his time. It would have been easy for him to take advantage of the impractical, dreamy scientist. Instead, he arranged that the inventor of the process should reap its rewards, and it is wholly owing to his insistence that control reverted to our family, where it has remained for more than a century.

All honor to these two exceptional men!

Neither, it is true, probably envisioned the great changes that would be wrought by the discovery. My ancestor remained to the end of his days dreamy and aloof, concerned solely with his futile efforts to trap the energy which he was sure he had released. The wealth which rolled up for him through Plastoscene Products, Inc.—apparently the largest individual fortune of his time—was to him a vague abstraction. I find a few references to it in his diary, but they are written in a spirit of annoyance. He goes so far as to mention once—apparently exasperated because the responsibilities of his position called him away from his experiments for a few hours—that he would like to convert the millions into hard currency and pour them into a conversion hopper, where at least they might be turned into something useful.

It is strange, by the way, that the problem he posed has never been demonstrably solved. Scientists still are divided in their allegiance to two major theories—one, that the force generated by this conversion of elements escapes into the fourth dimension; the other that it is generated in the form of radiations akin to cosmic rays, which are dissipated with a velocity approaching the infinite. These rays do not affect ordinary matter, according to the theory, because they do not impinge upon it, but instead pass through it, as light passes through a transparent substance.

August 5, 2065. I have read and reread my grandfather's diary, and confess that I more and more find in him a kindred spirit. His way of life seems to me infinitely more appealing than that which inheritance has imposed upon me. The responsibilities resting on my shoulders, as reigning head of the Baxter dynasty, become exceedingly onerous at times. I even find myself wondering whether plastoscene has, after all, proved such an unmixed blessing for mankind.

Perhaps the greatest benefits may lie in the future. Certainly each stage in its development has been marked by economic readjustments—some of them well-night world-shattering. I have often been glad that I did not live through those earlier days of stress, when industry after industry was wiped out by the remorseless juggernaut of technological progress. When, for example, hundreds of thousands were thrown out of employment in the metal-mining and -refining and allied industries. It was inevitable that plastoscene substitutes, produced at a fraction of the cost from common dirt of the fields, should wipe out this industry—but the step could have been taken, it seems to me, without subjecting the dispossessed workers and employers to such hardship, thereby precipitating what amounted to a civil war. When we pause to think of it, almost every article in common use today represents one or more of those industries which was similarly wiped out, and on which vast numbers of people depended for their livelihood.

We have, at length, achieved a form of stable society—but I, for one, am not wholly satisfied with it. What do we have? A small owning class—a cluster of corporations grouped around the supercorporation, Plastoscene Products, Inc., of which I am—heaven help me!—the hereditary ruler. Next, a situation-holding class, ranging from scientists, executives and technicians down to the mechanical workers. Here again—because there are so few situations open, compared with the vast reservoir of potential producers—the situation holders have developed what amounts to a system of hereditary succession. I am told that it is almost impossible for one whose father was not a situation holder even to obtain the training necessary to qualify him for any of the jealously guarded positions.

Outside of this group is that great, surging mass, the major part of human society. These millions, I grant, are fed and clothed and housed and provided with a standard of living which their ancestors would have regarded as luxurious. Nevertheless, their lot is pitiful. They have no incentives; their status is that of a subject class. Particularly do I find distasteful the law which makes it a crime for any member of this enforced leisure group to be caught engaging in useful labor. The appalling number of convictions in our courts for this crime shows that there is in mankind an instinct to perform useful service, which cannot be eradicated merely by passing laws.

The situation is unhealthy as well from another standpoint. To me it seems a normal thing that society should progress. Yet we cannot close our eyes to the fact that the most highly skilled scientific minds the world has ever known have failed to produce a worthwhile advance in technology for over a quarter of a century. Has science become sterile? No. In fact, every schoolboy knows the answer.

Our scientists do not dare to announce their discoveries. I am supposed to shut my eyes to what I know—that every vital discovery along the lines of technology has been suppressed. The plain, blunt truth is that we dare not introduce any technical advance which would eliminate more situation holders. A major discovery—one that reduced an entire class of situation holders to enforced leisure—would precipitate another revolution.

Is human society, as a result of its greatest discovery, doomed to sterility?

October 17, 2089. It has been nearly a quarter of a century since I first read the diary of my great-grandfather, Frank Baxter. I felt an impulse to get it out to show to my son, and before I realized it I had reread the volume in its entirety. It stirred me even more than it did back in my younger days. I must preserve its crumbling pages in facsimile, on permanent plastoscene parchment, so that later descendants—finding our two journals wrapped together— will thrill as I have thrilled to that early record of achievement.

The reading has crystallized thoughts long dormant in my mind. I am nearing the end of the trail. Soon I will turn over the presidency of Plastoscene Products, Inc. to my son—if he desires it. Perhaps he will have other ideas. He is now a full-fledged Pl. T.D. Doctor of Plastoscene Technology. It may be that power and position will mean as little to him as they have come to mean to me. I shall send for him tomorrow.

October 18, 2089. I have had my discussion with Philip, but I fear I bungled matters. He talked quite freely of his experiments. It seems that he has been working along the line of approach started by Levinson some years ago. As we know, the plastoscene principle in use involves the making of very complex adjustments. That is to say, if we wish to manufacture some new type of object—say a special gyroscope bearing—the engineer in charge first sets the machine to produce material of a certain specific hardness and temper, then he adjusts the controls which govern size and shape, and finally, having roughly achieved the desired result, he refines the product with micrometer adjustments—but largely through the trial-and-error method—until the quality, dimensions and so on meet the tests of his precision instruments. If the object involved is complex—involving two or more compounds, for example—the adjustments are correspondingly more difficult. We have not succeeded in producing palatable foodstuffs, though our engineers have turned out some messes which are claimed to have nourishing qualities. I suspect that the engineers have purposely made them nauseating to the taste.

True, once the necessary adjustments have been made, they are recorded on microfilm. Thereafter, it is only necessary to feed this film into the control box, where the electric eye automatically makes all the adjustments for which the skill of the technician was initially required. Levinson, however, proposed to reproduce natural objects in plastoscene by photographic means.

It is this process which Philip appparently has perfected. His method involves a three-dimensional "scanning" device which records the texture, shape and the exact molecular structure of the object to be reproduced. The record is made on microfilm, which then needs only to be passed through the control box to re-create the object as many times as may be required.

"Think of the saving of effort!" Philip remarked enthusiastically. "Not only can objects of the greatest intricacy be reproduced without necessity of assembling, but even natural foods can be created in all their flavor and nourishing quality. I have eaten synthetic radishes—I have even tasted synthetic chicken—that could not be told from the original which formed its matrix."

"You mean," I demanded in some alarm, "that you can reproduce life?"

His face clouded. "No. That is a quality that seems to elude the scanner. But I can reproduce the animal, identical with its live prototype down to the last nerve tip and hair, except that it is inert—lifeless. The radishes I spoke of will not grow in soil—they cannot reproduce themselves—but chemically and in cell structure they image the originals."

"Philip," I declared, "this is an amazing achievement! It removes the last limitation upon the adaptability of plastoscene. It means that we can produce not merely machine parts but completely assembled machines. It means that foodstuffs can be—"

I stopped, brought to myself by his sudden change in expression.

"True, Father," he observed coldly, "except that it happens to be a pipe dream. I did not expect that you would be taken in by my fairy tale. I have an engagement and must go."

He hurried from the room before I could get my wits about me.

October 23, 2089. Philip has been avoiding me, but I managed at last to corner him.

I began this time by mentioning that it would soon be necessary for me to turn over the burden of Plastoscene Products, Inc. to him as my logical successor.

He hesitated, then blurted, "Father, I know this is going to hurt you, but I don't want to carry on the succession. I prefer to remain just a cog in the engineering department."

"Responsibility," I reminded him, "is something that cannot be honorably evaded."

"Why should it be my responsibility?" he demanded vehemently. "I didn't ask to be your son."

"Nor," I countered, "did I ask to be my father's son, nor the great-grandson of a certain inventor who died in the twentieth century. Philip, I want you to do one thing for me. Take this little book, read it, then bring it back and tell me what you think of it." I handed him Frank Baxter's diary.

October 24, 2089. Philip brought back the diary today. He admitted that he had sat up all night reading it.

"But I'm afraid the effect isn't what you expected," he told me frankly. "Instead of instilling the idea that we Baxters have a divine mission to carry on the dynasty, it makes me feel that our responsibility is rather to undo the damage already caused by our meddling. That old fellow back there—Frank Baxter—didn't intend to produce this hideous stuff."

"Hideous stuff?" I demanded.

"Don't be shocked, Father," he said, a trifle apologetically. "I can't help feeling rather deeply about this. Perhaps you think we're better off than people in your great-grandfather's time. I doubt it. They had work to do. There may have been employment problems, but it wasn't the enforced idleness of our day. Look at Frank Baxter—he could work and invent things with the assurance that he was doing something to advance mankind. He wasn't compelled to cover up his discoveries for fear they'd cause further—"

He stopped suddenly, as if realizing that he had said more than he intended.

"My boy," I told him, speaking slowly, "I know just how you feel—and knowing it gives me more satisfaction than you can realize."

He stared at me, bewildered. "You mean—you don't want me to take on the succession?"

I unfolded my plan.

FROM THE DIARY OF RAN RAXLER, TENTH-RANKING HONOR STUDENT, NORTH-CENTRAL FINALS, CLASS OF 2653

December 28, 2653. I have had two thrills today—an exciting discovery right on the heels of winning my diploma in the finals. Being one of the high twenty practically assures me of a chance to serve in the production pits this year.

But the discovery—I must record that first of all. It consists of a couple of old diaries. I found them in a chestful of family heirlooms which I rescued as they were about to be tossed into the waste tube. In another minute, they would have been on their way to the community plastoscene converter.

There has been a legend in our family that we are descended from the original discoverer of plastoscene, and this find surely tends to prove it. Even the name is significant. Frank Baxter. Given names as well as surnames are passed down through the generations. My grandfather before me was Ran Raxler. The dropping of a letter here, the corruption of another there, could easily have resulted in the modification of Frank Baxter to Ran Raxler.

What a thrill it will be to present to the world the authentic diary of the man who discovered the plastoscene principle! Not the impossible legendary figure, but the actual, flesh-and-blood man. And what a shock it will be to many! For it appears that Frank Baxter stumbled upon this discovery quite by accident, and regarded it to the end of his days as an unimportant by-product of his experiments.

And this later Baxter—Quentin—who wrote the companion diary and sealed the two together. What a martyr to progress he proved himself—he and his son, Philip. The diary throws an altogether different light on their motives than has been recorded in history. Instead of being selfish oligarchs who were overthrown by a mass uprising, this diary reveals that they themselves engineered the revolution.

The final entry in Quentin Baxter's diary consists of these words: "I unfolded my plan." The context—when taken with the undisputed facts of history—makes it clear what the plan must have been. As I reconstruct it, the Baxters, father and son, determined to abolish the control of plastoscene by a closed corporation of hereditary owners, and to make it the property of the whole people.

The son had perfected the scanning principle which gives plastoscene its present unlimited range. His impulse was to withhold it—in fact, it had become a point of honor among technicians to bury such discoveries, after showing them to a few trusted associates. Incomprehensible? Perhaps so at first, but not when we understand the upheavals such discoveries might cause in the form of society then existing. To make this clear, I should, perhaps, point to the record of history, which proves that up to the time of plastoscene, foodstuffs had been largely produced by growing them in the soil. This was accomplished through a highly technical process, which I cannot explain, but I am told that the University of Antarctica maintains an experimental laboratory in which the method is actually demonstrated to advanced classes. Moreover, we know what these foods were like through the microfilm matrices which still reproduce some of them for us.

The right to produce such foods for humanity's needs was jealously guarded by the great agricultural aristocracy. And, of course, this entire situation-holding class, together with many others, would be abolished by Philip's invention.

We know what happened. Despite the laws prohibiting the operation of plastoscene converters except by licensed technicians and situation holders, contraband machines suddenly began to appear everywhere among the people. Since these machines were equipped with the new scanning principle, it is obvious, in view of the diary, that they must have been deliberately distributed at strategic points by the Baxters.

At first, the contraband machines were confiscated and destroyed—but since they were, of course, capable of reproducing themselves through the matrix library of microfilm which was standard equipment, the effort to keep pace with their spread through the masses was hopeless. The ruling hierarchies appealed to the law, and to the Baxters, whose hereditary control of the plastoscene monopoly had been supposedly a safeguard against its falling into the hands of the people as a whole. The Baxters, father and son, then played their trump card. They issued a proclamation deeding the plastoscene principle in perpetuity to all the people. History implies that they were forced to do this—but fails to explain how or why. There was a great deal of confusion and bloodshed during this period; no wonder that historians jumped at conclusions—even assuming that the Baxters were assassinated by revolutionists, along with others of the small owning group who made a last stand, trying to preserve their monopolies. In light of Quentin Baxter's diary, there is far better ground for believing that they were executed by members of their own class, who regarded them as traitors.

We should be thankful indeed that those ancient days of war and bloodshed are over. Surely such conditions can never reappear on Earth. What possible reason can there be for people to rise up against each other? Just as we can supply all our needs with plastoscene, so can our neighbors on every continent supply theirs.

March 30, 2654. I have completed my service in the production pits, and thrilling weeks they have been. To have a part in the great process which keeps millions of people alive, even for a brief four weeks' period, makes one feel that life has not been lived in vain.

One could hardly realize, without such experience, what enormous quantities of raw material are required for the sustenance and needs of the human race. How fortunate I am to

THE DWINDLING SPHERE

have been one of the few to earn this privilege of what the ancients called "work."

The problem must have been more difficult in the early days. Where we now distribute raw-material concentrates in the form of plastoscene-B, our forefathers had to transport the actual rock as dredged from the gravel pits. Even though the process of distribution was mechanical and largely automatic, still it was cumbersome, since material for conversion is required in a ratio of about twenty to one as compared with the finished product.

Today, of course, we have the intermediate process, by which soil and rock are converted at the pits into blocks of plastoscene-B. This represents, in a sense, the conversion process in an arrested stage. The raw material emerges in these blocks reduced to a tenth of its original weight and an even smaller volume than it will occupy in the finished product—since the mass has been increased by close packing of molecules.

A supply of concentrate sufficient to last the ordinary family for a year can now easily be stored in the standard-sized converter, and even the huge community converters have a capacity sufficient to provide for all the building, paving of roadways, recarpeting of recreation grounds, and like purposes, that are likely to be required in three months' time. I understand that experimental stations in South America are successfully introducing liquid concentrate, which can be piped directly to the consumers from the vast production pits.

I was amused on my last day by a question asked by a ten-year-old boy, the son of one of the supervisors. We stood on a rampart overlooking one of the vast production pits, several hundred feet deep and miles across—the whole space filled with a bewildering network of towers, girders, cranes, spires and cables, across and through which flashed transports of every variety. Far below us, the center of all this activity, could be discerned the huge conversion plant, in which the rock is reduced to plastoscene-B.

The little boy looked with awe at the scene, then turned his face upward, demanding, "What are we going to do when this hole gets so big that it takes up the whole world?"

We laughed, but I could sympathize with the question. Man is such a puny creature that it is difficult for him to realize what an infinitesimal thing on the Earth's surface is a cavity which to him appears enormous. The relationship, I should say, is about the same as a pinprick to a ball which a child can toss in the air.

FROM THE INTRODUCTION TO OUR EIGHTY YEARS' WAR, SIGNED BY GLUX GLUXTON, CHIEF HISTORIAN, THE NAPHALI INSTITUTE OF SCIENCE (DATED AS OF THE SIXTH DAY, SIXTH LUNAR MONTH, YEAR 10,487)

The Eighty Years' War is over. It has been concluded by a treaty of eternal amity signed at Latex on the morning of the twenty-ninth day of the fifth month.

By the terms of the treaty, all peoples of the world agree to subject themselves to the control by the World Court. The Court, advised through surveys continuously conducted by the International Institute of Science, will have absolute authority over the conversion of basic substance into plastoscene, to the end that further disputes between regions and continents shall be impossible.

To my distinguished associates and to myself was allotted the task of compiling a history of the causes behind this prolonged upheaval and of its course. How well we have succeeded posterity must judge. In a situation so complex, how, indeed, may one declare with assurance which were the essential causes? Though known as *the* Eighty Years' War, a more accurate expression would be "the Eighty Years *of* War," for the period has been one marked by a constant succession of wars—of outbreaks originating spontaneously and from divers causes in various parts of the world.

Chief among the basic causes, of course, were the disputes between adjoining districts over the right to extend their conversion pits beyond certain boundaries. Nor can we overlook the serious situation precipitated when it was realized that the Antarctican sea-water conversion plants were sucking up such great quantities that the level of the oceans was actually being lowered—much as the Great Lakes once found on the North American continent were drained of their water centuries ago. Disputes, alliances and counteralliances, regions arrayed against each other, and finally engines of war raining fearful destruction. What an unprecedented bath of blood the world has endured!

The whole aim, from this time forth, will be to strip off the earth's surface evenly, so that it shall become smooth and even, not rough and unsightly and covered with abandoned pits as now viewed from above. To prevent a too rapid lowering of sea level, it is provided that Antarctica and some other sections which have but a limited amount of land surface shall be supplied with concentrate from the more favored regions.

Under such a treaty, signed with fervent good will by the representatives of a war-weary world population, is it farfetched to assert that permanent peace has been assured? Your historian holds that it is not.

FROM THE REPORT OF RAGNAR DUGH, DELEGATE TO THE WORLD PEACE CONFERENCE, TO THE 117th DISTRICT (CIRCUIT 1092, REV. 148)

Honored confrères: It gives me pleasure to present, on behalf of the district which has honored me as its representative, concurrence in the conditions for peace as proposed in the majority report.

As I view your faces in the televisor, I see in them the same sense of deep elation that I feel in the thought that this exhausting era of bloodshed and carnage has run its course, and that war is to be rendered impossible from this time forth. Is this too strong a statement? I read in your eyes that it is not, for we are at last abolishing the cause of war— namely, the overcrowding of the earth's surface.

The proposed restrictions may seem drastic, but the human race will accustom itself to them. And let us remember that they would be even more drastic if the wars themselves had not resulted in depopulating the world to a great extent. I am glad that it has not been found necessary to impose a ten-year moratorium on all childbearing. As matters stand, by limiting childbirth to a proportion of one child per circuit of the sun for each three deaths within any given district, scientists agree that the population of the earth will be reduced at a sufficient rate to relieve the tension.

The minority report, which favors providing more room for the population by constructing various levels or concentric shells, which would gird the world's surface and to which addditional levels would be added as needed, I utterly condemn. It is impractical chiefly for the reason that the conversion of so much material into these various dwelling surfaces would cause a serious shrinkage in the earth's mass.

Let us cast our votes in favor of the majority proposition, thus insuring a long life for the human race and for the sphere on which we dwell, and removing the last cause of war between peoples of the earth.

FROM THE MEMOIRS OF XLAR XVII, PRINCEP OF PLES

Cycle 188, 400-43. What an abomination is this younger generation! I am glad the new rules limit offspring to not more than one in a district per cycle. My nephew, Ryk LVX, has been saturating himself with folklore at the Museum of Antiquity, and had the audacity to assure me that there are records which suggest the existence of mankind before plastoscope. Why will people befog their minds with the supernatural?

"There is a theory," he brazenly declared, "that at one time the world was partly composed of food, which burst up through its crust ready for the eating. It is claimed that even the carpet we now spread over the earth's surface had its correspondence in a substance which appeared there spontaneously."

"In that case," I retorted sarcastically, "what became of this—this exudation of the rocks?"

Of course, he had an answer ready: "Plastoscene was discovered and offered mankind an easier method of supplying its needs, with the result that the surface of the earth, containing the growth principle, was stripped away. I do not say that this is a fact," he hastened to add, "but merely that it may have some basis."

Here is what I told my nephew. I sincerely tried to be patient and to appeal to his common sense. "The basis in fact is this: It is true that the earth's surface has been many times stripped during the long existence of the human race. There is only one reasonable theory of life on this planet. Originally man—or rather his evolutionary predecessor—possessed within himself a digestive apparatus much wider in scope than at present. He consumed the rock, converted it into food, and thence into the elements necessary to feed his tissues, all within his own body. Eventually, as he developed intelligence, man learned how to produce plastoscene by mechanical means. He consumed this product as food, as well as using it for the myriad other purposes of his daily life. As a result, the organs within his own body no longer were needed to produce plastoscene directly from the rock. They

THE DWINDLING SPHERE

gradually atrophied and disappeared, leaving only their vestiges in the present digestive tract."

This silenced the young man for a time, but I have no doubt he will return later with some other fantastic delusion. On one occasion it was the legend that, instead of being twin planets, our earth and Luna were at one time of differing sizes, and that Luna revolved around the earth as some of the distant moons revolve around their primaries. This theory has been thoroughly discredited. It is true that there is a reduction of the earth's mass every time we scrape its surface to produce according to our needs; but it is incredible that the earth could ever have been several times the size of its companion planet, as these imaginative theorists would have us believe. They forget, no doubt, that the volume and mass of a large sphere is greater, in proportion to its area and consequent human population, than that of a smaller sphere. Our planet even now would supply man for an incomprehensible time, yet it represents but a tiny fraction of such a mass as these theorists would have us believe in. They forget that diminution would proceed at an ever-mounting rate as the size decreased; that such a huge sphere as they proposed would have lasted forever.

It is impossible. As impossible as to imagine that a time will come when there will be no more Earth for man's conversion—

THE AUTOMATIC PISTOL

Weird Tales
May

by Fritz Leiber (1910-   )

Fritz Leiber has been getting away with murder for many years in the sense that he is a major science fiction writer who writes mainly fantasy. He has won six Hugo and two Nebula Awards for stories and novels like "Gonna Roll the Bones" (1967) and The Big Time *(1958), but it is his "Gray Mouser" stories that have the most devoted following. Two of his early novels are classics:* Conjure Wife *(Unknown, 1943) and* Gather, Darkness, *originally a three-part serial in Astounding in 1943. Few writers have maintained such a high standard over so long a period.*

"The Automatic Pistol" is one of his best short stories, despite the fact that it was passed over in The Best of Fritz Leiber *in 1974.*

(The thing about Fritz that is entirely unfair—and I've complained about this in print before—is that he is tall, distinguished and good-looking. He looks like a Shakespearian actor and, in fact, his father *was* one, and a good one. Why is this unfair? Because writers are supposed to be eccentric and peculiar, darn it. I get away with murder because of that notion. I can be sloppy or do childish things and everyone smiles and says, forgivingly, "Oh, well, you know what writers are like." Then they see Fritz and suddenly I find myself held to an impossibly high standard. Oh, well. I.A.)

Inky never let anyone but himself handle his automatic pistol, or even touch it. It was blue-black and hefty and when you just pressed the trigger once, eight .45 caliber slugs came out of it almost on top of each other.

Inky was something of a mechanic, as far as his automatic went. He would break it down and put it together again, and every once in a while carefully rub a file across the inside trigger catch.

Glasses once told him, "You will make that gun into such a hair-trigger that it will go off in your pocket and blast off all your toes. You will only have to think about it and it will start shooting."

Inky smiled at that, I remember, and didn't bother to say anything. He was a little wiry man with a pale face, from which he couldn't ever shave off the blue-black of his beard, no matter how close he shaved. His hair was black too. When he talked, there was a foreign sound to his voice. He got together with Anton Larsen just after prohibition came, in the days when sea-skiffs with converted automobile motors used to play tag with revenue cutters in New York Bay and off the Jersey coast, both omitting to use lights in order to make the game more difficult. Larsen and Kozacs used to get their booze off a steamer and run it in near the Twin Lights in New Jersey.

It was there that Glasses and I started to work for them. Glasses, who looked like a cross between a college professor and an automobile salesman, came from I don't know where in New York City, and I was a local small-town policeman until I determined to lead a more honest life. We used to ride the stuff back toward Newark in a truck.

Inky always rode in with us; Larsen only occasionally. Neither of them used to talk much; Larsen, because he didn't see any sense in talking unless to give a guy orders or make a proposition; and Inky, well, I guess because he wasn't any too happy talking American. And there wasn't a ride Inky took with us but he didn't slip out his automatic and sort of pet it and mutter at it under his breath. Once when we were restfully chugging down the highway Glasses asked him, polite but inquiring:

"Just what is it makes you so fond of that gun? After all, there must be thousands identically like it."

"You think so?" says Inky, giving us a quick stare from his little, glinty black eyes and making a speech for once. "Let me tell you, Glasses" (he made the word sound like 'Hlasses'), "nothing is alike in this world. People, guns, bottles of Scotch—nothing. Everything in the world is different. Every man has different fingerprints; and, of all guns made in the same factory as this one, there is not one like mine. I could pick mine out from a hundred. Yes, even if I hadn't filed the trigger catch, I could do that."

We didn't contradict him. It sounded pretty reasonable. He sure loved that gun, all right. He slept with it under his pillow. I don't think it ever got more than three feet away from him as long as he lived. There is something crazy in a man feeling that way about a gun.

Once when Larsen was riding in with us, he remarked sarcastically in his heavy voice, "That is a pretty little gun, Inky, but I am getting very tired of hearing you talk to it so much, especially when no one can understand what you are saying. Doesn't it ever talk back to you?"

Inky didn't smile at this. "My gun only knows eight words," he said, "and they are practically all alike. They are eight lead slugs."

This was such a good crack that we laughed.

"Let's have a look at it," said Larsen, reaching out his hand.

But Inky put it back in his pocket and didn't take it out for the rest of the trip.

After that Larsen was always kidding Inky about the gun, and trying to get his goat. He was a persistent guy with a very peculiar sense of humor, and he kept it up for a long time after it had stopped being funny. Finally he took to acting as if he wanted to buy it, making Inky crazy offers of one or two hundred dollars.

"Two hundred and seventy-five dollars, Inky," he said one evening as we were rattling past Keansburg with a load of cognac and Irish whisky. "That's my last offer, and you better take it."

Inky shook his head and made a funny grimace that was almost like a snarl. Then, to my great surprise (I almost ran the truck off the pavement) Larsen lost his temper.

"Hand over that damn gun!" he bellowed, grabbing Inky's shoulders and shaking him. I was almost knocked off the seat. Somebody would have been hurt, or worse, if a motorcycle cop hadn't stopped us just at that moment to ask for his hush-money. By the time he was gone, Larsen and Inky were both cooled down below the danger point, and there was no more fighting. We got our load safely into the warehouse, nobody saying a word.

Afterward, when Glasses and I were having a cup of coffee

at a little open-all-night restaurant, I said, "Those two guys are crazy, and I don't like it a bit. Why the devil do they have to act that way, now that the business is going so swell? I haven't got the brains Larsen has, but you won't ever find me fighting about a gun as if I was a kid."

Glasses only smiled as he poured a precise half-spoonful of sugar into his cup.

"And Inky's as bad as *he* is," I went on. "I tell you, Glasses, it ain't natural or normal for a man to feel that way about a piece of metal. I can understand him being fond of it and feeling lost without it. I feel the same way about my lucky half-dollar. It's the way he pets it and makes love to it that gets on my nerves. And now Larsen's acting the same way."

Glasses shrugged. "We're all getting a little jittery, although we won't admit it," he said. "Too many bootleggers being shot up by hijackers. And so we start getting on each other's nerves and fighting about trifles—such as automatic pistols."

"There may be something there."

Glasses winked at me. "Why, certainly, No Nose; that's something else again. I even have another explanation of tonight's events."

"What?"

He leaned over and whispered in a mock-mysterious way, "Maybe there's something queer about the gun itself."

I told him in impolite language to go chase himself.

From that night, however, things were changed. Larsen and Inky Kozacs never spoke to each other any more except in the line of business. And there was no more talk, kidding or serious, about the gun. Inky only brought it out when Larsen wasn't along.

Well, the years kept passing and the bootlegging business stayed good except that the hijackers became more numerous and Inky got a couple of chances to show us what a nice noise his automatic made. Then, too, we got into a row with another gang in our line under an Irishman named Luke Dugan, and had to watch our step very carefully and change our routes about every other trip.

Still, business was good. I continued to support almost all my relatives, and Glasses put away a few dollars every month for what he called his Persian Cat Fund. Larsen, I believe, spent about everything he got on women and all that goes with them. He was the kind of guy who would take all the pleasures of life without cracking a smile, but who lived for them just the same.

As for Inky Kozacs, we never knew what happened to the money he made. We never heard of him spending much, so we finally figured he must be saving it—probably in bills in a safety deposit box, if I know his kind. Maybe he was planning to go back to the Old Country, wherever that was, and be somebody. At any rate he never told us. By the time Congress took our profession away from us, he must have had a whale of a lot of dough. We hadn't had a big racket, but we'd been very careful.

Finally the night came when we ran our last load. We'd have had to quit the business pretty soon anyway, because the big syndicates were demanding more protection money each week. There was no chance left for a small independent operator, even if he was as clever as Larsen. So Glasses and I took a couple of months off for vacation before thinking what to do next for his Persian cats and my shiftless relatives. For the time being we stuck together.

Then one morning I read in the paper that Inky Kozacs had been taken for a ride. He'd been found shot dead on a dump heap near Elizabeth, New Jersey.

"I guess Luke Dugan finally got him," said Glasses.

"A nasty break," I said, "especially figuring all that money he hadn't gotten any fun out of. I am glad that you and I, Glasses, aren't important enough for Dugan to bother about."

"Yeah. Say, No Nose, does it say if they found Inky's gun on him?"

I said it told that the dead man was unarmed and that no weapon was found on the scene.

Glasses remarked that it was queer to think of Inky's gun being in anyone else's pocket. I agreed, and we spent some time wondering whether Inky had had a chance to defend himself.

About two hours later Larsen called and told us to meet him at the hideout. He said Luke Dugan was gunning for him too.

The hideout is a three-room frame bungalow with a big corrugated iron garage next to it. The garage was for the truck, and sometimes we would store a load of booze there when we heard that the police were going to make some arrests for the sake of variety. It is near Keansburg, and is about a mile and a half from the cement highway and about a quarter of a mile from the bay and the little inlet in which we used to hide our boat. Stiff, knife-edged sea-grass, taller than a man, comes up near to the house on the bay side, which is north, and on the west too. Under the sea-grass the ground is marshy, though in hot weather and when the tides aren't high, it gets dry and caked; here and there creeks of tidewater go through it. Even a little breeze will make the blades of sea-grass scrape each other with a funny dry sound.

To the east are some fields, and beyond them, Keansburg. Keansburg is a very cheap summer resort town and many of the houses are built up on poles because of the tides and storms. It has a little lagoon for the boats of the fishermen who go out after crabs.

To the south of the hideout is the dirt road leading to the cement highway. The nearest house is about half a mile away.

It was late in the afternoon when Glasses and I got there. We brought groceries for a couple of days, figuring Larsen might want to stay. Then, along about sunset, we heard Larsen's coupé turning in, and I went out to put it in the big, empty garage and carry in his suitcase. When I got back Larsen was talking to Glasses. He was a big man and his shoulders were broad both ways, like a wrestler's. His head was almost bald and what was left of his hair was a dirty yellow. His eyes were little and his face wasn't given much to expression. And there wasn't any expression to it when he said, "Yeah, Inky got it."

"Luke Dugan's crazy gunmen sure hold a grudge," I observed.

Larsen nodded his head and scowled.

"Inky got it," he repeated, taking up his suitcase and starting for the bedroom. "And I'm planning to stay here for a few days, just in case they're after me too. I want you and Glasses to stay here with me."

Glasses gave me a funny wink and began throwing a meal together. I turned on the lights and pulled down the blinds, taking a worried glance down the road, which was empty. This waiting around in a lonely house for a bunch of gunmen to catch up with you didn't appeal to me. Nor to Glasses either, I guessed. It seemed to me that it would have been a lot more sensible for Larsen to put a couple of thousand miles between him and New York. But, knowing Larsen, I had sense enough not to make any comments.

After canned corned-beef hash and beans and beer, we sat around the table drinking coffee.

Larsen took an automatic out of his pocket and began fooling with it, and right away I saw it was Inky's. For about five minutes nobody said a word. The silence was so thick you could have cut it in chunks and sold it for ice cubes. Glasses played with his coffee, pouring in the cream one drop at a time. I wadded a piece of bread into little pellets and kicked myself for feeling so uneasy and sick at the stomach.

Finally Larsen looked up at us and said, "Too bad Inky didn't have this with him when he was taken for a ride. He gave it to me just before he planned sailing for the old country. He didn't want it with him any more, now that the racket's all over."

"I'm glad the guy that killed him hasn't got it now," said Glasses quickly. He talked nervously and at random, as if he didn't want the silence to settle down again. "It's a funny thing, Inky giving up his gun—but I can understand his feeling; he mentally associated the gun with our racket; when the one was over he didn't care about the other."

Larsen grunted, which meant for Glasses to shut up.

"What's going to happen to Inky's dough?" I asked.

Larsen shrugged his shoulders and went on fooling with the automatic, throwing a shell into the chamber, cocking it, and so forth. It reminded me so much of the way Inky used to handle it that I got fidgety and began to imagine I heard Luke Dugan's gunmen creeping up through the sea-grass. Finally I got up and started to walk around.

It was then that the accident happened. Larsen, after cocking the gun, was bringing up his thumb to let the hammer down easy, when it slipped out of his hand. As it hit the floor it went off with a flash and a bang, sending the slug gouging the floor too near my foot for comfort.

As soon as I realized I wasn't hit, I yelled without thinking, "I always told Inky he was putting too much of a hair-trigger on his gun! The crazy fool!"

"Inky is too far away to hear you," remarked Glasses.

Larsen sat with his pig eyes staring down at the gun where it lay between his feet. Then he gave a funny little snort, picked it up and put it on the table.

"That gun ought to be thrown away. It's too dangerous to handle. It's bad luck," I said to Larsen—and then wished I hadn't, for he gave me the benefit of a dirty look and some fancy Swedish swearing.

"Shut up, No Nose," he finished, "and don't tell me what I

can do and what I can't. I can take care of you, and I can take care of Inky's gun. Right now I'm going to bed."

He shut the bedroom door behind him, leaving it up to me and Glasses to guess that we were supposed to take our blankets and sleep on the floor.

But we didn't want to go to sleep right away, if only because we were still thinking about Luke Dugan. So we got out a deck of cards and started a game of stud poker, speaking very low. Stud poker is like the ordinary kind, except that four of the five cards are dealt face up and one at a time.

You bet each time a card is dealt, and so considerable money is apt to change hands, even when you're playing with a ten-cent limit, like we were. It's a pretty good game for taking money away from suckers, and Glasses and I used to play it by the hour when we had nothing better to do. But since we were both equally dumb or equally wise (whichever way you look at it) neither one of us won consistently.

It was very quiet, except for Larsen's snoring and the rustling of the sea-grass and the occasional chink of a dime.

After about an hour, Glasses happened to look down at Inky's automatic lying on the other side of the table, and something about the way his body twisted around sudden made me look too. Right away I felt something was wrong, but I couldn't tell what; it gave me a funny feeling in the back of the neck. Then Glasses put out two thin fingers and turned the gun halfway around, and I realized what had been wrong—or what I thought had been wrong. When Larsen had put the gun down, I thought it had been pointing at the outside door; but when Glasses and I looked at it, it was pointing more in the direction of the bedroom door. When you have the fidgets your memory gets tricky.

A half-hour later we noticed the gun pointed toward the bedroom door again. This time Glasses spun it around quick, and I got the fidgets for fair. Glasses gave a low whistle and got up, and tried putting the gun on different parts of the table and jiggling the table to see if the gun would move.

"I see what happened now," he whispered finally. "When the gun is lying on its side, it sort of balances on its safety catch.

"Now this table has got a wobble to it, and when we are playing cards the wobble is persistent enough to edge the gun slowly around in a circle."

"I don't care about that," I whispered back. "I don't want to be shot in my sleep just because the table has a persistent wobble. I think the rumble of a train two miles away would be enough to set off that crazy hair-trigger. Give me it."

Glasses handed it over and, taking care always to point it at the floor, I unloaded it, put it back on the table, and put the bullets in my coat pocket. Then we tried to go on with our card game.

"My red bullet bets ten cents," I said. (A "bullet" means an ace, and I called mine a red bullet because it was the ace of hearts.)

"My king raises you ten cents," responded Glasses.

But it was no use. Between Inky's automatic and Luke Dugan I couldn't concentrate on my cards.

"Do you remember, Glasses," I said, "the evening you said that there was maybe something queer about Inky's gun?"

"I do a lot of talking, No Nose, and not much of it is worth remembering. We'd better stick to our cards. My pair of sevens bets a nickel."

I followed his advice, but didn't have much luck, and lost five or six dollars. By two o'clock we were both pretty tired and not feeling quite so jittery; so we got the blankets and wrapped up in them and tried to grab a little sleep. I listened to the sea-grass and the tooting of a locomotive about two miles away, and worried some over the possible activities of Luke Dugan, but finally dropped off.

It must have been about sunrise that the clicking noise woke me up. There was a faint, greenish light coming in through the shades. I lay still, not knowing exactly what I was listening for, but so on edge that it didn't occur to me how prickly hot I was from sleeping without sheets, or how itchy my face and hands were from mosquito bites. Then I heard it again, and it sounded like nothing but the sharp click the hammer of a gun makes when it snaps down on an empty chamber. Twice I heard it. It seemed to be coming from the inside of the room. I slid out of my blankets and rustled Glasses awake.

"It's that damned automatic of Inky's," I whispered shakily. "It's trying to shoot itself."

When a person wakes up sudden and before he should, he's apt to feel just like I did and say crazy things without thinking. Glasses looked at me for a moment, and then he rubbed his eyes and smiled. I could hardly see the smile in the dim light, but I could feel it in his voice when he said, "No Nose, you are getting positively psychic."

"I tell you I'd swear to it," I insisted. "It was the click of the hammer of a gun."

Glasses yawned. "Next you will be telling me that the gun was Inky's familiar."

"Familiar what?" I asked him, scratching my head and beginning to get mad and feel foolish. There are times when Glasses' college professor stuff gets me down.

"No Nose," he continued, "have you ever heard of witches?"

I was walking around to the windows and glancing out from behind the blinds to make sure there was no one around. I didn't see anyone. For that matter, I didn't really expect to.

"What d'you mean?" I said. "Sure I have. Why, I knew a guy, a Pennsylvania Dutchman, and he told me about witches putting what he called hexes on people. He said his uncle had a hex put on him, and he died afterward. He was a traveling salesman—the Dutchman that told me all that, I mean."

Glasses nodded his head, and then went on, "Well, No Nose, the devil gives each witch a pet black cat or dog or maybe a toad to follow them around and instruct them and protect them and revenge injuries. Those little creatures were called familiars—stooges sent out by the Big Boy in hell to watch over his chosen, you might say. The witches used to talk to them in a language no one else could understand. Now this is what I'm getting at. Times change and styles change—and the style in familiars along with them. Inky's gun is black, isn't it? And he used to mutter at it in a language we couldn't understand, didn't he? And—"

"You're crazy," I told him, not wanting to be kidded and made a fool of.

"Why, No Nose," he said, giving me a very innocent look, "you were telling me yourself just now that you thought the gun had a life of its own, that it could cock itself and shoot itself without any human assistance. Weren't you?"

"You're crazy," I repeated, feeling like an awful fool and wishing I hadn't waked Glasses up. "See, the gun's here where I left it on the table, and the bullets are still in my pocket."

"Luckily," he said in a stagy voice he tried to make a sound like an undertaker's. "Well, now that you've called me early, I shall wander off and avail us of our neighbor's newspaper. Meanwhile, you may run my bath."

I waited until I was sure he was gone, because I didn't

want him to make a fool of me again. Then I went over and examined the gun. First I looked for the trademark or the name of the maker. I found a place which had been filed down, where it may have once been, but that was all. Before this I would have sworn I could have told the make after a quick inspection, but now I couldn't. Not that *in general* it didn't look like an ordinary automatic; it was the details—the grip, the trigger guard, the safety catch—that were different and *unfamiliar*. I figured it was some foreign make I'd never happened to see before.

After I'd been handling it for about two minutes I began to notice something queer about the feel of the metal. As far as I could see it was just ordinary blued steel, but somehow it was too smooth and slick and made me want to keep stroking the barrel back and forth. I can't explain it any better; the metal just didn't seem *right* to me. Finally I realized that the gun was getting on my nerves and making me imagine things; so I put it down on the mantel.

When Glasses got back, the sun was up and he wasn't smiling any more. He shoved a newspaper on my lap and pointed. It was open to page five. I read:

ANTON LARSEN SOUGHT
IN KOZACS KILLING

Police Believe Ex-Bootlegger
Slain by Pal

I looked up to see Larsen standing in the bedroom door. He was in his pajama trousers and looked yellow and seedy, his eyelids puffed and his pig eyes staring at us.

"Good morning, boss," said Glasses slowly. "We just noticed in the paper that they are trying to do you a dirty trick. They're claiming you, not Dugan, had Inky shot."

Larsen grunted, came over and took the paper, looked at it quickly, grunted again, and went to the sink to splash some cold water on his face.

"So," he said, turning to us. "So. All the better that we are here at the hideout."

That day was the longest and most nervous I've ever gone through. Somehow Larsen didn't seem to be completely waked up. If he'd have been a stranger I'd have diagnosed it as a laudanum jag. He just sat around in his pajama trousers, so that by noon he still looked as if he'd only that minute rolled out of bed. The worst thing was that he wouldn't talk or tell us anything about his plans. Of course he never did much talking, but this time there was a difference. His funny pig eyes began to give me the jim-jams; no matter how still he sat they were always moving—like a guy in a laudanum nightmare who's about to run amok.

Finally it started to get on Glasses' nerves, which surprised me, for Glasses usually knows how to take things quietly. He began by making little suggestions—that we should get a later paper, that we should call up a certain lawyer in New York, that I should get my cousin Jake to mosey around to the police station at Keansburg and see if anything was up, and so on. Each time Larsen shut him up quick.

Once I thought he was going to take a crack at Glasses. And Glasses, like a fool, kept on pestering. I could see a blow-up coming, plain as the No Nose in front of my face. I couldn't figure what was making him do it. I guess when the college professor type gets the jim-jams they get them worse than a dummy like me. They've got trained brains which they can't stop from pecking away at ideas, and that's a disadvantage sometimes.

As for me, I tried to keep hold of my nerves. I kept saying to myself, "Larsen is O.K. He's just a little on edge. We all are. Why, I've known him ten years. He's O.K." I only half realized I was saying those things because I was beginning to believe that Larsen *wasn't* O.K.

The blow-up came at about two o'clock. Larsen's eyes opened wide, as if he'd just remembered something, and he jumped up so quick that I started to look around for Luke Dugan's firing-squad—or the police. But it wasn't either of those. Larsen had spotted the automatic on the mantel. Right away, as he began fingering it, he noticed it was unloaded.

"Who monkeyed with this?" he asked in a very nasty, thick voice. "And why?"

Glasses couldn't keep quiet.

"I thought you might hurt yourself with it," he said.

Larsen walked over to him and slapped him on the side of the face, knocking him down. I took firm hold of the chair I had been sitting on, ready to use it like a club—and waited. Glasses twisted on the floor for a moment, until he got control of the pain. Then he looked up, tears beginning to drip out of his left eye—the side he had been hit on. He had sense enough not to say anything, or to smile. Some fools might have smiled in such a situation, thinking it showed courage. It would have showed courage, I admit, but not good sense.

After about twenty seconds Larsen decided not to kick him in the face.

"Well, are you going to keep your mouth shut?" he asked.

Glasses nodded. I let go my grip on the chair.

"Where's the load?" asked Larsen.

I took the bullets out of my pocket and put them on the table, moving deliberately.

Larsen reloaded the gun. It made me sick to see his big hands sliding along the blue-black metal, because I remembered the *feel* of it.

"Nobody touches this but me, see?" he said.

And with that he walked into the bedroom and closed the door.

All I could think was, "Glasses was right when he said Larsen was crazy on the subject of Inky's automatic. And it's just the same as it was with Inky. He has to have the gun close to him. That's what was bothering him all morning, only he didn't know."

Then I kneeled down by Glasses, who was still lying on the floor, propped up on his elbows looking at the bedroom door. The mark of Larsen's hand was brick-red on the side of his face, with a little trickle of blood on the cheekbone, where the skin was broken.

I whispered, very low, just what I thought of Larsen. "Let's beat it first chance and get the police on him," I finished. "Or else maybe jump him when he comes out."

Glasses shook his head a little. He kept staring at the door, his left eye blinking spasmodically. Then he shivered, and gave a funny grunt deep down in his throat.

"I can't believe it," he said. "It's horrible!"

"He killed Inky," I whispered in his ear. "I'm almost sure of it. And he was within an inch of killing you."

"I don't mean that," said Glasses.

"What do you mean then?"

Glasses shook his head, as if he were trying to change the subject of his thoughts.

"Something I saw," he said, "or, rather, something I realized."

"The . . . the gun?" I questioned. My lips were dry and it was hard for me to say the word.

He gave me a funny look and got up.

"We'd better both be sensible from now on," he said, and

then added in a whisper, "We can't do anything now. He's on guard and we're unarmed. Maybe we'll get a chance tonight."

After a long while Larsen called to me to heat some water so he could shave. I brought it to him, and by the time I was frying hash he came out and sat down at the table. He was all washed and shaved and the straggling patches of hair around his bald head were brushed smooth. He was dressed and had his hat on. But in spite of everything he still had that yellow, seedy, laudanum-jag look. We ate our hash and beans and drank our beer, no one talking. It was dark now, and a tiny wind was making the blades of sea-grass scrape together and whine.

Finally Larsen got up and walked around the table once and said, "Let's have a game of stud poker."

While I was clearing off the dishes he brought out his suitcase and planked it down on the side table. Then he took Inky's automatic out of his pocket and looked at it a second. A fleeting expression passed across his stolid face—an expression in which it seemed to me indecision and puzzlement and maybe even fear were mingled. Then he laid the automatic in the suitcase, and shut it and strapped it tight.

"We're leaving after the game," he said.

I wasn't quite sure whether to feel relieved or not.

We played with a ten-cent limit, and right from the start Larsen began to win. It was a queer game, what with me feeling so jittery, and Glasses sitting there with the left side of his face all swollen, squinting through the right lens of his spectacles because the left lens had been cracked when Larsen hit him, and Larsen all dressed up as if he were waiting for a train. The shades were all down and the hanging light bulb, which was shaded with a foolscap of newspaper, threw a bright circle of light on the table but left the rest of the room shadowy. And afterward we were going to leave, he'd said. For where?

It was after Larsen had won about five dollars from each of us that I began hearing the noise. At first I couldn't be sure, because it was very low and because of the dry whining of the sea-grass, but right from the first it bothered me.

Larsen turned up a king and raked in another pot.

"You can't lose tonight," observed Glasses, smiling—and winced because the smile hurt his cheek.

Larsen scowled. He didn't seem pleased at his luck, or at Glasses' remark. His pig eyes were moving in the same way that had given us the jim-jams earlier in the day. And I kept thinking, "Maybe he killed Inky Kozacs. Glasses and me are just small fry to him. Maybe he's trying to figure out whether to kill us too. Or maybe he's got a use for us, and he's wondering how much to tell us. If he starts anything I'll shove the table over on him; that is, if I get the chance." He was beginning to look like a stranger to me, although I'd known him for ten years and he'd been my boss and paid me good money.

Then I heard the noise again, a little plainer this time. It was very peculiar and hard to describe—something like the noise a rat would make if it were tied up in a lot of blankets and trying to work its way out. I looked up and saw that Glasses' face was pale. It made the bruise on his left cheek stand out plainer.

"My black bullet bets ten cents," said Larsen, pushing a dime into the pot.

"I'm with you," I answered, shoving in two nickels. My voice sounded so dry and choked it startled me.

Glasses put in his money and dealt another card to each of us.

Then *I* felt my face going pale, for it seemed to me that the noise was coming from Larsen's suitcase, and I remembered that he had put Inky's automatic into the suitcase with its muzzle pointing *away* from us.

The noise was louder now. Glasses couldn't bear to sit still without saying anything. He pushed back his chair and started to whisper, "I think I hear—"

Then he saw the crazy, murderous look that came into Larsen's eyes, and he had sense enough to finish lamely, "I think I hear the eleven o'clock train."

"Sit still," said Larsen, "very still. It's only ten forty-five. You don't hear anything. My ace bets another ten cents."

"I'll raise you," I croaked.

I didn't know what I was saying. I wanted to jump up. I wanted to throw Larsen's suitcase out the door. I wanted to run out myself. Yet I sat tight. We all sat tight. We didn't dare make a move, for if we had, it would have shown that we believed the impossible was happening. And if a man does that he's crazy. I kept rubbing my tongue against my dry lips.

I stared at the cards, trying to shut out everything else. The hand was all dealt now. I had a jack and some little ones, and I knew my face-down card was a jack. That made a pair of jacks. Glasses had a king showing. Larsen's ace of clubs was the highest card on the board.

And still the sound kept coming. Something twisting, straining, scuffling. A muffled sound.

"And I raise *you* ten cents," said Glasses loudly. I got the idea he did it just to make a noise, not because he thought his cards were especially good.

I turned to Larsen, trying to pretend I was interested in whether he would raise or stop betting. His eyes had stopped moving and were staring straight ahead at the suitcase. His mouth was twisted in a funny, set way. After a while his lips began to move. His voice was so low I could barely catch the words.

"Ten cents more. *I killed Inky, you know.* What does your jack say, No Nose?"

"It raises you," I said automatically.

His reply came in the same almost inaudible voice. "You haven't a chance of winning, No Nose. *But, you see, he didn't bring the money with him, like he said he would. However, I found out where he keeps it hidden in his room. I can't pull the job myself; the cops would recognize me. But you two ought to be able to do it for me. That's why we're going to New York tonight. I raise you ten cents more.* What do you say?"

"I'll see you," I heard myself saying.

The noise stopped, not gradually but all of a sudden. Right away I wanted ten times worse to jump up and do something. But I was frozen to my seat.

Larsen turned up the ace of diamonds. Again I barely heard his words.

"Two aces. *Inky's little gun didn't protect him, you know. He didn't have a chance to use it.* Clubs and diamonds. A pair of bullets. I win."

Then it happened.

I don't need to tell you much about what we did afterward. We buried the body in the sea-grass. We cleaned everything up and drove the coupé a couple of miles inland before abandoning it. We carried the gun away with us and took it apart and hammered it out of shape and threw it into the bay, part by part. We never found out anything more about Inky's money, or tried to. The police never bothered us. We counted ourselves lucky that we had enough sense left to get away safely, after what happened.

For, with smoke and flame squirting through the little round holes and the whole suitcase jerking and shaking with the recoils, eight slugs drummed out and almost cut Anton Larsen in two.

HINDSIGHT

Astounding Science Fiction
May

by Jack Williamson (1908-   )

1978 marked the fiftieth anniversary of Jack Williamson as a published science fiction writer, and he is still going strong as the current "Dean" of sf authors. From his first story, "The Metal Man," in the December 1928 issue of Amazing Stories, he has produced a steady stream of first-rate science fiction and fantasy. His long list of serials in the sf pulps of the thirties earned him his reputation, but he steadily improved his work, both in content and in style.

It is often charged (and with considerable validity) that Golden Age sf lacked character development. This powerful story of betrayal and realization, written at a time of intense nationalism in the United States, offers proof that there were some notable exceptions.

(Jack Williamson is one of the most lovable people in the entire lovable band of science fiction writers. He is quiet and gentle and yet doesn't in the least mind being surrounded by such loudmouths as Randall Garrett, Lester del Rey, Harlan Ellison and myself. In fact, Jack was the very first professional writer to accept me. When my very first published story appeared—"Marooned Off Vesta" in the March 1939 *Amazing*—I at once received a postcard from Jack which read, "Welcome to the ranks." I valued that tremendously. It was my union card, even more than the story was, and I've never forgotten it. Jack has, for I've asked him if he remembered and he looked blank—but I haven't. I.A.)

Something was wrong with the cigar.

But Brek Veronar didn't throw it away. Earth-grown tobacco was precious, here on Ceres. He took another bite off the end, and pressed the lighter cone again. This time, imperfectly, the cigar drew—with an acrid, puzzling odor of scorching paper.

Brek Veronar—born William Webster, Earthman—was sitting in his well-furnished office, adjoining the arsenal laboratory. Beyond the perdurite windows, magnified in the crystalline clarity of the asteroid's synthetic atmosphere, loomed a row of the immense squat turret forts that guarded the Astrophon base—their mighty twenty-four-inch rifles, coupled to the Veronar autosight, covered with their theoretical range everything within Jupiter's orbit. A squadron of the fleet lay on the field beyond, seven tremendous dead-black cigar shapes. Far off, above the rugged red palisades of a second plateau, stood the many-colored domes and towers of Astrophon itself, the Astrarch's capital.

A tall, gaunt man, Brek Veronar wore the bright, close-fitting silks of the Astrarchy. Dyed to conceal the increasing streaks of gray, his hair was perfumed and curled. In abrupt contrast to the force of his gray, wide-set eyes, his face was white and smooth from cosmetic treatments. Only the cigar could have betrayed him as a native of Earth, and Brek Veronar never smoked except here in his own locked laboratory.

He didn't like to be called the Renegade.

Curiously, that whiff of burning paper swept his mind away from the intricate drawing of a new rocket-torpedo gyropilot pinned to a board on the desk before him, and back across twenty years of time. It returned him to the university campus, on the low yellow hills beside the ancient Martian city of Toran—to the fateful day when Bill Webster had renounced allegiance to his native Earth, for the Astrarch.

Tony Grimm and Elora Ronee had both objected. Tony was the freckled, irresponsible redhead who had come out from Earth with him six years before, on the other of the two annual engineering scholarships. Elora Ronee was the lovely dark-eyed Martian girl—daughter of the professor of geodesics, and a proud descendant of the first colonists—whom they both loved.

He walked with them, that dry, bright afternoon, out from the yellow adobe buildings, across the rolling, stony, ocher-colored desert. Tony's sunburned, blue-eyed face was grave for once, as he protested.

"You can't do it, Bill. No Earthman could."

"No use talking," said Bill Webster, shortly. "The Astrarch wants a military engineer. His agents offered me twenty thousand eagles a year, with raises and bonuses—ten times what any research scientist could hope to get, back on Earth."

The tanned, vivid face of Elora Ronee looked hurt. "Bill—what about your own research?" the slender girl cried. "Your new reaction tube! You promised you were going to break the Astrarch's monopoly on space transport. Have you forgotten?"

"The tube was just a dream," Bill Webster told her, "but probably it's the reason he offered the contract to me, and not Tony. Such jobs don't go begging."

Tony caught his arm. "You can't turn against your own world, Bill," he insisted. "You can't give up everything that means anything to an Earthman. Just remember what the Astrarch is—a superpirate."

Bill Webster's toe kicked up a puff of yellow dust. "I know history," he said. "I know that the Astrarchy had its beginnings from the space pirates who established their bases in the asteroids, and gradually turned to commerce instead of raiding."

His voice was injured and defiant. "But, so far as I'm concerned, the Astrarchy is just as respectable as such planet nations as Earth and Mars and the Jovian Federation. And it's a good deal more wealthy and powerful than any of them."

Tense-faced, the Martian girl shook her dark head. "Don't blind yourself, Bill," she begged urgently. "Can't you see that the Astrarch really is no different from any of the old pirates? His fleets still seize any independent vessel, or make the owners ransom it with his space-patrol tax."

She caught an indignant breath. "Everywhere—even here on Mars—the agents and residents and traders of the Astrarchy have brought graft and corruption and oppression. The Astrarch is using his wealth and his space power to undermine the government of every independent planet. He's planning to conquer the system!"

Her brown eyes flashed. "You won't aid him, Bill. You—couldn't!"

Bill Webster looked into the tanned, intent loveliness of her face—he wanted suddenly to kiss the smudge of yellow dust on her impudent little nose. He had loved Elora Ronee, had once hoped to take her back to Earth. Perhaps he still loved her. But now it was clear that she had always wanted Tony Grimm.

Half angrily, he kicked an iron-reddened pebble. "If things had been different, Elora, it might have been—" With an abrupt little shrug, he looked back at Tony. "Anyhow," he said flatly, "I'm leaving for Astrophon tonight."

That evening, after they had helped him pack, he made a bonfire of his old books and papers. They burned palely in the thin air of Mars, with a cloud of acrid smoke.

That sharp odor was the line that had drawn Brek Veronar back across the years, when his nostrils stung to the scorched-paper scent. The cigar came from a box that had just arrived from Earth—made to his special order.

He could afford such luxuries. Sometimes, in fact, he almost regretted the high place he had earned in the Astrarch's favor. The space officers, and even his own jealous subordinates in the arsenal laboratory, could never forget that he was an Earthman—the Renegade.

The cigar's odor puzzled him.

Deliberately, he crushed out the smoldering tip, peeled off the brown wrapper leaves. He found a tightly rolled paper cylinder. Slipping off the rubber bands, he opened it. A glimpse of the writing set his heart to thudding.

It was the hand of Elora Ronee!

Brek Veronar knew that fine graceful script. For once Bill Webster had received a little note that she had written him, when they were still in school. He read it eagerly:

DEAR BILL: This is the only way we can hope to get word to you, past the Astrarch's spies. Your old name, Bill, may seem strange to you. But both Tony and I—want you to remember that you are an Earthman.

You can't know the oppression that Earth now is suffering, under the Astrarch's heel. But independence is almost gone. Weakened and corrupted, the government yields everywhere. Every Earthman's life is burdened with taxes and unjust penalties and the unfair competition of the Astrarch traders.

The Earth, Bill, has not completely yielded. We are going to strike for liberty. Many years of our lives—Tony's and mine—have gone into the plan. And the toil and the sacrifices of millions of our fellow Earthmen. We have at least a chance to recover our lost freedom.

But we need you, Bill—desperately.

For your own world's sake, come back. Ask for a vacation trip to Mars. The Astrarch will not deny you that. On April 8th, a ship will be waiting for you in the desert outside Toran—where we walked the day you left.

Whatever your decision, Bill, we trust you to destroy this letter and keep its contents secret. But we believe that you will come back. For Earth's sake, and for your old friends,

Tony and Elora

Brek Veronar sat for a long time at his desk, staring at the charred, wrinkled sheet. His eyes blurred a little, and he saw the tanned vital face of the Martian girl, her brown eyes imploring. At last he sighed and reached slowly for the lighter cone. He held the letter until the flame had consumed it.

Next day four space officers came to the laboratory. They were insolent in the gaudy gold and crimson of the Astrarch, and the voice of the captain was suave with a triumphant hate:

"Earthman, you are under technical arrest, by the Astrarch's order. You will accompany us at once to his quarters aboard the *Warrior Queen*."

Brek Veronar knew that he was deeply disliked, but very seldom had the feeling been so openly shown. Alarmed, he locked his office and went with the four.

Flagship of the Astrarch's space fleets, the *Warrior Queen* lay on her cradle, at the side of the great field beyond the low gray forts. A thousand feet and a quarter of a million tons of fighting metal, with sixty-four twenty-inch rifles mounted in eight bulging spherical turrets, she was the most powerful engine of destruction the system had ever seen.

Brek Veronar's concern was almost forgotten in a silent pride, as a swift electric car carried them across the field. It was his autosight—otherwise the Veronar achronic field detector geodesic achron-integration self-calculating range finder—that directed the fire of those mighty guns. It was the very fighting brain of the ship—of all the Astrarch's fleet.

No wonder these men were jealous.

"Come, Renegade!" The bleak-faced captain's tone was ominous. "The Astrarch is waiting."

Bright-uniformed guards let them into the Astrarch's compact but luxurious suite, just aft the console room and forward of the autosight installation, deep in the ship's armored bowels. The Astrarch turned from a chart projector, and crisply ordered the two officers to wait outside.

"Well, Veronar?"

A short, heavy, compact man, the dictator of the Astrarchy was vibrant with a ruthless energy. His hair was waved and perfumed, his face a rouged and powdered mask, his silk-swathed figure loaded with jewels. But nothing could hide the power of his hawklike nose and his burning black eyes.

The Astrarch had never yielded to the constant pressure of jealousy against Brek Veronar. The feeling between them had grown almost to friendship. But now the Earthman sensed, from the cold inquiry of those first words, and the probing flash of the ruler's eyes, that his position was gravely dangerous.

Apprehension strained his voice. "I'm under arrest?"

The Astrarch smiled, gripped his hand. "My men are overzealous, Veronar." The voice was warm, yet Brek Veronar could not escape the sense of something sharply critical, deadly. "I merely wish to talk with you, and the impending movements of the fleet allowed little time."

Behind that smiling mask, the Astrarch studied him. "Veronar, you have served me loyally. I am leaving Astrophon for a cruise with the fleet, and I feel that you, also, have earned a holiday. Do you want a vacation from your duties here—let us say, to Mars?"

Beneath those thrusting eyes, Brek Veronar flinched. "Thank you, Gorro," he gulped—he was among the few privileged to call the Astrarch by name. "Later, perhaps. But the torpedo guide isn't finished. And I've several ideas for improving the autosight. I'd much prefer to stay in the laboratory."

For an instant, the short man's smile seemed genuine. "The Astrarchy is indebted to you for the autosight. The increased accuracy of fire had in effect quadrupled our fleets." His eyes were sharp again, doubtful. "Are further improvements possible?"

Brek Veronar caught his breath. His knees felt a little weak. He knew that he was talking for his life. He swallowed, and his words came at first unsteadily.

"Geodesic analysis and integration is a completely new

science," he said desperately. "It would be foolish to limit the possibilities. With a sufficiently delicate pick-up, the achronic detector fields ought to be able to trace the world lines of any object almost indefinitely. Into the future—"

He paused for emphasis. "Or into the past!"

An eager interest flashed in the Astrarch's eyes. Brek felt confidence returning. His breathless voice grew smoother.

"Remember, the principle is totally new. The achronic field can be made a thousand times more sensitive than any telescope—I believe, a million times! And the achronic beam eliminates the time lag of all electromagnetic methods of observation. Timeless, paradoxically it facilitates the exploration of time."

"Exploration?" questioned the dictator. "Aren't you speaking rather wildly, Veronar?"

"Any range finder, in a sense, explores time," Brek assured him urgently. "It analyzes the past to predict the future—so that a shell fired from a moving ship and deflected by the gravitational fields of space may move thousands of miles to meet another moving ship, minutes in the future.

"Instruments depending on visual observation and electromagnetic transmission of data were not very successful. One hit in a thousand used to be good gunnery. But the autosight has solved the problem—now you reprimand gunners for failing to score two hits in a hundred."

Brek caught his breath. "Even the newest autosight is just a rough beginning. Good enough, for a range finder. But the detector fields can be made infinitely more sensitive, the geodesic integration infinitely more certain.

"It ought to be possible to unravel the past for years, instead of minutes. It ought to be possible to foretell the position of a ship for weeks ahead—to anticipate every maneuver, and even watch the captain eating his breakfast!"

The Earthman was breathless again, his eyes almost feverish. "From geodesic analysis," he whispered, "there is one more daring step—control. You are aware of the modern view that there is no absolute fact, but only probability. I can prove it! And probability can be manipulated through pressure of the achronic field.

"It is possible, even, I tell you—"

Brek's rushing voice faltered. He saw that doubt had drowned the flash of interest in the Astrarch's eyes. The dictator made an impatient gesture for silence. In a flat, abrupt voice he stated: "Veronar, you are an Earthman."

"Once I was an Earthman."

The black flashing eyes probed into him. "Veronar," the Astrarch said, "trouble is coming with Earth. My agents have uncovered a dangerous plot. The leader of it is an engineer named Grimm, who has a Martian wife. The fleet is moving to crush the rebellion." He paused. "Now, do you want the vacation?"

Before those ruthless eyes, Brek Veronar stood silent. Life, he was now certain, depended on his answer. He drew a long, unsteady breath. "No," he said.

Still the Astrarch's searching tension did not relax. "My officers," he said, "have protested against serving with you, against Earth. They are suspicious."

Brek Veronar swallowed. "Grimm and his wife," he whispered hoarsely, "once were friends of mine. I had hoped that it would not be necessary to betray them. But I have received a message from them."

He gulped again, caught his breath. "To prove to your men that I am no longer an Earthman—a ship that they have sent for me will be waiting on April 8th, Earth calendar, in the desert south of the Martian city of Toran."

The white, lax mask of the Astrarch smiled. "I'm glad you told me, Veronar," he said. "You have been very useful—and I like you. Now I call tell you that my agents read the letter in the cigar. The rebel ship was overtaken and destroyed by the space patrol, just a few hours ago."

Brek Veronar swayed to a giddy weakness.

"Entertain no further apprehensions." The Astrarch touched his arm. "You will accompany the fleet, in charge of the autosight. We take off in five hours."

The long black hull of the *Warrior Queen* lifted on flaring reaction tubes, leading the squadron. Other squadrons moved from the bases on Pallas, Vesta, Thule, and Eros. The Second Fleet came plunging sunward from its bases on the Trojan planets. Four weeks later, at the rendezvous just within the orbit of Mars, twenty-nine great vessels had come together.

The armada of the Astrarchy moved down upon Earth.

Joining the dictator in his chartroom, Brek was puzzled. "Still I don't see the reason for such a show of strength," he said. "Why have you gathered three fourths of your space forces to crush a handful of plotters?"

"We have to deal with more than a handful of plotters." Behind the pale mask of the Astrarch's face, Brek could sense a tension of worry. "Millions of Earthmen have labored for years to prepare for this rebellion. Earth has built a space fleet."

Brek was astonished. "A fleet?"

"The parts were manufactured secretly, mostly in underground mills," the Astrarch told him. "The ships were assembled by divers, under the surface of fresh-water lakes. Your old friend, Grimm, is clever and dangerous. We shall have to destroy his fleet before we can bomb the planet into submission."

Steadily, Brek met the Astrarch's eyes. "How many ships?" he asked.

"Six."

"Then we outnumber them five to one." Brek managed a confident smile. "Without considering the further advantage of the autosight. It will be no battle at all."

"Perhaps not," said the Astrarch, "but Grimm is an able man. He has invented a new type reaction tube, in some regards superior to our own." His dark eyes were somber. "It is Earthman against Earthman," he said softly. "And one of you shall perish."

Day after day, the armada dropped Earthward.

The autosight served also as the eyes of the fleet, as well as the fighting brain. In order to give longer base lines for the automatic triangulations, additional achronic-field pick-ups had been installed upon half a dozen ships. Tight achronic beams brought their data to the immense main instrument, on the *Warrior Queen*. The autosight steered every ship, by achronic beam control, and directed the fire of its guns.

The *Warrior Queen* led the fleet. The autosight held the other vessels in accurate line behind her, so that only one circular cross section might be visible to the telescopes of Earth.

The rebel planet was still twenty million miles ahead, and fifty hours at normal deceleration, when the autosight discovered the enemy fleet.

Brek Veronar sat at the curving control table.

Behind him, in the dim-lit vastness of the armored room, bulked the main instrument. Banked thousands of green-painted cases—the intricate cells of the mechanical brain—whirred with geodesic analyzers and integrators. The achronic-field pick-ups—sense organs of the brain—were housed in insignificant black boxes. And the web of achronic transmission beams—instantaneous, ultrashort, nonelectromagnetic waves of the subelectronic order—the nerve fibers that joined the busy cells—was quite invisible.

Before Brek stood the twenty-foot cube of the stereoscreen, through which the brain communicated its findings. The cube was black, now, with the crystal blackness of space. Earth, in it, made a long misty crescent of wavering crimson splendor. The moon was a smaller scimitar, blue with the dazzle of its artificial atmosphere.

Brek touched intricate controls. Th moon slipped out of the cube. Earth grew—and turned. So far had the autosight conquered time and space. It showed the planet's sunward side.

Earth filled the cube, incredibly real. The vast white disk of one low-pressure area lay upon the Pacific's glinting blue. Another, blotting out the winter brown of North America, reached to the bright cap of the arctic.

Softly, in the dim room, a gong clanged. Numerals of white fire flickered against the image in the cube. An arrow of red flame pointed. At its point was a tiny fleck of black.

The gong throbbed again, and another black mote came up out of the clouds. A third followed. Presently there were six. Watching, Brek Veronar felt a little stir of involuntary pride, a dim numbness of regret.

Those six vessels were the mighty children of Tony Grimm and Elora, the fighting strength of Earth. Brek felt an aching tenseness in his throat, and tears stung his eyes. It was too bad that they had to be destroyed.

Tony would be aboard one of those ships. Brek wondered how he would look, after twenty years. Did his freckles still show? Had he grown stout? Did concentration still plow little furrows between his blue eyes?

Elora—would she be with him? Brek knew she would. His mind saw the Martian girl, slim and vivid and intense as ever. He tried to thrust away the image. Time must have changed her. Probably she looked worn from the years of toil and danger; her dark eyes must have lost their sparkle.

Brek had to forget that those six little blots represented the lives of Tony and Elora, and the independence of the Earth. They were only six little lumps of matter, six targets for the autosight.

He watched them, rising, swinging around the huge, luminous curve of the planet. They were only six mathematical points, tracing world lines through the continuum, making a geodesic pattern for the analyzers to unravel and the integrators to project against the future—

The gong throbbed again.

Tense with abrupt apprehension, Brek caught up a telephone.

"Give me the Astrarch. . . . An urgent report. . . . No, the admiral won't do. . . . Gorro, the autosight has picked up the Earth's fleet . . . Yes, only six ships, just taking off from the sunward face. But there is one alarming thing."

Brek Veronar was hoarse, breathless. "Already, behind the planet, they have formed a cruising line. The axis extends exactly in our direction. That means that they know our precise position, before they have come into telescopic view. That suggests that Tony Grimm has invented an autosight of his own!"

Strained hours dragged by. The Astrarch's fleet decelerated, to circle and bombard the mother world, after the battle was done. The Earth ships came out at full normal acceleration.

"They must stop," the Astrarch said. "That is our advantage. If they go by us at any great velocity, we'll have the planet bombed into submission before they can return. They must turn back—and then we'll pick them off."

Puzzlingly, however, the Earth fleet kept up acceleration, and a slow apprehension grew in the heart of Brek Veronar. There was but one explanation. The Earthmen were staking the life of their planet on one brief encounter.

As if certain of victory!

The hour of battle neared. Tight achronic beams relayed telephoned orders from the Astrarch's chartroom, and the fleet deployed into battle formation—into the shape of an immense bowl, so that every possible gun could be trained upon the enemy.

The hour—and the instant!

Startling in the huge dim space that housed the autosight, crackling out above the whirring of the achron-integrator, the speaker that was the great brain's voice counted off the minutes.

"Minus four—"

The autosight was set, the pick-ups tuned, the director relays tested, a thousand details checked. By the control table, Brek Veronar tried to relax. His part was done.

A space battle was a conflict of machines. Humans beings were too puny, too slow, even to comprehend the play of the titanic forces they had set loose. Brek tried to remember that he was the autosight's inventor; he fought an oppression of helpless dread.

"Minus three—"

Sodium bombs filled the void ahead with vast silver plumes and streamers—for the autosight removed the need of telescopic eyes, and enabled ships to fight from deep smoke screens.

"Minus two—"

The two fleets came together at a relative velocity of twelve hundred thousand miles an hour. Maximum useful range of twenty-inch guns, even with the autosight, was only twenty thousand miles in free space.

Which meant, Brek realized, that the battle could last just two minutes. In that brief time lay the destinies of Astrarchy and Earth—and Tony Grimm's and Elora's and his own.

"Minus one—"

The sodium screens made little puffs and trails of silver in the great black cube. The six Earth ships were visible behind them, through the magic of the achronic-field pick-ups, now spaced in a close ring, ready for action.

Brek Veronar looked down at the jeweled chronometer on his wrist—a gift from the Astrarch. Listening to the rising hum of the achron-integrators, he caught his breath, tensed instinctively.

"Zero!"

The *Warrior Queen* began quivering to her great guns, a salvo of four firing every half-second. Brek breathed again, watched the chronometer. That was all he had to do. And in two minutes—

The vessel shuddered, and the lights went out. Sirens wailed, and air valves clanged. The lights came on, went off again. And abruptly the cube of the stereoscreen was dark. The achron-integrators clattered and stopped.

The guns ceased to thud.

"Power!" Brek gasped into a telephone. "Give me power! Emergency! The autosight has stopped and—"

But the telephone was dead.

There were no more hits. Smothered in darkness, the great room remained very silent. After an eternal time, feeble emergency lights came on. Brek looked again at his chronometer, and knew that the battle was ended.

But who was the victor?

He tried to hope that the battle had been won before some last chance broadside crippled the flagship—until the Astrarch came stumbling into the room, looking dazed and pale.

"Crushed," he muttered. "You failed me, Veronar."

"What are the losses?" whispered Brek.

"Everything." The shaken ruler dropped wearily at the control table. "Your achronic beams are dead. Five ships remain able to report defeat by radio. Two of them hope to make repairs.

"The *Queen* is disabled. Reaction batteries shot away, and main power plant dead. Repair is hopeless. And our present orbit will carry us far too close to the sun. None of our ships able to undertake rescue. We'll be baked alive."

His perfumed dark head sank hopelessly. "In those two minutes, the Astrarchy was destroyed." His hollow, smoldering eyes lifted resentfully to Brek. "Just two minutes!" He crushed a soft white fist against the table. "If time could be recaptured—"

"How were we beaten?" demanded Brek. "I can't understand!"

"Marksmanship," said the tired Astrarch. "Tony Grimm has something better than your autosight. He shot us to pieces before we could find the range." His face was a pale mask of bitterness. "If my agents had employed him, twenty years ago, instead of you—" He bit blood from his lip. "But the past cannot be changed."

Brek was staring at the huge, silent bulk of the autosight. "Perhaps"—he whispered—"it can be!"

Trembling, the Astrarch rose to clutch his arm. "You spoke of that before," gasped the agitated ruler. "Then I wouldn't listen. But now—try anything you can, Veronar. To save us from roasting alive, at perihelion. Do you really think—" The Astrarch shook his pale head. "I'm the madman," he whispered. "To speak of changing even two minutes of the past!" His hollow eyes clung to Brek. "Though you have done amazing things, Veronar."

The Earthman continued to stare at his huge creation. "The autosight itself brought me one clue, before the battle," he breathed slowly. "The detector fields caught a beam of Tony Grimm's, and analyzed the frequencies. He's using achronic radiation a whole octave higher than anything I've tried. That must be the way to the sensitivity and penetration I have hoped for."

Hope flickered in the Astrarch's eyes. "You believe you can save us? How?"

"If the high-frequency beam can search out the determiner factors," Brek told him, "it might be possible to alter them, with a sufficiently powerful field. Remember that we deal with probabilities, not with absolutes. And that small factors can determine vast results.

"The pick-ups will have to be rebuilt. And we'll have to have power. Power to project the tracer fields. And a river of power—if we can trace out a decisive factor and attempt to change it. But the power plants are dead."

"Rebuild your pick-ups," the Astrarch told him. "And you'll have power—if I have to march every man aboard into the conversion furnaces, for fuel."

Calm again, and confident, the short man surveyed the tall, gaunt Earthman with wondering eyes.

"You're a strange individual, Veronar," he said. "Fighting time and destiny to crush the planet of your birth! It isn't strange that men call you the Renegade."

Silent for a moment, Brek shook his haggard head. "I don't want to be baked alive," he said at last. "Give me power—and we'll fight that battle again."

The wreck dropped sunward. A score of expert technicians toiled, under Brek's expert direction, to reconstruct the achronic pick-ups. And a hundred men labored, beneath the ruthless eye of the Astrarch himself, to repair the damaged atomic converters.

They had crossed the orbit of Venus, when the autosight came back to humming life. The Astrarch was standing beside Brek, at the curved control table. The shadow of doubt had returned to his reddened, sleepless eyes. "Now," he demanded, "what can you do about the battle?"

"Nothing, directly," Brek admitted. "First we must search the past. We must find the factor that caused Tony Grimm to invent a better autosight than mine. With the high-frequency field—and the full power of the ship's converters, if need be—we must reverse the factor. Then the battle should have a different outcome."

The achron-integrators whirred, as Brek manipulated the controls, and the huge black cube began to flicker with the passage of ghostly images. Symbols of colored fire flashed and vanished within it.

"Well?" anxiously rasped the Astrarch.

"It works!" Brek assured him. "The tracer fields are following all the world lines that intersected at the battle, back across the months and years. The analyzers will isolate the smallest—and hence most easily altered—essential factor."

The Astrarch gripped his shoulder. "There—in the cube—yourself!"

The ghostly shape of the Earthman flickered out, and came again. A hundred times, Brek Veronar glimpsed himself in the cube. Usually the scene was the great arsenal laboratory, at Astrophon. Always he was differently garbed, always younger.

Then the background shifted. Brek caught his breath as he recognized glimpses of barren, stony, ocher-colored hills, and low, yellow adobe buildings. He gasped to see a freckled, red-haired youth and a slim, tanned, dark-eyed girl.

"That's on Mars!" he whispered. "At Toran. He's Tony Grimm. And she's Elora Ronee—the Martian girl we loved."

The racing flicker abruptly stopped, upon one frozen tableau. A bench on the dusty campus, against a low adobe wall. Elora Ronee, with a pile of books propped on her knees to support pen and paper. Her dark eyes were staring away across the campus, and her sun-brown face looked tense and troubled.

In the huge dim room aboard the wrecked warship, a gong throbbed softly. A red arrow flamed in the cube, pointing down at the note on the girl's knee. Cryptic symbols flashed above it. And Brek realized that the humming of the achron-integrators had stopped.

"What's this?" rasped the anxious Astrarch. "A schoolgirl writing a note—what has she to do with a space battle?"

Brek scanned the fiery symbols. "She was deciding the battle—that day twenty years ago!" His voice rang with elation. "You see, she had a date to go dancing in Toran with Tony Grimm that night. But her father was giving a special lecture on the new theories of achronic force. Tony broke the date, to attend the lecture."

As Brek watched the motionless image in the cube his voice turned a little husky. "Elora was angry—that was before she knew Tony very well. I had asked her for a date. And, at the moment you see, she has just written a note, to say that she would go dancing with me."

Brek gulped. "But she is undecided, you see. Because she loves Tony. A very little would make her tear up the note to me, and write another to Tony, to say that she would go to the lecture with him."

The Astrarch stared cadaverously. "But how could that decide the battle?"

"In the past that we have lived," Brek told him, "Elora sent the note to me. I went dancing with her, and missed the lecture. Tony attended it—and got the germ idea that finally caused his autosight to be better than mine.

"But, if she had written to Tony instead, he would have offered, out of contrition, to cut the lecture—so the analyzers indicate. I should have attended the lecture in Tony's place, and my autosight would have been superior in the end."

The Astrarch's waxen head nodded slowly. "But—can you really change the past?"

Brek paused for a moment, solemnly. "We have all the power of the ship's converters," he said at last. "We have the high-frequency achronic field, as a lever through which to apply it. Surely, with the millions of kilowatts to spend, we can stimulate a few cells in a schoolgirl's brain. We shall see."

His long, pale fingers moved swiftly over the control keys. At last, deliberately, he touched a green button. The converters whispered again through the silent ship. The achron-integrators whirred again. Beyond, giant transformers began to whine.

And that still tableau came to sudden life.

Elora Ronee tore up the note that began, "Dear Bill—" Brek and the Astrarch leaned forward, as her trembling fingers swiftly wrote: "Dear Tony—I'm so sorry that I was angry. May I come with you to father's lecture? Tonight—"

The image faded.

"Minus four—"

The metallic rasp of the speaker brought Brek Veronar to himself with a start. Could he have been dozing—with contact just four minutes away? He shook himself. He had a queer, unpleasant feeling—as if he had forgotten a nightmare dream in which the battle was fought and lost.

He rubbed his eyes, scanned the control board. The autosight was set, the pick-ups were tuned, the director relays tested. His part was done. He tried to relax the puzzling tension in him.

"Minus three—"

Sodium bombs filled the void ahead with vast silver plumes and streamers. Staring into the black cube of the screen, Brek found once more the six tiny black motes of Tony Grimm's ships. He couldn't help an uneasy shake of his head.

Was Tony mad? Why didn't he veer aside, delay the contact? Scattered in space, his ships could harry the Astrarchy's commerce, and interrupt bombardment of the Earth. But, in a head-on battle, they were doomed.

Brek listened to the quiet hum of the achron-integrators. Under these conditions, the new autosight gave an accuracy of fire of forty percent. Even if Tony's gunnery was perfect, the odds were still two to one against him.

"Minus two—"

Two minutes! Brek looked down at the jeweled chronometer on his wrist. For a moment he had an odd feeling that the design was unfamiliar. Strange, when he had worn it for twenty years.

The dial blurred a little. He remembered the day that Tony and Elora gave it to him—the day he left the university to come to Astrophon. It was too nice a gift. Neither of them had much money.

He wondered if Tony had ever guessed his love for Elora. Probably it was better that she had always declined his attentions. No shadow of jealousy had ever come over their friendship.

"Minus one—"

This wouldn't do! Half angrily, Brek jerked his eyes back to the screen. Still, however, in the silvery sodium clouds, he saw the faces of Tony and Elora. Still he couldn't forget the oddly unfamiliar pressure of the chronometer on his wrist—it was like the soft touch of Elora's fingers, when she had fastened it there.

Suddenly the black flecks in the screen were not targets any more. Brek caught a long gasping breath. After all, he was an Earthman. After twenty years in the Astrarch's generous pay, this timepiece was still his most precious possession.

His gray eyes narrowed grimly. Without the autosight, the Astrarch's fleet would be utterly blind in the sodium clouds. Given any sort of achronic range finder, Tony Grimm could wipe it out.

Brek's gaunt body trembled. Death, he knew, would be the sure penalty. In the battle or afterward—it didn't matter. He knew that he would accept it without regret.

"Zero!"

The achron-integrators were whirring busily, and the *Warrior Queen* quivered to the first salvo of her guns. Then

Brek's clenched fists came down on the carefully set keyboard. The autosight stopped humming. The guns ceased to fire.

Brek picked up the Astrach's telephone. "I've stopped the autosight." His voice was quiet and low. "It is quite impossible to set it again in two minutes."

The telephone clicked and was dead.

The vessel shuddered and the lights went out. Sirens wailed. Air valves clanged. The lights came on, went off again. Presently, there were no more hits. Smothered in darkness, the great room remained very silent.

The tiny racing tick of the chronometer was the only sound.

After an eternal time, feeble emergency lights came on. The Astrarch came stumbling into the room, looking dazed and pale.

A group of spacemen followed him. Their stricken, angry faces made an odd contrast with their gay uniforms. Before their vengeful hatred, Brek felt cold and ill. But the Astrarch stopped their ominous advance.

"The Earthman has doomed himself as well," the shaken ruler told them. "There's not much more that you can do. And certainly no haste about it."

He left them muttering at the door and came slowly to Brek.

"Crushed," he whispered. "You destroyed me, Veronar." A trembling hand wiped at the pale waxen mask of his face. "Everything is lost. The *Queen* disabled. None of our ships able to undertake the rescue. We'll be baked alive."

His hollow eyes stared dully at Brek. "In those two minutes, you destroyed the Astrarchy." His voice seemed merely tired, strangely without bitterness. "Just two minutes," he murmured wearily. "If time could be recaptured—"

"Yes," Brek said, "I stopped the autosight." He lifted his gaunt shoulders defiantly, and met the menacing stares of the spacemen. "And they can do nothing about it?"

"Can you?" Hope flickered in the Astrarch's eyes.

"Once you told me, Veronar, that the past could be changed. Then I wouldn't listen. But now—try anything you can. You might be able to save yourself from the unpleasantness that my men are planning."

Looking at the muttering men, Brek shook his head. "I was mistaken," he said deliberately. "I failed to take account of the two-way nature of time. But the future, I see now, is as real as the past. Aside from the direction of entropy change and the flow of consciousness, future and past cannot be distinguished.

"The future determines the past, as much as the past does the future. It is possible to trace out the determiner factors, and even, with sufficient power, to cause a local deflection of the geodesics. But world lines are fixed in the future, as rigidly as in the past. However the factors are rearranged, the end result will always be the same."

The Astrarch's waxen face was ruthless. "Then, Veronar, you are doomed."

Slowly, Brek smiled. "Don't call me Veronar," he said softly. "I remembered, just in time, that I am William Webster, Earthman. You can kill me in any way you please. But the defeat of the Astrarchy and the new freedom of Earth are fixed in time—forever."

POSTPAID TO PARADISE   *Argosy*
June

by Robert Arthur (1909-1969)

Robert Arthur (Robert A. Feder) is a neglected writer of sf and fantasy, best known as a television and radio producer and scriptwriter. This is unfortunate, because he produced a number of excellent stories, many of them outside the sf magazines. In the science fiction field his reputation resides with his "Murchison Morks" series of which this story was the first.

"Postpaid to Paradise" has an interesting publishing history, since it was reprinted by The Magazine of Fantasy and Science Fiction *in 1950 and, in spite of its non-original status, was selected for inclusion in the first* Best From F & SF.

(Nowadays, of course, with the vast increase in the number of science fiction writers, I am not surprised that there are so many I haven't met—or having met them, that they don't stick in my aging mind. It bothers me, though, that I never met some of the old-timers. I never met Robert Arthur, for instance, but I was always particularly fond of his stories. I.A.)

It was Hobby Week at the Club, and Malcolm was displaying his stamp collection.

"Now take these triangulars," he said. "Their value is not definitely known, since they've never been sold as a unit. But they make up the rarest and most interesting complete set known to philatelists. They—"

"I once had a set of stamps that was even rarer and more

interesting," Murchison Morks interrupted, his voice melancholy. Morks is a small, wispy man who usually sits by the fireplace and smokes his pipe, silently contemplating the coals. I do not believe he particularly cares for Malcolm, who is our only millionaire and likes what he owns to be better than what anybody else owns.

"You own a set of stamps *rarer* than my triangulars?" Malcolm asked incredulously, a dark tinge of annoyance creeping into his ruddy cheeks.

"Not own, no." Morks shook his head in gentle correction. "Owned."

"Oh!" Malcolm snorted. "I suppose they got burned? Or stolen?"

"No"—and Morks uttered a sigh—"I used them. For postage, I mean. Before I realized their utter uniqueness."

Malcolm gnawed at his lip.

"This set of stamps," he said with great positiveness, laying a possessive hand on the glass covering the triangular bits of paper, "cost the life of at least one man."

"Mine," Morks replied, "cost me my best friend."

"Cost you the *life* of your best friend?" Malcolm demanded.

Morks shook his head, his face expressing a reflective sadness, as if in his mind he were living again a bit of the past that it still hurt him to remember.

"I don't know," he answered the philatelist. "I really don't. I suspect not. I honestly think that Harry Norris—that was my friend—at this moment is a dozen times happier than any man here. And when I reflect that but for a bit of timidity on my part I might be with him—

"But I had better tell you the whole story," he said more briskly, "so you can fully understand."

I am not a stamp collector myself [he began, with a pleasant nod toward Malcolm] but my father was. He died some years ago, and among other things he left me his collection.

It was not a particularly good one—he had leaned more toward picturesqueness in his items than toward rarity or value—and when I sold it, I hardly got enough for it to repay me for the trouble I went to in having it appraised.

I even thought for a time of keeping it; for some of his collection, particularly those stamps from tropical countries that featured exotic birds and beasts, were highly decorative.

But in the end I sold them all—except one set of five

which the dealer refused to take, because he said they were forgeries.

Forgeries! If he had only guessed.

But naturally I took his word for it. I assumed he knew. Especially since the five stamps differed considerably from any I had ever seen before, and had not even been pasted into my father's album. Instead, they had been loose in an envelope tucked in at the rear of the book.

But forgeries or not, they were both interesting and attractive. The five were in differing denominations: ten cents, fifty cents, one dollar, three dollars, and five dollars.

All were unused, in mint condition—that's the term, isn't it, Malcolm?—and in the gayest of colors; vermillion and ultramarine, emerald and yellow, orange and azure, chocolate and ivory, black and gold.

And since they were all large—their size was roughly four times that of the current airmail stamps, with which you are all familiar—the scenes they showed had great vividness and reality.

In particular the three-dollar one, portraying the native girl with the platter of fruit on her head—

However, that's getting ahead of my story. Let me say simply that, thinking they were forgeries, I put them away in my desk and forgot about them.

I found them again one night, quite by accident, when I was rummaging around in the back of a drawer, looking for an envelope in which to post a letter I had just written to my best friend, Harry Norris. Harry was at the time living in Boston.

It so happened that the only envelope I could find was the one in which I had been keeping those stamps of my father's. I emptied them out, addressed the envelope, and then, after I had sealed the letter inside, found my attention attracted to those five strange stamps.

I have mentioned that they were all large and rectangular: almost the size of baggage labels, rather than of conventional postage stamps. But then, of course, these were not conventional postage stamps.

Across the top of them was a line in bold print: FEDERATED STATES OF EL DORADO. Then, on either side, about the center, the denomination. And at the bottom, another line, *Rapid Post*.

Being unfamiliar with such things, I had assumed when first I found them that El Dorado was one of these small Indian states, or perhaps it was in Central America someplace. Rapid Post, I judged, would probably correspond to our own airmail.

Since the denominations were in cents and dollars, I rather leaned to the Latin American theory: there are a lot of little countries down there that I'm always getting confused, like San Salvador and Colombia. But until that moment I had never really given the matter much thought.

Now, staring at them, I began to wonder whether that dealer had known his business. They were done so well, the engraving executed with such superb verve, the colors so bold and attractive, that it hardly seemed likely any forger could have gotten them up.

It is true the subjects they depicted were far from usual. The ten-cent value, for instance, pictured a unicorn standing erect, head up, spiral horn pointing skyward, mane flowing, the very breathing image of life.

It was almost impossible to look at it without *knowing* that the artist had worked with a real unicorn for a model. Except, of course, that there aren't any unicorns any more.

The fifty-center showed Neptune, trident held aloft, riding a pair of harnessed dolphins through a foaming surf. It was just as real as the first.

The one-dollar value depicted Pan playing on his pipes, with a Greek temple in the background, and three fauns dancing on the grass. Looking at it, I could almost hear the music he was making.

I'm not exaggerating in the least. I must admit I was a little puzzled that a tropical country should be putting Pan on one of its stamps, for I thought he was purely a Greek monopoly. But when I moved on to the three-dollar stamp, I forgot all about him.

I probably can't put into words quite the impression that stamp made upon me—and upon Harry Norris, later.

The central figure was a girl; I believe I spoke of that.

A native girl, against a background of tropical flowers, a girl of about sixteen, I should say, just blossomed into womanhood, smiling a little secret smile that managed to combine the utter innocence of girlhood with all the inherited wisdom of a woman.

Or am I making myself clear? Not very? Well, no matter. Let it go at that. I'll only add that on her head, native fashion, she was carrying a great flat platter piled high with fruit of every kind you can imagine; and that platter, together with some flowers at her feet, was her only attire.

I looked at her for quite a long time, before I examined the last of the set—the five-dollar value.

This one was relatively uninteresting, by comparison—just a map. It showed several small islands set down in an expanse of water labeled, in neat letters, *Sea of El Dorado*. I assumed that the islands represented the Federated States of El Dorado itself, and that the little dot on the largest, marked by the word Nirvana, was the capital of the country.

Then an idea occurred to me. Harry had a nephew who collected stamps. Just for the fun of it, I might put one of those El Dorado forgeries—if they were forgeries—on my letter to Harry, along with the regular stamp, and see whether it wouldn't go through the post office. If it did, Harry's nephew might get a rarity, a foreign stamp with an American cancellation.

It was a silly idea, but it was late at night and finding the stamps had put me in a gay mood. I promptly licked the ten-cent El Dorado, pasted it onto the corner of Harry's letter, and then got up to hunt a regulation stamp to put with it.

The search took me into my bedroom, where I found the necessary postage in the wallet I had left in my coat. While I was gone, I left the letter itself lying in plain sight on my desk.

And when I got back into the library, the letter was gone.

I don't need to say I was puzzled. There wasn't any place it could have gone to. There wasn't anybody who could have taken it. The window was open, but it was a penthouse window overlooking twenty floors of empty space, and nobody had come in through it.

Nor was there any breeze that might have blown the envelope to the floor. I looked. In fact, I looked everywhere, growing steadily more puzzled.

And then, as I was about to give up, my phone began ringing.

It was Harry Norris, calling me from Boston. His voice, as he said hello, was a little strained. I quickly found out why.

Three minutes before, as he was getting ready for bed, the letter I had just finished giving up for lost had come swooping in his window, hung for a moment in midair as he stared at it, and then fluttered to the floor.

The next afternoon, Harry Norris arrived in New York. I had promised him over the phone, after explaining about the

El Dorado stamp on the letter, not to touch the others except to put them safely away.

It was obvious that the stamp was responsible for what had happened. In some manner it had carried that letter from my library straight to Harry Norris' feet in an estimated time of three minutes, or at an average rate of approximately five thousand miles an hour.

It was a thought to stagger the imagination. Certainly it staggered mine.

Harry arrived just at lunch time, and over lunch I told him all I knew; just what I've told you now. He was disappointed at the meagerness of my information. But I couldn't add a thing to the facts we already knew, and those facts spoke for themselves.

Basically, they reduced to this: I had put the El Dorado stamp on Harry's letter, and promptly that letter had delivered itself to him with no intermediary processes whatever.

"No, that's not quite right!" Harry burst out. "Look. I brought the letter with me. And—"

He held it out to me, and I saw I had been wrong. There *had* been an intermediary process of some kind, for the stamp was canceled. Yes, and the envelope was postmarked, too, in a clearly legible, pale purple ink.

Federated States of El Dorado, the postmark said. It was circular, like our own; and in the center of the circle, where the time of cancellation usually is, was just the word *Thursday*.

"Today is Thursday," Harry remarked. "It was after midnight when you put the stamp on the letter?"

"Just after," I told him. "Seems queer these El Dorado people pay no attention to the hour and the minute, doesn't it?"

"Only proves they're a tropical country," Harry suggested. "Time means little or nothing in the tropics, you know. But what I was getting at, the Thursday postmark goes to show El Dorado is probably down in Central America, as you suggested. If it were in India, or the Orient, it would have been marked Wednesday, wouldn't it? On account of the time difference?"

"Or would it have been Friday?" I asked, rather doubtfully, not knowing much about those things. "In any case we can find out easily enough. We've just to look in the atlas. I don't know why I didn't think of it before."

Harry brightened.

"Of course," he said. "Where do you keep yours?"

But it turned out I hadn't any atlas in the house—not even a small one. So we phoned downtown to one of the big bookstores to send up their latest and largest atlas. And while we waited for it we examined the letter again and speculated upon the method by which it had been transmitted.

"Rapid post!" Harry explained. "I should say so! It beats airmail all hollow. Why, if that letter not only traveled from here to Boston between the time you missed it and it fell at my feet, but actually went all the way to Central America, was canceled and postmarked, and *then* went on to Boston, its average speed must have been—"

We did a little rough calculation and hit upon two thousand miles a minute as a probable speed. When we'd done that, we looked at each other.

"Good Lord!" Harry gasped. "The Federated States of El Dorado may be a tropical country, but they've really hit upon something new in this thing! I wonder why we haven't heard about it before?"

"May be keeping it a secret," I suggested. "No, that won't do, because I've had the stamps for several years, and of course, my father had them before that."

"I tell you, there's something queer here," Harry suggested, darkly. "Where are those others you told me about? I think we ought to make a few tests with them while we're waiting for that atlas."

With that I brought out the four remaining unused stamps, and handed them to him. Now Harry, among other things, was a rather good artist; and his whistle at the workmanship was appreciative. He examined each with care, but it was— I'd thought it would be—the three-dollar value that really caught his eye. The one with the native girl on it, you remember.

"Lord!" Harry said aloud. "What a beauty!"

Presently, however, Harry put that one aside and finished examining the others. Then he turned to me.

"The thing I can't get over," he commented, "is the *lifelikeness* of the figures. You know what I'd suspect if I didn't know better? I'd suspect these stamps were never engraved at all. I'd believe that the plates they came from were prepared from photographs."

"From photographs!" I exclaimed; and Harry nodded.

"Of course, you know and I know they can't have been," he added. "Unicorns and Neptunes and Pans aren't running around to be photographed, these days. But that's the feeling they give me."

I confessed that I had had the same feeling. But since we both agreed on the impossibility of its being so, we dismissed that phase of the matter and went back again to the problem of the method used in transporting the letter.

"You say you were out of the room when it vanished," Harry remarked. "That means you didn't see it go. You don't actually know what happened when you put that stamp on and turned your back, do you?"

I agreed that was so, and Harry sat in thoughtful silence. At last he looked up.

"*I* think," he said, "we ought to find out by using one of these other stamps to mail something with."

Why that hadn't occurred to me before I can't imagine. As soon as Harry said it, I recognized the rightness of the idea. The only thing was to decide what to send, and to whom.

That held us up for several minutes. There wasn't anybody else either of us cared to have know about this just now; and we couldn't send anything to each other very well, being both there together.

"I'll tell you!" Harry exclaimed at last. "We'll send something to El Dorado itself!"

I agreed to that readily enough, but how it came about that we decided to send, not a letter, but Thomas à Becket, my aged and ailing Siamese cat, I can't remember.

I do know that I told myself it would be a kind way to dispose of the creature. Transmission through space at the terrific velocity of one hundred and twenty thousand miles an hour would surely put him out of his sufferings, quickly and painlessly.

Thomas à Becket was asleep under the couch, breathing asthmatically and with difficulty. I found a cardboard box the right size and we punched some air holes in it. Then I gathered up Thomas and placed him in the container. He opened rheumy old eyes, gazed at me vaguely, and relapsed into slumber again. With a pang I put the lid on and we tied the box.

"Now," Harry said thoughtfully, "there's the question of how to address him, of course. However, any address will do for our purpose."

He took up a pen and wrote with rapidity. *Mr. Henry Smith, 711 Elysian Fields Avenue, Nirvana, Federated*

States of El Dorado. And beneath that he added, *Perishable! Handle With Care!*

"But—" I began. Harry cut me off.

"No," he said, "of course I don't know of any such address. I just made it up. But the post-office people won't know that, will they?"

"But what will happen when—" I began again, and again he had had the answer before I'd finished the question.

"It'll go to the dead letter office, I expect," he told me. "And if he *is* dead, they'll dispose of him. If he's alive, I've no doubt they'll take good care of him. From the stamps I've gotten a notion living is easy there."

That silenced my questions, and Harry picked up a stamp—the fifty-cent value—licked it, and placed it firmly on the box. Then he withdrew his hand and stepped back beside me.

Intently, we watched the parcel.

For a moment, nothing whatever happened.

And then, just as disappointment was gathering on Harry Norris' countenance, the box holding Thomas à Becket rose slowly into the air, turned like a compass needle, and began to drift with increasing speed toward the open window.

By the time it reached the window, it was moving with racehorse velocity. It shot through and into the open. We rushed to the window and saw it moving upward in a westerly direction, above the Manhattan skyline.

And then, as we stared, it began to be vague in outline, misty; and an instant later had vanished entirely. Because of its speed, I suggested, the same way a rifle bullet is invisible.

But Harry had another idea. He shook his head as we stepped back toward the center of the room.

"No," he began, "I don't think that's the answer. I have a notion—"

What his notion was I never did find out. Because just then he stopped speaking, with his mouth still open, and I saw him stiffen. He was looking past me, and I turned to see what had affected him so.

Outside the window was the package we had just seen vanish. It hung there for a moment, then moved slowly into the room, gave a little swoop, and settled lightly onto the table from which, not two minutes before, it had left.

Harry and I rushed over to it, and our eyes must have bugged out a bit.

Because the package was all properly canceled and postmarked, just as the letter had been. With the addition that across the corner, in large purple letters, somebody had stamped, RETURN TO SENDER. NO SUCH PERSON AT THIS ADDRESS.

"Well!" Harry said at last. It wasn't exactly adequate, but it was all either of us could think of. Then, inside the box, Thomas à Becket let out a squall.

I cut the cords and lifted the lid. Thomas à Becket leaped out with an animation he had not shown in years.

There was no denying it. Instead of killing him, his trip to El Dorado, brief as it was, had done him good. He looked five years younger.

Harry Norris was turning the box over in his hands, perplexed.

"What I can't get over," he remarked, "is that there really *is* such an address as 711 Elysian Fields Avenue. I swear I just made it up."

"There's more to it than that," I reminded him. "The very fact that the package came back. We didn't put any return address on it."

"So we didn't," Harry agreed. "Yet they knew just where to return it, didn't they?"

He pondered for a moment longer. Then he put the box down.

"I'm beginning to think," he said, an odd expression on his face, "that there is more to this than we realize. A great deal more. I suspect the whole truth is a lot more exciting than we have any notion. As for this Federated States of El Dorado, I have a theory—"

But he didn't tell me what his theory was. Instead, that three-dollar chocolate-and-ivory stamp caught his eye again.

"Jove!" he whispered, more to himself than to me—he was given occasionally to these archaic ejaculations—"she's beautiful. Heavenly! With a model like that an artist might paint—"

"He might forget to paint, too," I put in. Harry nodded.

"He might indeed," he agreed. "Though I think he'd be inspired in the end to work he'd never on earth have dreamed of doing, otherwise." His gaze at the stamp was almost hungry. "This girl," he declared, "is the one I've been waiting all my life to find. To meet her I'd give—I'd give— Well, almost anything."

"I'm afraid you'd have to go to El Dorado to do that," I suggested flippantly, and Harry started.

"So I would! And I'm perfectly willing to do it, too. Listen! These stamps suggest this El Dorado place must be rather fascinating. What do you say we both pay it a visit? We neither of us have any ties to keep us, and—"

"Go there just so you can meet the girl who was the model for that stamp?" I demanded.

"Why not? Can you think of a better reason?" he asked me. "I can give you more. For one thing, the climate. Look how much better the cat is. His little excursion took years off his age. Must be a highly healthful place. Maybe it'll make a young man of you again. And besides—"

But he didn't have to go on. I was already convinced.

"All right," I agreed. "We'll take the first boat. But when we get there, how will we—"

"By logic," Harry shot back. "Purely by logic. The girl must have posed for an artist, mustn't she? And the postmaster general of El Dorado must know who the artist is, mustn't he? We'll go straight to the postmaster general. He'll direct us to the artist. The artist will give us her name and address. Could anything be simpler?"

I hadn't realized how easy it would be. Now some of his impatience was getting into my own blood.

"Maybe we won't have to take a boat," I suggested. "Maybe there's a plane service. That would save—"

"Boat!" Harry Norris snorted, stalking back and forth across the room and waving his hands. "Plane! You can take boats and planes if you want to. I've got a better idea. I'm going to El Dorado by mail!"

Until I saw how beautifully simple his idea was, I was a bit stunned. But he quickly pointed out that Thomas à Becket had made the trip, and come back, without injury. If a cat could do it, a man could.

There wasn't a thing in the way except the choice of a destination. It would be rather wasted effort to go, only to be sent back ignominiously for want of proper addressing.

"I have that figured out too," Harry told me promptly when I voiced the matter. "The first person I'd go to see anyway when I got there would be the postmaster general. *He* must exist, certainly. And mail addressed to him would be the easiest of all to deliver. So why not kill two birds with one stone by posting myself to his office?"

That answered all my objections. It was as sound and sensible a plan as I'd ever heard.

"Why," Harry Norris added with rising excitement, "I may

be having dinner with the girl tonight! Wine and pomegranates beneath a gold-washed moon, with Pan piping in the shadows and nymphs dancing on the velvet green!"

"But"—I felt I had to prepare him for possible disappointment—"suppose she's married by now?"

He shook his head.

"She won't be. I have a feeling. Just a feeling. Now to settle the details. We've got three stamps left—nine dollars' worth altogether. That should be enough. I'm a bit lighter; you've been taking on weight lately, I see. Four dollars should carry me—the one and the three. That leaves the five-dollar for you.

"As for the address, we'll write that on tags and tie them to our wrists. You have tags, haven't you? Yes, here's a couple in this drawer. Now give me that pen and ink. Something like this ought to do very well..."

He wrote, then held the tags out to me. They were just alike. *Office of the Postmaster General,* they said. *Nirvana, Federated States of El Dorado. Perishable. Handle With Care.*

"Now," he said, "we'll each tie one to our wrist—"

But I drew back. Somehow I couldn't quite nerve myself to it. Delightful as the prospects he had painted of the place, the idea of posting myself into the unknown, the way I had sent off Thomas à Becket, did something queer to me.

I told him I would join him. I would take the first boat, or plane, and meet him there, say at the principal hotel.

Harry was disappointed, but he was too impatient by now to argue.

"Well," he agreed, "all right. But if for any reason you can't get a boat or plane, you'll use that last stamp to join me?"

I promised faithfully that I would. With that he held out his right wrist and I tied a tag about it. Then he took up the one-dollar stamp, moistened it, and applied it to the tag. He had the three-dollar one in his hand when the doorbell rang.

"In a minute," he was saying, "or maybe in less, I shall probably be in the fairest land man's combined imagination has ever been able to picture."

"Wait!" I called, and hurried out to answer the bell. I don't know whether he heard me or not. He was just lifting that second stamp to his tongue to moisten it when I turned away, and that was the last I ever saw of him.

When I came back, with the package in my hands—the

ring had been the messenger from the bookshop, with the atlas we had ordered—Harry Norris was gone.

Thomas à Becket was sitting up and staring toward the window. The curtains were still fluttering. I hurried over. But Norris was not in sight.

Well, I thought, he must have put on that stamp he had in his hand, not knowing I'd left the room. I could see him, in my mind's eye, that very moment being deposited on his feet in the office of an astonished postmaster general.

Then it occurred to me I might as well find out just where the Federated States of El Dorado were, after all. So I ripped the paper off the large volume the bookstore had sent and began to leaf through it.

When I had finished, I sat in silence for a while. From time to time I glanced at that unused tag, and that uncanceled stamp still lying on my desk. Then I made my decision.

I got up and fetched Harry's bag. It was summer, luckily, and he had brought mostly light clothing. To it I added anything of mine I thought he might be able to use, including a carton of cigarettes, and pen and ink on the chance he might want to write me.

As an afterthought I added a small Bible—just in case.

Then I strapped the bag shut and affixed the tag to it. I wrote *Harry Norris* above the address, pasted that last El Dorado stamp to it, and waited.

In a moment the bag rose in the air, floated to the window, out, and began to speed away.

It would reach there, I figured, before Harry had had time to leave the postmaster general's office, and I hoped he might send me a postcard or something by way of acknowledgment. But he didn't. Perhaps he couldn't.

. . . At this point Morks stopped, as if he had finished his story. But unnoticed Malcolm had left our little group for a moment. Now he came pushing back into it with a large atlas-gazeteer in his hands.

"So that's what became of your set of rarities!" he said, with a scarcely veiled sneer. "Very interesting and entertaining. But there's one point I want to clear up. The stamps were issued by the Federated States of El Dorado, you say. Well, I've just been looking through this atlas, and there's no such place on earth."

Morks looked at him, his melancholy countenance calm.

"I know it," he said. "That's why, after glancing through my own atlas that day, I didn't keep my promise to Harry Norris and use that last stamp to join him. I'm sorry now. When I think of how Harry must be enjoying himself there—

"But it's no good regretting what I did or didn't do. I couldn't help it. The truth is that my nerve failed me, just for a moment then, when I discovered there *was* no such place as the Federated States of El Dorado—on earth, I mean."

And sadly he shook his head.

"I've often wished I knew where my father got those stamps," he murmured, almost to himself; then fell into a meditative silence.

COVENTRY*   *Astounding Science Fiction*
July

by Robert A. Heinlein

> "Coventry" is a sequel to "If This Goes On . . ." (ASF, February, 1940) and with the addition of "Misfit" (see Volume One) was published as *Revolt in 2100* in 1953 by Shasta, one of the early specialist science fiction publishers. The present selection is perhaps Heinlein's finest statement of his position on, and commitment to, individualism, privacy, and the necessity to *earn* liberty. It can also be read as an indictment of synthetic contemporary Western civilization.

(Although Bob and I have been good friends for forty years now, whe don't see eye-to-eye politically. I, for instance, am suspicious of any doctrine that tells us we must *earn* liberty. Who decides when we have earned it and who has the right to withhold it if we haven't earned it? It bothers me.

I'm also suspicious of those who equate liberty with "small government," meaning less interference from Washington over the details of our life. I don't believe there can be less interference; just a change of interference. If Washington bows out, then it is the local bully on the block who will take over, and I'd rather have Washington. Every once in a while through history, places have tried "small government" and replaced a tyrannical central power with local "self-help." It's called "feudalism" and it's also called "dark ages" and I don't want it. —But I must say Bob preaches his point of view charmingly. I.A.)

---

* See note following end of Introduction.

INTO THE DARKNESS

Astonishing Stories
June

by Ross Rocklynne (1913-   )

> *One of the best of the "second rank" writers of the late thirties and forties, Ross Rocklynne (real name Ross L. Rocklin), has been a neglected figure in science fiction, largely because he produced very little long fiction. The best of his work, including stories like "Jackdaw" (1942), "Jaywalker" (1950), and "Time Wants a Skeleton" can be found in his two Ace Books collections* The Men and the Mirror *and* The Sun Destroyers, *both 1973. He has continued to write and has produced some interesting work in recent years, especially "Ching Witch" in* Again Dangerous Visions *(1972) and "Randy-Tandy Man" in* Universe 3.
>
> *"Into the Darkness" is a remarkable story, very different from the "usual" sf of 1940—with a little polishing, it would find little difficulty fitting in to the so-called "New Wave" of the 1960s. As Terry Carr reminds us, this story was written in 1934, but none of the editors of the day would touch it until Fred Pohl published it in* Astonishing.

(I'm not sure how you define "New Wave," a name given to stories that appeared in the 1960s except to say that they were characterized by writing that was experimental and different and by tales that broke new ground.

Well, what about 1940? Who ever heard about "New Wave" then? I remember that in the April, 1940 *Astonishing Stories,* I published a story called "The Callistan Menace," the second story I ever wrote and it was Old Wave; it was Ancient Wave; it was Antediluvian Wave.

Yet one issue later, one little issue, in the June, 1940 *Astonishing* Ross Rocklynne published "Into the Darkness." What do you make of it? It never slips. It stays inside the minds of creatures and life and conditions altogether different from ours. It breaks new ground; it is experimental and different. The style and literary gloss may not be quite as high and polished as was the writing of the 1960s, but "Into the Darkness" is surely New Wave a quarter-century before its time. Fred Pohl was the editor who accepted it. Not surprising. I.A.)

I. Birth of "Darkness"

Out in space, on the lip of the farthest galaxy, and betwixt two star clusters, there came into being a luminiferous globe that radiated for light-years around. A life had been born!

It became aware of light; one of its visions had become activated. First it saw the innumerable suns and nebulae whose radiated energy now fed it. Beyond that it saw a dense, impenetrable darkness.

The darkness intrigued it. It could understand the stars, but the darkness it could not. The babe probed outward several light-years and met only lightlessness. It probed farther, and farther, but there was no light. Only after its visions could not delve deeper did it give up, but a strange seed had been sown; that there was light on the far edge of the darkness became its innate conviction.

Wonders never seemed to cease parading themselves before this newly born. It became aware of another personality hovering near, an energy creature thirty millions of miles across. At its core hung a globe of subtly glowing green light one million miles in diameter.

He explored this being with his vision, and it remained still during his inspection. He felt strange forces plucking at him, forces that filled him to overflowing with peacefulness. At once, he discovered a system of energy waves having marvelous possibilities.

"Who are you?" these waves were able to inquire of that other life.

Softly soothing, he received answer.

"I am your mother."

"You mean—?"

"You are my son—my creation. I shall call you—

Darkness. Lie here and grow, Darkness, and when you are many times larger, I will come again."

She had vanished, swallowed untraceably by a vast spiral nebula—a cloud of swiftly twisting stardust.

He lay motionless, strange thoughts flowing. Mostly he wondered about the sea of lightlessness lapping the shore of this galaxy in which he had been born. Sometime later, he wondered about life, what life was, and its purpose.

"When *she* comes again, I shall ask her," he mused. "Darkness, she called me—Darkness!"

His thoughts swung back to the darkness.

For five million years he bathed himself in the rays that permeate space. He grew. He was ten million miles in diameter.

His mother came; he saw her hurtling toward him from a far distance. She stopped close.

"You are much larger, Darkness. You grow faster than the other newly born." He detected pride in her transmitted thoughts.

"I have been lying here, thinking," he said. "I have been wondering, and I have come to guess at many things. There are others, like you and myself."

"There are thousands of others. I am going to take you to them. Have you tried propellents?"

"I have not tried, but I shall." There was a silence. "I have discovered the propellents," said Darkness, puzzled, "but they will not move me."

She seemed amused. "That is one thing you do not know, Darkness. You are inhabiting the seventeenth band of hyperspace; propellents will not work there. See if you can expand."

All these were new things, but instinctively he felt himself expand to twice his original size.

"Good. I am going to snap you into the first band. . . . There. Try your propellents."

He tried them, and, to his intense delight, the flaring lights that were the stars fled past. So great was his exhilaration that he worked up a speed that placed him several light-years from his mother.

She drew up beside him. "For one so young, you have speed. I shall be proud of you. I feel, Darkness," and there was wistfulness in her tone, "that you will be different from the others."

She searched his memory swirls. "But try not to be too different."

Puzzled at this, he gazed at her, but she turned away. "Come."

He followed her down the aisles formed by the stars, as she accommodated her pace to his.

They stopped at the sixth galaxy from the abyss of lightlessness. He discerned thousands of shapes that were his kind moving swiftly past and around him. These, then, were his people.

She pointed them out to him. "You will know them by their vibrations, and the varying shades of the colored globes of light at their centers."

She ran off a great list of names which he had no trouble in impressing on his memory swirls.

"Radiant, Vibrant, Swift, Milky, Incandescent, Great Power, Sun-eater, Light-year...."

"Come, I am going to present you to Oldster."

They whirled off to a space seven light-years distant. They stopped, just outside the galaxy. There was a peculiar snap in his consciousness.

"Oldster has isolated himself in the sixth band of hyperspace," said his mother.

Where before he had seen nothing save inky space, dotted with masses of flaming, tortured matter, he now saw an energy creature whose aura fairly radiated old age. And the immense purple globe which hung at his core lacked a certain vital luster which Darkness had instinctively linked with his own youth and boundless energy.

His mother caught the old being's attention, and Darkness felt his thought-rays contact them.

"Oh, it's you, Sparkle," the old being's kindly thoughts said. "And who is it with you?"

Darkness saw his mother, Sparkle, shoot off streams of crystalline light.

"This is my first son."

The newly born felt Oldster's thought rays going through his memory swirls.

"And you have named him Darkness," said Oldster slowly. "Because he has wondered about it." His visions withdrew, half-absently. "He is so young, and yet he is a thinker; already he thinks about life."

For long and long Oldster bent a penetrating gaze upon him. Abruptly, his vision rays swung away and centered on a tiny, isolated group of stars. There was a heavy, dragging silence.

"Darkness," Oldster said finally, "your thoughts are useless." The thoughts now seemed to come from an immeasurable distance, or an infinitely tired mind. "You are young, Darkness. Do not think so much—so much that the happiness of life is destroyed in the over-estimation of it. When you wish, you may come to see me. I shall be in the sixth band for many millions of years."

Abruptly, Oldster vanished. He had snapped both mother and son back in the first band.

She fixed her vision on him. "Darkness, what he says is true—every word. Play for a while—there are innumerable things to do. And once in great intervals, if you wish, go to see Oldster; but for a long time do not bother him with your questions."

"I will try," answered Darkness, in sudden decision.

II. Cosmic Children

Darkness played. He played for many millions of years. With playmates of his own age, he roamed through and through the endless numbers of galaxies that composed the universe. From one end to another he dashed in a reckless obedience to Oldster's command.

He explored the surfaces of stars, often disrupting them into fragments, sending scalding geysers of belching flame millions of miles into space. He followed his companions into the swirling depths of the green-hued nebulae that hung in intergalactic space. But to disturb these mighty creations of nature was impossible. Majestically they rolled around and around, or coiled into spirals, or at times condensed into matter that formed beautiful, hot suns.

Energy to feed on was rampant here, but so densely and widely was it distributed that he and his comrades could not even dream of absorbing more than a trillionth part of it in all their lives.

He learned the mysteries of the forty-seven bands of hyperspace. He learned to snap into them or out again into the first or true band at will. He knew the delights of blackness impenetrable in the fifteenth band, of a queerly illusory multiple existence in the twenty-third, and an equally strange sensation of speeding away from himself in an opposite direction in the thirty-first, and of the forty-seventh, where all space turned into a nightmarish concoction of cubistic suns and galaxies.

Incomprehensible were those forty-seven bands. They were coexistent in space, yet they were separated from each other by a means which no one had ever discovered. In each band were unmistakable signs that it was the same universe. Darkness only knew that each band was one of forty-seven subtly differing faces which the universe possessed, and the powers of his mind experienced no difficulty in allowing him to cross the unseen bridges which spanned the gulfs between them.

And he made no attempts toward finding the solution—he was determined to cease thinking, for the time being at least. He was content to play, and to draw as much pleasure and excitement as he could from every new possibility of amusement.

But the end of all *that* came, as he had suspected it would. He played, and loved all this, until. . . .

He had come to his fifty-millionth year, still a youth. The purple globe at his core could have swallowed a sun a million miles in diameter, and his whole body could have displaced fifty suns of that size. For a period of a hundred thousand years he lay asleep in the seventh band, where a soft, colorless light pervaded the universe.

He awoke, and was about to transfer himself to the first band and rejoin the children of Radiant, Light-year, Great Power and all those others.

He stopped, almost dumbfounded, for a sudden, overwhelming antipathy for companionship had come over him. He discovered, indeed, that he never wanted to join his friends again. While he had slept, a metamorphosis had come about, and he was as alienated from his playmates as if he had never known them.

What had caused it? Something. Perhaps, long before his years, he had passed into the adult stage of mind. Now he was rebelling against the friendships which meant nothing more than futile play.

Play! Bouncing huge suns around like rubber balls, and then tearing them up into solar systems; chasing one another up the scale through the forty-seven bands, and back again; darting about in the immense spaces between galaxies, rendering themselves invisible by expanding to ten times normal size.

He did not want to play, and he never wanted to see his

friends again. He did not hate them, but he was intolerant of the characteristics which bade them to disport among the stars for eternity.

He was not mature in size, but he felt he had become an adult, while they were still children—tossing suns the length of a galaxy, and then hurling small bits of materialized energy around them to form planets; then just as likely to hurl huger masses to disrupt the planetary systems they so painstakingly made.

He had felt it all along—this superiority. He had manifested it by besting them in every form of play they conceived. They generally bungled everything, more apt to explode a star into small fragments than to whirl it until centrifugal force threw off planets.

"I have become an adult in mind, if not in body; I am at the point where I must accumulate wisdom, and perhaps sorrow," he thought whimsically. "I will see Oldster, and ask him my questions—the questions I have thus far kept in the background of my thoughts. But," he added thoughtfully, "I have a feeling that even his wisdom will fail to enlighten me. Nevertheless, there must be answers. What is life? Why is it? And there must be—another universe beyond the darkness that hems this one in."

Darkness reluctantly turned and made a slow trail across that galaxy and into the next, where he discovered those young energy creatures with whom it would be impossible to enjoy himself again.

He drew up, and absently translated his time standard to one corresponding with theirs, a rate of consciousness at which they could observe the six planets whirling around a small, white-hot sun as separate bodies, and not mere rings of light.

They were gathered in numbers of some hundreds around this sun, and Darkness hovered on the outskirts of the crowd, watching them moodily.

One of the young purple lights, Cosmic by name, threw a mass of matter a short distance into space, reached out with a tractor ray and drew it in. He swung it 'round and 'round on the tip of that ray, gradually forming ever-decreasing circles. To endow the planet with a velocity that would hurl it unerringly between the two outermost planetary orbits required a delicate sense of compensatory adjustment between the factors of mass, velocity, and solar attraction.

When Cosmic had got the lump of matter down to an angular velocity that was uniform, Darkness knew an irritation he had never succeeded in suppressing. An intuition, which had unfailingly proved itself accurate, told him that anything but creating an orbit for that planet was likely to ensue.

"Cosmic." He contacted the planet-maker's thought rays. "Cosmic, the velocity you have generated is too great. The whole system will break up."

"Oh, Darkness." Cosmic threw a vision on him. "Come on, join us. You say the speed is wrong? Never; you are! I've calculated everything to a fine point."

"To the wrong point," insisted Darkness stubbornly. "Undoubtedly, your estimation of the planet's mass is the factor which makes your equation incorrect. Lower the velocity. You'll see."

Cosmic continued to swing his lump of matter, but stared curiously at Darkness.

"What's the matter with you?" he inquired. "You don't sound just right. What does it matter if I do calculate wrong, and disturb the system's equilibrium? We'll very probably break up the whole thing later, anyway."

A flash of passion came over Darkness. "That's the trouble," he said fiercely. "It doesn't matter to any of you. You will always be children. You will always be playing. Careful construction, joyous destruction—that is the creed on which you base your lives. Don't you feel as if you'd like, sometime, to quit playing, and do something—worthwhile?"

As if they had discovered a strangely different set of laws governing an alien galaxy, the hundreds of youths, greens and purples, stared at Darkness.

Cosmic continued swinging the planet he had made through space, but he was plainly puzzled. "What's wrong with you, Darkness? What else is there to do except to roam the galaxies, and make suns? I can't think of a single living thing that might be called more worthwhile."

"What good is playing?" answered Darkness. "What good is making a solar system? If you made one, and then, perhaps, vitalized it with life, that would be worthwhile! Or think, think! About yourself, about life, why it is, and what it means in the scheme of things! Or," and he trembled a little, "try discovering what lies beyond the veil of lightlessness which surrounds the universe."

The hundreds of youths looked at the darkness.

Cosmic stared anxiously at him. "Are you crazy? We all know there's nothing beyond. Everything that is is right here in the universe. That blackness is just empty, and it stretches away from here forever."

"Where did you get that information?" Darkness inquired scornfully. "You don't know that. Nobody does. But I am going to know! I awoke from sleep a short while ago, and I couldn't bear the thought of play. I wanted to do something substantial. So I am going into the darkness."

He turned his gaze hungrily on the deep abyss hemming in the stars. There were thousands of years, even under its lower time-standard, in which awe dominated the gathering. In his astonishment at such an unheard-of intention, Cosmic entirely forgot his circling planet. It lessened in velocity, and then tore loose from the tractor ray that had become weak, in a tangent to the circle it had been performing.

It sped toward that solar system, and entered between the orbits of the outmost planets. Solar gravitation seized it; the lone planet took up an erratic orbit, and then the whole system had settled into complete stability, with seven planets where there had been six.

"You see," said Darkness, with a note of unsteady mirth, "if you had used your intended speed, the system would have coalesced. The speed of the planet dropped, and then escaped you. Some blind chance sent it in the right direction. It was purely an accident. Now throw in a second sun, and watch the system break up. That has always amused you." His aura quivered. "Goodbye, friends."

III. Oldster

He was gone from their sight forever. He had snapped into the sixth band.

He ranged back to the spot where Oldster should have been. He was not.

"Probably in some other band," thought Darkness, and went through all the others, excepting the fifteenth, where resided a complete lack of light. With a feeling akin to awe, since Oldster was apparently in none of them, he went into the fifteenth, and called out.

There was a period of silence. Then Oldster answered, in his thoughts a cadence of infinite weariness.

"Yes, my son; who calls me?"

"It is I, Darkness, whom Sparkle presented to you nearly fifty million years ago." Hesitating, an unexplainable feeling, as of sadness unquenchable, came to him.

"I looked for you in the sixth," he went on in a rush of words, "but did not expect to find you here, isolated, with no light to see by."

"I am tired of seeing, my son. I have lived too long. I have tired of thinking and of seeing. I am sad."

Darkness hung motionless, hardly daring to interrupt the strange thought of this incredible ancient. He ventured timidly, "It is just that I am tired of playing, Oldster, tired of doing nothing. I should like to accomplish something of some use. Therefore, I have come to you, to ask you three questions, the answers to which I must know."

Oldster stirred restlessly. "Ask your questions."

"I am curious about life." Oldster's visitor hesitated nervously, and then went on. "It has a purpose, I know, and I want to know that purpose. That is my first question."

"But why, Darkness? What makes you think life *has* a purpose, an ultimate purpose?"

"I don't know," came the answer, and for the first time Darkness was startled with the knowledge that he really didn't! "But there must be some purpose!" he cried.

"How can you say 'must'? Oh, Darkness, you have clothed life in garments far too rich for its ordinary character! You have given it the sacred aspect of meaning! There is no meaning to it. Once upon a time the spark of life fired a blob of common energy with consciousness of its existence. From that, by some obscure evolutionary process, we came. That is all. We are born. We live, and grow, and then we die! After that, there is nothing! Nothing!"

Something in Darkness shuddered violently, and then rebellilously. But his thoughts were quiet and tense. "I won't believe that! You are telling me that life is only meant for death, then. Why—why, if that were so, why should there be life? No, Oldster! I feel that there must be something which justifies my existence."

Was it pity that came flowing along with Oldster's thoughts? "You will never believe me. I knew it. All my ancient wisdom could not change you, and perhaps it is just as well. Yet you may spend a lifetime in learning what I have told you."

His thoughts withdrew, absently, and then returned.

"Your other questions, Darkness."

For a long time Darkness did not answer. He was of half a mind to leave Oldster, and leave it to his own experiences to solve his other problems. His resentment was hotter than a dwarf sun, for a moment. But it cooled and though he was beginning to doubt the wisdom to which Oldster laid claim, he continued with his questioning.

"What is the use of the globe of purple light which forever remains at my center, and even returns, no matter how far I hurl it from me?"

Such a wave of mingled agitation and sadness passed from the old being that Darkness shuddered. Oldster turned on him with extraordinary fierceness. "Do not learn *that* secret! I will not tell you! What might I not have spared myself had I not sought and found the answer to that riddle! I was a thinker, Darkness, like you! Darkness, if you value— Come, Darkness," he went on in a singularly broken manner, "your remaining question." His thought rays switched back and forth with an uncommon sign of utter chaos of mind.

Then they centered on Darkness again. "I know your other query, Darkness. I know, knew when first Sparkle brought you to me, eons ago.

"What is beyond the darkness? That has occupied your mind since your creation. What lies on the fringe of the lightless section by which this universe is bounded?

"I do not know, Darkness. Nor does anyone know."

"But you *must* believe there is something beyond," cried Darkness.

"Darkness, in the dim past of our race, beings of your caliber have tried—five of them I remember in my time, billions of years ago. But, they never came back. They left the universe, hurling themselves into that awful void, and they never came back."

"How do you know they didn't reach that foreign universe?" asked Darkness breathlessly.

"Because they didn't come back," answered Oldster, simply. "If they could have gotten across, at least one or two of them would have returned. They never reached that universe. Why? All the energy they were able to accumulate for that staggering voyage was exhausted. And they dissipated— died—in the energiless emptiness of the darkness."

"There must be a way to cross!" said Darkness violently. "There must be a way to gather energy for the crossing! Oldster, you are destroying my life-dream! I have wanted to cross. I want to find the edge of the darkness. I want to find life there—perhaps then I will find the meaning of all life!"

"Find the—" began Oldster pityingly, then stoppped, realizing the futility of completing the sentence.

"It is a pity you are not like the others, Darkness. Perhaps they understand that it is as purposeful to lie sleeping in the seventh band as to discover the riddle of the darkness. They are truly happy, you are not. Always, my son, you overestimate the worth of life."

"Am I wrong in doing so?"

"No. Think as you will, and think that life is high. There is no harm. Dream your dream of great life, and dream your dream of another universe. There is joy even in the sadness of unattainment."

Again that long silence, and again the smoldering flame of resentment in Darkness' mind. This time there was no quenching of that flame. It burned fiercely.

"I will not dream!" said Darkness furiously. "When first my visions became activated, they rested on the darkness, and my newborn thought-swirls wondered about the darkness, and knew that something lay beyond it!

"And whether or not I die in that void, I am going into it!"

Abruptly, irately, he snapped from the fifteenth band into the first, but before he had time to use his propellents, he saw Oldster, a giant body of intense, swirling energies of pure light, materialize before him.

"Darkness, stop!" and Oldster's thoughts were unsteady. "Darkness," he went on, as the younger energy creature stared spellbound, "I had vowed to myself never to leave the band of lightlessness. I have come from it, a moment, for—you!

"You will die. You will dissipate in the void! You will never cross it, if it can be crossed, with the limited energy your body contains!"

He seized Darkness' thought-swirls in tight bands of energy.

"Darkness, there is knowledge that I possess. Receive it!"

With newborn wonder, Darkness erased consciousness. The mighty accumulated knowledge of Oldster sped into him in a swift flow, a great tide of space lore no other being had ever possessed.

The inflow ceased, and as from an immeasurably distant space came Oldster's parting words:

"Darkness, farewell! Use your knowledge, use it to further your dream. Use it to cross the darkness."

Again fully conscious, Darkness knew that Oldster had gone again into the fifteenth band of utter lightlessness, in his vain attempt at peace.

He hung tensely motionless in the first band, exploring the knowledge that now was his. At the portent of one particular portion of it, he trembled.

In wildest exhilaration, he thrust out his propellents, dashing at full speed to his mother.

He hung before her.

"Mother, I am going into the darkness!"

There was a silence, pregnant with her sorrow. "Yes, I know. It was destined when first you were born. For that I named you Darkness." A restless quiver of sparks left her. Her gaze sad and loving. She said, "Farewell, Darkness, my son."

She wrenched herself from true space, and he was alone. The thought stabbed him. He was alone—alone as Oldster.

Struggling against the vast depression that overwhelmed him, he slowly started on his way to the very farthest edge of the universe, for there lay the Great Energy.

Absently he drifted across the galaxies, the brilliant denizens of the cosmos, lying quiescent on their eternal black beds. He drew a small sun into him, and converted it into energy for the long flight.

And suddenly afar off he saw his innumerable former companions. A cold mirth seized him. Playing! The folly of children, the aimlessness of stars!

He sped away from them, and slowly increased his velocity, the thousands of galaxies flashing away behind. His speed mounted, a frightful acceleration carrying him toward his goal.

IV. Beyond Light

It took him seven millions of years to cross the universe, going at the tremendous velocity he had attained. And he was in a galaxy whose far flung suns hung out into the darkness, were themselves traveling into the darkness at the comparatively slow pace of several thousand miles a second.

Instantaneously, his vision rested on an immense star, a star so immense that he felt himself unconsciously expand in an effort to rival it. So titanic was its mass that it drew all light rays save the short ultraviolet back into it.

It was hot, an inconceivable mass of matter a billion miles across. Like an evil, sentient monster of the skies it hung, dominating the tiny suns of this galaxy that were perhaps its children, to Darkness flooding the heavens with ultraviolet light from its great expanse of writhing, coiling, belching surface; and mingled with that light was a radiation of energy so virulent that it ate its way painfully into his very brain.

Still another radiation impinged on him, an energy which, were he to possess its source, would activate his propellents to such an extent that his velocity would pale any to which his race had attained in all its long history!—would hurl him into the darkness at such an unthinkable rate that the universe would be gone in the infinitesimal part of a second!

But how hopeless seemed the task of rending it from that giant of the universe! The source of that energy, he knew with knowledge that was sure, was matter, matter so incomparably dense, its electrons crowding each other till they touched, that even that furiously molten star could not destroy it.

He spurred back several millions of miles, and stared at it. Suddenly he knew fear, a cold fear. He felt that the sun was animate, that it knew he was waiting there, that it was prepared to resist his pitiable onslaughts. And as if in support of his fears, he felt rays of such intense repelling power, such alive, painful malignancy that he almost threw away his mad intentions of splitting it.

"I have eaten suns before," he told himself, with the air of one arguing against himself. "I can at least split that one open, and extract the morsel that lies in its interior."

He drew into him as many of the surrounding suns as he was able, converting them into pure energy. He ceased at last, for no longer could his body, a giant complexity of swarming intense fields sixty millions of miles across, assimilate more.

Then, with all the acceleration he could muster, he dashed headlong at the celestial monster.

It grew and expanded, filling all the skies until he could no longer see anything but it. He drew near its surface. Rays of fearful potency smote him until he convulsed in the whiplash agony of it. A frightful velocity, he contacted the heaving surface, and—made a tiny dent some millions of miles in depth.

He strove to push forward, but streams of energy repelled him, energy that flung him away from the star in acceleration.

He stoppped his backward flight, fighting his torment, and threw himself upon the star again. It repulsed him with an uncanny likeness to a living thing. Again and again he went through the agonizing process, to be as often thrust back.

He could not account for those repelling rays, which seemed to operate in direct contrariness to the star's obviously great gravitational field, nor did he try to account for them. There were mysteries in space which even Oldster had never been able to solve.

But there was a new awe in him. He hung in space, spent and quivering.

"It is *almost* alive," he thought, and then adopted new tactics. Rushing at the giant, he skimmed over and through its surface in titanic spirals, until he had swept it entirely free of raging, incandescent gases. Before the star could replenish its surface, he spiraled it again, clinging to it until he could no longer resist the repelling forces, or the burning rays which impinged upon him.

The star now lay in the heavens diminished by a tenth of its former bulk. Darkness, hardly able to keep himself together, retired a distance from it and discarded excess energy.

He went back to the star.

Churning seas of pure light flickered fitfully across. Now and then there were belchings of matter bursting within itself.

Darkness began again. He charged, head on. He contacted, bored millions of miles, and was thrown back with mounting velocity. Hurtling back into space, Darkness finally knew that all these tactics would in the last analysis prove useless. His glance roving, it came to rest on a dense, redly glowing sun. For a moment it meant nothing, and then he knew, knew that here at last lay the solution.

He plucked that dying star from its place, and swinging it in huge circles on the tip of a tractor ray, flung it with the utmost of his savage force at the gargantuan star.

Fiercely, he watched the smaller sun appproach its parent. Closer, closer, and then—they collided! A titanic explosion ripped space, sending out wave after wave of cosmic rays, causing an inferno of venomous, raging flames that extended far into the skies, licking it in a fury of utter abandon. The mighty sun split wide open, exhibiting a violet hot, gaping maw more than a billion miles wide.

Darkness activated his propellents, and dropped into the awful cavity until he was far beneath its rim, and had approached the center of the star where lay that mass of matter which was the source of the Great Energy. To his sight, it was invisible, save as a blank area of nothingness, since light rays of no wavelength whatsoever could leave it.

Darkness wrapped himself exotically around the sphere, and at the same time the two halves of the giant star fell together, imprisoning him at its core.

This possibility he had not overlooked. With concentrated knots of force, he ate away the merest portion of the surface of the sphere, and absorbed it in him. He was amazed at the metamorphosis. He became aware of a vigor so infinite that he felt nothing could withstand him.

Slowly, he began to expand. He was inexorable. The star could not stop him; it gave. It cracked, great gaping cracks which parted with displays of blinding light and pure heat. He continued to grow, pushing outward.

With the sphere of Great Energy, which was no more than ten million miles across, in his grasp, he continued inflation. A terrific blast of malignant energy ripped at him; cracks millions of miles in length appeared, cosmic displays of pure energy flared. After that, the gargantua gave way before Darkness so readily that he had split it up into separate parts before he ever knew it.

He then became aware that he was in the center of thousands of large and small pieces of the star that were shooting away from him in all directions, forming new suns that would chart individual orbits for themselves.

He had conquered. He hung motionless, grasping the sphere of Great Energy at his center, along with the mystic globe of purple light.

He swung his vision on the darkness, and looked at it in fascination for a long time. Then, without a last look at the universe of his birth, he activated his propellents with the nameless Great Energy, and plunged into that dark well.

All light, save that he created, vanished. He was hemmed in on all sides by the vastness of empty space. Exaltation, coupled with an awareness of the infinite power in his grasp, took hold of his thoughts and made them soar. His acceleration was minimum rather than maximum, yet in a brief space of his time standard he traversed uncountable billions of light-years.

Darkness ahead, and darkness behind, and darkness all around—that had been his dream. It had been his dream all through his life, even during those formless years in which he had played, in obedience to Oldster's admonishment. Always there had been the thought—what lies at the other end of the darkness? Now he was in the darkness, and a joy such as he had never known claimed him. He was on the way! Would he find another universe, a universe which had bred the same kind of life as he had known? He could not think otherwise.

His acceleration was incredible! Yet he knew that he was using a minimum of power. He began to step it up, swiftly increasing even the vast velocity which he had attained. Where lay that other universe? He could not know, and he had chosen no single direction in which to leave his own universe. There had been no choice of direction. Any line stretching into the vault of the darkness might have ended in that alien universe....

Not until a million years had elapsed did his emotions subside. Then there were other thoughts. He began to feel a dreadful fright, a fright that grew on him as he left his universe farther behind. He was hurtling into the darkness that none before him had crossed, and few had dared to try crossing, at a velocity which he finally realized he could attain, but not comprehend. Mind could not think it, thoughts could not say it!

And—he was alone! *Alone!* An icy hand clutched at him. He had never known the true meaning of that word. There were none of his friends near, nor his mother, nor greatbrained Oldster—there was no living thing within innumerable light-centuries. *He* was the only life in the void!

Thus, for almost exactly ninety millions of years he wondered and thought, first about life, then the edge of the darkness, and lastly the mysterious energy field eternally at his core. He found the answer to two, and perhaps, in the end, the other.

Ever, each infinitesimal second that elapsed, his visions were probing hundreds of light-years ahead, seeking the first sign of that universe he believed in; but no, all was darkness so dense it seemed to possess mass.

The monotony became agony. A colossal loneliness began to tear at him. He wanted to do anything, even play, or slice huge stars up into planets. But there was only one escape from the phantasmal horror of the unending ebon path. Now and anon he seized the globe of light with a tractor ray and hurled it into the curtain of darkness behind him at terrific velocity.

It sped away under the momentum imparted to it until sight of it was lost. But always, though millions of years might elapse, it returned, attached to him by invisible strings of energy. It was part of him, it defied penetration of its secret, and it would never leave him, until, perhaps, of itself it revealed its true purpose.

Infinite numbers of light-years, so infinite that if written a sheet as broad as the universe would have been required, reeled behind.

Eighty millions of years passed. Darkness had not been as old as that when he had gone into the void for which he had been named. Fear that he had been wrong took a stronger foothold in his thoughts. But now he knew that he would never go back.

Long before the eighty-nine-millionth year came, he had exhausted all sources of amusement. Sometimes he expanded or contracted to incredible sizes. Sometimes he automatically went through the motions of traversing the forty-seven bands. He felt the click in his consciousness which told him that if there had been hyperspace in the darkness, he would have been transported into it. But how could there be different kinds of darkness? He strongly doubted the existence of hyperspace here, for only matter could occasion the dimensional disturbances which obtained in his universe.

But with the eighty-nine-millionth year came the end of his pilgrimage. It came abruptly. For one tiny space of time, his visions contacted a stream of light, light that was left as the outward trail of a celestial body. Darkness' body, fifty millions of miles in girth, involuntarily contracted to half its size. Energy streamed together and formed molten blobs of flaring matter that sped from him in the chaotic emotions of the moment.

A wave of shuddering thankfulness shook him, and his thoughts rioted sobbingly in his memory swirls.

"Oldster, Oldster, if only your great brain could know this...."

Uncontrollably inflating and deflating, he tore onward, shearing vast quantities of energy from the tight matter at his core, converting it into propellent power that drove him at a velocity that was more than unthinkable, toward the universe from whence had come that light-giving body.

V. The Colored Globes

In the ninety-millionth year a dim spot of light rushed at him, and, as he hurtled onward, the spot of light grew, and expanded, and broke up into tinier lights, tinier lights that in turn broke up into their components—until the darkness was blotted out, giving way to the dazzling, beautiful radiance of an egg-shaped universe.

He was out of the darkness; he had discovered its edge. Instinctively, he lessened his velocity to a fraction of its former self, and then, as if some mightier will than his had overcome him, he lost consciousness, and sped unknowingly, at steady speed, through the outlying fringe of the outer galaxy, through it, through its brothers, until, unconscious, he was in the midst of that alien galactic system.

First he made a rigid tour of inspection, flying about from star to star, tearing them wantonly apart, as if each and every atom belonged solely to him. The galaxies, the suns, the very elements of construction, all were the same as he knew them. All nature, he decided, was probably alike, in this universe, or in that one.

But was there life?

An abrupt wave of restlessness, of unease, passed over him. He felt unhappy, and unsated. He looked about on the stars, great giants, dwarfs fiercely burning, other hulks of matter cooled to black, forbidding cinders, intergalactic nebulae wreathing unpurposefully about, assuming weird and beautiful formations over periods of thousands of years. He, Darkness, had come to them, had crossed the great gap of nothing, but they were unaffected by this unbelievable feat, went swinging on their courses knowing nothing of him. He felt small, without meaning. Such thoughts seemed the very apostasy of sense, but there they were—he could not shake them off. It was with a growing feeling of disillusionment that he drifted through the countless galaxies and nebulae that unrolled before him, in search of life.

And his quest was rewarded. From afar off, the beating flow of the life-energy came. He drove toward its source, thirty or forty light-years, and hung in its presence.

The being was a green-light, that one of the two classes in which Darkness had divided the life he knew. He himself was a purple-light, containing at his core a globe of pure light, the purpose of which had been one of the major problems of his existence.

The green-light, when she saw him, came to a stop. They stared at each other.

Finally she spoke, and there was wonder and doubt in her thoughts.

"Who are you? You seem—alien."

"You will hardly believe me," Darkness replied, now trembling with a sensation which, inexplicably, could not be defined by the fact that he was in converse with a being of another universe. "But I am alien. I do not belong to this universe."

"But that seems quite impossible. Perhaps you are from another space, beyond the forty-seventh. But that is more impossible!" She eyed him with growing puzzlement and awe.

"I am from no other space," said Darkness somberly. "I am from another universe beyond the darkness."

"From beyond the darkness?" she said faintly, and then she involuntarily contracted. Abruptly she turned her visions on the darkness. For a long, long time she stared at it, and then she returned her vision rays to Darkness.

"So you have crossed the darkness," she whispered. "They used to tell me that that was the most impossible thing it was possible to dream of—to cross that terrible section of lightlessness. No one could cross, they said, because there was nothing on the other side. But I never believed, purple-light, I never believed them. And there have been times when I have desperately wanted to traverse it myself. But there were tales of beings who had gone into it, and never returned. . . . And you have crossed it!"

A shower of crystalline sparks fled from her. So evident was the sudden hero worship carried on her thought waves, that Darkness felt a wild rise in spirits. And suddenly he was able to define the never before experienced emotions which had enwrapped him when first this green-light spoke.

"Green-light, I have journeyed a distance the length of which I cannot think to you, seeking the riddle of the darkness. But perhaps there was something else I was seeking, something to fill a vacant part of me. I know now what it was. A mate, green-light, a thinker. And you are that thinker, that friend with whom I can journey, voyaging from universe to universe, finding the secrets of all that is. Look! The Great Energy which alone made it possible for me to cross the darkness, has been barely tapped!"

Imperceptibly she drew away. There was an unexplainable wariness that seemed half sorrow in her thoughts.

"You are a thinker," he exclaimed. "Will you come with me?"

She stared at him, and he felt she possessed a natural wisdom he could never hope to accumulate. There was a strange shrinkage of his spirits. What was that she was saying?

"Darkness," she said gently, "you would do well to turn and leave me, a green-light, forever. You are a purple-light, I a green. Green-light and purple-light—is that all you have thought about the two types of life? Then you must know that beyond the difference in color, there is another: the greens have a knowledge not vouchsafed the purples, until it is . . . too late. For your own sake, then, I ask you to leave me forever."

He looked at her puzzled. Then slowly, "That is an impossible request, now that I have found you. You are what I need," he insisted.

"But don't you understand?" she cried. "I know something you have not even guessed at! Darkness—leave me!"

He became bewildered. What was she driving at? What was it she knew that he could not know? For a moment he hesitated. Far down in him a voice was bidding him to do as she asked, and quickly. But another voice, that of a growing emotion he could not name, bid him stay; for she was the complement of himself, the half of him that would make him complete. And the second voice was stronger.

"I am not going," he said firmly, and the force of his thoughts left no doubt to the unshakable quality of his decision.

She spoke faintly, as if some outside will had overcome her. "No, Darkness, now you are not going; it is too late! Learn the secret of the purple globe!"

Abruptly, she wrenched herself into a hyperspace, and all his doubts and fears were erased as she disappeared. He followed her delightedly up the scale, catching sight of her in one band just as she vanished into the next.

And so they came to the forty-seventh, where all matter, its largest and smallest components, assumed the shapes of unchangeable cubes; even he and the green-light appeared as cubes, gigantic cubes millions of miles in extent, a geometric figure they could never hope to distort.

Darkness watched her expectantly. Perhaps she would now start a game of chopping chunks off these cubed suns, and swing them around as planets. Well, he would be willing to do that for a while, in her curious mood of playfulness, but after that they must settle down to discovering possible galactic systems beyond this one.

As he looked at her she vanished.

"Hmm, probably gone down the scale," thought Darkness, and he dropped through the lower bands. He found her in none.

"Darkness . . . try the . . . forty-eighth. . . ." Her thought came faintly.

"The forty-eighth!" he cried in astonishment. At the same time, there was a seething of his memory-swirls as if the knowledge of his life were being arranged to fit some new fact, a strange alchemy of the mind by which he came to know that there *was* a forty-eighth.

Now he knew, as he had always known, that there was a forty-eighth. He snapped himself into it.

Energy became rampant in a ceaseless shifting about him. A strange energy, reminding him of nothing so much as the beating flow of an energy creature approaching him from a near distance. His vision sought out the green-light.

She was facing him somberly, yet with a queerly detached arrogance. His mind was suddenly choked with the freezing sensation that he was face to face with horror.

"I have never been here before," he whispered faintly.

He thought he detected pity in her, but it was overwhelmed by the feeling that she was under the influence of an outside will that could not know pity.

Yet she said, "I am sadder than ever before. But too late. You are my mate, and this is the band of—life!"

Abruptly while he stared, she receded, and he could not follow, save with his visions. Presently, as if an hypnotist had clamped his mind, she herself disapppeared, all that he saw of her being the green globe of light she carried. He saw nothing else, knew nothing else. It became his whole universe, his whole life. A peacefulness, complete and uncorroded by vain striving, settled on him like stardust.

The green globe of light dimmed, became smaller, until it was less than a pinpoint, surrounded by an infinity of colorless white energy.

Then, so abruptly it was in the nature of a shock, he came from his torpor, and was conscious. Far off he still saw the green globe of light, but it was growing in size, approaching—approaching a purple globe of light that in turn raced toward it at high velocity.

"It is my own light," he thought, startled. "I must have unwittingly hurled it forth when she settled that hypnotic influence over me. No matter. It will come back."

But would it come back? Green globe of light was expanding in apparent size, approaching purple which, in turn, dwindled toward it at increasing speed.

"At that rate," he thought in panic, "they will collide. Then how will my light come back to me?"

He watched intently, a poignantly cold feeling clutching at him. Closer . . . closer. He quivered. Green globe and purple globe had crashed.

They met in a blinding crescendo of light that brightened space for light-years around. A huge mistiness of light formed into a sphere, in the center of which hung a brilliant ball. The misty light slowly subsided until it had been absorbed into the brighter light that remained as motionless as Darkness himself. Then it commenced pulsating with a strange, rhythmic regularity.

Something about that pulsing stirred ancient memories, something that said, "You, too, were once no more than that pulsing ball."

Thoughts immense in scope, to him, tumbled in his mind.

"That globe is life," he thought starkly. "The green-light and I have created life. That was her meaning, when she said this was the band of life. Its activating energy flows rampant here.

"That is the secret of the purple globe; with the green globe it creates life. And I had never known the forty-eighth band until she made it known to me!

"The purpose of life—to create life." The thought of that took fire in his brain. For one brief, intoxicating moment he thought that he had solved the last and most baffling of his mighty problems.

As with all other moments of exaltation he had known, disillusionment followed swiftly after. To what end was that? The process continued on and on, and what came of it? Was creation of life the only use of life? A meaningless circle! He recalled Oldster's words of the past, and horror claimed him.

"Life, my life," he whispered dully. "A dead sun and life—one of equal importance with the other. That is unbelievable!" he burst out.

He was aware of the green-light hovering near; yes, she possessed a central light, while his was gone!

She looked at him sorrowfully. "Darkness, if only you had listened to me!"

Blankly, he returned her gaze. "Why is it that you have a light, while I have none?"

"A provision of whatever it was that created us, endows the green-lights with the ability to replace their lights three times. Each merging of a purple and green light may result in the creation of one or several newly born. Thus the number born over-balances the number of deaths. When my fourth light has gone, as it will some day, I know, I too, will die."

"You mean, I will—die?"

"Soon."

Darkness shuddered, caught halfway between an emotion of blind anger and mental agony. "There is death everywhere," he whispered, "and everything is futile!"

"Perhaps," she said softly, her grief carrying poignantly to him. "Darkness, do not be sad. Darkness, death does indeed come to all, but that does not say that life is of no significance.

"Far past in the gone ages of our race, we were pitiful, tiny blobs of energy which crept along at less than light speed. An energy creature of that time knew nothing of any but the first and forty-eighth bands of hyperspace. The rest he could not conceive of as being existent. He was ignorant, possessing elementary means of absorbing energy for life. For countless billions of years he never knew there was an edge to the universe. He could not conceive an edge.

"He was weak, but he gained in strength. Slowly, he evolved, and intelligence entered his mind.

"Always, he discovered things he had been formerly unable to conceive in his mind, and even now there are things that lie beyond the mind; one of them is the end of all space. And the greatest is, why life exists. Both are something we cannot conceive, but in time evolution of mental powers will allow us to conceive them, even as we conceived the existence of hyperspace, and those other things. Dimly, so dimly, even now I can see some reason, but it slips the mind. But Darkness! All of matter is destined to break down to an unchanging state of maximum entropy; it is life, and life alone, that builds in an upward direction. So . . . faith!"

She was gone. She had sown what comfort she could.

Her words shot Darkness full of the wild fire of hope. That

was the answer! Vague and promissory it was, but no one could arrive nearer to the solution than that. For a moment he was suffused with the blissful thought that the last of his problems was disposed of.

Then, in one awful space of time, the green-light's philosophy was gone from his memory as if it had never been uttered. He felt the pangs of an unassailable weariness, as if life energies were seeping away.

Haggardly, he put into effect one driving thought. With lagging power, he shot from the fatal band of life . . . and death . . . down the scale. Something unnameable, perhaps some natal memory, made him pause for the merest second in the seventeenth band. Afar off, he saw the green-light and her newly born. They had left the highest band, come to the band where propellents became useless. So it had been at his own birth.

He paused no more and dropped to the true band, pursuing a slow course across the star-beds of this universe, until he at last emerged on its ragged shore. He went on into the darkness, until hundreds of light-years separated him from the universe his people had never known existed.

VI. Dissipation

He stopped and looked back at the lens of misty radiance. "I have not even discovered the edge of the darkness," he thought. "It stretched out and around. That galactic system and my own are just pinpoints of light, sticking up, vast distances apart, through an unlimited ebon cloth. They are so small in the darkness they barely have the one dimension of existence!"

He went on his way, slowly, wearily, as if the power to activate his propellents were diminishing. There came a time, in his slow, desperate striving after the great velocity he had known in crossing the lightless section, when that universe, that pinpoint sticking up, became as a pinpoint to his sight.

He stopped, took one longing look at it, and accelerated until it was lost to view.

"I am alone again," he thought vaguely. "I am more alone than Oldster ever was. How did he escape death from the green-lights? Perhaps he discovered their terrible secret, and fled before they could wreak their havoc on him. He was a lover of wisdom, and he did not want to die. Now he is living, and he is alone, marooning himself in the lightless band, striving not to think. He could make himself die, but he is afraid to, even though he is so tired of life, and of thinking his endless thoughts.

"I will die. But no . . . ! Ah, yes, I will."

He grew bewildered. He thought, or tried to think, of what came after death. Why, there would be nothing! He would not be there, and without him nothing else could exist!

"I would not be there, and therefore there would be nothing," he thought starkly. "Oh, that is inconceivable. Death! Why, forever after I died, I would be—dead!"

He strove to alleviate the awfulness of the eternal unconsciousness. "I was nothing once, that is true; why cannot that time come again? But it is unthinkable. I feel as if I am the center of everything, the cause, the focal point, and even the foundation."

For some time this thought gave him a kind of gloating satisfaction. Death was indeed not so bad, when one could thus drag to oblivion the very things which had sponsored his life. But at length reason supplanted dreams. He sighed. "And that is vanity!"

Again he felt the ineffably horrible sensation of an incapacity to activate his propellents the full measure, and an inability to keep himself down to normal size. His memory swirls were pulsating, and striving, sometimes, to obliterate themselves.

Everything seemed meaningless. His very drop into the darkness, at slow acceleration, was without purpose.

"I could not reach either universe now," he commented to himself, "because I am dying. Poor Mother! Poor Oldster! They will not even know I crossed. That seems the greatest sorrow—to do a great thing, and not be able to tell of it. Why did they not tell me of the central lights? With Oldster, it was fear that I should come to the same deathless end as he. With Mother—she obeyed an instinct as deeply rooted as space. There must be perpetuation of life.

"Why? Was the green-light right? Is there some tangible purpose to life which we are unable to perceive? But where is my gain, if I have to die to bring to ultimate fruition that purpose? I suppose Oldster knew the truth. Life just is, had an accidental birth, and exists haphazardly, like a star, or an electron.

"But, knowing these things, why do I not immediately give way to the expanding forces within me? Ah, I do not know!"

Convulsively he applied his mind to the continuance of life within his insistently expanding body. For a while he gloried in the small increase of his fading vigor.

"Making solar systems!" his mind took up the thread of a lost thought. "Happy sons of Radiant, Incandecsent, Great Power, and all the others!"

He concentrated on the sudden thought that struck him. He was dying, of that he was well aware, but he was dying without doing anything. What had he actually done, in this life of his?

"But what can I do? I am alone," he thought vaguely. Then, "I could make a planet, and I could put the life germ on it. Oldster taught me that."

Suddenly he was afraid he would die before he created this planet. He set his mind to it, and began to strip from the sphere of tight matter vast quantities of energy, then condensed it to form matter more attenuated. With lagging power, he formed mass after mass of matter, ranging all through the ninety-eight elements that he knew.

Fifty thousand years saw the planet's first stage of completion. It had become a tiny sphere some fifteen thousand miles in diameter. With a heat ray he then boiled it, and with another ray cooled its crust, at the same time forming oceans and continents on its surface. Both water and land, he knew, were necessary to life which was bound by nature of its construction to the surface of a planet.

Then came the final, completing touch. No other being had ever deliberately done what Darkness did then. Carefully, he created an infinitesimal splash of life-perpetuating protoplasm; he dropped it aimlessly into a tiny wrinkle on the planet's surface.

He looked at the finished work, the most perfect planet he or his playmates had ever created, with satisfaction, notwithstanding the dull pain of weariness that throbbed through the complex energy fields of his body.

Then he took the planet up in a tractor ray, and swung it around and around, as he now so vividly recalled doing in his childhood. He gave it a swift angular velocity, and then shot it off at a tangent, in a direction along the line of which he was reasonably sure lay his own universe. He watched it with dulling visions. It receded into the darkness that would surround it for ages, and then it was a pinpoint, and then nothing.

"It is gone," he said, somehow wretchedly lonely because

of that, "but it will reach the universe; perhaps for millions of years it will traverse the galaxies unmolested. Then a sun will reach out and claim it. There will be life upon it, life that will grow until it is intelligent, and will say it has a soul, and purpose in existing."

Nor did the ironic humor of the ultimate swift and speedy death of even that type of life, once it had begun existence, escape him. Perhaps for one or ten million years it would flourish, and then even it would be gone—once upon a time nothing and then nothing again.

He felt a sensation that brought blankness nearer, a sensation of expansion, but now he made no further attempts to prolong a life which was, in effect, already dead. There was a heave within him, as if some subconscious force were deliberately attempting to tear him apart.

He told himself that he was no longer afraid. "I am simply going into another darkness—but it will be a much longer journey than the other."

Like a protecting cloak, he drew in his vision rays about him, away from the ebon emptiness. He drifted, expanding through the vast, interuniversal space.

The last expansion came, the expansion that dissipated his memory swirls. A vast compact sphere of living drew itself out until Darkness was only free energy distributed over light-years of space.

And death, in that last moment, seemed suddenly to be a far greater and more astounding occurrence than birth had ever seemed.

DARK MISSION

Astounding Science Fiction
July

by Lester del Rey (1915-   )

> *Many people believe that July was a special month in the history of* Astounding Science Fiction *because so many excellent and influential stories seemed to fill that issue during the Golden Age. Heinlein's "Coventry" dominated the July, 1940 ASF and may have been partially responsible for the relative neglect of this fine story of tragedy and sacrifice. It was first reprinted in del Rey's 1948 collection from Prime Press* . . . And Some Were Human, *one of the pioneer single-author collections in science fiction.*

(Lester del Rey always reminds me of Harlan Ellison; or, rather, vice versa, since I've known Lester much longer. He's another one of the brotherhood who goes back forty years with me. —Astonishing how many of us have survived and are still active. Maybe science fiction has a preservative effect.

In any case, Lester, like Harlan, is short, and loud, and quarrelsome and prickly. And, as in the case of Harlan, if you can make your way through the prickles and stay alive—by no means certain—you'll find Lester is soft as mush underneath and will do anything for you. A true, trusty friend who will give you anything but a kind word.

And he's an excellent cook. If you've never eaten a Passover meal that he's cooked, you haven't truly lived.—I.A.)

The rays of the Sun lanced down over the tops of the trees and into the clearing, revealing a scene of chaos and havoc.

Yesterday there had been a wooden frame house there, but now only pieces of it remained. One wall had been broken away, as by an explosion, and lay on the ground in fragments; the roof was crushed in, as if some giant had stepped on it and passed on.

But the cause of the damage was still there, lying on the ruins of the house. A tangled mass of buckled girders and metal plates lay mixed with a litter of laboratory equipment that had been neatly arranged in one room of the house, and parts of a strange engine lay at one side. Beyond was a tube that might have been a rocket. The great metal object that lay across the broken roof now only hinted at the sleek cylinder it had once been, but a trained observer might have guessed that it was the wreck of a rocketship. From the former laboratory, flames were licking up at the metal hull, and slowly spreading toward the rest of the house.

In the clearing, two figures lay outstretched, of similar size and build, but otherwise unlike. One was of a dark man of middle age, completely naked, with a face cut and battered beyond all recognition. The odd angle of the head was unmistakable proof that his neck was broken. The other man might have been a brawny sea viking of earlier days, both from his size and appearance, but his face revealed something finer and of a higher culture. He was fully clothed, and the slow movement of his chest showed that there was still life in him. Beside him, there was a broken beam from the roof, a few spots of blood on it. There was more blood on the man's head, but the cut was minor, and he was only stunned.

Now he stirred uneasily and groped uncertainly to his feet, shaking his head and fingering the cut on his scalp. His eyes traveled slowly across the clearing and to the ruins that were burning merrily. The corpse claimed his next attention, and he turned it over to examine the neck. He knit his brows and shook his head savagely, trying to call back the memories that eluded him.

They would not come. He recognized what his eyes saw, but his mind produced no words to describe them, and the past was missing. His first memory was of waking to find his head pounding with an ache that was almost unbearable. Without surprise, he studied the rocket and saw that it had come down on the house, out of control, but it evoked no pictures in his mind, and he gave up. He might have been in the rocket or the house at the time; he had no way of telling which. Probably the naked man had been asleep at the time in the house.

Something prickled gently in the back of his mind, growing stronger and urging him to do something. He must not waste time here, but must fulfill some vital mission. What mission? For a second, he almost had it, and then it was gone again, leaving only the compelling urge that must be obeyed. He shrugged and started away from the ruins toward the little trail that showed through the trees.

Then another impulse called him back to the corpse, and he obeyed it because he knew of nothing else to do. Acting without conscious volition, he tugged at the corpse, found it strangely heavy, and dragged it toward the house. The flames were everywhere now, but he found a place where the heat was not too great and pulled the corpse over a pile of combustibles.

With the secondary impulse satisfied, the first urge returned, and he set off down the trail, moving slowly. The shoes hurt his feet, and his legs were leaden, but he kept on grimly, while a series of questions went around his head in circles. Who was he, where, and why?

Whoever had lived in the house, himself or the corpse, had obviously chosen the spot for privacy; the trail seemed to go on through the woods endlessly, and he saw no signs of houses along it. He clumped on mechanically, wondering if there was no end, until a row of crossed poles bearing wires caught his eye. Ahead, he made out a broad highway, with vehicles speeding along it in both directions, and hastened forward, hoping to meet someone.

Luck was with him. Pulled up at the side of the road was one of the vehicles, and a man was doing something at the front end of the car. Rough words carried back to him suggesting anger. He grinned suddenly and hastened toward the car, his eyes riveted on the man's head. A tense feeling shot through his brain and left, just as he reached the machine.

"Need help?" The words slipped out unconsciously, and now other words came pouring into his head, along with ideas and knowledge that had not been there before. But the sight of the man, or whatever had restored that section of his memory, had brought back no personal knowledge, and that seemed wrong somehow. The driving impulse he felt was still unexplained.

The man had looked up at his words, and relief shot over the sweating face. "Help's the one thing I need," he replied gratefully. "I been fussing with this blasted contraption darned near an hour, and nobody's even stopped to ask, so far. Know anything about it?"

"Um-m-m." The stranger, as he was calling himself for want of a better name, tested the wires himself, vaguely troubled at the simplicity of the engine. He gave up and went around to the other side, lifting the hood and inspecting the design. Then sureness came to him as he reached for the tool kit. "Probably the ... um ... timing pins," he said.

It was. A few minutes later the engine purred softly and the driver turned to the stranger. "O. K. now, I guess. Good thing you came along: worst part of the road and not a repair shop for miles. Where you going?"

"I—" The stranger caught himself. "The big city," he said, for want of a better destination.

"Hop in, then. I'm going to Elizabeth, right on your way. Glad to have you along; gets so a man talks to himself on these long drives, unless he has something to do. Smoke?"

"Thank you, no. I never do." He watched the other light up, feeling uncomfortable about it. The smell of the smoke, when it reached him, was nauseating, as were the odor of gasoline and the man's own personal effluvium, but he pushed them out of his mind as much as possible. "Have you heard or read anything about a rocketship of some kind?"

"Sure. Oglethorpe's, you mean? I been reading what the papers had to say about it." The drummer took his eyes off the road for a second, and his beady little eyes gleamed. "I been wondering a long time why some of these big-shot financiers don't back up the rockets, and finally Oglethorpe does. Boy, now maybe we'll find out something about this Mars business."

The stranger grinned mechanically. "What does his ship look like?"

"Picture of it in the *Scoop*, front page. Find it back of the seat, there. Yeah, that's it. Wonder what the Martians look like?"

"Hard to guess," the stranger answered. Even rough halftones of the picture showed that it was not the ship that had crashed, but radically different. "No word of other rockets?"

"Nope, not that I know of. You know, I kinda feel maybe the Martians might look like us. Sure." He took the other's skepticism for granted without looking around. "Wrote a story about that once, for one of these science-fiction magazines, but they sent it back. I figured out maybe a long time ago there was a civilization on Earth—Atlantis, maybe—and they went over and settled on Mars. Only Atlantis sunk on them, and there they were, stranded. I figured maybe one day they came back, sort of lost out for a while, but popped up again and started civilization humming. Not bad, eh?"

"Clever," the stranger admitted. "But it sounds vaguely familiar. Suppose we said instead there was a war between the mother world and Mars that wrecked both civilizations, instead of your Atlantis sinking. Wouldn't that be more logical?"

"Maybe, I dunno. Might try it, though mostly they seem to want freaks— Darned fool, passing on a hill!" He leaned out to shake a pudgy fist, then came back to his rambling account. "Read one the other day with two races, one like octopuses, the others twenty feet tall and all blue."

Memory pricked tantalizingly and came almost to the surface. Blue— Then it was gone again, leaving only a troubled feeling. The stranger frowned and settled down in the seat, answering in monosyllables to the other's monologue, and watching the patchwork of country and cities slip by.

"There's Elizabeth. Any particular place you want me to drop you?"

The stranger stirred from the half-coma induced by the cutting ache in his head, and looked about. "Any place," he answered. Then the urge in the back of his mind grabbed at him again, and he changed it. "Some doctor's office."

That made sense, of course. Perhaps the impulse had been only the logical desire to seek medical aid, all along. But it was still there, clamoring for expression, and he doubted the logic of anything connected with it. The call for aid could not explain the sense of disaster that accompanied it. As the car stopped before a house with a doctor's shingle, his pulse was hammering with frenzied urgency.

"Here we are." The drummer reached out toward the door hangle, almost brushing one of the other's hands. The stranger jerked it back savagely, avoiding contact by a narrow margin, and a cold chill ran up his back and quivered its way down again. If that hand had touched him— The half-opened door closed again, but left one fact impressed on him. Under no conditions must he suffer another to make a direct contact with his body, lest something horrible should happen! Another crazy angle, unconnected with the others, but too strong for disobedience.

He climbed out, muttering his thanks, and made up the walk toward the office of Dr. Lanahan, hours 12:00 to 4:00.

The doctor was an old man, with the seamed and rugged good-nature of the general practitioner, and his office fitted him. There was a row of medical books along one wall, a glass-doored cabinet containing various medicaments, and a clutter of medical instruments. He listened to the stranger's account quietly, smiling encouragement at times, and tapping the desk with his pencil.

"Amnesia, of course," he agreed, finally. "Rather peculiar in some respects, but most cases of that are individual. When the brain is injured, its actions are usually unpredictable. Have you considered the possibility of hallucinations in connection with those impulses you mention?"

"Yes." He had considered it from all angles, and rejected the solutions as too feeble. "If they were ordinary impulses, I'd agree with you. But they're far deeper than that, and there's a good reason for them, somewhere. I'm sure of that."

"Hm-m-m." The doctor tapped his pencil again and considered. The stranger sat staring at the base of his neck, and the tense feeling in his head returned, as it had been when he first met the drummer. Something rolled around in his mind and quieted. "And you have nothing on you in the way of identification?"

"Uh!" The stranger grunted, feeling foolish, and reached into his pockets. "I hadn't thought of that." He brought out a package of cigarettes, a stained handkerchief, glasses, odds and ends that meant nothing to him, and finally a wallet stuffed with bills. The doctor seized on that and ran through its contents quickly.

"Evidently you had money. . . . Hm-m-m, no identification card, except for the letters. L.H. Ah, here we are; a calling card." He passed it over, along with the wallet, and smiled in self-satisfaction. "Evidently you're a fellow physician, Dr. Lurton Haines. Does that recall anything?"

"Nothing." It was good to have a name, in a way, but that was his only response to the sight of the card. And why was he carrying glasses and cigarettes for which he had no earthly use?

The doctor was hunting through his pile of books, and finally came up with a dirty red volume. "Who's Who," he explained. "Let's see. Hm-m-m! Here we are. 'Lurton R. Haines, M.D.' Odd, I thought you were younger than that. Work along cancer research. No relatives mentioned. The

address is evidently that of the house you remember first—
'Surrey Road, Danesville.' Want to see it?"

He passed the volume over, and the stranger—or
Haines—scanned it carefully, but got no more out of it than
the other's summary, except for the fact that he was forty-
two years old. He put the book back on the desk, and
reached for his wallet, laying a bill on the pad where the
other could reach it.

"Thank you, Dr. Lanahan." There was obviously nothing
more the doctor could do for him, and the odor of the little
room and the doctor was stifling him; apparently he was allergic to the smell of other men. "Never mind the cut on the
head—it's purely superficial."

"But—"

Haines shrugged and mustered a smile, reached for the
door, and made for the outside again. The urge was gone
now, replaced by a vast sense of gloom, and he knew that his
mission had ended in failure.

They knew so little about healing, though they tried so
hard. The entire field of medicine ran through Haines' mind
now, with all its startling successes and hopeless failures, and
he knew that even his own problem was beyond their ability.
And the knowledge, like the sudden return of speech, was a
mystery; it had come rushing into his mind while he stared at
the doctor, at the end of the sudden tenseness, and a numb-
ing sense of failure had accompanied it. Strangely, it was
not the knowledge of a specialist in cancer research, but such
common methods as a general practitioner might use.

One solution suggested itself, but it was too fantastic for
belief. The existence of telepaths was suspected, but not ones
who could steal whole pages of knowledge from the mind of
another, merely by looking at him. No, that was more illogical than the sudden wakening of isolated fields of memory by
the sight of the two men.

He stopped at a corner, weary under the load of despon-
dency he was carrying, and mulled it over dully. A newsboy
approached hopefully. *"Time* a' *News* out!" the boy sing-
songed his wares. "*Scoop* 'n' *Juhnal!* Read awl about the big
train wreck! Paper, mister?"

Haines shrugged dully. "No paper!"

"Blonde found moidehed in bathtub," the boy insinuated.
"Mahs rocket account!" The man must have an Achilles' heel
somewhere.

But the garbled jargon only half registered on Haines' ears. He started across the street, rubbing his temples, before the second driving impulse caught at him and sent him back remorselessly to the paper boy. He found some small change in his pocket, dropped a nickel on the pile of papers, disregarding the boy's hand, and picked up a copy of the *Scoop*. "Screwball," the boy decided aloud, and dived for the nickel.

The picture was no longer on the front page of the tabloid, but Haines located the account with some effort. "Mars Rocket Take-off Wednesday," said the headline in conservative twenty-four-point type, and there was three-quarters of a column under it. "Man's first flight to Mars will not be delayed, James Oglethorpe told reporters here today. Undismayed by the skepticism of the scientist, the financier is going ahead with his plans, and expects his men to take off for Mars Wednesday, June 8, as scheduled. Construction had been completed, and the rocket machine is now undergoing tests."

Haines scanned down the page, noting the salient facts. The writer had kept his tongue in his cheek, but under the faintly mocking words there was the information he wanted. The rocket might work; man was at last on his way toward the conquests of the planets. There was no mention of another rocket. Obviously then, that one must have been built in secret in a futile effort to beat Oglethorpe's model.

But that was unimportant. The important thing was that he must stop the flight! Above all else, man must not make that trip! There was no sanity to it, and yet somehow it was beyond mere sanity. It was his duty to prevent any such voyage, and that duty was not to be questioned.

He returned quickly to the newsboy, reached out to touch his shoulder, and felt his hand jerk back to avoid the touch. The boy seemed to sense it, though, for he turned quickly. "Paper?" he began brightly before recognizing the stranger. "Oh, it's you. Watcha want?"

"Where can I find a train to New York?" Haines pulled a quarter from his pocket and tossed it on the pile of papers.

The boy's eyes brightened again.

"Four blocks down, turn right, and keep going till you come to the station. Can't miss it. Thanks, mister."

The discovery of the telephone book as a source of information was Haines' single major triumph, and the fact that the first Oglethorpe he tried was a colored street cleaner failed to take the edge off it. Now he trudged uptown, counting the numbers that made no sense to him; apparently the only system was one of arithmetical progression, irrespective of streets.

His shoulders were drooping, and the lines of pain around his eyes had finally succeeded in drawing his brows together. A coughing spell hit him, torturing his lungs for long minutes, and then passed. That was a new development, as was the pressure around his heart. And everywhere was the irritating aroma of men, gasoline, and tobacco, a stale mixture that he could not escape. He thrust his hands deeper into his pockets to avoid chance contact with someone on the street, and crossed over toward the building that bore the number for which he was searching.

Another man was entering the elevator, and he followed mechanically, relieved that he would not have to plod up the stairs. "Oglethorpe?" he asked the operator, uncertainly.

"Fourth floor, Room 405." The boy slid the gate open, pointing, and Haines stepped out and into the chromium-trimmed reception room. There were half a dozen doors leading from it, but he spotted the one marked "James H. Oglethorpe, Private," and slouched forward.

"Were you expected, sir?" The girl popped up in his face, one hand on the gate that barred his way. Her face was a study in frustration, which probably explained the sharpness of her tone. She delivered an Horatius-guarding-the-bridge formula. "Mr. Oglethorpe is busy now."

"Lunch," Haines answered curtly. He had already noticed that men talked more freely over food.

She flipped a little book in her hand and stared at it. "There's no record here of a luncheon engagement, Mr.—"

"Haines. Dr. Lurton Haines." He grinned wryly, wiggling a twenty-dollar bill casually in one hand. Money was apparently the one disease to which nobody was immune. Her eyes dropped to it, and hesitation entered her voice as she consulted her book.

"Of course, Mr. Oglethorpe might have made it some time ago and forgotten to tell me—" She caught his slight nod, and followed the bill to the corner of the desk. "Just have a seat, and I'll speak to Mr. Oglethorpe."

She came out of the office a few minutes later, and winked quickly. "He'd forgotten," she told Haines, "but it's all right now. He'll be right out, Dr. Haines. It's lucky he's having lunch late today."

James Oglethorpe was a younger man than Haines had expected, though his interest in rocketry might have been some clue to that. He came out of his office, pushing a Homburg down on curly black hair, and raked the other with his eyes. "Dr. Haines?" he asked, thrusting out a large hand. "Seems we have a luncheon engagement."

Haines rose quickly and bowed before the other had a chance to grasp his hand. Appparently Oglethorp did not notice, for he went on smoothly. "Easy to forget these telephone engagements, sometimes. Aren't you the cancer man? One of your friends was in a few months ago for a contribution to your work."

They were in the elevator then, and Haines waited until it opened and they headed for the lunchroom in the building before answering. "I'm not looking for money this time, however. It's the rocket you're financing that interests me. I think it may work."

"It will, though you're one of the few that believes it." Caution, doubt, and interest were mingled on Oglethorpe's face. He ordered before turning back to Haines. "Want to go along? If you do, there's still room for a physician in the crew."

"No, nothing like that. Toast and milk only, please—" Haines had no idea of how to broach the subject, with nothing concrete to back up his statements. Looking at the set of the other's jaw and the general bulldog attitude of the man, he gave up hope and only continued because he had to. He fell back on imagination, wondering how much of it was true.

"Another rocket made that trip, Mr. Oglethorpe, and returned. But the pilot was dying before he landed. I can show you the wreck of his machine, though there's not much left after the fire—perhaps not enough to prove it was a rocketship. Somewhere out on Mars there's something man should never find. It's—"

"Ghosts?" suggested Oglethorpe, brusquely.

"Death! I'm asking you—"

Again Oglethorpe interrupted. "Don't. There was a man in to see me yesterday who claimed he'd been there—offered to show me the wreck of *his* machine. A letter this morning explained that the Martians had visited the writer and threatened all manner of things. I'm not calling you a liar, Dr. Haines, but I've heard too many of those stories; whoever told you this one was either a crank or a horror-monger. I can show you a stack of letters that range from astrology to zombies, all explaining why I can't go, and some offer photographs for proof."

"Suppose I said I'd made the trip in that rocket?" The card in the wallet said he was Haines, and the wallet had been in the suit he was wearing; but there had also been the glasses and cigarettes for which he had no use.

Oglethorpe twisted his lips, either in disgust or amusement. "You're an intelligent man, Dr. Haines; let's assume I am, also. It may sound ridiculous to you, but the only reason I had for making the fortune I'm credited with was to build that ship, and it's taken more work and time than the layman would believe. If a green ant, seven feet high, walked into my office and threatened Armageddon, I'd still go."

Even the impossible impulse recognized the impossible. Oglethorpe was a man who did things first and worried about them when the mood hit him—and there was nothing moody about him. The conversation turned to everyday matters and Haines let it drift as it would, finally dragging out into silence.

At least, he was wiser by one thing: he knew the location of the rocket ground and the set-up of guards around it—something even the newspapermen had failed to learn, since all pictures and information had come through Oglethorpe. There could no longer be any question of his ability to gain desired information by some hazy telepathic process. Either he was a mental freak, or the accident had done things to him that should have been surprising but weren't.

Haines had taken a cab from the airport, giving instructions that caused the driver to lift his eyebrows; but money was still all-powerful. Now they were slipping through country even more desolate than the woods around Haines' house, and the end of the road came into view, with a rutted muddy trail leading off, marked by the tires of the trucks Oglethrope had used for his freighting. The cab stopped there.

"This the place?" the driver asked uncertainly.

"It is." Haines added a bill to what had already been paid and dismissed him. Then he dragged his way out to the dirt road and followed it, stopping for rest frequently. His ears were humming loudly now, and each separate little vertebra of his back protested at his going on. But there was no turning back; he had tried that at the airport and found the urge strong enough to combat his weakening will.

"Only a little rest!" he muttered thickly, but the force in

his head lifted his leaden feet and sent them marching toward the rocket camp. Above him the gray clouds passed over the Moon, and he looked up at Mars shining in the sky. Words from the lower part of the drummer's vocabulary came into his throat, but the effort of saying them was more than the red planet merited. He plowed on in silence.

Mars had moved over several degrees in the sky when he first sighted the camp, lying in a long, narrow valley. At one end were the shacks of the workmen, at the other a big structure that housed the rocket from chance prying eyes. Haines stopped to cough out part of his lungs, and his breath was husky and labored as he worked his way down.

The guards should be strung out along the edge of the valley. Oglethorpe was taking no chances with the cranks who had written him letters and denounced him as a godless fool leading his men to death. Rockets at best were fragile things, and only a few men would be needed to ruin the machine once it was discovered. Haines ran over the guards' positions, and skirted through the underbrush, watching for periods when the Moon was darkened. Once he almost tripped an alarm, but missed it in time.

Beyond there was no shrubbery, but his suit was almost the shade of the ground in the moonlight, and by lying still between dark spells, he crawled forward toward the rocket shed, undetected. He noticed the distance of the houses and the outlying guards and nodded to himself; they should be safe from any explosion.

The coast looked clear. Then, in the shadow of the building, a tiny red spark gleamed and subsided slowly; a man was there, smoking a cigarette. By straining his eyes, Haines made out the long barrel of a rifle against the building. This guard must be an added precaution, unknown to Oglethorpe.

A sudden rift in the thickening clouds came, and Haines slid himself flat against the ground, puzzling over the new complication. For a second he considered turning back, but realized that he could not—his path now was clearly defined, and he had no choice but to follow it. As the Moon slid out of sight again, he came to his feet quietly and moved toward the figure waiting there.

"Hello!" His voice was soft, designed to reach the man at the building but not the guards behind the outskirts. "Hello, there. Can I come forward? Special inspector from Oglethorpe."

A beam of light lanced out from the shadow, blinding him,

and he walked forward at the best pace he could muster. The light might reveal him to the other guards, but he doubted it; their attention was directed outward, away from the buildings.

"Come ahead," the answer came finally. "How'd you get past the others?" The voice was suspicious, but not unusually so. The rifle, Haines saw, was directed at his midsection, and he stopped a few feet away, where the other could watch him.

"Jimmy Durham knew I was coming," he told the guard. According to the information he had stolen from Oglethorpe's mind, Durham was in charge of the guards. "He told me he hadn't had time to notify you, but I took a chance."

"Hm-m-m. Guess it's all right, since they let you through; but you can't leave here until somebody identifies you. Keep your hands up." The guard came forward cautiously to feel for concealed weapons. Haines held his hands up out of the other's reach, where there was no danger of a direct skin to skin contact. "O.K., seems all right. What's your business here?"

"General inspection; the boss got word there might be a little trouble brewing and sent me here to make sure guard was being kept, and to warn you. All locked up here?"

"Nope. A lock wouldn't do much good on this shack; that's why I'm here. Want I should signal Jimmy to come and identify you so you can go?"

"Don't bother." Conditions were apparently ideal, except for one thing. But he would not murder the guard! There must be some other way, without adding that to the work he was forced to do. "I'm in no hurry, now that I've seen everything. Have a smoke?"

"Just threw one away. 'Smatter, no matches? Here."

Haines rubbed one against the friction surface of the box and lit the cigarette gingerly. The raw smoke stung against his burning throat, but he controlled the cough, and blew it out again; in the dark, the guard could not see his eyes watering, nor the grimaces he made. He was waging a bitter fight with himself against the impulse that had ordered the smoke to distract the guard's attention, and he knew he was failing. "Thanks!"

One of the guard's hands met his, reaching for the box. The next second the man's throat was between the stranger's hands, and he was staggering back, struggling to tear away and cry for help. Surprise confused his efforts for the split second necessary, and one of Haines' hands came free and out, then chopped down sharply to strike the guard's neck with the edge of the palm. A low grunt gurgled out, and the figure went limp.

Impulse had conquered again! The guard was dead, his neck broken by the sharp blow. Haines leaned against the building, catching his breath and fighting back the desire to lose his stomach's contents. When some control came back, he picked up the guard's flashlight, and turned into the building. In the darkness, the outlines of the great rocketship were barely visible.

With fumbling fingers Haines groped forward to the hull, then struck a match and shaded it in his hands until he could make out the airport, standing open. Too much light might show through a window and attract attention.

Inside, he threw the low power of the flashlight on and moved forward, down the catwalk and toward the rear where the power machinery would be housed. It had been simple, after all, and only the quick work of destruction still remained.

He traced the control valves easily, running an eye over the uncovered walls and searching out the pipes that led from them. From the little apparatus he saw, this ship was obviously inferior to the one that had crashed, yet it had taken years to build and drained Oglethorpe's money almost to the limit. Once destroyed, it might take men ten more years to replace it; two was the minimum, and in those two years—

The thought slipped from him, but some memories were coming back. He saw himself in a small metal room, fighting against the inexorable exhaustion of fuel, and losing. Then there had been a final burst from the rockets, and the ship had dropped sickeningly through the atmosphere. He had barely had time to get to the air locks before the crash. Miraculously, as the ship's fall was cushioned by the house, he had been thrown free into the lower branches of a tree, to catch, and lose momentum before striking Earth.

The man who had been in the house had fared worse; he had been thrown out with the wrecked wall, already dead. Roughly, the stranger remembered a hasty transfer of clothing from the corpse, and then the beam had dropped on him, shutting out his memory in blackness. So he was not Haines, after all, but someone from the rocket, and his story to Oglethorpe had been basically true.

Haines—he still thought of himself under that name—caught himself as his knees gave under him, and hauled himself up by the aid of a protruding bar. There was work to be done; after that, what happened to his own failing body was another matter. It seemed now that from his awakening he had expected to meet death before another day, and had been careless of the fact.

He ran his eyes around the rocket room again, until he came to a tool kit that lay invitingly open with a large wrench sticking up from it. That would serve to open the valves. The flashlight lay on the floor where he had dropped it, and he kicked it around with his foot to point at the wall, groping out for the wrench. His fingers were stiff as they clasped around the handle.

And, in the beam of light, he noticed his hand for the first time in hours. Dark-blue veins rose high on the flesh that was marked with a faint pale-blue. He considered it dully, thrusting out his other hand and examining it; there, too, was the blue flush, and on his palms, as he turned them upward, the same color showed. Blue!

The last of his memory flashed through his brain in a roaring wave, bringing a slow tide of pictures with it. With one part of his mind, he was working on the valves with the wrench, while the other considered the knowledge that had returned to him. He saw the streets of a delicate, fairy city, half deserted, and as he seemed to watch, a man staggered out of a doorway, clutching at his throat with blue hands, to fall writhing to the ground! The people passed on quickly, avoiding contact with the corpse, fearful even to touch each other.

Everywhere, death reached out for the people. The planet was riddled with it. It lay on the skin of an infected person, to be picked up by the touch of another, and passed on to still more. In the air, a few seconds sufficed to kill the germs, but new ones were being sent out from the pores of the skin, so that there were always a few active ones lurking there. On contact, the disease began an insidious conquest, until, after months without a sign, it suddenly attacked the body housing it, turned it blue, and brought death in a few painful hours.

Some claimed it was the result of an experiment that had gone beyond control, others that it had dropped as a spore from space. Whatever it was, there was no cure for it on Mars. Only the legends that spoke of a race of their people on the mother world of Earth offered any faint hope, and to that they had turned when there was no other chance.

He saw himself undergoing examinations that finally resulted in his being chosen to go in the rocket they were building feverishly. He had been picked because his powers of telepathy were unusual, even to the mental science of Mars; the few remaining weeks had been used in developing that power systematically, and implanting in his head the duties that he must perform, so long as a vestige of life remained to him.

Haines watched the first of the liquid from the fuel pipes splash out, and dropped the wrench. Old Leán Dagh had doubted his ability to draw knowledge by telepathy from a race of a different culture, he reflected; too bad the old man had died without knowing of the success his methods had met, even though the mission had been a failure, due to man's feeble knowledge of the curative sciences. Now his one task was to prevent the race of this world from dying in the same manner.

He pulled himself to his feet and went staggering down the catwalk, muttering disconnected sentences. The blue of his skin was darker now, and he had to force himself across the space from the ship to the door of the building, grimly commanding his failing muscles, to the guard's body that still lay where he had left it.

Most of the strength left him was useless against the pull of this heavier planet and the torture movement had become. He tried to drag the corpse behind him, then fell on hands and knees and backed toward the ship, using one arm and his teeth on the collar to pull it after him. He was swimming in a world that was bordering on unconsciousness, now, and once darkness claimed him; he came out of it to find himself inside the rocket, still dragging his burden, the implanted impulses stronger than his will.

Bit by bit, he dragged his burden behind him down the catwalk, until the engine room was reached, and he could drop it on the floor, where the liquid fuel had made a thin film. The air was heavy with vapors, and chilled by the evaporation, but he was only partly conscious of that. Only a spark was needed now, and his last duty would be finished.

Inevitably, a few of the dead on Mars would be left unburned, where men might find the last of that unfortunate race, and the germs would still live within them. Earthmen must not face that. Until such a time as the last Martian had crumbled to dust and released the plague into the air to be destroyed, the race of Earth must remain within the confines of its own atmosphere, and safe.

There was only himself and the corpse he had touched left here to carry possible germs, and the ship to carry the men to other sources of infection; all that was easily remedied.

The stranger from Mars groped in his pocket for the guard's match box, smiling faintly. Just before the final darkness swept over him, he drew one of the matches from the box and scraped it across the friction surface. Flame danced from the point and outward—

IT

Unknown
August

by Theodore Sturgeon (1918-   )

Ted Sturgeon is as good a writer of fantasy as he is of science fiction. For evidence, the reader is directed to stories like The Dreaming Jewels, *"The Professor's Teddy-Bear," "Bianca's Hands," "A God In the Garden," and "Talent."*

Although he is considered to be a master of portraying human relationships and the complexities of the emotion called love, Sturgeon can also chill. Witness this story—simply one of the finest horror tales of all time.

(When Marty says "one of the finest horror tales of all time" he's not just whistling Dixie. The trouble with horror tales is that most of them don't horrify you. Nothing by Lovecraft ever horrified me for instance because he labored so hard over the atmosphere and spent so much time *telling* you it was horrible, that you grew bored. Not so here. If you've never read this before, read it now, and it will be a long time before you can look garbage in the face again.

Theodore Sturgeon is very adept at prickling your mind and spine and yet, like so many horror experts, he neither looks nor sounds it. Of course, he's not young anymore. (Who is, other than myself?) But when he was young, he could have posed for anyone wanting to draw a pixie. No retouching necessary. And to this day his voice is soft and winning. You have to keep these gentle people away from the typewriter if you don't want grue. Robert Bloch is, and Fredric Brown was, just the same—I.A.)

125

It walked in the woods.

It was never born. It existed. Under the pine needles the fires burn, deep and smokeless in the mold. In heat and in darkness and decay there is growth. There is life and there is growth. It grew, but it was not alive. It walked unbreathing through the woods, and thought and saw and was hideous and strong, and it was not born and it did not live. It grew and moved about without living.

It crawled out of the darkness and hot damp mold into the cool of a morning. It was huge. It was lumped and crusted with its own hateful substances, and pieces of it dropped off as it went its way, dropped off and lay writhing, and stilled, and sank putrescent into the forest loam.

It had no mercy, no laughter, no beauty. It had strength and great intelligence. And—perhaps it could not be destroyed. It crawled out of its mound in the wood and lay pulsing in the sunlight for a long moment. Patches of it shone wetly in the golden glow, parts of it were nubbled and flaked. And whose dead bones had given it the form of a man?

It scrabbled painfully with its half-formed hands, beating the ground and the bole of a tree. It rolled and lifted itself up on its crumbling elbows, and it tore up a great handful of herbs and shredded them against its chest, and it paused and gazed at the gray-green juices with intelligent calm. It wavered to its feet, and seized a young sapling and destroyed it, folding the slender trunk back on itself again and again, watching attentively the useless, fibered splinters. And it snatched up a fear-frozen field-creature, crushing it slowly, letting blood and pulpy flesh and fur ooze from between its fingers, run down and rot on the forearms.

It began searching.

Kimbo drifted through the tall grasses like a puff of dust, his bushy tail curled tightly over his back and his long jaws agape. He ran with an easy lope, loving his freedom and the power of his flanks and furry shoulders. His tongue lolled listlessly over his lips. His lips were black and serrated, and each tiny pointed liplet swayed with his doggy gallop. Kimbo was all dog, all healthy animal.

He leaped high over a boulder and landed with a startled yelp as a long-eared cony shot from its hiding place under the rock. Kimbo hurtled after it, grunting with each great thrust of his legs. The rabbit bounced just ahead of him, keeping its distance, its ears flattened on its curving back and its little legs nibbling away at distance hungrily. It stopped, and Kimbo pounced, and the rabbit shot away at a tangent and popped into a hollow log. Kimbo yelped again and rushed snuffling at the log, and knowing his failure, curvetted but once around the stump and ran on into the forest. The thing that watched from the wood raised its crusted arms and waited for Kimbo.

Kimbo sensed it there, standing dead-still by the path. To him it was a bulk which smelled of carrion not fit to roll in, and he snuffled distastefully and ran to pass it.

The thing let him come abreast and dropped a heavy twisted fist on him. Kimbo saw it coming and curled up tight as he ran, and the hand clipped stunningly on his rump, sending him rolling and yipping down the slope. Kimbo straddled to his feet, shook his head, shook his body with a deep growl, came back to the silent thing with green murder in his eyes. He walked stiffly, straight-legged, his tail as low as his lowered head and a ruff of fury round his neck. The thing raised its arms again, waited.

Kimbo slowed, then flipped himself through the air at the monster's throat. His jaws closed on it; his teeth clicked together through a mass of filth, and he fell choking and snarling at its feet. The thing leaned down and struck twice, and after the dog's back was broken, it sat beside him and began to tear him apart.

"Be back in an hour or so," said Alton Drew, picking up his rifle from the corner behind the wood box. His brother laughed.

"Old Kimbo 'bout runs your life, Alton," he said.

"Ah, I know the ol' devil," said Alton. "When I whistle for him for half an hour and he don't show up, he's in a jam or he's treed something wuth shootin' at. The ol' son of a gun calls me by not answerin'."

Cory Crew shoved a full glass of milk over to his nine-year-old daughter and smiled. "You think as much o' that houn' dog o' yours as I do of Babe here."

Babe slid off her chair and ran to her uncle. "Gonna catch me the bad fella, Uncle Alton?" she shrilled. The "bad fella" was Cory's invention—the one who lurked in corners ready to pounce on little girls who chased the chickens and played around mowing machines and hurled green apples with a powerful young arm at the sides of the hogs, to hear the synchronized thud and grunt; little girls who swore with an

Austrian accent like an ex-hired man they had had; who dug caves in haystacks till they tipped over, and kept pet crawfish in tomorrow's milk cans, and rode work horses to a lather in the night pasture.

"Get back here and keep away from Uncle Alton's gun!" said Cory. "If you see the bad fella, Alton, chase him back here. He has a date with Babe here for that stunt of hers last night." The preceding evening, Babe had kind-heartedly poured pepper on the cows' salt block.

"Don't worry, kiddo," grinned her uncle, "I'll bring you the bad fella's hide if he don't get me first."

Alton Drew walked up the path toward the wood, thinking about Babe. She was a phenomenon—a pampered farm child. Ah well—she had to be. They'd both loved Clissa Drew, and she'd married Cory, and they had to love Clissa's child. Funny thing, love. Alton was a man's man, and thought things out that way; and his reaction to love was a strong and frightened one. He knew what love was because he felt it still for his brother's wife and would feel it as long as he lived for Babe. It led him through his life, and yet he embarrassed himself by thinking of it. Loving a dog was an easy thing, because you and the old devil could love one another completely without talking about it. The smell of gunsmoke and wet fur in the rain were perfume enough for Alton Drew, a grunt of satisfaction and the scream of something hunted and hit were poetry enough. They weren't like love for a human, that choked his throat so he could not say words he could not have thought of anyway. So Alton loved his dog Kimbo and his Winchester for all to see, and let his love for his brother's women, Clissa and Babe, eat at him quietly and unmentioned.

His quick eyes saw the fresh indentations in the soft earth behind the boulder, which showed where Kimbo had turned and leaped with a single surge, chasing the rabbit. Ignoring the tracks, he looked for the nearest place where a rabbit might hide, and strolled over to the stump. Kimbo had been there, he saw, and had been there too late. "You're an ol' fool," muttered Alton. "Y' can't catch a cony by chasin' it. You want to cross him up some way." He gave a peculiar trilling whistle, sure that Kimbo was digging frantically under some nearby stump for a rabbit that was three counties away by now. No answer. A little puzzled, Alton went back to the path. "He never done this before," he said softly.

He cocked his .32-40 and cradled it. At the county fair someone had once said of Alton Drew that he could shoot at a handful of corn and peas thrown in the air and hit only the corn. Once he split a bullet on the blade of a knife and put two candles out. He had no need to fear anything that could be shot at. That's what he believed.

The thing in the woods looked curiously down at what it had done to Kimbo, and tried to moan the way Kimbo had before he died. It stood a minute storing away facts in its foul, unemotional mind. Blood was warm. The sunlight was warm. Things that moved and bore fur had a muscle to force the thick liquid through tiny tubes in their bodies. The liquid coagulated after a time. The liquid on rooted green things was thinner and the loss of a limb did not mean loss of life. It was very interesting, but the thing, the mold with a mind, was not pleased. Neither was it displeased. Its accidental urge was a thirst for knowledge, and it was only—interested.

It was growing late, and the sun reddened and rested awhile on the hilly horizon, teaching the clouds to be inverted flames. The thing threw up its head suddenly, noticing the dusk. Night was ever a strange thing, even for those of us who have known it in life. It would have been frightening for the monster had it been capable of fright, but it could only be curious; it could only reason from what it had observed.

What was happening? It was getting harder to see. Why? It threw its shapeless head from side to side. It was true—things were dim, and growing dimmer. Things were changing shape, taking on a new and darker color. What did the creatures it had crushed and torn apart see? How did they see? The larger one, the one that had attacked, had used two organs in its head. That must have been it, because after the thing had torn off two of the dog's legs it had struck at the hairy muzzle; and the dog, seeing the blow coming, had dropped folds of skin over the organs—closed its eyes. Ergo, the dog saw with its eyes. But then after the dog was dead, and its body still, repeated blows had had no effect on the eyes. They remained open and staring. The logical conclusion was, then, that a being that had ceased to live and breathe and move about lost the use of its eyes. It must be that to lose sight was, conversely, to die. Dead things did not walk about. They lay down and did not move. Therefore the thing in the wood concluded that it must be dead, and so it lay down by the path, not far away from Kimbo's scattered body, lay down and believed itself dead.

Alton Drew came up through the dusk to the wood. He was frankly worried. He whistled again, and then called, and there was still no response, and he said again, "The ol' fleabus never done this before," and shook his heavy head. It was past milking time, and Cory would need him. "Kimbo!" he roared. The cry echoed through the shadows, and Alton flipped on the safety catch of his rifle and put the butt on the ground beside the path. Leaning on it, he took off his cap and scratched the back of his head, wondering. The rifle butt sank into what he thought was soft earth; he staggered and stepped into the chest of the thing that lay beside the path. His foot went up to the ankle in its yielding rottenness, and he swore and jumped back.

"*Whew!* Somp'n sure dead as hell there! Ugh!" He swabbed at his boot with a handful of leaves while the monster lay in the growing blackness with the edges of the deep footprint in its chest sliding into it, filling it up. It lay there regarding him dimly out of its muddy eyes, thinking it was dead because of the darkness, watching the articulation of Alton Drew's joints, wondering at this new uncautious creature.

Alton cleaned the butt of his gun with more leaves and went on up the path, whistling anxiously for Kimbo.

Clissa Drew stood in the door of the milk shed, very lovely in red-checked gingham and a blue apron. Her hair was clean yellow, parted in the middle and stretched tautly back to a heavy braided knot. "Cory! Alton!" she called a little sharply.

"Well?" Cory responded gruffly from the barn, where he was stripping off the Ayrshire. The dwindling streams of milk plopped pleasantly into the froth of a full pail.

"I've called and called," said Clissa. "Supper's cold, and Babe won't eat until you come. Why—where's Alton?"

Cory grunted, heaved the stool out of the way, threw over the stanchion lock and slapped the Ayrshire on the rump. The cow backed and filled like a towboat, clattered down the line and out into the barnyard. "Ain't back yet."

"Not back?" Clissa came in and stood beside him as he sat by the next cow, put his forehead against the warm flank. "But, Cory, he said he'd—"

"Yeh, yeh, I know. He said he'd be back fer the milkin'. I heard him. Well, he ain't."

"And you have to— Oh, Cory, I'll help you finish up. Alton would be back if he could. Maybe he's—"

"Maybe he's treed a blue jay," snapped her husband. "Him an' that damn dog," He gestured hugely with one hand while the other went on milking. "I got twenty-six head o' cows to milk. I got pigs to feed an' chickens to put to bed. I got to toss hay for the mare and turn the team out. I got harness to mend and a wire down in the night pasture. I got wood to split an' carry." He milked for a moment in silence, chewing on his lip. Clissa stood twisting her hands together, trying to think of something to stem the tide. It wasn't the first time Alton's hunting had interfered with the chores. "So I got to go ahead with it. I can't interfere with Alton's spoorin.' Every damn time that hound o' his smells out a squirrel I go without my supper. I'm gettin' sick and—"

"Oh, I'll help you!" said Clissa. She was thinking of the spring, when Kimbo had held four hundred pounds of raging black bear at bay until Alton could put a bullet in its brain, the time Babe had found a bearcub and started to carry it home, and had fallen into a freshet, cutting her head. You can't hate a dog that has saved your child for you, she thought.

"You'll do nothin' of the kind!" Cory growled. "Get back to the house. You'll find work enough there. I'll be along when I can. Dammit, Clissa, don't cry! I didn't mean to— Oh, shucks!" He got up and put his arms around her. "I'm wrought up," he said. "Go on now. I'd no call to speak that way to you. I'm sorry. Go back to Babe. I'll put a stop to this for good tonight. I've had enough. There's work here for four farmers an' all we've got is me an' that . . . that huntsman.

"Go on now, Clissa."

"All right," she said into his shoulder. "But, Cory, hear him out first when he comes back. He might be unable to come back. He might be unable to come back this time. Maybe he . . . he—"

"Ain't nothin' kin hurt my brother that a bullet will hit. He can take care of himself. He's got no excuse good enough this time. Go on, now. Make the kid eat."

Clissa went back to the house, her young face furrowed. If Cory quarreled with Alton now and drove him away, what with the drought and the creamery about to close and all, they just couldn't manage. Hiring a man was out of the question. Cory'd have to work himself to death, and he just wouldn't be able to make it. No one man could. She sighed and went into the house. It was seven o'clock, and the milking not done yet. Oh, why did Alton have to—

Babe was in bed at nine when Clissa heard Cory in the shed, slinging the wire cutters into a corner. "Alton back yet?" they both said at once as Cory stepped into the kitchen; and as she shook her head he clumped over to the stove, and lifting a lid, spat into the coals. "Come to bed," he said.

She laid down her stitching and looked at his broad back. He was twenty-eight, and he walked and acted like a man ten years older, and looked like a man five years younger. "I'll be up in a while," Clissa said.

Cory glanced at the corner behind the wood box where Alton's rifle usually stood, then made an unspellable, disgusted sound and sat down to take off his heavy muddy shoes.

"It's after nine," Clissa volunteered timidly. Cory said nothing, reaching for house slippers.

"Cory, you're not going to—"

"Not going to what?"

"Oh, nothing. I just thought that maybe Alton—"

"Alton," Cory flared. "The dog goes hunting field mice. Alton goes hunting the dog. Now you want me to go hunting Alton. That's what you want?"

"I just— He was never this late before."

"I won't do it! Go out lookin' for him at nine o'clock in the night? I'll be damned! He has no call to use us so, Clissa."

Clissa said nothing. She went to the stove, peered into the wash boiler, set aside at the back of the range. When she turned around, Cory had his shoes and coat on again.

"I knew you'd go," she said. Her voice smiled though she did not.

"I'll be back durned soon," said Cory. "I don't reckon he's strayed far. It is late. I ain't feared for him, but—" He broke his 12-gauge shotgun, looked through the barrels, slipped two shells in the breech and a box of them into his pocket. "Don't wait up," he said over his shoulder as he went out.

"I won't," Clissa replied to the closed door, and went back to her stitching by the lamp.

The path up the slope to the wood was very dark when Cory went up it, peering and calling. The air was chill and quiet, and a fetid odor of mold hung in it. Cory blew the taste of it out through impatient nostrils, drew it in again with the next breath, and swore. "Nonsense," he muttered. "Houn' dawg. Huntin', at ten in th' night, too. Alton!" he bellowed. "Alton Drew!" Echoes answered him, and he entered the wood. The huddled thing he passed in the dark heard him and felt the vibrations of his footsteps and did not move because it thought it was dead.

Cory strode on, looking around and ahead and not down since his feet knew the path.

"Alton!"

"That you, Cory?"

Cory Drew froze. That corner of the wood was thickly set and as dark as a burial vault. The voice he heard was choked, quiet, penetrating.

"Alton?"

"I found Kimbo, Cory."

"Where the hell have you been?" shouted Cory furiously. He disliked this pitch-darkness; he was afraid at the tense hopelessness of Alton's voice, and he mistrusted his ability to stay angry at his brother.

"I called him, Cory. I whistled at him, an' the ol' devil didn't answer."

"I can say the same for you, you . . . you louse. Why weren't you to milkin'? Where are you? You caught in a trap?"

"The houn' never missed answerin' me before, you know," said the tight, monotonous voice from the darkness.

"Alton! What the devil's the matter with you? What do I care if your mutt didn't answer? Where—"

"I guess because he ain't never died before," said Alton, refusing to be interrupted.

"You *what?*" Cory clicked his lips together twice and then said, "Alton, you turned crazy? What's that you say?"

"Kimbo's dead."

"Kim . . . oh! Oh!" Cory was seeing that picture again in his mind— Babe sprawled unconscious in the freshet, and Kimbo raging and snapping against a monster bear, holding her back until Alton could get there. "What happened, Alton?" he asked more quietly.

"I aim to find out. Someone tore him up."

"Tore him up?"

"There ain't a bit of him left tacked together, Cory. Every damn joint in his body tore apart. Guts out of him."

"Good God! Bear, you reckon?"

"No bear, nor nothin' on four legs. He's all here. None of him's been et. Whoever done it just killed him an'—tore him up."

"Good God!" Cory said again. "Who could've—" There

was a long silence, then. "Come 'long home," he said almost gently. "There's no call for you to set up by him all night."

"I'll set. I aim to be here at sunup, an' I'm going to start trackin', an' I'm goin' to keep trackin' till I find the one done this job on Kimbo."

"You're drunk or crazy, Alton."

"I ain't drunk. You can think what you like about the rest of it. I'm stickin' here."

"We got a farm back yonder. Remember? I ain't going to milk twenty-six head o' cows again in the mornin' like I did jest now, Alton."

"Somebody's got to. I can't be there. I guess you'll just have to, Cory."

"You dirty scum!" Cory screamed. "You'll come back with me now or I'll know why!"

Alton's voice was still tight, half-sleepy. "Don't you come no nearer, bud."

Cory kept moving toward Alton's voice.

"I said"—the voice was very quiet now—"*stop where you are.*" Cory kept coming. A sharp click told of the release of the .32-40's safety. Cory stopped.

"You got your gun on me, Alton?" Cory whispered.

"Thass right, bud. You ain't a-trompin' up these tracks for me. I need 'em at sunup."

A full minute passed, and the only sound in the blackness was that of Cory's pained breathing. Finally:

"I got my gun, too, Alton. Come home."

"You can't see to shoot me."

"We're even on that."

"We ain't. I know just where you stand, Cory. I been here four hours."

"My gun scatters."

"My gun kills."

Without another word Cory Drew turned on his heel and stamped back to the farm.

Black and liquidescent it lay in the blackness, not alive, not understanding death, believing itself dead. Things that were alive saw and moved about. Things that were not alive could do neither. It rested its muddy gaze on the line of trees at the crest of the rise, and deep within it thoughts trickled wetly. It lay huddled, dividing its newfound facts, dissecting them as it had dissected live things when there was light, comparing, concluding, pigeonholing.

The trees at the top of the slope could just be seen, as their trunks were a fraction of a shade lighter than the dark sky behind them. At length they, too, disappeared, and for a moment sky and trees were a monotone. The thing knew it was dead now, and like many a being before it, it wondered how long it must stay like this. And then the sky beyond the trees grew a little lighter. That was a manifestly impossible occurrence, thought the thing, but it could see it and it must be so. Did dead things live again? That was curious. What about dismembered dead things? It would wait and see.

The sun came hand over hand up a beam of light. A bird somewhere made a high yawning peep, and as an owl killed a shrew, a skunk pounced on another, so that the night shift deaths and those of the day could go on without cessation. Two flowers nodded archly to each other, comparing their pretty clothes. A dragon-fly nymph decided it was tired of looking serious and cracked its back open, to crawl out and dry gauzily. The first golden ray sheared down between the trees, through the grasses, passed over the mass in the shadowed bushes. "I am alive again," thought the thing that could not possibly live. "I am alive, for I see clearly." It stood up on its thick legs, up into the golden glow. In a little while the wet flakes that had grown during the night dried in the sun, and when it took its first steps, they cracked off and a small shower of them fell away. It walked up the slope to find Kimbo, to see if he, too, was alive again.

Babe let the sun come into her room by opening her eyes. Uncle Alton was gone—that was the first thing that ran through her head. Dad had come home last night and had shouted at mother for an hour. Alton was plumb crazy. He'd turned a gun on his own brother. If Alton ever came ten feet into Cory's land, Cory would fill him so full of holes, he'd look like a tumbleweed. Alton was lazy, shiftless, selfish, and one or two other things of questionable taste but undoubted vividness. Babe knew her father. Uncle Alton would never be safe in this county.

She bounced out of bed in the enviable way of the very young, and ran to the window. Cory was trudging down to the night pasture with two bridles over his arm, to get the team. There were kitchen noises from downstairs.

Babe ducked her head in the washbowl and shook off the water like a terrier before she toweled. Trailing clean shirt and dungarees, she went to the head of the stairs, slid into the shirt, and began her morning ritual with the trousers. One step down was a step through the right leg. One more, and she was into the left. Then, bouncing step by step on both feet, buttoning one button per step, she reached the bottom fully dressed and ran into the kitchen.

"Didn't Uncle Alton come back a-tall, Mum?"

"Morning, Babe. No, dear." Clissa was too quiet, smiling too much Babe thought shrewdly. Wasn't happy.

"Where'd he go, Mum?"

"We don't know, Babe. Sit down and eat your breakfast."

"What's a misbegotten, Mum?" the Babe asked suddenly. Her mother nearly dropped the dish she was drying. "Babe! You must never say that again!"

"Oh. Well, why is Uncle Alton, then?"

"Why is he what?"

Babe's mouth muscled around an outsize spoonful of oatmeal. "A misbe—"

"Babe!"

"All right, Mum," said Babe with her mouth full. "Well, why?"

"I told Cory not to shout last night," Clissa said half to herself.

"Well, whatever it means, he isn't," said Babe with finality. "Did he go hunting again?"

"He went to look for Kimbo, darling."

"Kimbo? Oh Mummy, is Kimbo gone, too? Didn't he come back either?"

"No dear. Oh, please, Babe, stop asking questions!"

"All right. Where do you think they went?"

"Into the north woods. Be quiet."

Babe gulped away at her breakfast. An idea struck her; and as she thought of it she ate slower and slower, and cast more and more glances at her mother from under the lashes of her tilted eyes. It would be awful if daddy did anything to Uncle Alton. Someone ought to warn him.

Babe was halfway to the woods when Alton's .32-40 sent echoes giggling up and down the valley.

Cory was in the south thirty, riding a cultivator and cussing at the team of grays when he heard the gun. "Hoa," he called to the horses, and sat a moment to listen to the sound. "One-two-three. Four," he counted. "Saw someone, blasted away at him. Had a chance to take aim and give him another, careful. My God!" He threw up the cultivator points and steered the team into the shade of three oaks. He hobbled the gelding with swift tosses of a spare strap, and headed for the woods. "Alton a killer," he murmured, and doubled back to the house for his gun. Clissa was standing just outside the door.

"Get shells!" he snapped and flung into the house. Clissa followed him. He was strapping his hunting knife on before she could get a box off the shelf. "Cory—"

"Hear that gun, did you? Alton's off his nut. He don't waste lead. He shot at someone just then, and he wasn't fixin' to shoot pa'tridges when I saw him last. He was out to get a man. Gimme my gun."

"Cory, Babe—"

"You keep her here. Oh, God, this is a helluva mess. I can't stand much more." Cory ran out the door.

Clissa caught his arm: "Cory I'm trying to tell you. Babe isn't here. I've called, and she isn't here."

Cory's heavy, young-old face tautened. "Babe— Where did you last see her?"

"Breakfast." Clissa was crying now.

"She say where she was going?"

"No. She asked a lot of questions about Alton and where he'd gone."

"Did you say?"

Clissa's eyes widened, and she nodded, biting the back of her hand.

"You shouldn't ha' done that, Clissa," he gritted, and ran toward the woods, Clissa looking after him, and in that moment she could have killed herself.

Cory ran with his head up, straining with his legs and lungs and eyes at the long path. He puffed up the slope to the woods, agonized for breath after the forty-five minutes' heavy going. He couldn't even notice the damp smell of mold in the air.

He caught a movement in a thicket to his right, and dropped. Struggling to keep his breath, he crept forward until he could see clearly. There was something in there, all right. Something black, keeping still. Cory relaxed his legs and torso completely to make it easier for his heart to pump some strength back into them, and slowly raised the 12-gauge until it bore on the thing hidden in the thicket.

"Come out!" Cory said when he could speak.

Nothing happened.

"Come out or by God I'll shoot!" rasped Cory.

There was a long moment of silence, and his finger tightened on the trigger.

"You asked for it," he said, and as he fired, the thing leaped sideways into the open, screaming.

It was a thin little man dressed in sepulchral black, and bearing the rosiest baby-face Cory had ever seen. The face was twisted with fright and pain. The man scrambled to his feet and hopped up and down saying over and over, "Oh, my hand. Don't shoot again! Oh, my hand. Don't shoot again!" He stopped after a bit, when Cory had climbed to his feet, and he regarded the farmer out of sad china-blue eyes. "You shot me," he said reproachfully, holding up a little bloody hand. "Oh, my goodness."

Cory said, "Now, who the hell are you?"

The man immediately became hysterical, mouthing such a flood of broken sentences that Cory stepped back a pace and half-raised his gun in self-defense. It seemed to consist mostly of "I lost my papers," and "I didn't do it," and "It was horrible. Horrible. Horrible," and "The dead man," and "Oh, don't shoot again."

Cory tried twice to ask him a question, and then he stepped over and knocked the man down. He lay on the ground writhing and moaning and blubbering and putting his bloody hand to his mouth where Cory had hit him.

"Now what's going on around here?"

The man rolled over and sat up. "I didn't do it!" he sobbed. "I didn't. I was walking along and I heard the gun and I heard some swearing and an awful scream and I went over there and peeped and I saw the dead man and I ran away and you came and I hid and you shot me and—"

"*Shut up!*" The man did, as if a switch had been thrown. "Now," said Cory, pointing along the path, "you say there's a dead man up there?"

The man nodded and began crying in earnest. Cory helped him up. "Follow this path back to my farmhouse," he said. "Tell my wife to fix up your hand. *Don't* tell her anything else. And wait there until I come. Hear?"

"Yes. Thank you. Oh, thank you. *Snff.*"

"Go on now." Cory gave him a gentle shove in the right direction and went alone, in cold fear, up the path to the spot where he had found Alton the night before.

He found him here now, too, and Kimbo. Kimbo and Alton had spent several years together in the deepest friendship; they had hunted and fought and slept together, and the lives they owed each other were finished now. They were dead together.

It was terrible that they died the same way. Cory Drew was a strong man, but he gasped and fainted dead away when he saw what the thing of the mold had done to his brother and his brother's dog.

The little man in black hurried down the path, whimpering and holding his injured hand as if he rather wished he could limp with it. After a while the whimper faded away, and the hurried stride changed to a walk as the gibbering terror of the last hour receded. He drew two deep breaths, said: "My goodness!" and felt almost normal. He bound a linen handkerchief around his wrist, but the hand kept bleeding. He tried the elbow, and that made it hurt. So he stuffed the handkerchief back in his pocket and simply waved the hand stupidly in the air until the blood clotted. He did not see the great moist horror that clumped along behind him, although his nostrils crinkled with its foulness.

The monster had three holes close together on its chest, and one hole in the middle of its slimy forehead. It had three close-set pits in its back and one on the back of its head. These marks were where Alton Drew's bullets had struck and passed through. Half of the monster's shapeless face was sloughed away, and there was a deep indentation on its shoulder. This was what Alton Drew's gun butt had done after he clubbed it and struck at the thing that would not lie down after he put his four bullets through it. When these things happened the monster was not hurt or angry. It only wondered why Alton Drew acted that way. Now it followed the little man without hurrying at all, matching his stride step by step and dropping little particles of muck behind it.

The little man went on out of the wood and stood with his back against a big tree at the forest's edge, and he thought. Enough had happened to him here. What good would it do to stay and face a horrible murder inquest, just to continue this silly, vague search? There was supposed to be the ruin of an old, old hunting lodge deep in this wood somewhere, and perhaps it would hold the evidence he wanted. But it was a vague report—vague enough to be forgotten without regret. It would be the height of foolishness to stay for all the hicktown red tape that would follow that ghastly affair back in the wood. Ergo, it would be ridiculous to follow that farmer's advice, to go to his house and wait for him. He would go back to town.

The monster was leaning against the other side of the big tree.

The little man snuffled disgustedly at a sudden overpowering odor of rot. He reached for his handkerchief, fumbled and dropped it. As he bent to pick it up, the monster's arm *whuffed* heavily in the air where his head had been—a blow that would certainly have removed that baby-face protuberance. The man stood up and would have put the handkerchief to his nose had it not been so bloody. The creature behind the tree lifted its arm again just as the little man tossed the handkerchief away and stepped out into the field, heading across country to the distant highway that would take him back to town. The monster pounced on the handkerchief, picked it up, studied it, tore it across several times and inspected the tattered edges. Then it gazed vacantly at the disappearing figure of the little man, and finding him no longer interesting, turned back into the woods.

Babe broke into a trot at the sound of the shots. It was important to warn Uncle Alton about what her father had said, but it was more interesting to find out what he had bagged. Oh, he'd bagged it, all right. Uncle Alton never fired without killing. This was about the first time she had ever heard him blast away like that. Must be a bear, she thought excitedly, tripping over a root, sprawling, rolling to her feet again, without noticing the tumble. She'd love to have another bearskin in her room. Where would she put it? Maybe they could line it and she could have it for a blanket. Uncle Alton could sit on it and read to her in the evening— Oh, no. No. Not with this trouble between him and dad. Oh, if she could only do something! She tried to run faster, worried and anticipating, but she was out of breath and went more slowly instead.

At the top of the rise by the edge of the woods she stopped and looked back. Far down in the valley lay the south thirty. She scanned it carefully, looking for her father. The new furrows and the old were sharply defined, and her keen eyes saw immediately that Cory had left the line with the cultivator and had angled the team over to the shade trees without finishing his row. That wasn't like him. She could see the team now, and Cory's pale-blue denim was nowhere in sight. She giggled lightly to herself as she thought of the way she would fool her father. And the little sound of laughter drowned out, for her, the sound of Alton's hoarse dying scream.

She reached and crossed the path and slid through the brush beside it. The shots came from up around here somewhere. She stopped and listened several times, and then suddenly heard something coming toward her, fast. She ducked under cover, terrified, and a little baby-faced man in black, his blue eyes wide with horror, crashed blindly past her, the leather case he carried catching on the branches. It spun a moment and then fell right in front of her. The man never missed it.

Babe lay there for a long moment and then picked up the case and faded into the woods. Things were happening too fast for her. She wanted Uncle Alton, but she dared not call. She stopped again and strained her ears. Back toward the edge of the wood she heard her father's voice, and another's—probably the man who had dropped the briefcase. She dared not go over there. Filled with enjoyable terror, she thought hard, then snapped her fingers in triumph. She and Alton had played Injun many times up here; they had a whole repertoire of secret signals. She had practiced bird calls until she knew them better than the birds themselves. What would it be? Ah—blue jay. She threw back her head and by some youthful alchemy produced a nerve-shattering screech that would have done justice to any jay that ever flew. She repeated it, and then twice more.

The response was immediate—the call of a blue jay, four times, spaced two and two. Babe nodded to herself happily. That was the signal that they were to meet immediately at The Place. The Place was a hideout that he had discovered and shared with her, and not another soul knew of it; an angle of rock beside a stream not far away. It wasn't exactly a cave, but almost. Enough so to be entrancing. Babe trotted happily away toward the brook. She had just known that Uncle Alton would remember the call of the blue jay, and what it meant.

In the tree that arched over Alton's scattered body perched a large jay bird, preening itself and shining in the sun. Quite unconscious of the presence of death, hardly noticing the Babe's realistic cry, it screamed again four times, two and two.

It took Cory more than a moment to recover himself from what he had seen. He turned away from it and leaned weakly against a pine, panting. Alton. That was Alton lying there, in—parts.

"God! God, God, God—"

Gradually his strength returned, and he forced himself to turn again. Stepping carefully, he bent and picked up the .32-40. Its barrel was bright and clean, but the butt and stock were smeared with some kind of stinking rottenness. Where had he seen the stuff before? Somewhere—no matter. He cleaned it off absently, throwing the befouled bandanna away afterward. Through his mind ran Alton's words—was that only last night?—*"I'm goin' to start trackin'. An' I'm goin' to keep trackin' till I find the one done this job on Kimbo."*

Cory searched shrinkingly until he found Alton's box of shells. The box was wet and sticky. That made it—better, somehow. A bullet wet with Alton's blood was the right thing to use. He went away a short distance, circled around till he found heavy footprints, then came back.

"I'm a-trackin' for you, bud," he whispered thickly, and began. Through the brush he followed its wavering spoor, amazed at the amount of filthy mold about, gradually associating it with the thing that had killed his brother. There was nothing in the world for him any more but hate and doggedness. Cursing himself for not getting Alton home last night, he followed the tracks to the edge of the woods. They led him to a big tree there, and there he saw something else—the footprints of the little city man. Nearby lay some tattered scraps of linen, and—what was that?

Another set of prints—small ones. Small, stub-toed ones.

"Babe!"

No answer. The wind sighed. Somewhere a blue jay called.

Babe stopped and turned when she heard her father's voice, faint with distance, piercing.

"Listen at him holler," she crooned delightedly. "Gee, he sounds mad." She sent a jay bird's call disrespectfully back to him and hurried to The Place.

It consisted of a mammoth boulder beside the brook. Some upheaval in the glacial age had cleft it, cutting out a huge V-shaped chunk. The widest part of the cleft was at the water's edge, and the narrowest was hidden by bushes. It made a little ceilingless room, rough and uneven and full of pot-holes and cavelets inside, and yet with quite a level floor. The open end was at the water's edge.

Babe parted the bushes and peered down the cleft.

"Uncle Alton!" she called softly. There was no answer. Oh,

well, he'd be along. She scrambled in and slid down to the floor.

She loved it here. It was shaded and cool, and the chattering stream filled it with shifting golden lights and laughing gurgles. She called again, on principle, and then perched on an outcropping to wait. It was only then she realized that she still carried the little man's briefcase.

She turned it over a couple of times and then opened it. It was divided in the middle by a leather wall. On one side were a few papers in a large yellow envelope, and on the other some sandwiches, a candy bar, and an apple. With a youngster's complacent acceptance of manna from heaven, Babe fell to. She saved one sandwich for Alton, mainly because she didn't like its highly spiced bologna. The rest made quite a feast.

She was a little worried when Alton hadn't arrived, even after she had consumed the apple core. She got up and tried to skim some flat pebbles across the rolling brook, and she stood on her hands, and she tried to think of a story to tell herself, and she tried just waiting. Finally, in desperation, she turned again to the briefcase, took out the papers, curled up by the rocky wall and began to read them. It was something to do, anyway.

There was an old newspaper clipping that told about strange wills that people had left. An old lady had once left a lot of money to whoever would make the trip from the Earth to the Moon and back. Another had financed a home for cats whose masters and mistresses had died. A man left thousands of dollars to the first person who could solve a certain mathematical problem and prove his solution. But one item was blue-penciled. It was:

> One of the strangest of wills still in force is that of Thaddeus M. Kirk, who died in 1920. It appears that he built an elaborate mausoleum with burial vaults for all the remains of his family. He collected and removed caskets from all over the country to fill the designated niches. Kirk was the last of his line; there were no relatives when he died. His will stated that the mausoleum was to be kept in repair permanently, and that a certain sum was to be set aside as a reward for whoever could produce the body of his grandfather, Roger Kirk, whose niche is

still empty. Anyone finding this body is eligible to receive a substantial fortune.

Babe yawned vaguely over this, but kept on reading because there was nothing else to do. Next was a thick sheet of business correspondence, bearing the letterhead of a firm of lawyers. The body of it ran:

> In regard to your query regarding the will of Thaddeus Kirk, we are authorized to state that his grandfather was a man about five feet, five inches, whose left arm had been broken and who had a triangular silver plate set into his skull. There is no information as to the whereabouts of his death. He disappeared and was declared legally dead after the lapse of fourteen years.
>
> The amount of the reward as stated in the will, plus accrued interest, now amounts to a fraction over sixty-two thousand dollars. This will be paid to anyone who produces the remains, providing that said remains answer descriptions kept in our private files.

There was more, but Babe was bored. She went on to the little black notebook. There was nothing in it but penciled and highly abbreviated records of visits to libraries; quotations from books with titles like "History of Angelina and Tyler Counties" and "Kirk Family History." Babe threw that aside, too. Where could Uncle Alton be?

She began to sing tunelessly, "Tumalumalum tum, ta ta ta," pretending to dance a minuet with flowing skirts like a girl she had seen in the movies. A rustle of the bushes at the entrance to The Place stopped her. She peeped upward, saw them being thrust aside. Quickly she ran to a tiny cul-de-sac in the rock wall, just big enough for her to hide in. She giggled at the thought of how surprised Uncle Alton would be when she jumped out at him.

She heard the newcomer come shuffling down the steep slope of the crevice and land heavily on the floor. There was something about the sound— What was it? It occurred to her that though it was a hard job for a big man like Uncle Alton to get through the little opening in the bushes, she could hear no heavy breathing. She heard no breathing at all!

Babe peeped out into the main cave and squealed in utmost horror. Standing there was, not Uncle Alton, but a massive caricature of a man: a huge thing like an irregular mud doll, clumsily made. It quivered and parts of it glistened and parts of it were dried and crumbly. Half of the lower part of its face was gone, giving it a lopsided look. It had no perceptible mouth or nose, and its eyes were crooked, one higher than the other, both a dingy brown with no whites at all. It stood quite still looking at her, its only movement a seedy unalive quivering.

It wondered about the queer little noise Babe had made.

Babe crept far back against a little pocket of stone, her brain running round and round in tiny circles of agony. She opened her mouth to cry out, and could not. Her eyes bulged and her face flamed with the strangling effort, and the two golden ropes of her braided hair twitched and twitched as she hunted hopelessly for a way out. If only she were out in the open—or in the wedge-shaped half-cave where the thing was—or home in bed!

The thing clumped toward her, expressionless, moving with a slow inevitability that was the sheer crux of horror. Babe lay wide-eyed and frozen, mounting pressure of terror stilling her lungs, making her heart shake the whole world. The monster came to the mouth of the little pocket, tried to walk to her and was stopped by the sides. It was such a narrow little fissure, and it was all Babe could do to get it. The thing from the wood stood straining against the rock at its shoulders, pressing harder and harder to get to Babe. She sat up slowly, so near to the thing that its odor was almost thick enough to see, and a wild hope burst through her voiceless fear. It couldn't get in! It couldn't get in because it was too big!

The substance of its feet spread slowly under the tremendous strain and at its shoulder appeared a slight crack. It widened as the monster unfeelingly crushed itself against the rock, and suddenly a large piece of the shoulder came away and the being twisted slushily three feet farther in. It lay quietly with its muddy eyes fixed on her, and then brought one thick arm up over its head and reached.

Babe scrambled in the inch farther she had believed impossible, and the filthy clubbed hand stroked down her back, leaving a trail of muck on the blue denim of the shirt she wore. The monster surged suddenly and, lying full length now, gained that last precious inch. A black hand seized one of her braids, and for Babe the lights went out.

When she came to, she was dangling by her hair from that

same crusted paw. The thing held her high, so that her face and its featureless head were not more than a foot apart. It gazed at her with a mild curiosity in its eyes, and it swung her slowly back and forth. The agony of her pulled hair did what fear could not do—gave her a voice. She screamed. She opened her mouth and puffed up her powerful young lungs, and she sounded off. She held her throat in the position of the first scream, and her chest labored and pumped more air through the frozen throat. Shrill and monotonous and infinitely piercing, her screams.

The thing did not mind. It held her as she was, and watched. When it had learned all it could from this phenomenon, it dropped her jarringly, and looked around the half-cave, ignoring the stunned and huddled Babe. It reached over and picked up the leather briefcase and tore it twice across as if it were tissue. It saw the sandwich Babe had left, picked it up, crushed it, dropped it.

Babe opened her eyes, saw that she was free, and just as the thing turned back to her she dove between its legs and out into the shallow pool in front of the rock, paddled across and hit the other bank screaming. A vicious little light of fury burned in her; she picked up a grapefruit-sized stone and hurled it with all her frenzied might. It flew low and fast, and struck squashily on the monster's ankle. The thing was just taking a step toward the water; the stone caught it off balance, and its unpracticed equilibrium could not save it. It tottered for a long, silent moment at the edge and then splashed into the stream. Without a second look Babe ran shrieking away.

Cory Drew was following the little gobs of mold that somehow indicated the path of the murderer, and he was nearby when he first heard her scream. He broke into a run, dropping his shotgun and holding the .32-40 ready to fire. He ran with such deadly panic in his heart that he ran right past the huge cleft rock and was a hundred yards past it before she burst out through the pool and ran up the bank. He had to run hard and fast to catch her, because anything behind her was that faceless horror in the cave, and she was living for the one idea of getting away from there. He caught her in his arms and swung her to him, and she screamed on and on and on.

Babe didn't see Cory at all, even when he held her and quieted her.

The monster lay in the water. It neither liked nor disliked this new element. It rested on the bottom, its massive head a foot beneath the surface, and it curiously considered the facts that it had garnered. There was the little humming noise of Babe's voice that sent the monster questing into the cave. There was the black material of the briefcase that resisted so much more than green things when he tore it. There was the little two-legged one who sang and brought him near, and who screamed when he came. There was this new cold moving thing he had fallen into. It was washing his body away. That had never happened before. That was interesting. The monster decided to stay and observe this new thing. It felt no urge to save itself; it could only be curious.

The brook came laughing down out of its spring, ran down from its source beckoning to the sunbeams and embracing freshets and helpful brooklets. It shouted and played with streaming little roots, and nudged the minnows and pollywogs about in its tiny backwaters. It was a happy brook. When it came to the pool by the cloven rock it found the monster there, and plucked at it. It soaked the foul substances and smoothed and melted the molds, and the waters below the thing eddied darkly with its diluted matter. It was a thorough brook. It washed all it touched, persistently. Where it found filth, it removed filth; and if there was layer on layer of foulness, then layer by foul layer it was removed. It was a good brook. It did not mind the poison of the monster, but took it up and thinned it and spread it in little rings round rocks downstream, and let it drift to the rootlets of water plants, that they might grow greener and lovelier. And the monster melted.

"I am smaller," the thing thought. "That is interesting. I could not move now. And now this part of me which thinks is going, too. It will stop in just a moment, and drift away with the rest of the body. It will stop thinking and I will stop being, and that, too, is a very interesting thing."

So the monster melted and dirtied the water, and the water was clean again, washing and washing the skeleton that the monster had left. It was not very big, and there was a badly healed knot on the left arm. The sunlight flickered on the triangular silver plate set into the pale skull, and the skeleton was very clean now. The brook laughed about it for an age.

They found the skeleton, six grim-lipped men who came to find a killer. No one had believed Babe, when she told her story days later. It had to be days later because Babe had screamed for seven hours without stopping, and had lain like a dead child for a day. No one believed her at all, because her story was all about the bad fella, and they knew that the bad fella was simply a thing that her father had made up to frighten her with. But it was through her that the skeleton was found, and so the men at the bank sent a check to the Drews for more money than they had ever dreamed about. It was old Roger Kirk, sure enough, that skeleton, though it was found five miles from where he had died and sank into the forest floor where the hot molds built around his skeleton and emerged—a monster.

So the Drews had a new barn and fine new livestock and they hired four men. But they didn't have Alton. And they didn't have Kimbo. And Babe screams at night and has grown very thin.

VAULT OF THE BEAST

Astounding Science Fiction
August

by A. E. van Vogt (1912-   )

The shape-changer is among the most fearsome creatures in the canon of science fiction and fantasy. Here, A. E. van Vogt, one of the brightest stars of the 1940s, presents a most unusual shape-changer— a robot. "The Tower" which holds the key to the defeat of the Beast is one of the most memorable edifices in science fiction and rightly captured the imagination of the readers of Astounding. *This was one of the most talked about and written about stories in the magazine's history, both because of its qualities as fiction and its very strange mathematics. There was never an ultimate prime number like this one!*

(I saw science fiction through John Campbell's eyes during the magic years of 1938 to 1942, when I was learning how to write under that great editor's tutelage. Each month I would come to his office and each month he would tell me of the great stories he had received and my mouth would water and my heart would yearn to be able to duplicate such marvels and have John speak of *me* and *my* stories that way.

And in those years there was no question at all which writers John admired most and which absolutely bestrode the field like colossi. They were Robert Heinlein and A. E. van Vogt. How fortunate those two were. Never again will the field be bestridden like that. It's now too large for any one or two writers to set the pace. But while it lasted it was those two on one side and everyone else on the other. I.A.)

The creature crept. It whimpered from fear and pain, a thing, slobbering sound horrible to hear. Shapeless, formless thing yet changing shape and form with every jerky movement.

It crept along the corridor of the space freighter, fighting the terrible urge of its elements to take the shape of its surroundings. A gray blob of disintegrating stuff, it crept, it cascaded, it rolled, flowed, dissolved, every movement an agony of struggle against the abnormal need to become a stable shape.

Any shape! The hard, chilled-blue metal wall of the Earthbound freighter, the thick, rubbery floor. The floor was easy to fight. It wasn't like the metal that pulled and pulled. It would be easy to become metal for all eternity.

But something prevented it. An implanted purpose. A purpose that drummed from electron to electron, vibrated from atom to atom with an unvarying intensity that was like a special pain: *Find the greatest mathematical mind in the solar system, and bring it to the vault of the Martian ultimate metal. The Great One must be freed! The prime number time lock must be opened!*

That was the purpose that hummed with unrelenting agony through its elements. That was the thought that had been seared into its fundamental consciousness by the great and evil minds that had created it.

There was movement at the far end of the corridor. A door opened. Footsteps sounded. A man whistling to himself. With a metallic hiss, almost a sigh, the creature dissolved, looking momentarily like diluted mercury. Then it turned brown like the floor. It became the floor, a slightly thicker stretch of dark-brown rubber spread out for yards.

It was ecstasy just to lie there, to be flat and to have shape, and to be so nearly dead that there was no pain. Death was so sweet, so utterly desirable. And life such an unbearable torment of agony, such a throbbing, piercing nightmare of anguished convulsion. If only the life that was approaching would pass swiftly. If the life stopped, it would pull it into shape. Life could do that. Life was stronger than metal, stronger than anything. The approaching life meant torture, struggle, pain.

The creature tensed its now flat, grotesque body—the body that could develop muscles of steel—and waited in terror for the death struggle.

Spacecraftsman Parelli whistled happily as he strode along

the gleaming corridor that led from the engine room. He had just received a wireless from the hospital. His wife was doing well, and it was a boy. Eight pounds, the radiogram had said. He suppressed a desire to whoop and dance. A boy. Life sure was good.

Pain came to the thing on the floor. Primeval pain that sucked through its elements like acid burning, burning. The brown floor shuddered in every atom as Parelli strode over it. The aching urge to pull toward him, to take his shape. The thing fought its horrible desire, fought with anguish and shivering dread, more consciously now that it could think with Parelli's brain. A ripple of floor rolled after the man.

Fighting didn't help. The ripple grew into a blob that momentarily seemed to become a human head. Gray, hellish nightmare of demoniac shape. The creature hissed metallically in terror, then collapsed palpitating, slobbering with fear and pain and hate as Parelli strode on rapidly—too rapidly for its creeping pace.

The thin, horrible sound died; the thing dissolved into brown floor, and lay quiescent yet quivering in every atom from its unquenchable, uncontrollable urge to live—live in spite of pain, in spite of abysmal terror and primordial longing for stable shape. To live and fulfill the purpose of its lusting and malignant creators.

Thirty feet up the corridor, Parelli stopped. He jerked his mind from its thoughts of child and wife. He spun on his heels, and stared uncertainly along the passageway from the engine room.

"Now, what the devil was that?" he pondered aloud.

A sound—a queer, faint yet unmistakably horrid sound was echoing and re-echoing through his consciousness. A shiver ran the length of his spine. That sound—that devilish sound.

He stood there, a tall, magnificently muscled man, stripped to the waist, sweating from the heat generated by the rockets that were decelerating the craft after its meteoric flight from Mars. Shuddering, he clenched his fists, and walked slowly back the way he had come.

The creature throbbed with the pull of him, a gnawing, writhing, tormenting struggle that pierced into the deeps of every restless, agitated cell, stabbing agonizingly along the alien nervous system; and then became terrifyingly aware of the inevitable, the irresistible need to take the shape of the life.

Parelli stopped uncertainly. The floor moved under him, a visible wave that reared brown and horrible before his incredulous eyes and grew into a bulbous, slobbering, hissing mass. A venomous demon head reared on twisted, half-human shoulders. Gnarled hands on apelike, malformed arms clawed at his face with insenate rate—and changed even as they tore at him.

"Good God!" Parelli bellowed.

The hands, the arms that clutched him grew more normal, more human, brown, muscular. The face assumed familiar lines, sprouted a nose, eyes, a red gash of mouth. The body was suddenly his own, trousers and all, sweat and all.

"—God!" his image echoed; and pawed at him with letching fingers and an impossible strength.

Gasping, Parelli fought free, then launched one crushing blow straight into the distorted face. A drooling scream of agony came from the thing. It turned and ran, dissolving as it ran, fighting dissolution, uttering strange half-human cries.

And, struggling against horror, Parelli chased it, his knees weak and trembling from sheer funk and incredulity. His arm reached out and plucked at the disintegrating trousers. A piece came away in his hand, a cold, slimy, writhing lump like wet clay.

The feel of it was too much. His gorge rising in disgust, he faltered in his stride. He heard the pilot shouting ahead:

"What's the matter?"

Parelli saw the open door of the storeroom. With a gasp, he dived in, came out a moment later, wild-eyed, an ato-gun in his fingers. He saw the pilot, standing with staring, horrified brown eyes, white face and rigid body, facing one of the great windows.

"There it is!" the man cried.

A gray blob was dissolving into the edge of the glass, becoming glass. Parelli rushed forward, ato-gun poised. A ripple went through the glass, darkening it; and then, briefly, he caught a glimpse of a blob emerging on the other side of the glass into the cold of space.

The officer stood gaping beside him; the two of them watched the gray, shapeless mass creep out of sight along the side of the rushing freight liner.

Parelli sprang to life. "I got a piece of it!" he gasped. "Flung it down on the floor of the storeroom."

VAULT OF THE BEAST

It was Lieutenant Morton who found it. A tiny section of floor reared up, and then grew amazingly large as it tried to expand into human shape. Parelli with distorted, crazy eyes scooped it up in a shovel. It hissed; it nearly became a part of the metal shovel, but couldn't because Parelli was so close. Changing, fighting for shape, it slobbered and hissed as Parelli staggered with it behind his superior officer. He was laughing hysterically. "I touched it," he kept saying, "I touched it."

A large blister of metal on the outside of the space freighter stirred into sluggish life, as the ship tore into the Earth's atmosphere. The metal walls of the freighter grew red, then white-hot, but the creature, unaffected, continued its slow transformation into gray mass. Vague thought came to the thing, realization that it was time to act.

Suddenly, it was floating free of the ship, falling slowly, heavily, as if somehow the gravitation of Earth had no serious effect upon it. A minute distortion in its electrons started it falling faster, as in some alien way it suddenly became more allergic to gravity.

The Earth was green below; and in the dim distance a gorgeous and tremendous city of spires and massive buildings glittered in the sinking sun. The thing slowed, and drifted like a falling leaf in a breeze toward the still-distant Earth. It landed in an arroyo beside a bridge at the outskirts of the city.

A man walked over the bridge with quick, nervous steps. He would have been amazed, if he had looked back, to see a replica of himself climb from the ditch to the road, and start walking briskly after him.

Find the—greatest mathematician!

It was an hour later; and the pain of the throbbing thought was a dull, continuous ache in the creature's brain, as it walked along the crowded street. There were other pains, too. The pain of fighting the pull of the pushing, hurrying mass of humanity that swarmed by with unseeing eyes. But it was easier to think, easier to hold form now that it had the brain and body of a man.

Find—mathematician!

"Why?" asked the man's brain of the thing; and the whole body shook with startled shock at such heretical questioning. The brown eyes darted in fright from side to side, as if expecting instant and terrible doom. The face dissolved a little in that brief moment of mental chaos, became successively the man with the hooked nose who swung by, the tanned face of the tall woman who was looking into the shop window, the—

With a second gasp, the creature pulled its mind back from fear, and fought to readjust its face to that of the smooth-shaven young man who sauntered idly in from a side street. The young man glanced at him, looked away, then glanced back again startled. The creature echoed the thought in the man's brain: "Who the devil is that? Where have I seen that fellow before?"

Half a dozen women in a group approached. The creature shrank aside as they passed, its face twisted with the agony of the urge to become woman. Its brown suit turned just the faintest shade of blue, the color of the nearest dress, as it momentarily lost control of its outer atoms. Its mind hummed with the chatter of clothes and "My dear, didn't she look dreadful in that awful hat?"

There was a solid cluster of giant buildings ahead. The thing shook its human head consciously. So many buildings meant metal; and the forces that held metal together would pull and pull at its human shape. The creature comprehended the reason for this with the understanding of the slight man in a dark suit who wandered by dully. The slight man was a clerk; the thing caught his thought. He was thinking enviously of his boss who was Jim Brender, of the financial firm of J. P. Brender & Co.

The overtones of that thought struck along the vibrating elements of the creature. It turned abruptly and followed Lawrence Pearson, bookkeeper. If people ever paid attention to other people on the street, they would have been amazed after a moment to see two Lawrence Pearsons proceeding down the street, one some fifty feet behind the other. The second Lawrence Pearson had learned from the mind of the first that Jim Brender was a Harvard graduate in mathematics, finance and political economy, the latest of a long line of financial geniuses, thirty years old, and the head of the tremendously wealthy J. P. Brender & Co. Jim Brender had just married the most beautiful girl in the world; and this was the reason for Lawrence Pearson's discontent with life.

"Here I'm thirty, too," his thoughts echoed in the creature's mind, "and I've got nothing. He's got everything—everything while all I've got to look forward to is the same old boarding house till the end of time."

It was getting dark as the two crossed the river. The creature quickened its pace, striding forward with aggressive alertness that Lawrence Pearson in the flesh could never have managed. Some glimmering of its terrible purpose communicated itself in that last instant to the victim. The slight man turned; and let out a faint squawk as those steel-muscled fingers jerked at his throat, a single, fearful snap.

The creature's brain went black with dizziness as the brain of Lawrence Pearson crashed into the night of death. Gasping whimpering, fighting dissolution, it finally gained control of itself. With one sweeping movement, it caught the dead body and flung it over the cement railing. There was a splash below, then a sound of gurgling water.

The thing that was now Lawrence Pearson walked on hurriedly, then more slowly till it came to a large, rambling brick house. It looked anxiously at the number, suddenly uncertain if it had remembered rightly. Hesitantly, it opened the door.

A streamer of yellow light splashed out, and laughter vibrated in the thing's sensitive ears. There was the same hum of many thoughts and many brains, as there had been in the street. The creature fought against the inflow of thought that threatened to crowd out the mind of Lawrence Pearson. A little dazed by the struggle, it found itself in a large, bright hall, which looked through a door into a room where a dozen people were sitting around a dining table.

"Oh, it's you, Mr. Pearson," said the landlady from the head of the table. She was a sharp-nosed, thin-mouthed woman at whom the creature stared with brief intentness. From her mind, a thought had come. She had a son who was a mathematics teacher in a high school. The creature shrugged. In one penetrating glance, the truth throbbed along the intricate atomic structure of its body. This woman's son was as much of an intellectual lightweight as his mother.

"You're just in time," she said incuriously. "Sarah, bring Mr. Pearson's plate."

"Thank you, but I'm not feeling hungry," the creature replied; and its human brain vibrated to the first silent, ironic laughter that it had ever known. "I think I'll just lie down."

All night long it lay on the bed of Lawrence Pearson, bright-eyed, alert, becoming more and more aware of itself. It thought:

"I'm a machine, without a brain of my own. I use the brains of other people, but somehow my creators made it possible for me to be more than just an echo. I use people's brains to carry out my purpose."

It pondered about those creators, and felt a surge of panic sweeping along its alien system, darkening its human mind. There was a vague physiological memory of pain unutterable, and of tearing chemical action that was frightening.

The creature rose at dawn, and walked the streets till half past nine. At that hour, it approached the imposing marble entrance of J. P. Brender & Co. Inside, it sank down in the comfortable chair initialed L. P.; and began painstakingly to work at the books Lawrence Pearson had put away the night before.

At ten o'clock, a tall young man in a dark suit entered the arched hallway and walked briskly through the row after row of offices. He smiled with easy confidence to every side. The thing did not need the chorus of "Good morning, Mr. Brender" to know that its prey had arrived.

Terrible in its slow-won self-confidence, it rose with a lithe, graceful movement that would have been impossible to the real Lawrence Pearson, and walked briskly to the washroom. A moment later, the very image of Jim Brender emerged from the door and walked with easy confidence to the door of the private office which Jim Brender had entered a few minutes before.

The thing knocked and walked in—and simultaneously became aware of three things: The first was that it had found the mind after which it had been sent. The second was that its image mind was incapable of imitating the finer subtleties of the razor-sharp brain of the young man who was staring up from dark-gray eyes that were a little startled. And the third was the large metal bas-relief that hung on the wall.

With a shock that almost brought chaos, it felt the overpowering tug of that metal. And in one flash it knew that this was ultimate metal, product of the fine craft of the ancient Martians, whose metal cities, loaded with treasures of furniture, art and machinery, were slowly being dug up by enterprising human beings from the sands under which they had been buried for thirty or fifty million years.

The ultimate metal! The metal that no heat would even warm, that no diamond or other cutting device, could scratch, never duplicated by human beings, as mysterious as the *ieis* force which the Martians made from apparent nothingness.

VAULT OF THE BEAST

All these thoughts crowded the creature's brain, as it explored the memory cells of Jim Brender. With an effort that was a special pain, the thing wrenched its mind from the metal, and fastened its eyes on Jim Brender. It caught the full flood of the wonder in his mind, as he stood up.

"Good lord," said Jim Brender, "who are you?"

"My name's Jim Brender," said the thing, conscious of grim amusement, conscious, too, that it was progress for it to be able to feel such an emotion.

The real Jim Brender had recovered himself. "Sit down, sit down," he said heartily. "This is the most amazing coincidence I've ever seen."

He went over to the mirror that made one panel of the left wall. He stared, first at himself, then at the creature. "Amazing," he said. "Absolutely amazing."

"Mr. Brender," said the creature, "I saw your picture in the paper, and I thought our astounding resemblance would make you listen, where otherwise you might pay no attention. I have recently returned from Mars, and I am here to persuade you to come back to Mars with me."

"That," said Jim Brender, "is impossible."

"Wait," the creature said, "until I have told you why. Have you ever heard of the Tower of the Beast?"

"The Tower of the Beast!" Jim Brender repeated slowly. He went around his desk and pushed a button.

A voice from an ornamental box said: "Yes, Mr. Brender?"

"Dave, get me all the data on the Tower of the Beast and the lengendary city of Li in which it is supposed to exist."

"Don't need to look it up," came the crisp reply. "Most Martian histories refer to it as the beast that fell from the sky when Mars was young—some terrible warning connected with it—the beast was unconscious when found—said to be the result of its falling out of sub-space. Martians read its mind; and were so horrified by its subconscious intentions they tried to kill it, but couldn't. So they built a huge vault, about fifteen hundred feet in diameter and a mile high—and the beast, apparently of these dimensions, was locked in. Several attempts have been made to find the city of Li, but without success. Generally believed to be a myth. That's all, Jim."

"Thank you!" Jim Brender clicked off the connection, and turned to his visitor. "Well?"

"It is not a myth. I know where the Tower of the Beast is; and I also know that the beast is still alive."

"Now, see here," said Brender good-humoredly, "I'm intrigued by your resemblance to me; and as a matter of fact I'd like Pamela—my wife—to see you. How about coming over to dinner? But don't, for Heaven's sake, expect me to believe such a story. The beast, if there is such a thing, fell from the sky when Mars was young. There are some authorities who maintain that the Martian race died out a hundred million years ago, though twenty-five million is the conservative estimate. The only things remaining of their civilization are their constructions of ultimate metal. Fortunately, toward the end they built almost everything from that indestructible metal."

"Let me tell you about the Tower of the Beast," said the thing quietly. "It is a tower of gigantic size, but only a hundred feet or so projected above the sand when I saw it. The whole top is a door, and that door is geared to a time lock, which in turn has been integrated along a line of *ieis* to the ultimate prime number."

Jim Brender stared; and the thing caught his startled thought, the first uncertainty, and the beginning of belief.

"Ultimate prime number!" Brender ejaculated. "What do you mean?" He caught himself. "I know of course that a prime number is a number divisible only by itself and by one."

He snatched at a book from the little wall library beside his desk, and rippled through it. "The largest known prime is—ah, here it is—is 230584300921393951. Some others, according to this authority, are 77843839397, 182521213001, and 78875943472201."

He frowned. "That makes the whole thing ridiculous. The ultimate prime would be an indefinite number." He smiled at the thing. "If there is a beast, and it is locked up in a vault of ultimate metal, the door of which is geared to a time lock, integrated along a line of *ieis* to the ultimate prime number—then the beast is caught. Nothing in the world can free it."

"To the contrary," said the creature. "I have been assured by the beast that it is within the scope of human mathematics to solve the problem, but that what is required is a born mathematical mind, equipped with all the mathematical training that Earth science can afford. You are that man."

"You expect me to release this evil creature—even if I could perform this miracle of mathematics."

"Evil nothing!" snapped the thing. "That ridiculous fear of the unknown which made the Martians imprison it has resulted in a very grave wrong. The beast is a scientist from another space, accidentally caught in one of his experiments. I say 'his' when of course I do not know whether this race has a sexual differentiation."

"You actually talked with the beast?"

"It communicated with me by mental telepathy."

"It has been proven that thoughts cannot penetrate ultimate metal."

"What do humans know about telepathy? They cannot even communicate with each other except under special conditions." The creature spoke contemptuously.

"That's right. And if your story is true, then this is a matter for the Council."

"This is a matter for two men, you and I. Have you forgotten that the vault of the beast is the central tower of the great city of Li—billions of dollars' worth of treasure in furniture, art and machinery? The beast demands release from its prison before it will permit anyone to mine that treasure. You can release it. We can share the treasure."

"Let me ask you a question," said Jim Brender. "What is your real name?"

"P-Pierce Lawrence!" the creature stammered. For the moment, it could think of no greater variation of the name of its first victim than reversing the two words, with a slight change on "Pearson." Its thoughts darkened with confusion as the voice of Brender pounded:

"On what ship did you come from Mars?"

"O-on *F 4961*," the thing stammered chaotically, fury adding to the confused state of its mind. It fought for control, felt itself slipping, suddenly felt the pull of the ultimate metal that made up the bas-relief on the wall, and knew by that tug that it was dangerously near dissolution.

"That would be a freighter," said Jim Brender. He pressed a button. "Carltons, find out if the *F 4961* had a passenger or person aboard, named Pierce Lawrence. How long will it take?"

"About a minute, sir."

"You see," said Jim Brender, leaning back, "this is mere formality. If you were on that ship, then I shall be compelled to give serious attention to your statements. You can understand, of course, that I could not possibly go into a thing like this blindly. I—"

The buzzer rang. "Yes?" said Jim Brender.

"Only the crew of two was on the *F 4961* when it landed yesterday. No such person as Pierce Lawrence was aboard."

"Thank you." Jim Brender stood up. He said coldly, "Good-bye, Mr. Lawrence. I cannot imagine what you hoped to gain by this ridiculous story. However, it has been most intriguing, and the problem you presented was very ingenious indeed—"

The buzzer was ringing. "What is it?"

"Mr. Gorson to see you, sir."

"Very well, send him right in."

The thing had greater control of its brain now, and it saw in Brender's mind that Gorson was a financial magnate, whose business ranked with the Brender firm. It saw other things, too, things that made it walk out of the private office, out of the building, and wait patiently until Mr. Gorson emerged from the imposing entrance. A few minutes later, there were two Mr. Gorsons walking down the street.

Mr. Gorson was a vigorous man in his early fifties. He had lived a clean, active life; and the hard memories of many climates and several planets were stored away in his brain. The thing caught the alertness of this man on its sensitive elements, and followed him warily, respectfully, not quite decided whether it would act.

It thought: "I've come a long way from the primitive life that couldn't hold its shape. My creators, in designing me, gave to me powers of learning, developing. It is easier to fight dissolution, easier to be human. In handling this man, I must remember that my strength is invincible when properly used."

With minute care, it explored in the mind of its intended victim the exact route of his walk to his office. There was the entrance to a large building clearly etched on his mind. Then a long, marble corridor, into an automatic elevator up to the eighth floor, along a short corridor with two doors. One door led to the private entrance of the man's private office. The other to a storeroom used by the janitor. Gorson had looked into the place on various occasions; and there was in his mind, among other things, the memory of a large chest—

The thing waited in the storeroom till the unsuspecting Gorson was past the door. The door creaked. Gorson turned, his eyes widening. He didn't have a chance. A fist of solid steel smashed his face to a pulp, knocking the bones back into his brain.

This time, the creature did not make the mistake of keeping its mind tuned to that of its victim. It caught him viciously as he fell, forcing its steel fist back to a semblance of human flesh. With furious speed, it stuffed the bulky and athletic form into a large chest, and clamped the lid down tight.

Alertly, it emerged from the storeroom, entered the private office of Mr. Gorson, and sat down before the gleaming desk of oak. The man who responded to the pressing of a button saw John Gorson sitting there, and heard John Gorson say:

"Crispins, I want you to start selling these stocks through the secret channels right away. Sell until I tell you to stop, even if you think it's crazy. I have information of something big on."

Crispins glanced down the row after row of stock names; and his eyes grew wider and wider. "Good lord, man!" he gasped finally, with that familiarity which is the right of a trusted adviser, "these are all the gilt-edged stocks. Your whole fortune can't swing a deal like this."

"I told you I'm not in this alone."

"But it's against the law to break the market," the man protested.

"Crispins, you heard what I said. I'm leaving the office. Don't try to get in touch with me. I'll call you."

The thing that was John Gorson stood up, paying no attention to the bewildered thoughts that flowed from Crispins. It went out of the door by which it had entered. As it emerged from the building, it was thinking: "All I've got to do is kill half a dozen financial giants, start their stocks selling, and then—"

By one o'clock it was over. The exchange didn't close till three, but at one o'clock the news was flashed on the New York tickers. In London, where it was getting dark, the papers brought out an extra. In Hankow and Shanghai, a dazzling new day was breaking as the newsboys ran along the streets in the shadows of skyscrapers, and shouted that J. P. Brender & Co. had assigned; and that there was to be an investigation—

"We are facing," said the chairman of the investigation committee, in his opening address the following morning, "one of the most astounding coincidences in all history. An ancient and respected firm, with world-wide affiliations and branches, with investments in more than a thousand companies of every description, is struck bankrupt by an unexpected crash in every stock in which the firm was interested. It will require months to take evidence on the responsibility for the short-selling which brought about this disaster. In the meantime, I see no reason, regrettable as the action must be to all the old friends of the late J. P. Brender, and of his son, why the demands of the creditors should not be met, and the properties liquidated through auction sales and such other methods as may be deemed proper and legal—"

"Really, I don't blame her," said the first woman, as they wandered through the spacious rooms of the Brenders' Chinese palace. "I have no doubt she does love Jim Brender, but no one could seriously expect her to remain married to him *now*. She's a woman of the world, and it's utterly impossible to expect her to live with a man who's going to be a mere pilot or space hand or something on a Martian spaceship—"

Commander Hughes of Interplanetary Spaceways entered the office of his employer truculently. He was a small man, but extremely wiry; and the thing that was Louis Dyer gazed at him tensely, conscious of the force and power of this man.

Hughes began: "You have my report on this Brender case?"

The thing twirled the mustache of Louis Dyer nervously; then picked up a small folder, and read out loud:

"Dangerous for psychological reasons . . . to employ Brender. . . . So many blows in succession. Loss of wealth, position and wife. . . . No normal man could remain normal under . . . circumstances. Take him into office . . . befriend him . . . give him a sinecure, or position where his undoubted great ability . . . but not on a spaceship, where the utmost hardiness, both mental, moral, spiritual and physical is required—"

Hughes interrupted: "Those are exactly the points which I am stressing. I knew you would see what I meant, Louis."

"Of course, I see," said the creature, smiling in grim amusement, for it was feeling very superior these days. "Your thoughts, your ideas, your codes and your methods are stamped irrevocably on your brain and"—it added hastily—"you have never left me in doubt as to where you stand. However, in this case I must insist. Jim Brender will not take an ordinary position offered by his friends. And it is ridiculous to ask him to subordinate himself to men to whom he is in every way superior. He has commanded his own space yacht; he knows more about the mathematical end of the work than our whole staff put together; and that is no reflection on our staff. He knows the hardships connected with space flying, and believes that it is exactly what he needs. I, therefore, command you, for the first time in our long association, Peter, to put him on space freighter *F 4961* in the place of Spacecraftsman Parelli who collapsed into a nervous breakdown after that curious affair with the creature from space, as Lieutenant Morton described it— By the way, did you find the . . . er . . . sample of that creature yet?"

"No, sir, it vanished the day you came in to look at it. We've searched the place high and low—queerest stuff you ever saw. Goes through glass as easy as light; you'd think it was some form of light-stuff—scares me, too. A pure sympodial development—actually more adaptable to environment than anything hitherto discovered; and that's putting it mildly. I tell you, sir— But see here, you can't steer me off the Brender case like that."

"Peter, I don't understand your attitude. This is the first time I've interferred with your end of the work and—"

"I'll resign," groaned that sorely beset man.

The thing stifled a smile. "Peter, you've built up the staff of Spaceways. It's your child, your creation; you can't give it up, you know you can't—"

The words hissed softly into alarm; for into Hughes' brain had flashed the first real intention of resigning. Just hearing of his accomplishments and the story of his beloved job brought such a rush of memories, such a realization of how tremendous an outrage was this threatened interference. In one mental leap, the creature saw what this man's resignation would mean: The discontent of the men; the swift perception of the situation by Jim Brender; and his refusal to accept the job. There was only one way out—that Brender would get to the ship without finding out what had happened. Once on it, he must carry through with one trip to Mars; and that was all that was needed.

The thing pondered the possibility of imitating Hughes' body; then agonizingly realized that it was hopeless. Both Louis Dyer and Hughes must be around until the last minute.

"But, Peter, listen!" the creature began chaotically. Then it said, "Damn!" for it was very human in its mentality; and the realization that Hughes took its words as a sign of weakness was maddening. Uncertainty descended like a black cloud over its brain.

"I'll tell Brender when he arrives in five minutes how I feel about all this!" Hughes snapped; and the creature knew that the worst had happened. "If you forbid me to tell him then I resign. I— Good God, man, your face!"

Confusion and horror came to the creature simultaneously. It knew abruptly that its face had dissolved before the threatened ruin of its plans. It fought for control, leaped to its feet, seeing the incredible danger. The large office just beyond the frosted glass door—Hughes' first outcry would bring help—

With a half sob, it sought to force its arm into an imitation of a metal fist, but there was no metal in the room to pull it into shape. There was only the solid maple desk. With a harsh cry, the creature leaped completely over the desk, and sought to bury a pointed shaft of stick into Hughes' throat.

Hughes cursed in amazement, and caught at the stick with furious strength. There was sudden commotion in the outer office, raised voices, running feet—

It was quite accidental the way it happened. The surface cars swayed to a stop, drawing up side by side as the red light blinked on ahead. Jim Brender glanced at the next car.

A girl and a man sat in the rear of the long, shiny, streamlined affair, and the girl was desperately striving to crouch down out of his sight, striving with equal desperation not to be too obvious in her intention. Realizing that she was seen, she smiled brilliantly, and leaned out of the window.

"Hello, Jim, how's everything?"

"Hello, Pamela!" Jim Brender's fingers tightened on the steering wheel till the knuckles showed white, as he tried to keep his voice steady. He couldn't help adding: "When does the divorce become final?"

"I get my papers tomorrow," she said, "but I suppose you won't get yours till you return from your first trip. Leaving today, aren't you?"

"In about fifteen minutes." He hesitated. "When is the wedding?"

The rather plump, white-faced man who had not participated in the conversation so far, leaned forward.

"Next week," he said. He put his fingers possessively over Pamela's hand. "I wanted it tomorrow but Pamela wouldn't—er, good-bye."

His last words were hastily spoken, as the traffic lights switched, and the cars rolled on, separating at the first corner.

The rest of the drive to the spaceport was a blur. He hadn't expected the wedding to take place so soon. Hadn't, when he came right down to it, expected it to take place at all. Like a fool, he had hoped blindly—

Not that it was Pamela's fault. Her training, her very life made this the only possible course of action for her. But— *one week!* The spaceship would be one fourth of the long trip to Mars—

He parked his car. As he paused beside the runway that led to the open door of F 4961—a huge globe of shining metal, three hundred feet in diameter—he saw a man running toward him. Then he recognized Hughes.

The thing that was Hughes approached, fighting for calmness. The whole world was a flame of cross-pulling forces. It shrank from the thoughts of the people milling about in the office it had just left. Everything had gone wrong. It had never intended to do what it now had to do. It had intended to spend most of the trip to Mars as a blister of metal on the outer shield of the ship. With an effort, it controlled its funk, its terror, its brain.

"We're leaving right away," it said.

Brender looked amazed. "But that means I'll have to figure out a new orbit under the most difficult—"

"Exactly," the creature interrupted. "I've been hearing a lot about your marvelous mathematical ability. It's time the words were proved by deeds."

Jim Brender shrugged. "I have no objection. But how is it that you're coming along?"

"I always go with a new man."

It sounded reasonable. Brender climbed the runway, closely followed by Hughes. The powerful pull of the metal was the first real pain the creature had known for days. For a long month, it would now have to fight the metal, fight to retain the shape of Hughes—and carry on a thousand duties at the same time.

That first stabbing pain tore along its elements, and smashed the confidence that days of being human had built up. And then, as it followed Brender through the door, it heard a shout behind it. It looked back hastily. People were streaming out of several doors, running toward the ship.

Brender was several yards along the corridor. With a hiss that was almost a sob, the creature leaped inside, and pulled the lever that clicked the great door shut.

There was an emergency lever that controlled the antigravity plates. With one jerk, the creature pulled the heavy lever hard over. There was a sensation of lightness and a sense of falling.

Through the great plate window, the creature caught a flashing glimpse of the field below, swarming with people. White faces turning upward, arm waving. Then the scene grew remote, as a thunder of rockets vibrated through the ship.

"I hope," said Brender, as Hughes entered the control room, "you wanted me to start the rockets."

"Yes," the thing replied, and felt brief panic at the chaos in its brain, the tendency of its tongue to blur. "I'm leaving the mathematical end entirely in your hands."

It didn't dare to stay so near the heavy metal engines, even with Brender's body there to help it keep its human shape. Hurriedly, it started up the corridor. The best place would be the insulated bedroom—

Abruptly, it stopped in its headlong walk, teetered for an instant on tiptoes. From the control room it had just left, a thought was trickling—a thought from Brender's brain. The creature almost dissolved in terror as it reailzed that Brender was sitting at the radio, answering an insistent call from Earth.

It burst into the control room, and braked to a halt, its eyes widening with humanlike dismay. Brender whirled from before the radio with a single twisting step. In his fingers, he held a revolver. In his mind, the creature read a dawning comprehension of the whole truth. Brender cried:

"You're the . . . thing that came to my office, and talked about prime numbers and the vault of the beast."

He took a step to one side to cover an open doorway that led down another corridor. The movement brought the telescreen into the vision of the creature. In the screen was the image of the real Hughes. Simultaneously, Hughes saw the thing.

"Brender," he bellowed, "it's the monster that Morton and Parelli saw on their trip from Mars. It doesn't react to heat or any chemicals, but we never tried bullets. Shoot, you fool!"

It was too much, there was too much metal, too much confusion. With a whimpering cry, the creature dissolved. The pull of the metal twisted it horribly into thick half metal; the struggle to be human left it a malignant structure of bulbous head, with one eye half gone, and two snakelike arms attached to the half metal of the body.

Instinctively, it fought closer to Brender, letting the pull of his body make it more human. The half metal became fleshlike stuff that sought to return to its human shape.

"Listen, Brender!" Hughes' voice came urgently. "The fuel vats in the engine room are made of ultimate metal. One of them is empty. We caught a part of this thing once before, and it couldn't get out of the small jar of ultimate metal. If you could drive it into the vat while it's lost control of itself, as it seems to do very easily—"

"I'll see what lead can do!" Brender rapped in a brittle voice.

Bang! The half-human creature screamed from its half-formed slit of mouth, and retreated, its legs dissolving into gray dough.

"It hurts, doesn't it?" Brender ground out. "Get over into the engine room, you damned thing, into the vat!"

"Go on, go on!" Hughes was screaming from the telescreen.

Brender fired again. The creature made a horrible slobbering sound, and retreated once more. But it was bigger again, more human; and in one caricature hand a caricature of Brender's revolver was growing.

It raised the unfinished, unformed gun. There was an explosion, and a shriek from the thing. The revolver fell, a shapeless, tattered blob, to the floor. The little gray mass of it scrambled frantically toward the parent body, and attached itself like some monstrous canker to the right foot.

And then, for the first time, the mighty and evil brains that had created the thing, sought to dominate their robot. Furious, yet conscious that the game must be carefully played, the Controller forced the terrified and utterly beaten thing to its will. Scream after agonized scream rent the air, as the change was forced upon the unstable elements. In an instant, the thing stood in the shape of Brender, but instead of a revolver, there grew from one browned, powerful hand a pencil of shining metal. Mirror bright, it glittered in every facet like some incredible gem.

The metal glowed ever so faintly, an unearthly radiance. And where the radio had been, and the screen with Hughes' face on it, there was a gaping hole. Desperately, Brender pumped bullets into the body before him, but though the shape trembled, it stared at him now, unaffected. The shining weapon swung toward him.

"When you are quite finished," it said, "perhaps we can talk."

It spoke so mildly that Brender, tensing to meet death, lowered his gun in amazement. The thing went on:

"Do not be alarmed. This which you hear and see is a robot, designed by us to cope with your space and number world. Several of us are working here under the most difficult conditions to maintain this connection, so I must be brief.

"We exist in a time world immeasurably more slow than your own. By a system of synchronization, we have geared a number of these spaces in such fashion that, though one of our days is millions of your years, we can communicate. Our purpose is to free our colleague, Kalorn, from the Martian vault. Kalorn was caught accidentally in a time warp of his own making and precipitated onto the planet you know as Mars. The Martians, needlessly fearing his great size, constructed a most diabolical prison, and we need your knowledge of the mathematics peculiar to your space and number world—and to it alone—in order to free him."

The calm voice continued, earnest but not offensively so, insistent but friendly. He regretted that their robot had killed human beings. In greater detail, he explained that every space was constructed on a different numbers system, some all negative, some all positive, some a mixture of the two, the whole an infinite variety, and every mathematic interwoven into the very fabric of the space it ruled.

Ieis force was not really mysterious. It was simply a flow from one space to another, the result of a difference in potential. This flow, however, was one of the universal forces, which only one other force could affect, the one he had used a few minutes before. Ultimate metal was *actually* ultimate.

In their space they had a similar metal, built up from negative atoms. He could see from Brender's mind that the Martians had known nothing about minus numbers, so that they must have built it up from ordinary atoms. It could be done that way, too, though not so easily. He finished:

"The problem narrows down to this: Your mathematics must tell us how, with our universal force, we can short-circuit the ultimate prime number—that is, factor it—so that the door will open any time. You may ask how a prime can be factored when it is divisible only by itself and by one.

That problem is, for your system, solvable only by your mathematics. Will you do it?"

Brender realized with a start that he was still holding his revolver. He tossed it aside. His nerves were calm as he said:

"Everything you have said sounds reasonable and honest. If you were desirous of making trouble, it would be the simplest thing in the world to send as many of your kind as you wished. Of course, the whole affair must be placed before the Council—"

"Then it is hopeless—the Council could not possibly accede—"

"And you expect me to do what you do not believe the highest governmental authority in the System would do?" Brender exclaimed.

"It is inherent in the nature of a democracy that it cannot gamble with the lives of its citizens. We have such a government here; and its members have already informed us that, in a similar condition, they would not consider releasing an unknown beast upon their people. Individuals, however, can gamble where governments must not. You have agreed that our argument is logical. What system do men follow if not that of logic?"

The Controller, through its robot, watched Brender's thoughts alertly. It saw doubt and uncertainty, opposed by a very human desire to help, based upon the logical conviction that it was safe. Probing his mind, it saw swiftly that it was unwise, in dealing with men, to trust too much to logic. It pressed on:

"To an individual we can offer—everything. In a minute, with your permission, we shall transfer this ship to Mars; not in thirty days, but in thirty seconds. The knowledge of how this is done will remain with you. Arrived at Mars, you will find yourself the only living person who knows the whereabouts of the ancient city of Li, of which the vault of the beast is the central tower. In this city will be found literally billions of dollars' worth of treasure made of ultimate metal; and according to the laws of Earth, fifty percent will be yours. Your fortune re-established, you will be able to return to Earth this very day, and reclaim your former wife, and your position. Poor silly child, she loves you still, but the iron conventions and training of her youth leave her no alternative. If she were older, she would have the character to defy those conventions. You must save her from herself. Will you do it?"

Brender was as white as a sheet, his hands clenching and unclencing. Malevolently, the thing watched the flaming thought sweeping through his brain—the memory of a pudgy white hand closing over Pamela's fingers, watched the reaction of Brender to its words, those words that expressed exactly what he had always thought. Brender looked up with tortured eyes.

"Yes," he said, "I'll do what I can."

A bleak range of mountains fell away into a valley of reddish gray sand. The thin winds of Mars blew a mist of sand against the building.

Such a building! At a distance, it had looked merely big. A bare hundred feet projected above the desert, a hundred feet of length and *fifteen hundred feet of diameter*. Literally thousands of feet must extend beneath the restless ocean of sand to make the perfect balance of form, the graceful flow, the fairylike beauty, which the long-dead Martians demanded of all their constructions, however massive. Brender felt suddenly small and insignificant as the rockets of his spacesuit pounded him along a few feet above the sand toward that incredible building.

At close range the ugliness of sheer size was miraculously lost in the wealth of the decorative. Columns and pilasters assembled in groups and clusters, broke up the façades, gathered and dispersed again restlessly. The flat surfaces of wall and roof melted into a wealth of ornaments and imitation stucco work, vanished and broke into a play of light and shade.

The creature floated beside Brender; and its Controller said: "I see that you have been giving considerable thought to the problem, but this robot seems incapable of following abstract thoughts, so I have no means of knowing the source of your speculations. I see however that you seem to be satisfied."

"I think I've got the answer," said Brender, "but first I wish to see the time lock. Let's climb."

They rose into the sky, dipping over the lip of the building. Brender saw a vast flat expanse; and in the center— He caught his breath!

The meager light from the distant sun of Mars shone down on a structure located at what seemed the exact center of the great door. The structure was about fifty feet high, and seemed nothing less than a series of quadrants coming together at the center, which was a metal arrow pointing straight up.

The arrow head was not solid metal. Rather it was as if the metal had divided in two parts, then curved together again. But not quite together. About a foot separated the two sections of metal. But that foot was bridged by a vague, thin, green flame of *ieis* force.

"The time lock!" Brender nodded. "I thought it would be something like that, though I expected it would be bigger, more substantial."

"Do not be deceived by its fragile appearance," answered the thing. "Theoretically, the strength of ultimate metal is infinite; and the *ieis* force can only be affected by the universal I have mentioned. Exactly what the effect will be, it is impossible to say as it involves the temporary derangement of the whole number system upon which that particular area of space is built. But now tell us what to do."

"Very well." Brender eased himself onto a bank of sand, and cut off his antigravity plates. He lay on his back, and stared thoughtfully into the blue-black sky. For the time being all doubts, worries and fears were gone from him, forced out by sheer will power. He began to explain:

"The Martian mathematic, like that of Euclid and Pythagoras, was based on endless magnitude. Minus numbers were beyond their philosophy. On Earth, however, beginning with Descartes, an analytical mathematic was evolved. Magnitude and perceivable dimensions were replaced by that of variable relation-values between positions in space.

"For the Martians, there was only one number between 1 and 3. Actually, the totality of such numbers is an infinite aggregate. And with the introduction of the idea of the square root of minus one—or i—and the complex numbers, mathematics definitely ceased to be a simple thing of magnitude, perceivable in pictures. Only the intellectual step from the infinitely small quantity to the lower limit of every possible finite magnitude brought out the conception of a variable number which oscillated beneath any assignable number that was not zero.

"The prime number, being a conception of pure magnitude, had no reality in *real* mathematics, but in this case was rigidly bound up with the reality of the *ieis* force. The Martians knew *ieis* as a pale-green flow about a foot in length and developing say a thousand horsepower. (It was actually 12.171 inches and 1021.23 horsepower, but that was unimportant.) The power produced never varied, the length never varied, from year end to year end, for tens of thousands of years. The Martians took the length as their basis of measurement, and called it one 'el'; they took the power as their basis of power and called it one 'rb.' And because of the absolute invariability of the flow they knew it was eternal.

"They knew furthermore that nothing could be eternal without being prime; their whole mathematic was based on numbers which could be factored, that is, disintegrated, destroyed, rendered less than they had been; and numbers which could not be factored, disintegrated, or divided into smaller groups.

"Any number which could be factored was incapable of being infinite. Contrariwise, the infinite number must be prime.

"Therefore, they built a lock and integrated it along a line of *ieis*, to operate when the *ieis* ceased to flow—which would be at the end of Time, provided it was not interfered with. To prevent interference, they buried the motivating mechanism of the flow in ultimate metal, which could not be destroyed or corroded in any way. According to their mathematic, that settled it."

"But you have the answer," said the voice of the thing eagerly.

"Simply this: The Martians set a value on the flow of one 'rb.' If you interfere with that flow to no matter what small degree, you no longer have an 'rb.' You have something less. The flow, which is a universal, becomes automatically less than a universal, less than infinite. The prime number ceases to be prime. Let us suppose that you interfere with it to the extent of *infinity minus one*. You will then have a number divisible by two. As a matter of fact, the number, like most large numbers, will immediately break into thousands of pieces, i.e., it will be divisible by tens of thousands of smaller numbers. If the present time falls anywhere near one of these breaks, the door would open then. In other words, the door will open immediately if you can so interfere with the flow that one of the factors occurs in immediate time."

"That is very clear," said the Controller with satisfaction and the image of Brender was smiling triumphantly. "We shall now use this robot to manufacture a universal; and Kalorn shall be free very shortly." He laughed aloud. "The poor robit is protesting violently at the thought of being destroyed, but after all it is only a machine, and not a very good one at that. Besides, it is interfering with my proper reception of your thoughts. Listen to it scream, as I twist it into shape."

The cold-blooded words chilled Brender, pulled him from the heights of his abstract thought. Because of the prolonged intensity of his thinking, he saw with sharp clarity something that had escaped him before.

"Just a minute," he said. "How is it that the robot, introduced from your world, is living at the same time rate as I am, whereas Kalorn continues to live at your time rate?"

"A very good question." The face of the robot was twisted into a triumphant sneer, as the Controller continued. "Because, my dear Brender, you have been duped. It is true that Kalorn is living in our time rate, but that was due to a shortcoming in our machine. The machine which Kalorn built, while large enough to transport him, was not large enough in its adaptive mechanism to adapt him to each new space as he entered it. With the result that he was transported but not adapted. It was possible of course for us, his helpers, to transport such a small thing as the robot, though we have no more idea of the machine's construction than you have.

"In short, we can use what there is of the machine, but the secret of its construction is locked in the insides of our own particular ultimate metal, and in the brain of Kalorn. Its invention by Kalorn was one of those accidents which, by the law of averages, will not be repeated in millions of our years. Now that you have provided us with the method of bringing Kalorn back, we shall be able to build innumerable interspace machines. Our purpose is to control all spaces, all worlds—particularly those which are inhabited. We intend to be absolute rulers of the entire Universe."

The ironic voice ended; and Brender lay in his prone position the prey of horror. The horror was twofold, partly due to the Controller's monstrous plan, and partly due to the thought that was pulsing in his brain. He groaned, as he realized that warning thought must be ticking away on the automatic receiving brain of the robot. "Wait," his thought was saying, "that adds a new factor. Time—"

There was a scream from the creature as it was forcibly dissolved. The scream choked to a sob, then silence. An intricate machine of shining metal lay there on that great gray-brown expanse of sand and ultimate metal.

The metal glowed; and then the machine was floating in the air. It rose to the top of the arrow, and settled over the green flame of *ieis*.

Brender jerked on his antigravity screen, and leaped to his feet. The violent action carried him some hundred feet into the air. His rockets sputtered into staccato fire, and he clamped his teeth against the pain of acceleration.

Below him, the great door began to turn, to unscrew, faster and faster, till it was like a flywheel. Sand flew in all directions in a miniature storm.

At top acceleration, Brender darted to one side.

Just in time. First, the robot machine was flung off that tremendous wheel by sheer centrifugal power. Then the door came off, and, spinning now at an incredible rate, hurtled straight into the air, and vanished into space.

A puff of black dust came floating up out of the blackness of the vault. Suppressing his horror, yet perspiring from awful relief, he rocketed to where the robot had fallen into the sand.

Instead of glistening metal, a time-dulled piece of junk lay there. The dull metal flowed sluggishly and assumed a quasi-human shape. The flesh remained gray and in little rolls as if it were ready to fall apart from old age. The thing tried to stand up on wrinkled, horrible legs, but finally lay still. Its lips moved, mumbled:

"I caught your warning thought, but I didn't let them know. Now, Kalorn is dead. They realized the truth as it was happening. End of Time came—"

It faltered into silence, and Brender went on: "Yes, end of Time came when the flow became momentarily less than eternal—came at the factor point which occurred a few minutes ago."

"I was . . . only partly . . . within its . . . influence, Kalorn all the way. . . . Even if they're lucky . . . will be years before . . . they invent another machine . . . and one of their years is billions . . . of yours. . . . I didn't tell them. . . . I caught your thought . . . and kept it . . . from them—"

"But why did you do it? Why?"

"Because they were hurting me. They were going to destroy me. Because . . . I liked . . . being human. I was . . . somebody!"

The flesh dissolved. It flowed slowly into a pool of lavalike gray. The lava crinkled, split into dry, brittle pieces. Brender touched one of the pieces. It crumbled into a fine powder of gray dust. He gazed out across that grim, deserted valley of sand, and said aloud, pityingly:

"Poor Frankenstein."

He turned toward the distant spaceship, toward the swift trip to Earth. As he climbed out of the ship a few minutes later, one of the first persons he saw was Pamela.

She flew into his arms. "Oh, Jim, Jim," she sobbed. "What a fool I've been. When I heard what had happened, and realized you were in danger, I— Oh, Jim!"

Later, he would tell her about their new fortune.

THE IMPOSSIBLE HIGHWAY
Thrilling Wonder Stories
August

by Oscar J. Friend (1897-1963)

Oscar J. Friend was one of the pioneer literary agents in the sf field, directing the briefly influential Otis Kline Literary Agency. He was also an editor of some note, editing Thrilling Wonder Stories *and its companion magazine* Startling Stories *from 1941–1944. In addition, he was a competent to good writer, and his stories appeared (often under pseudonyms) in a wide variety of pulp markets.*

"The Impossible Highway" is a superior example of the kind of enigmatic story that so entralled the science fiction readers of the 40s.

(Martin brought this story to my attention. I could have sworn there wasn't a story in the 1930s and 1940s I wasn't familiar with, but either I missed this issue of TWS, which doesn't seem likely, or I am softening as I approach early middle age.

In any case I read it fresh now and it brought back my youth. We had never heard of flying saucers then, but there is always this vague yearning for mysterious and all-powerful beings from beyond, even if their doings on Earth are not clear. This story is an example of the kind of thing that stirred what Sam Moskowitz called "the sense of wonder." We may have learned too much and grown too sophisticated to be impressed by this kind of story any longer, but to some extent that's our loss.—I.A.)

Dr. Albert Nelson looked at his young assistant, Robert Mackensie, and scowled.

"So this was just what I needed!" he snapped. "Leave my laboratory and take a walking tour with you in the Ozarks. Lovely vacation. Bah!"

"But, Doctor," Mackensie protested mildly, "you did need a vacation. I can't help it if we had an accident." A grin crept over his youthful face. "Besides, it's kind of funny— two erudite scientists helpless as babes in the woods!"

But Dr. Nelson could not see the humor in the situation. They were lost—lost deep in the Ozark Mountains, their compass hopelessly smashed. And that annoyed him no end.

For Dr. Nelson was an orderly soul. He had always been a logical thinker. He had a mathematical mind that clicked like a machine. No loose ends existed for him. That was why he made such an excellent biologist. He traced everything to its source and pigeonholed it permanently within his brain before letting go of it.

To Dr. Nelson, two plus two equaled four, and he had to get that answer before he quit. Every positive had a negative, every cause an effect. There was never any unfinished research work in his laboratory, no litter of paper on his desk, no clutter of stuff in is mind. He repudiated everything which did not have a logical explanation. He had no patience with unfinished symphonies, lady-and-tiger stories, enigmas, or unsolved mysteries. Quite a definite, positive chap.

That's why he was peeved and exasperated when he and Mackensie came upon the end of the road. It wasn't the cumulative effect of the facts that they were lost, that their compass had accidentally been broken, that they had been pushing on since early morning and it was three o'clock in the afternoon now, that they were weary and scratched up and hungry and thirsty. None of this. It was the inexplicable fact of the road itself.

"What is that ahead of us?" Dr. Nelson panted as his keen eyes caught sight of a shining, white expanse through the trees and underbrush. They had been climbing steadily for the past hour, seeking a high spot from which they might survey the surrounding terrain and get their bearings. "An expanse of water, or the sky?"

Mackensie puffed on ahead. His young voice floated back in eager accents.

"It's a road, Doctor! A concrete highway! Thank God, we can find our way back to civilization now."

It was a road, all right. Nelson wrinkled his brows in thought as he quickened his pace to overtake his companion.

But what was a concrete road doing here in the heart of a wild country which sane white men never even trod on foot? How could there be a cement highway up here in these mountains where there weren't even country side roads, where only wild game lived and an occasional blue jay raised his raucous voice or a lone turkey buzzard wheeled in solitary splendor overhead? And there was something else.

There was nothing peculiar about the concrete slab itself. It was a quite normal specimen of the engineer's and road builder's art. Twenty feet wide, fully eight inches thick, it stretched suddenly away before the two men in a properly graded, sweet white expanse that curved through the pines and elms and cedars and dipped gracefully out of sight over the brow of a slope.

No, it wasn't the construction or condition of the road; it was the very fact of its sudden presence here. Dr. Nelson became aware of the fact that he had used the adverb "suddenly" twice in as many seconds in thinking of this thoroughfare. That described the thing. Abruptly—just like that—the road began, its near end as squarely chopped off and finished as the shoulders running along the side edges of the best-behaved highways. In the midst of a primordial wilderness the road just suddenly began.

There was no evidence that it was intended to continue in this direction. No blazed trees, no surveyor's marks, no grading, no sand or gravel or lumber piles, no machinery, no tools, no barricade, no road marker, no detour sign. Nothing. Not even a dirt road, trail, or footpath leading in any direction from the end of the concrete slab. Simply a wild and untrammeled hillside in the heart of uncharted mountains, and there, as abruptly as a pistol shot—the near end of a gleaming highway!

The incongruity of it must have finally struck Mackensie in spite of his relief, for the young biologist was standing just short of the end of the paving and staring around him in perplexity as Nelson joined him. His bright blue eyes met the steady brown eyes of the older man, and his face twisted quizzically. He wagged his hands helplessly.

"Why doesn't it go on?" he asked. "Can it be an abandoned project?"

"Who ever heard of even an abandoned trail that didn't lead at least to a house or a shack?" snorted Nelson irritably.

"Can it be a test stretch of road?" suggested Mackensie.

Wordlessly, Dr. Nelson pointed at the road's unsullied surface. There wasn't a drop of oil, a tire mark, a clamp of caked dirt from a hoof, a footprint—anything, to mar the slab's virgin purity. And yet the road, beginning here in the thick of the forest, curved out of sight before them as though it led on forever, an important artery of transportation.

"It's a senseless riddle!" snapped Nelson. "And I detest riddles."

"Well, although it begins spontaneously, Doctor, it seems to lead somewhere," Mackensie said. "At least, it will lead us back to civilization. We can solve its mystery at the other end. Are you too tired to go on?"

"No. No," repeated Nelson irritably, frowning along the road. But he felt a vague reluctance to set foot on the slab. Why, he did not know. He hesitated, mopped his perspiring brow with a handkerchief, and gazed around at the deep woods through which they had come. Then he shrugged and stepped up on the end of the road.

Mackensie stepped up beside him and set off along the paving in a swinging stride. Perforce, Nelson fell in step, and they marched together in silence. For a brief space there was no sound at all save the rhythmic tramping of their boots and the occasional slithering noises which came from Nelson's knapsack. This was the little green lizard the biologist had captured some time before noon.

"Always the indefatigable scientist," Mackensie had observed when Nelson had adroitly caught the little reptile sunning itself on a rock and had popped it into an emptied sandwich box to study later.

Now, the noise of the little lizard was the only sound outside themselves which kept them company. It was the queer significance of this that caused Nelson to put his hand on Mackensie's arm and stop suddenly.

"Why are we stopping?" asked the younger man in surprise. "This beats tearing our way through brambles and underbrush by a house and farm."

"Listen," said Nelson.

Mackensie did so tensely. All around was utter silence. There wasn't even a breath of wind stirring the leaves on the trees.

"I don't hear anything," he said.

"That's just it," commented Nelson. "Not even the buzz of an insect—not a bird in the sky—not a rustle in the thickets alongside the road. What became of the blue jays and the gnats that kept us company and annoyed us before we reached this road?"

Mackensie's blue eyes looked startled. Nelson turned to stare along the section of road they had already traversed. It stretched there for twenty yards, white and spotless save for the faint markings of their own recent passage. It was as though they stood alone in a dead and lifeless world. No, it wasn't like that exactly. All around them was the evidence of floral life, but a life in arrested motion. That was it—a Technicolor, three-dimensional still—a rigid, frozen world in which only they themselves had the power of motion. It was uncanny.

"Not a bug crawling across the road," whispered Mackensie in awe. "Not even a distant sound to indicate that anything or anybody is on this planet. But I have a queer sort of feeling deep inside me that—that the forces of life are surging all about us. Doctor, I feel as though this very road is quivering and teeming with life even as it lies rigid beneath our feet. What in God's name is all this?"

Nelson lowered his gaze to the area about his feet. Mackensie was right. There was a psychic sort of hum or quiver to the concrete, to the very air about them, and yet everything was so still and silent. Slowly an odd impression upon the perturbed scientist.

It was as though his eyes penetrated the fraction of an inch below the smooth surface of the concrete slab. He felt, rather than saw, that this was an incredible highway of life, that billions and billions of living entities had trod this way before him in endless, teeming throngs.

"Come on," said Nelson in a muffled voice. "Let's go on."

It was around the next curve, where the forest thinned away and the road appeared to wind majestically across a series of plateaus on top of the world, that they came upon the first variation to the smooth progress of the road. This was a concrete pedestal about waist high on the left-hand shoulder of the highway, an integral part of the concrete itself. It was as though the road had paused and flung up a sort of pseudopodium at its edge.

On top of this slim pedestal was a cube of what appeared to be quartz glass. At least it was crystal of some sort, faintly iridescent and sparkling under the rays of the afternoon sun. As they approached, they saw that it was a hollow cube which enclosed a powerful binocular microscope. Its twin eye-pieces, capped against the weather, protruded outside the case. On the flaring top of the pedestal, just below the glass cube and easily discernible without stopping or squinting, was a bronze plate containing raised letters. The inscription was in English.

Both men halted in amazement at the further incongruity of this. A fine microscope mounted like a museum display in a wilderness which contained only a deserted concrete highway! What did it mean?

"My God!" murmured Mackensie. "Look! Read it, Dr. Nelson." Together they stared at the dark but clearly legible plaque.

UNIVERSAL LIFE SPORTS—PAN-COSMIC

> These minute cellular specimens are the tiniest evolved seeds of that phenomenon called life, whether floral or faunal, which are self-contained and practically immortal. They are propelled throughout the universe on beams of light. Peculiarly deathless, they settle like a fungoid mold upon the most barren and arid planet and father all forms of living matter. Their primary origin is unknown.

Nelson whipped the caps from the binocular eyepieces and glued his eyes to the lenses. He was conscious of a queer sort of magnetic thrill as he touched the glass-encased instrument. The crystal cabinet scintillated and glowed as though endowed with a life force of its own. It was impossible to adjust the controls of the microscope since they were within the glass shell, but this proved needless.

On the field before his eyes, perfectly adjusted, was a typical stained glass slide similar to thousands the biologist had examined. There, immobile, deathless, changeless, were hundreds of tiny gray cells which resembled the various fern molds he had studied more than once, and yet they were different. They were cellular; they were undoubtedly bacteria—but they had a sharply distinct rim or shell which might well have been impervious to the darkness and cold and cosmic rays of outer space. Certainly, Dr. Nelson had never seen their exact like before.

After a careful study, he raised his head, stepped aside, and motioned Mackensie to look. The young man did so.

"Good heavens, Doctor," he murmured. "They don't even take the stain the least bit. They reject it completely, standing out like dots against a field of pale pink."

"Precisely," Nelson agreed, frowning thoughtfully. "And you notice that they are motionless, inert—as though arrested by magic in the midst of their activity."

"Yes," nodded Mackensie, still looking. "Doubtless they are dead."

"I wonder," said Nelson.

"I can't understand it," pursued Mackensie. "Even the most minute organisms would show at least molecular motion."

"Let's go on," said Nelson, recapping the eyepieces. "I see another pedestal a few yards beyond, on the opposite side of this infernal road."

Mackensie was the first to reach the second queer pedestal with its faintly glowing and pulsing glass case enclosing another microscope. He was already peering through the eyepieces when Nelson read the bronze plaque below the crystal case.

LEPTOTHRIX—A GENUS OF THE FAMILY CHLAMYDOBACTERIACEAE

One of the earliest forms of cellular life on this planet, dating from archaeozoic rocks at least one billion years old. Filamental in form, with unbranched segments, it reproduces by fission from one end only. Walls of filaments are of iron deposited around the living cells by accretion. Man and beast are fueled by plants which consume earth elements and build up by chlorophyl sun power, but LEPTOTHRIX literally eats iron. Most veins of iron ore have been built by the action of this bacterium.

When Mackensie, dazed and uncertain, removed his eyes from the microscope, Nelson looked. He recognized the specimens instantly. And these bacteria were caught in an immobile net, frozen rigid as statues in the midst of life. When he looked up, Mackensie was already running on to the next pedestal twenty or thirty feet beyond. Nelson followed more slowly.

"Algae!" cried out Mackensie.

Nelson read the bronze plaque and then stared at the familiar blue-green strands of the primitive water plant which becomes visible to the naked eye as the greenish scum on stagnant pond water. And once again he noted the frozen and arrested condition of the specimens.

"Plankton!" shouted Mackensie next, reaching the fourth

pedestal. "Good Lord, Doctor, this is like—like going through an open-air penny arcade of bacteriology." He smiled.

That was precisely what Nelson was thinking. He still hadn't solved the enigma of the road itself. The additional mystery of high-powered microscopes mounted here in the open in queer crystal cases he thrust to the background of his mind to be explained in due and proper course. It was, as Mackensie said, like a laboratory of the gods. Almost fearfully Nelson looked up at the sky as though he half expected the head and shoulders of some superscientist to materialize from behind a fleecy cloud. But nothing happened. It was still three o'clock in the afternoon. Nothing lived or moved save the two men and the confined little lizard.

One thing was significant to the methodical Nelson as he plodded along this weird and unaccountable highway. There had been no unnecessary or haphazard placements of specimens. Everything was in logical and chronological order as far as he could determine. The trend was precisely and steadily upward in the mighty cycle of life.

Coming into view before them, lining the highway like trees in a park, were crystal specimen cases of varying sizes and shapes. No longer did a microscope accompany each exhibit. Life specimens now were in forms discernible to the naked eye. A distinct line of cleavage between plant and animal life had come into being, both being carried forward in faithful progression. And in each case every specimen was perfectly preserved and apparently lifeless.

The entire array of crystal cases pulsed and glowed in the sun with an eerie life of their own.

Up through the ages ran this bizarre story of life. Through the day of the fossils, the fern forests, the primordial piscine life of the sea, the first conifers, the first reptiles, the age of gigantic reptilian mammals—along the ladder of life they marched, seeing actual specimens no man, presumably, had seen before. It was like a tour through a marvelous combination of laboratory, botanical garden, aquarium, and the Smithsonian Institution.

The two biologists forgot their hunger, their thirst, their weariness. They lost all track of time, although it must have been hours and hours that they marched along this corridor of still life. It was like looking at color plates in a three-dimensional magazine of the future, or like gazing at stereopticon enlargements of the screen of life. And the sun hung brilliantly in the sky at three o'clock in the afternoon.

The written matter on the various bronze plaques—which was always there, regardless of the size of the display cabinet or the nature of its contents—would have composed a complete and unique thumbnail history of the surging course of that tenacious, fragile, but indestructible thing called life. Nelson began to regret that he had not copied down each one of them, realizing as he did so that it would have been impossible. He wouldn't have had enough paper if his knapsack had been full of nothing else.

Mackensie began to mourn that he hadn't brought a camera with him. Some of the specimens were such as man, in filling in the gaps of life's history, had never even imagined. The main enigma still unsolved, Nelson pushed onward with a mounting fever which amazed him. He felt, without analysis, that he was being drawn onward by the hand of destiny, approaching a climax, a height, a fate that was inexorable.

The same fire must have imbued Mackensie, for the young man now marveled at the Gargantuan panorama, at the magnetic oddity of the crystal cases, at the puzzling thought and speculation of how this *outré* museum came to be, at the impossible fact that time stood still.

And then they came to the first empty display case. It was a little cabinet, and they paused to read the bronze plaque. They had long since passed into a comparatively modern era, reaching a stage of presentation which encompassed flora and fauna as it now existed. Primitive man had already appeared, and his image was in properly spaced and graded cabinets.

Nelson had got a start at his view of the first shaggy brute which was definitely the long-sought missing link between man and the lower animals. A queer and repulsive thing to the esthete, Nelson the biologist almost worshiped before the lifelike mammal. From there on the story of mankind was written graphically for the two amazed travelers to read.

But here was the first vacant case. Conscious of great annoyance, Nelson read the bronze plaque.

LACERTA VIRIDIS

This green lizard is a specimen of the small, four-legged reptile with tapering tail which, along with related families, form the suborder of all the LACERTILIA with the exception of geckos and chameleons, which see.

The biologist raised his eyes. But the case, pulsing and glowing with its faintly bluish-green sheen, unharmed and unbroken, was empty. There simply was nothing within it.

"That's funny," mused Mackensie aloud, as Nelson thoughtfully examined the crystal case which, in this instance, resembled a bell jar. "That's the first gap in all the series."

"Yes," almost growled Nelson as he tugged at the knob of the bell jar. To his surprise, he was able to remove it. Then he saw at the base of the jar, on the flaring ledge of the pedestal, the little wheel which controlled the air-exhausting and sealing apparatus.

He accidentally placed one hand on the spot which had been covered by the bell jar, and instantly he lost all feeling in the member. It was as though his entire hand, from the wrist down, was nothing but a lump of insensate matter. Hastily he snatched it back. At once life and feeling returned.

"What's the matter?" asked Mackensie quickly in professional interest. "Hot?"

"No," answered Nelson, replacing the bell jar carefully. "Just—nothing at all. No feeling. My hand went completely dead."

"Is it all right now?"

"Quite. There must be something about these magnetic pulsations that blanket and cut off the life force without destroying life."

"Then, if that's so, all those—those specimens we have seen are alive? Alive but dormant?"

"I wonder," said Nelson.

Mackensie shuddered silently.

"Come on," he said. "Let's go. I think I see a mountain lion yonder."

Knitting his brows in irritation at this minor break in this colossal display of specimens, Nelson followed on. The scampering, rattling, slithering sound of the little lizard in the lunchbox in his knapsack was like the annoying impulse scurrying around in his brain. They passed the chameleon, the specimens of wild game and small fauna, and reached the spot where the depicted story of this era of plant life was resumed.

Here, perhaps a couple of hundred yards on from the empty lizard case, Nelson halted in the fashion of a man who has firmly made up his mind. Mackensie looked at him in astonishment.

"Come," said Nelson. "We're going back."

"Back?" echoed the younger man incredulously. "Where? Why?"

"Only as far as the *Lacerta Viridis* case. I've got to. I've just got to. I can't go on."

"But—but, can we go—back?" whispered Mackensie.

This was a startling thought. Nelson had never considered such a possibility.

"Will we have time?" pursued his assistant biologist. "Night may overtake us as it is before we come to the end of this road."

For answer, Nelson pointed at the sun. It hung in the bright sky precisely at the three o'clock position.

"Come," ordered Nelson.

Obediently, almost like a man under the power of hypnosis, Mackensie turned and started back along the highway. Nelson paced him. It was as though they breasted a strong and resistant tide, as though they fought a steady and powerful wind. Nelson felt like a man in a dream, almost overpowered with a lethargy he could not understand. Only his indomitable will forced them both onward. And still nothing moved or lived along the entire ghastly highway save the two men, walking in the warm sunlight.

Slowly they retraced their steps and drew up before the empty lizard case.

"Well, we're here," panted Mackensie. "Now what?"

For answer Nelson removed his knapsack in a methodical fashion and took out the lunchbox. Pinioning the little lizard swiftly by the nape of the neck, he removed the bell jar and placed the squirming reptile on the pedestal.

Instantly the creature went rigid. Nelson withdrew his numbed hand and stared at the specimen. In lifelike manner the lizard rested on its four tiny feet, body half-coiled, head uplifted, beady little eyes glittering as it stared at nothing.

Primly Nelson covered it with the bell jar and turned the wheel to seal the vacuum. A faint hum resulted from within the base of the pedestal and then died into nothingness. The god of science accepting an offering. When Mackensie tried to lift the bell jar he found it immovable.

The two men stared at each other.

"At least, it is a passable specimen," observed Nelson. "It is similar to the Old World species. Let's go now."

With a quicker step he led the way. All annoyance over the empty case had vanished.

It must have been hours later, and God only knew how

many curving miles, when they reached the second and final empty specimen case.

"Look!" cried Mackensie in heartfelt relief. "We are coming to the end of the road!"

Nelson had lost interest in the road. The mighty story of life which had unfolded had swept him up and on in an irresistible surge. It was with a start that he came back to a realization of his surroundings and focused his attention on the distance.

Mackensie was right. About a hundred yards on, ending in a thicket of trees on a downward slope, was the end of the road.

Just as it started, so the road ended—abruptly, inexplicably. Not far from its termination was a specimen case which appeared to be about three feet tall upon its low pedestal. But Nelson was more interested in the seven-foot case opposite him.

TWENTIETH-CENTURY MAN

> This specimen of the warm-blooded biped mammal with the developing brainpan and thyroidal glands represents man at the physical peak of his evolution. As has been pointed out through the various case histories, animal and plant life, having come far from a common origin, differing principally in the matter of an atom of magnesium in chlorophyl structure instead of an atom of iron in the hemoglobin of blood, have now passed their separate evolution goals. From this point on, their parallel paths converge, finally uniting once more in a common structure which approaches the apex of mental development.

Dr. Nelson raised his eyes from the bronze plaque. The pulsating hollow cube was empty. There was no specimen. Instead, there was only a door of beveled glass which swung out over the road on invisible hinges, as if inviting a weary sojourner to enter and rest—for eternity.

The biologist frowned in utter exasperation. Why, of all specimen cases should this one be empty? He pulled restlessly at one ear as he turned to stare along the road. He was annoyed again, disappointed, to note there were no more specimen cases save the one three-foot case at the very end of the way.

The story was almost told. Past hundreds of thousands of

crystal cases they had walked for endless hours—only to find this most important case, as far as mankind was concerned, empty. Somehow, Nelson could not go on and leave it thus. His methodical nature seemed to be driving him onward with inexorable logic. His gaze fell upon his companion.

"Mackensie," he said in a queer voice. "Mackensie, come here."

The younger man paled and shrank away.

"No," he cried out, intuitively guessing the other's purpose. "No! You are mad, Doctor. Let's get away from this hellish thing. I . . ."

He ended in a cry of stark terror as Nelson pounced upon him. The biologist was twenty years older than Mackensie, but he was also the larger man physically. Mackensie had no chance against him. The struggle was as short as its meaning was horrible. In a matter of seconds, Nelson had his victim helpless.

"No!" screamed Mackensie, horror dawning in his eyes. "Dr. Nelson, you mustn't! You can't do this! You . . ."

He ended in shrill scream after scream of fainting madness as Nelson lifted him erect and carried him to the ajar door of the crystal cabinet.

"It is painless," murmured Nelson gently. "I know. *And why is the case empty*, if not for one of us? Answer me that!"

But Mackensie was past answering anything. He was passing into a state of cataleptic horror.

Like a man in a dream, like a puppet controlled by extra-terrestrial strings, Nelson shifted his burden dexterously around to face him and then, balancing himself carefully, he thrust the body of his companion squarely and smoothly into the empty crystal case. The change that took place was miraculous, instantaneous. The texture of Mackensie's body became like marble. Remaining erect, he rocked back against the rear of the cabinet and then forward like a tottering statue.

Nelson quickly pulled the heavy crystal door around, literally closing it in the set face of his companion. With a soft *whoosh* of air, the beveled edges of the door fitted smoothly into the beveled crystal frame—and the last case had its perfect specimen.

The biologist was trembling as he stared into the glazed eyes of his former laboratory assistant. Then he sighed, mopping his brow, and glanced at the sun. It was three o'clock in the afternoon.

Turning slowly, as though loath to part company with the man who had made this incredible journey with him, Nelson strode on to the end of the road.

Reaching that last case, he paused to study the specimen within. Almost in the shade of the thickening trees, the pulsating aura of the case was faintly phosphorescent. But it was the nature of the specimen that fascinated the biologist.

Squat, scarcely three feet tall, pallid and sickly brownish in tinge, the thing looked more like an overgrown mushroom than anything else. A mushroom with a bulging dome that was a horrible caricature of a human head. A pair of enormous orifices denoted what may have been meant for eyes. The mouth was nothing but a seam or a weal which indicated where a mouth once had been. The thing was sexless and stood upon three rootlike feet. At last Nelson brought himself to read the bronze plaque.

THYROIDICUS—PLANT MAN

> The final evolution of mammalian life upon this planet. Composed principally of a fibrous brain tissue and a free iodine-producing organism which is the development of what was formerly man's iodine plant, the thyroid gland located in the throat, this creature has neither blood nor chlorophyl.
> Like LEPTOTHRIX, this form of life has learned at long last to assimilate its food directly from the elements, transmuting it instantly and releasing free energy. THYROIDICUS, the ultimate goal of physical evolution, is practically all brain. The next stage of evolution, inevitably, crosses the boundary of animate existance, and life becomes purely spiritual.

That was all. The story was told. The end of the road was reached—abruptly. No blazed trees, no surveyor's marks, no grading, no material piles, no machinery, no tools, no barricades, no detour sign. Not even a dirt road, a trail, or a footpath leading in any direction from the end of the concrete slab.

Simply a wild and untrammeled hillside in the heart of uncharted mountains, and the road which had begun as suddenly as a pistol shot led nowhere and ended as precipitantly.

Dr. Nelson was a methodical and orderly soul. Ironically

so, he realized grimly. He hadn't been able to help himself. His cold logic had been tapped to the nth degree.

He thoughtfully turned and stared back along the way he had come. He felt that vague and incomprehensible tremble of vibrant life flowing onward in the road beneath his feet. Now there was not an empty case, not a broken thread in the two lines of specimen cases which stretched off into the illimitable distance there. The record was complete.

What record? Just what was this incredible scientific display? That it was not of Earth he was now firmly convinced. Was it a time trap or a gigantic trophy corridor of some superhunter from beyond the stars?

The doctor shrugged his shoulders as he gave up the enigma. He stepped off the near end of the Impossible Highway, relieved to feel the more prosaic sod and grass beneath his feet. He turned once more to look back on the concrete slab.

The highway had disappeared. There was nothing beyond but the tangled underbrush of the wilderness. The sun was sinking redly behind the western mountains.

QUIETUS

Astounding Science Fiction
September

by Ross Rocklynne (1913-   )

One of the best of the "second rank" writers of the late thirties and forties, Ross Rocklynne (real name Ross L. Rocklin), has been a neglected figure in science fiction, largely because he produced very little long fiction. The best of his work, including stories like "Jackdaw" (1942), "Jaywalker" (1950), and "Time Wants a Skeleton" can be found in his two Ace Books collections The Men and the Mirror *and* The Sun Destroyers, *both 1973. He has continued to write and has produced some interesting work in recent years, especially "Ching Witch" in* Again Dangerous Visions *(1972) and "Randy-Tandy Man" in* Universe 3.

"Quietus" is a lovely and tragic story about the difficulty of making life and death decisions, and the relative meaning of "intelligence."

(What an issue this one was. It contained this story and "Blowups Happen" which follows, and it also contained the first installment of A. E. van Vogt's "Slan" which may very well be the best first installment of any s.f. serial ever written. It's no wonder that the second story I sold to Campbell, "Homo Sol," which also appeared in this issue, sank without a trace.

I have always remembered Ross Rocklynne's stories with affection. He wrote a series of detective-adventure stories in which pursuer and pursued fell into a trap and had to rescue themselves by using a scientific principle. "The Men and the Mirror" was the best of these.—I.A.)

The creatures from Alcon saw from the first that Earth, as a planet, was practically dead; dead in the sense that it had given birth to life, and was responsible, indirectly, for its almost complete extinction.

"This type of planet is the most distressing," said Tark, absently smoothing down the brilliantly colored feathers of his left wing. "I can stand the dark, barren worlds which never have, and probably never will, hold life. But these that have been killed by some celestial catastrophe! Think of what great things might have come from their inhabitants."

As he spoke thus to his mate, Vascar, he was marking down in a book the position of this planet, its general appearance from space, and the number and kind of satellites it supported.

Vascar, sitting at the controls, both her claws and her vestigial hands at work, guided the spherical ship at slowly decreasing speed toward the planet Earth. A thousand miles above it, she set the craft into an orbital motion, and then proceeded to study the planet, Tark setting the account into his book, for later insertion into the Astronomical Archives of Alcon.

"Evidently," mused Vascar, her brilliant, unblinking eyes looking at the planet through a transparent section above the control board, "some large meteor, or an errant asteroid—that seems most likely—must have struck this specimen a terrible blow. Look at those great, gaping cracks that run from pole to pole, Tark. It looks as if volcanic eruptions are still taking place, too. At any rate, the whole planet seems entirely denuded—except for that single, short strip of green we saw as we came in."

Tark nodded. He was truly a bird, for in the evolutionary race on his planet, distant uncounted light years, his stock had won out over the others. His wings were short, true, and in another thousand years would be too short for flight, save in a dense atmosphere; but his head was large, and his eyes, red, small, set close together, showed intelligence and a kind benevolence. He and Vascar had left Alcon, their planet, a good many years ago; but they were on their way back now. Their outward-bound trip had taken them many light years north of the Solar System; but on the way back, they had decided to make it one of the stop-off points in their zigzag course. Probably their greatest interest in all this long cruise was in the discovery of planets—they were indeed few. And that pleasure might even be secondary to the discovery of life. To find a planet that had almost entirely died was, conversely, distressing. Their interest in the planet Earth was, because of this, a wistful one.

The ship made the slow circuit of Earth—the planet was a hodge-podge of tumbled, churned mountains; of abysmal, frightfully long cracks exuding unholy vapors; of volcanoes that threw their fires and hot liquid rocks far into the sky; of vast oceans disturbed from the ocean bed by cataclysmic eruptions. And of life they saw nothing save a single strip of green perhaps a thousand miles long, a hundred wide, in the Western Hemisphere.

"I don't think we'll find intelligent life, though," Tark said pessimistically. "This planet was given a terrific blow—I wouldn't be surprised if her rotation period was cut down considerably in a single instant. Such a charge would be unsupportable. Whole cities would literally be snapped away from their foundations—churned, ground to dust. The intelligent creatures who built them would die by the millions—the billions—in that holocaust; and whatever destruction was left incomplete would be finished up by the appearance of volcanoes and faults in the crust of the planet."

Vascar reminded him, "Remember, where there's vegetation, even as little as evidenced by that single strip down there, there must be some kind of animal life."

Tark ruffled his wings in a shrug. "I doubt it. The plants would get all the carbon dioxide they needed from volcanoes—animal life wouldn't have to exist. Still, let's take a look. Don't worry, I'm hoping there's intelligent life, too. If there is, it will doubtless need some help if it is to survive. Which ties in with our aims, for that is our principal purpose on this expedition—to discover intelligent life, and, wherever possible, to give it what help we can, if it needs help."

Vascar's vestigial hands worked the controls, and the ship dropped leisurely downward toward the green strip.

A rabbit darted out of the underbrush—Tommy leaped at it with the speed and dexterity of a thoroughly wild animal. His powerful hands wrapped around the creature—its struggles ceased as its vertebra was snapped. Tommy squatted, tore the skin off the creature, and proceeded to eat great mouthfuls of the still warm flesh.

Blacky cawed harshly, squawked, and his untidy form came flashing down through the air to land precariously on Tommy's shoulder. Tommy went on eating, while the crow fluttered its wings, smoothed them out, and settled down to a restless somnolence. The quiet of the scrub forest, save for the cries and sounds of movement of birds and small animals moving through the forest, settled down about Tommy as he ate. "Tommy" was what he called himself. A long time ago, he remembered, there used to be a great many people in the world—perhaps a hundred—many of whom, and particularly two people whom he had called Mom and Pop, had called him by that name. They were gone now, and the others with them. Exactly where they went, Tommy did not know. But the world had rocked one night—it was the night Tommy ran away from home, with Blacky riding on his shoulder—and when Tommy came out of the cave where he had been sleeping, all was in flames, and the city on the horizon had fallen so that it was nothing but a huge pile of dust—but in the end it had not mattered to Tommy. Of course, he was lonesome, terrified, at first, but he got over that. He continued to live, eating, drinking, sleeping, walking endlessly; and Blacky, his talking crow, was good company. Blacky was smart. He could speak every word that Tommy knew, and a good many others that he didn't. Tommy was not Blacky's first owner.

But though he had been happy, the last year had brought the recurrence of a strange feeling that had plagued him off and on, but never so strongly as now. A strange, terrible hunger was settling on him. Hunger? He knew this sensation. He had forthwith slain a wild dog, and eaten of the meat. He saw then that it was not a hunger of the belly. It was a hunger of the mind, and it was all the worse because he could not know what it was. He had come to his feet, restless, looking into the tangled depths of the second growth forest.

"Hungry," he had said, and his shoulders shook and tears coursed out of his eyes, and he sat down on the ground and sobbed without trying to stop himself, for he had never been told that to weep was unmanly. What was it he wanted?

He had everything there was all to himself. Southward in winter, northward in summer, eating of berries and small animals as he went, and Blacky to talk to and Blacky to talk the same words back at him. This was the natural life—he had lived it ever since the world went bang. But still he cried, and felt a panic growing in his stomach, and he didn't know what it was he was afraid of, or longed for, whichever it was. He was twenty-one years old. Tears were natural to him, to be indulged in whenever he felt like it. Before the world went bang—there were some things he remembered—the creature whom he called Mom generally put her arms around him and merely said, "It's all right, Tommy, it's all right."

So on that occasion, he arose from the ground and said, "It's all right, Tommy, it's all right."

Blacky, he with the split tongue, said harshly, as was his wont, "It's all right, Tommy, it's all right! I tell you, the price of wheat is going down!"

Blacky, the smartest crow anybody had—why did he say that? There wasn't anybody else, and there weren't any more crows—helped a lot. He not only knew all the words and sentences that Tommy knew, but he knew others that Tommy could never understand because he didn't know where they came from, or what they referred to. And in addition to all that, Blacky had the ability to anticipate what Tommy said, and frequently took whole words and sentences right out of Tommy's mouth.

Tommy finished eating his rabbit, and threw the skin aside, and sat quite still, a peculiarly blank look in his eyes. The strange hunger was on him again. He looked off across the lush plain of grasses that stretched away, searching into the distance, toward where the sun was setting. He looked to left and right. He drew himself softly to his feet, and peered into the shadows of the forest behind him. His heavily bearded lips began to tremble, and the tears started from his eyes again. He turned and stumbled from the forest, blinded.

Blacky clutched at Tommy's broad shoulder, and rode him, and a split second before Tommy, said, "It's all right, Tommy, it's all right."

Tommy said the words angrily to himself, and blinked the tears away.

He was a little bit tired. The sun was setting, and night would soon come. But it wasn't that that made him tired. It was a weariness of the mind, a feeling of futility, for, whatever it was he wanted, he could never, never find it, because he would not know where he should look for it.

His bare foot trampled on something wet—he stopped and looked at the ground. He stooped and picked up the skin of a recently killed rabbit. He turned it over and over in his hands, frowning. This was not an animal he had killed, certainly—the skin had been taken off in a different way. Someone else—no! But his shoulders began to shake with a wild excitement. Someone else? No, it couldn't be! There was no one—there could be no one—could there? The skin dropped from his nerveless fingers as he saw a single footprint not far ahead of him. He stooped over it, examining, and knew again that he had not done this, either. And certainly it could be no other animal than a man!

It was a small footprint at which he stared, as if a child, or an under-sized man, might have stepped in the soft humus. Suddenly he raised his head. He had definitely heard the crackling of a twig, not more than forty feet away, certainly. His eyes stared ahead through the gathering dusk. Something looking back at him? Yes! Something there in the bushes that was not an animal!

"No noise, Blacky," he whispered, and forgot Blacky's general response to that command.

"No noise, Blacky!" the big, ugly bird blasted out. "No noise, Blacky! Well, fer cryin' out loud!"

Blacky uttered a scared squawk as Tommy leaped ahead, a snarl contorting his features, and flapped from his master's shoulder. For several minutes Tommy ran after the vanishing figure, with all the strength and agility of his singularly powerful legs. But whoever—or whatever—it was that fled him, outdistanced him easily, and Tommy had to stop at last, panting. Then he stooped, and picked up a handful of pebbles and hurled them at the squawking bird. A single tail feather fell to earth as Blacky swooped away.

"Told you not to make noise," Tommy snarled, and the tears started to run again. The hunger was starting up in his mind again, too! He sat down on a log, and put his chin in his palms, while his tears flowed. Blacky came flapping through the air, almost like a shadow—it was getting dark. The bird tentatively settled on his shoulder, cautiously flapped away again and then came back.

Tommy turned his head and looked at it bitterly, and then turned away, and groaned.

"It's all your fault, Blacky!"

"It's all your fault," the bird said. "Oh, Tommy, I could spank you! I get so exasperated!"

Sitting there, Tommy tried to learn exactly what he had seen. He had been sure it was a human figure, just like himself, only different. Different! It had been smaller, had seemed to possess a slender grace—it was impossible! Every time he thought of it, the hunger in his mind raged!

He jumped to his feet, his fists clenched. This hunger had been in him too long! He must find out what caused it—he must find her—why did the word *her* come to his mind? Suddenly, he was flooded with a host of childhood remembrances.

"It was a girl!" he gasped. "Oh, Tommy must want a girl!"

The thought was so utterly new that it left him stunned; but the thought grew. He must find her, if it took him all the rest of his life! His chest deepened, his muscles swelled, and a new light came into his blue eyes. Southward in winter, northward in summer—eating—sleeping—truly, there was nothing in such a life. Now he felt the strength of a purpose swelling up in him. He threw himself to the ground and slept; and Blacky flapped to the limb of a tree, inserted his head beneath a wing, and slept also. Perhaps, in the last ten or fifteen years, he also had wanted a mate, but probably he had long ago given up hope—for, it seemed, there were no more crows left in the world. Anyway, Blacky was very old, perhaps twice as old as Tommy; he was merely content to live.

Tark and Vascar sent their spherical ship lightly plummeting above the green strip—it proved to be vegetation, just as they had supposed. Either one or the other kept constant watch of the ground below—they discovered nothing that might conceivably be classed as intelligent life. Insects they found, and decided that they worked entirely by instinct; small animals, rabbits, squirrels, rats, raccoons, otters, opossums, and large animals, deer, horses, sheep, cattle, pigs, dogs, they found to be just that—animals, and nothing more.

"Looks as if it was all killed off, Vascar," said Tark, "and not so long ago at that, judging by the fact that this forest must have grown entirely in the last few years."

Vascar agreed; she suggested they put the ship down for a few days and rest.

"It would be wonderful if we could find intelligent life after all," she said wistfully. "Think what a great triumph it would be if we were the ones to start the last members of that race on the upward trail again. Anyway," she added, "I think this atmosphere is dense enough for us to fly in."

He laughed—a trilling sound. "You've been looking for such an atmosphere for years. But I think you're right about this one. Put the ship down there, Vascar—looks like a good spot."

For five days Tommy followed the trail of the girl with a grim determination. He knew now that it was a woman; perhaps—indeed, very probably—the only one left alive. He had only the vaguest of ideas of why he wanted her—he thought it was for human companionship, that alone. At any rate, he felt that this terrible hunger in him—he could give it no other word—would be allayed when he caught up with her.

She was fleeing him, and staying just near enough to him to make him continue the chase, he knew that with a fierce exultation. And somehow her actions seemed right and proper. Twice he had seen her, once on the crest of a ridge, once as she swam a river. Both times she had easily outdistanced him. But by cross-hatching, he picked up her trail again—a bent twig or weed, a footprint, the skin of a dead rabbit.

Once, at night, he had the impression that she crept up close, and looked at him curiously, perhaps with the same great longing that he felt. He could not be sure. But he knew that very soon now she would be his—and perhaps she would be glad of it.

Once he heard a terrible moaning, high up in the air. He looked upward. Blacky uttered a surprised squawk. A large, spherical thing was darting overhead.

"I wonder what that is," Blacky squawked.

"I wonder what that is," said Tommy, feeling a faint fear. "There ain't nothin' like that in the yard."

He watched as the spaceship disappeared from sight. Then, with the unquestioning attitude of the savage, he dismissed the matter from his mind, and took up his tantalizing trail again.

"Better watch out, Tommy," the bird cawed.

"Better watch out, Tommy," Tommy muttered to himself. He only vaguely heard Blacky—Blacky always anticipated what Tommy was going to say, because he had known Tommy so long.

The river was wide, swirling, muddy, primeval in its surge of resistless strength. Tommy stood on the bank, and looked out over the waters—suddenly his breath soughed from his lungs.

"It's her!" he gasped. "It's her, Blacky! She's drownin'!"

No time to waste in thought—a figure truly struggled against the push of the treacherous waters, seemingly went under. Tommy dived cleanly, and Blacky spread his wings at the last instant and escaped a bath. He saw his master disappear beneath the swirling waters, saw him emerge, strike out with singularly powerful arms, slightly upstream, fighting every inch of the way. Blacky hovered over the waters, cawing frantically, and screaming.

"Tommy, I could spank you! I could spank you! I get so exasperated! You wait till your father comes home!"

A log was coming downstream. Tommy saw it coming, but knew he'd escape it. He struck out, paid no more attention to it. The log came down with a rush, and would have missed him had it not suddenly swung broadside on. It clipped the swimming man on the side of the head. Tommy went under, threshing feebly, barely conscious, his limbs like leaden bars. That seemed to go on for a very long time. He seemed to be breathing water. Then something grabbed hold of his long black hair—

When he awoke, he was lying on his back, and he was staring into her eyes. Something in Tommy's stomach fell out—perhaps the hunger was going. He came to his feet, staring at her, his eyes blazing. She stood only about twenty feet away from him. There was something pleasing about her, the slimness of her arms, the roundness of her hips, the strangeness of her body, her large, startled, timid eyes, the mass of ebon hair that fell below her hips. He started toward her. She gazed at him as if in a trance.

Blacky came flapping mournfully across the river. He was making no sound, but the girl must have been frightened as he landed on Tommy's shoulder. She tensed, and was away like a rabbit. Tommy went after her in long, loping bounds, but his foot caught in a tangle of dead grass, and he plummeted head foremost to the ground.

The other vanished over a rise of ground.

He arose again, and knew no disappointment that he had again lost her. He knew now that it was only her timidity, the timidity of a wild creature, that made her flee him. He started off again, for now that he knew what the hunger was, it seemed worse than ever.

The air of this planet was deliciously breathable, and was the nearest thing to their own atmosphere that Tark and Vascar had encountered.

Vascar ruffled her brilliant plumage, and spread her wings, flapping them. Tark watched her, as she laughed at him in her own way, and then made a few short, running jumps and took off. She spiraled, called down to him.

"Come on up. The air's fine, Tark."

Tark considered. "All right," he conceded, "but wait until I get a couple of guns."

"I can't imagine why," Vascar called down; but nevertheless, as they rose higher and higher above the second growth forest, each had a belt strapped loosely around the neck, carrying a weapon similar to a pistol.

"I can't help but hope we run into some kind of intelligent life," said Vascar. "This is really a lovely planet. In time the volcanoes will die down, and vegetation will spread all over. It's a shame that the planet has to go to waste."

"We could stay and colonize it," Tark suggested rakishly.

"Oh, not I. I like Alcon too well for that, and the sooner we get back there, the better—Look! Tark! Down there!"

Tark looked, caught sight of a medium large animal moving through the underbrush. He dropped a little lower. And then rose again.

"It's nothing," he said. "An animal, somewhat larger than the majority we've seen, probably the last of its kind. From the looks of it, I'd say it wasn't particularly pleasant on the eyes. Its skin shows—Oh, now I see what you mean, Vascar!"

This time he was really interested as he dropped lower, and a strange excitement throbbed through his veins. Could it be that they were going to discover intelligent life after all—perhaps the last of its kind?

It was indeed an exciting sight the two bird-creatures from another planet saw. They flapped slowly above and a number of yards behind the unsuspecting upright beast that moved swiftly through the forest, a black creature not unlike themselves in general structure riding its shoulder.

"It must mean intelligence!" Vascar whispered excitedly, her brilliant red eyes glowing with interest. "One of the first requisites of intelligent creatures is to put animals lower in the scale of evolution to work as beasts of burden and transportation."

"Wait awhile," cautioned Tark, "before you make any irrational conclusions. After all, there are creatures of different species which live together in friendship. Perhaps the creature which looks so much like us keeps the other's skin and hair free of vermin. And perhaps the other way around, too."

"I don't think so," insisted his mate. "Tark, the bird-creature is riding the shoulder of the beast. Perhaps that means its race is so old, and has used this means of transportation so long, that its wings have atrophied. That would almost certainly mean intelligence. It's talking now—you can hear it. It's probably telling its beast to stop—there, it has stopped!"

"It's voice is not so melodious," said Tark dryly.

She looked at him reprovingly; the tips of their flapping wings were almost touching.

"That isn't like you, Tark. You know very well that one of our rules is not to place intelligence on creatures who seem like ourselves, and neglect others while we do so. Its harsh voice proves nothing—to one of its race, if there are any left, its voice may be pleasing in the extreme. At any rate, it ordered the large beast of burden to stop—you saw that."

"Well, perhaps," conceded Tark.

They continued to wing their slow way after the perplexing duo, following slightly behind, skimming the tops of the trees. They saw the white beast stop, and place its paws on its hips. Vascar, listening very closely, because she was anxious to gain proof of her contention, heard the bird-creature say,

"Now what, Blacky?" and also the featherless beast repeat the same words: "Now what, Blacky?"

"There's your proof," said Vascar excitedly. "Evidently the white beast is highly imitative. Did you hear it repeat what its master said?"

Tark said uneasily, "I wouldn't jump to conclusions, just from a hasty survey like this. I admit that, so far, all the proof points to the bird. It seems truly intelligent; or at least more intelligent than the other. But you must bear in mind that we are naturally prejudiced in favor of the bird—it may not be intelligent at all. As I said, they may merely be friends in the sense that animals of different species are friends."

Vascar made a scornful sound.

"Well, let's get goin', Blacky," she heard the bird say; and heard the white, upright beast repeat the strange, alien words. The white beast started off again, traveling very stealthily, making not the least amount of noise. Again Vascar called this quality to the attention of her skeptical mate—such stealth was the mark of the animal, certainly not of the intelligent creature.

"We should be certain of it now," she insisted. "I think we ought to get in touch with the bird. Remember, Tark, that our primary purpose on this expedition is to give what help we can to the intelligent races of the planets we visit. What creature could be more in need of help than the bird-creature down there? It is evidently the last of its kind. At least, we could make the effort of saving it from a life of sheer boredom; it would probably leap at the chance to hold converse with intelligent creatures. Certainly it gets no pleasure from the company of dumb beasts."

But Tark shook his handsome, red-plumed head worriedly.

"I would prefer," he said uneasily, "first to investigate the creature you are so sure is a beast of burden. There is a chance—though, I admit, a farfetched one—that it is the intelligent creature, and not the other."

But Vascar did not hear him. All her feminine instincts had gone out in pity to the seemingly intelligent bird that rode Tommy's broad shoulder. And so intent were she and Tark on the duo, that they did not see, less than a hundred yards ahead, that another creature, smaller in form, more graceful, but indubitably the same species as the white-skinned, unfeathered beast, was slinking softly through the underbrush, now and anon casting indecisive glances behind her toward him who pursued her. He was out of sight, but she could hear—

Tommy slunk ahead, his breath coming fast; for the trail was very strong, and his keen ears picked up the sounds of footsteps ahead. The chase was surely over—his terrible hunger about to end! He felt wildly exhilarated. Instincts were telling him much that his experience could not. He and this girl were the last of mankind. Something told him that now mankind would rise again—yet he did not know why. He slunk ahead, Blacky on his shoulder, all unaware of the two brilliantly colored denizens of another planet who followed above and behind him. But Blacky was not so easy of mind. His neck feathers were standing erect. Nervousness made him raise his wings up from his body—perhaps he heard the soft swish of large-winged creatures, beating the air behind, and though all birds of prey had been dead these last fifteen years, the old fear rose up.

Tommy glued himself to a tree, on the edge of a clearing. His breath escaped from his lungs as he caught a glimpse of a white, unclothed figure. It was she! She was looking back at him. She was tired of running. She was ready, glad to give up. Tommy experienced a dizzy elation. He stepped forth into the clearing, and slowly, very slowly, holding her large, dark eyes with his, started toward her. The slightest swift motion, the slightest untoward sound, and she would be gone. Her whole body was poised on the balls of her feet. She was not at all sure whether she should be afraid of him or not.

Behind him, the two feathered creatures from another planet settled slowly into a tree, and watched. Blacky certainly did not hear them come to rest—what he must have noticed was that the beat of wings, nagging at the back of his mind, had disappeared. It was enough.

"No noise, Blacky!" the bird screamed affrightedly, and flung himself into the air and forward, a bundle of ebon feathers with tattered wings outspread, as it darted across the clearing. For the third time, it was Blacky who scared her, for again she was gone, and had lost herself to sight even before Tommy could move.

"Come back!" Tommy shouted ragingly. "I ain't gonna hurt you!" He ran after her full speed, tears streaming down his face, tears of rage and heartbreak at the same time. But already he knew it was useless! He stopped suddenly, on the edge of the clearing, and sobbing to himself, caught sight of Blacky, high above the ground, cawing piercingly, warningly. Tommy stooped and picked up a handful of pebbles. With deadly, murderous intent he threw them at the bird. It soared and swooped in the air—twice it was hit glancingly.

"It's all your fault, Blacky!" Tommy raged. He picked up a rock the size of his fist. He started to throw it, but did not. A tiny, sharp sound bit through the air. Tommy pitched forward. He did not make the slightest twitching motion to show that he had bridged the gap between life and death. He did not know that Blacky swooped down and landed on his chest; and then flung himself upward, crying, "Oh, Tommy, I could spank you!" He did not see the girl come into the clearing and stoop over him; and did not see the tears that began to gush from her eyes, or hear the sobs that racked her body. But Tark saw.

Tark wrested the weapon from Vascar with a trill of rage.

"Why did you do that?" he cried. He threw the weapon from him as far as it would go. "You've done a terrible thing, Vascar!"

Vascar looked at him in amazement. "It was only a beast, Tark," she protested. "It was trying to kill its master! Surely, you saw it. It was trying to kill the intelligent bird-creature, the last of its kind on the planet."

But Tark pointed with horror at the two unfeathered beasts, one bent over the body of the other. "But they were mates! You have killed their species! The female is grieving for its mate, Vascar. You have done a terrible thing!"

But Vascar shook her head crossly. "I'm sorry I did it then," she said acidly. "I suppose it was perfectly in keeping with our aim on this expedition to let the dumb beast kill its master! That isn't like you at all, Tark! Come, let us see if the intelligent creature will not make friends with us."

And she flapped away toward the cawing crow. When Blacky saw Vascar coming toward him, he wheeled and darted away.

Tark took one last look at the female bending over the male. He saw her raise her head, and saw the tears in her eyes, and heard the sobs that shook her. Then, in a rising, inchoate series of bewildering emotions, he turned his eyes away, and hurriedly flapped after Vascar. And all that day they pursued Blacky. They circled him, they cornered him; and Vascar tried to speak to him in friendly tones, all to no avail. It only cawed, and darted away, and spoke volumes of disappointingly incomprehensible words.

When dark came, Vascar alighted in a tree beside the strangely quiet Tark.

"I suppose it's no use," she said sadly. "Either it is terribly afraid of us, or it is not as intelligent as we supposed it was, or else it has become mentally deranged in these last years of loneliness. I guess we might as well leave now, Tark; let the poor creature have its planet to itself. Shall we stop by and see if we can help the female beast whose mate we shot?"

Tark slowly looked at her, his red eyes luminous in the gathering dusk. "No," he said briefly. "Let us go, Vascar."

The spaceship of the creatures from Alcon left the dead planet Earth. It darted out into space. Tark sat at the controls. The ship went faster and faster. And still faster. Fled at ever-increasing speed beyond the solar system and into the wastes of interstellar space. And still farther, until the star that gave heat to Earth was not even visible.

Yet even this terrible velocity was not enough for Tark. Vascar looked at him strangely.

"We're not in that much of a hurry to get home, are we, Tark?"

"No," Tark said in a low, terrible voice; but still he urged the ship to greater and greater speed, though he knew it was useless. He could run away from the thing that happened on the planet Earth; but he could never, never outrun his mind, though he passionately wished he could.

BLOWUPS HAPPEN*

Astounding Science Fiction
September

by Robert A. Heinlein

> Here is one of the earliest stories of the possibility of an accident at a nuclear power plant, one of several that would grace the pages of the scence fiction magazines in advance of the explosion of the first atomic device. Its emphasis on the *pressure* involved in working in such a plant anticipated Lester del Rey's classic "Nerves," published in 1942.

(In my opinion, this was one of the best stories Robert Heinlein ever wrote. It was an example of how he, more than any other science fiction writer in the business could anticipate the future. This was published less than a year after the discovery of fission so it must have been written only months after the discovery, and two years *before* the Manhattan Project began. Bob, of course, didn't get all the details right. It's not just uranium we use—he left out the graphite, cadmium, heavy water, things like that. Also nuclear fission reactors *can't* explode. However, he *did* spot danger, long before anyone else did, and he *did* suggest a solution, which is only now beginning to be a practical one for handling all kinds of dangerous technologies.—I.A.)

---

* See note following end of Introduction.

STRANGE PLAYFELLOW

Super Science Stories
September

by Isaac Asimov (1920-   )

I'm writing this introduction all by myself because I suspect Marty won't touch my stories with a ten-foot pole.

In any case, my early notoriety was based on three things: my story "Nightfall," my "Foundation series" and my "positronic robot series." My own feeling is that the last of these, with the "three laws of robotics" was most influential actually. And, as it happened, I started it first.

"Strange Playfellow," the first of the positronic robot series, was written in May, 1939, and John Campbell rejected it promptly. I did not manage to sell it till nearly a year later, when Fred Pohl took it.

I had called the story "Robbie" but Fred, an inveterate title-changer, made it "Strange Playfellow" to my indignation. I restored the name to "Robbie" when it appeared as the lead story in "I, Robot" in 1950, and it has kept that title ever since. "Strange Playfellow" was used only in this one case in the magazine, but I keep it here to maintain historical accuracy.

It is also here in its magazine version for the same reason. I polished it somewhat before it appeared in the book, but never mind. Let it be here as the 19-year-old-I-was wrote it.

By the way, you won't find the three laws of robotics here. I hadn't worked them out yet. You'll get a vague reference to the first law, though, if you look for it.—I.A.

"Ninety-eight—ninety-nine—one hundred."

Gloria withdrew her chubby little forearm from before her eyes and stood for a moment, wrinkling her nose and blinking in the sunlight. Then, she gazed about her and withdrew a few cautious steps from the tree against which she had been leaning.

She craned her neck to investigate the possibilities of a clump of bushes. The quiet was profound except for the incessant buzzing of insects and the occasional chirrup of some hardy bird, braving the midday sun.

Gloria pouted, "I'll bet he went inside the house, and I've told him a million times that that's not fair." With tiny lips pressed together tightly and a severe frown crinkling her forehead, she moved determinedly toward the two-story building on the other side of the fence.

Too late, she heard a rustling sound behind her, followed by the distinctive and rhythmic clump-clump of Robbie's heavy feet. She whirled about to see her traitorous companion emerge from hiding and make for the "home" tree at full speed.

Gloria shrieked in dismay. "Wait, Robbie! That wasn't fair, Robbie! You promised you wouldn't run before I found you." Her little feet could make no headway at all against Robbie's giant strides. Then, within ten feet of "home," Robbie's pace suddenly slowed to the merest of crawls, and Gloria with one final burst of wild speed touched the welcome bark of "home" first.

Gleefully, she turned on the faithful Robbie. "Robbie can't run," she shouted at the top of her eight-year-old voice. "I can beat him any day. He's a terrible runner!"

Robbie didn't answer—because he couldn't. In spite of all science could do, it was still impossible to equip robots with phonographic attachments of sufficient complexity—not without sacrificing mobility. Consequently, he contented himself with snatching her up in the air and whirling her about till she begged to be put down again.

"Anyway, Robbie, it's my turn to hide now," she insisted seriously, "because you've got longer legs and you promised not to run till I found you."

Robbie nodded his head and obediently faced the tree. A thin, metal film descended over his glowing eyes and from within his body came a steady metallic clicking—for all the world like a metronome counting off the seconds.

"Don't peek now—and don't skip any numbers," and Gloria scurried for cover.

At the hundredth second, up went the eyelids, and the glowing red of Robbie's eyes swept the prospect. They rested for a moment on a bit of colorful gingham that protruded from behind a boulder. Thereupon one tentacle slapped against his gleaming metal chest with a resounding clang and another pointed straight at the boulder. Gloria emerged sulkily.

"You peeked!" she exclaimed with gross unfairness. "Besides I'm tired of playing hide-and-seek. I want a ride."

But Robbie was hurt at the unjust accusation, so he seated himself carefully and shook his head ponderously from side to side.

Gloria changed her tone to one of gentle coaxing immediately. "Come on, Robbie. I didn't mean it about the peeking. Give me a ride. If you don't, I'm going to cry," and her face twisted into an appalling position.

Hard-hearted Robbie paid scant attention to this dreadful prospect, and Gloria found it necessary to play her trump card.

"If you don't," she exclaimed warmly, "I won't tell you any more fairy tales, so there!"

Robbie gave in immediately and unconditionally and nodded his head vigorously until the metal of his neck hummed. Carefully, he raised the little girl and placed her on his broad, flat shoulders.

Gloria's threatened tears vanished immediately and she crowed with delight. Robbie's metal skin, kept at the constant temperature of seventy degrees by the high resistance coils within, felt nice and comfortable, and the beautifully loud sound her shoes made as they bumped rhythmically against his chest was enchanting.

"I knew you'd let me ride for the fairy tales, Robbie," she giggled. "I knew it. She grasped him about the head and began bouncing up and down.

"Faster, Robbie, faster," and the robot increased his speed until the vibration forced out Gloria's happy laughter in convulsive jerks. Clear across the field he sped, to the patch of tall grass on the other side, where he stopped with a suddenness that evoked a shriek from his flushed rider, and tumbled her onto the soft, natural carpet.

Gloria gasped and panted and gave voice to intermittent whispered exclamations of "That was nice!"

Robbie waited until she had caught her breath and then lifted a tentacle with which he gently pulled her hair—a sign that he wished her attention.

"What do you want, Robbie," she asked roguishly, pretending an artless perplexity that fooled the wise Robbie not at all. He only pulled one golden curl the harder.

"Oh, I know! You want a story." Robbie nodded rapidly. "Which one?" Robbie curled one tentacular finger into a semi-circle. "But I've told you Cinderella a million times. Aren't you tired of it?" The semi-circle persisted.

"Oh, well." Gloria composed herself, ran over the details of the tale in her mind, and began.

"Are you ready? Well—once upon a time there was a beautiful little girl whose name was Ella. And she had a terribly cruel step-mother and two very ugly and very cruel step-sisters and—"

Gloria was reaching the very climax of the tale when the interruption came.

"Gloria!"

"Mama's calling me," said Gloria, not quite happily. "Carry me back to the house, Robbie."

Robbie obeyed with alacrity. Gloria's mother was a source of uneasiness to him.

"I've shouted myself hoarse, Gloria," Mrs. Weston said severely. "Where were you?"

"I was with Robbie," quavered Gloria. "I was telling him Cinderella, and I forgot it was dinnertime."

"Well, it's a pity Robbie forgot, too." Then, as if that reminded her of the robot's presence, she whirled toward him. "You may go, Robbie. She doesn't need you now." Then, brutally, "And don't come back till I call you."

Robbie turned to go, but hesitated as Gloria cried out in his defense. "Let him stay, Mama, please let him stay. I want to finish Cinderella for him."

"Gloria!"

"Honest and truly, Mama, he'll stay so quiet, you won't even know he's here. Won't you, Robbie?"

Robbie nodded his massive head up and down once, in manifest fear of the woman before him.

"Gloria, if you don't stop this at once, you shan't see Robbie for a whole week."

The girl's eyes fell. "All right! But Cinderella is his favorite story!"

The robot left with a disconsolate step and Gloria choked back a sob.

George Weston wasn't pleased when his wife walked in. After ten years of married life, he still was so unutterably foolish as to love her, and there was no question that he was always glad to see her—still Sunday afternoons just after dinner were sacred to him and his idea of solid comfort was to be left in utter solitude for two or three hours. Consequently, he fixed his eye firmly on the latest report of the Douglas expedition to the moon (which looked as if it might actually succeed) and pretended she wasn't there.

Mrs. Weston waited patiently for two minutes, then impatiently for two more, and finally broke the silence.

"George!"

"Hmpph!"

"George, I say! Will you put down that paper and look at me?"

The paper rustled to the floor and Weston turned a weary face toward his wife, "What is it, dear?"

"You know what it is, George. It's Gloria and that terrible machine."

"What terrible machine?"

"Now don't pretend you don't know what I'm talking about. It's that robot Gloria calls Robbie. He doesn't leave her for a moment."

"Well, why should he? He's not supposed to. And he certainly isn't a terrible machine. He's the best darn robot money can buy and Lord knows he set me back half a year's income. He's worth it, too—darn sight cleverer, he is, than half my office staff."

He made a move to pick up the paper again, but his wife was quicker and snatched it away.

"You listen to me, George. I won't have my daughter entrusted to a machine—and I don't care how clever it is. A child just isn't made to be guarded by a thing of metal."

"Dear! A robot is infinitely more to be trusted than a human nursemaid. Robbie was constructed for only one purpose—to be the companion of a little child. His entire 'mentality' has been created for the purpose. He just can't help being faithful and loving and kind. He's a machine—made so."

"Yes, but something might go wrong. Some—some—" Mrs. Weston was a bit hazy about the insides of a robot— "some little jigger will come loose and the awful thing will go berserk and—and—" She couldn't bring herself to complete the quite obvious thought.

"Nonsense," Weston denied. "You're jumping at shadows, Grace. Pretend Robbie's a dog. I've seen hundreds of children no less crazy about their pets."

"A dog is different. George, we must get rid of that horrible thing. You can easily sell it back to the company."

"That's out, Grace, and I don't want to hear of it again. You'd better stop reading 'Frankenstein'—if that's what you've been doing."

And with that he walked out of the room in a huff.

And yet he loved his wife—and what was worse, his wife knew it. George Weston, after all, was only a man, and his wife made full use of every art and wile which a clumsier and more scrupulous sex has learned from time immemorial to fear.

Ten times in the ensuing week, he would cry, "Robbie stays—and that's final!" and each time it was weaker and accompanied by a louder and more agonized groan.

Came the day, at last, when Weston approached his daughter guiltily and suggested a "beautiful" visivox show in the village.

Gloria clapped her hands happily. "Can Robbie go?"

"No, dear," and how his conscience did twinge, "they won't allow robots at the visivox—and besides you can tell him all about it when you get home." He stumbled over the last few words and decided within himself that he made a terribly poor liar.

Gloria came back from town bubbling over with enthusiasm, for the visivox had been a gorgeous spectacle indeed, and the antics of the famous comic, Francis Frin, amid the fierce "leopard-men of the Moon" had evoked delightfully hysterical bursts of laughter.

She ran into the house joyfully and stopped suddenly at the sight of a beautiful collie which regarded her out of serious brown eyes as it wagged its tail on the porch.

"Oh, what a nice dog." Gloria approached cautiously and patted it. "Is it for me, Daddy?"

Weston cleared his throat miserably and wondered whether the substitution would do any good. "Yes, dear!"

"Oh—! Thank you very much, Daddy." Then, turning precipitously, she ran down the basement steps, shouting as she went, "Oh Robbie! Come and see what Daddy's brought me, Robbie!"

In a minute she returned, a frightened little girl. "Mama, Robbie isn't in his room. Where is he?" There was no answer, and George Weston coughed and suddenly seemed to be extremely interested in an aimlessly drifting cloud. Gloria's voice quavered on the verge of tears. "Where's Robbie, Mama?"

Mrs. Weston sat down and drew her daughter gently to her. "Don't feel bad, Gloria. Robbie has—gone away."

"Gone away? Where? Where's he gone away, Mama?"

"No one knows, darling. He just walked away. We've looked and we've looked and we've looked for him, but we can't find him."

"You mean I'll never see him again?" Her eyes were round in horror.

"We may find him some day, and meanwhile, you can play with your nice new doggie. Look at him! His name is Lightning and he can—"

But Gloria's eyelids had overflowed. "I don't want the nasty dog—I want Robbie. I want you to find me Robbie." Her feelings became too deep for words, and she spluttered into a shrill wail.

Her mother groaned in defeat and left Gloria to her sorrow.

"Let her have her cry out," she told her husband. "Childish griefs are never lasting. In a few days, she'll forget that awful robot ever existed."

But time proved Mrs. Weston a bit too optimistic. To be sure, Gloria ceased crying, but she ceased smiling too, and the passing days seemed but to increase the inner hurt. Gradually, her attitude of passive unhappiness wore Mrs. Weston down, and all that kept her from yielding was the impossibility of admitting defeat to her husband.

Then, one evening, she flounced into the living room, sat down, folded her arms and looked boiling mad.

Her husband stretched his neck in order to see her over his newspaper, "What now, Grace?"

"It's that child, George. I had to send back the dog today. Gloria positively couldn't stand the sight of him. She's driving me into a nervous breakdown."

Weston laid down the paper and a hopeful gleam entered his eye. "Maybe—maybe we ought to get Robbie back. It might be done, you know. I can get in touch with—"

"No!" she replied grimly. "I won't hear of it. We're not giving up that easily. My child shall not be brought up by a robot if it takes years to break her of it. What Gloria needs is a change of environment. We're going to take her to New York."

"Oh, Lord," groaned the lesser half, "back to the frying pavements."

"You'll have to," was the unshaken response. "Gloria has lost five pounds in the last month and my little girl's health is more important to me than your comfort."

"It's a pity you didn't think of your little girl's health before you deprived her of her pet robot," he muttered—but to himself.

Gloria displayed immediate signs of improvement when told of the impending trip to the city. She began to smile, and to eat with something of her former appetite.

Mrs. Weston lost no opportunity to triumph over her still skeptical husband.

"You see, George, she chatters away as if she hadn't a care in the world. It's just as I told you—all we need to do is substitute other interests."

"Hmpph," was the skeptical response. "I hope so."

In high good-humor, the family drove down to the airport and entered the waiting liner.

"Come, Gloria," called Mrs. Weston, "I've saved you a seat near the window so you can watch the scenery."

"Yes, Mama," was Gloria's unenthusiastic rejoinder. She turned to her mother with a sudden mysterious air of secret knowledge.

"I know why we're going to the city, Mama."

"Do you?" Mrs. Weston was puzzled. "Why, dear?"

"You didn't tell me because you wanted it to be a surprise, but I know." For a moment she was lost in admiration at her own acute penetration, and then she laughed gaily. "We're going to New York so we can find Robbie, aren't we?"

Mrs. Weston maintained her composure, but she found her temper rather bent.

"Maybe," she retorted tartly. "Now sit and be still, for heaven's sake."

New York City, in this good year of 1982, is quite a place for an eight-year-old girl. Gloria's parents made the most of it.

Gloria was taken to the top of the half-mile-tall Roosevelt Building, to gaze down in awe upon the jagged panorama of rooftops, far off to where they blended into the fields of Long Island and New Jersey. They visited the zoos where Gloria stared in delicious fright at the "real live lion" (rather disappointed that the keepers fed him raw steaks, instead of human beings, as she had expected), and asked insistently and peremptorily to see "the whale."

The various museums came in for their share of attention, together with the parks and the beaches and the aquarium.

She was taken halfway up the Hudson in an excursion steamer fitted out in the delicious old-fashioned style of the "gay twenties." She traveled into the stratosphere on an exhibition trip, where the sky turned deep purple and the stars came out and the misty earth below looked like a huge concave bowl. Down under the waters of the Long Island Sound, she was taken in a glass-walled sub-sea vessel, where in a green and wavering world, quaint and curious sea-things ogled her and wiggled slowly to and fro.

In fact, when the month had nearly sped the Westons were convinced that everything conceivable had been done to take Gloria's mind once and for all off the departed Robbie—but they were not quite sure they had succeeded.

It was the episode at the Museum of Science and Industry, though, that finally convinced Mrs. Weston. She was standing totally absorbed in the exploits of a powerful electro-magnet when she suddenly became aware of the fact that Gloria was no longer with her. Initial panic gave way to calm decision and, enlisting the aid of three attendants, the Westons began a careful search.

Gloria's disappearance was simply enough explained. A huge sign on the third floor said, "This Way to see the Talking Robot." Having spelled it out to herself and having noticed that her parents did not seem to wish to move in the proper direction, she determined to see it for herself.

The "Talking Robot" as a scientific achievement left much to be desired. It sprawled its unwieldy mass of wires and coils through twenty-five square yards, and every robotical function had been subordinated to the vital attribute of speech. It worked—and was in this respect quite a victory—but as yet, it could translate only the simpler and more concrete thoughts into words. Certainly, it was not half so clever as Robbie in Gloria's opinion.

Gloria watched it silently for a while, waiting for the two or three who watched with her to depart. Then, when she stood there alone for the moment, she asked hurriedly, "Have you seen Robbie, Mr. Robot, sir?" She was not quite sure how polite one must be to a robot that could talk.

There was an oily whir of gears, and a metallically timbered voice boomed out in words that lacked accent and intonation, "Who—is—Robbie?"

"He's a robot, Mr. Robot, sir. Just like you, you know, only he can't talk, of course."

"A—robot—like—me?"

"Yes, Mr. Robot, sir."

But the talking robot's only response to this was an erratic splutter and occasional incoherent sound. The conception of other robots like him had stalled his "thinking" engine, for he had not the mental complexity to grasp the idea.

Gloria was still waiting, with carefully concealed impatience, for the machine's answer when she heard the cry behind her of "There she is," and recognized that cry as her mother's.

"What are you doing here, you bad girl?" cried Mrs. Weston, anxiety dissolving at once into anger. "Do you know you frightened your Mama and Daddy almost to death? Why did you run away?"

"I only came to see the talking robot, Mama. I thought he might know where Robbie was because they're both robots." And then, as the thought of Robbie was brought forcefully home to her, she burst into a sudden storm of tears. "And oh, Mama, I do want to see Robbie again. I miss him like anything."

Her mother gave forth a strangled cry, more than half a sob, and cried to her husband, "Come home, George. This is more than I can stand."

That night, George Weston left on a mysterious errand, and the next morning he approached his wife with something that looked suspiciously like smug complacence.

"I've got an idea, Grace."

"About what?" was the gloomy, uninterested query.

"About Gloria."

"Well, go ahead. I might as well listen to you. Nothing I've done seems to have been any good. But remember, I will not consent to buying back that awful robot."

"Of course not. That's understood. However, here's what I've been thinking. The whole trouble with Gloria is that she thinks of Robbie as a person and not as a machine. Naturally, she can't forget him. Now if we managed to convince her that Robbie was nothing more than a mess of steel and copper in the form of sheets and wires with electricity its juice of life, how long would this aberration last?"

Mrs. Weston frowned in thought. "It sounds good, but how are you going to do it?"

"Simple. Where do you suppose I was last night? I persuaded old Finmark of the Finmark Robot Corporation to arrange for a complete tour of his premises tomorrow. The three of us will go, and by the time we're through, Gloria will have it drilled into her that a robot is not alive."

His wife's eyes widened. "Why, George, how did you manage to think of that?" There was a gleam of determination in Mrs. Weston's eye. "Gloria is not going to miss a step of the process. We'll settle this once and for all!"

Mr. Struthers was a conscientious General Manager and naturally inclined to be a bit talkative. The combination resulted in a tour that was fully explained—perhaps even overabundantly explained—at every step. In spite of this, Mrs. Weston was not bored. Indeed, she stopped him several times and begged him to repeat his statements in simpler language so that Gloria might understand. Under the influence of this appreciation of his narrative powers, Mr. Struthers explained genially and became even more communicative—if possible.

Weston, himself, displayed an odd impatience, nevertheless—an almost angry impatience.

"Pardon me, Struthers," he broke in suddenly, in the midst of a lecture on the photo-electric cell, "I understand you have a section of the factory where only robot labor is employed?"

"Eh? Oh, yes! Yes, indeed!" He smiled at Mrs. Weston. "A vicious circle in a way—robots creating more robots. However we don't intend to make a general practice of it. You see," he tapped his pince-nez on one palm, "the robot—"

"Yes, yes, Struthers—may we see it? It would be a most interesting experience."

"Yes! Yes, of course." Mr. Struthers replaced his pince-nez in one convulsive movement and gave vent to a soft cough of discomfiture. "Follow me, please."

He was comparatively quiet, while leading the three through a long corridor and down a flight of stairs. Then, when they had entered a large well-lit room that buzzed with metallic activity, the sluices opened and the flood of explanation poured forth again.

"There you are," he said in part, and with quite a bit of pride in his voice. "Robots only! Five men act as overseers and they don't even stay in the room. In five years, ever since we began this project, not a single accident has occurred. Of course, very few robots here are intelligent—"

The General Manager's voice had long died to a rather soothing murmur in Gloria's ears. The whole trip seemed rather dull and pointless to her, though there were many robots in sight. None was even remotely like Robbie and she surveyed them all with open contempt.

Her glance fell upon six or seven robots busily engaged about a round table halfway across the room. Her eyes widened in incredulous surprise. One of the robots looked like—looked like—

"Robbie!" Her shriek pierced the air, and one of the robots about the table faltered and dropped the tool he was holding. Gloria went almost mad with joy. Squeezing through the railing before either parent could stop her, she dropped lightly to the floor a few feet below and ran toward her Robbie, arms waving and hair flying.

And the three horrified adults, as they stood frozen in their tracks, saw what the excited little girl did not see—a huge, lumbering tractor rolling blindly down its track.

It took a split second for Weston to come to his senses, but that split second meant everything, for Gloria could not be overtaken. Although Weston vaulted the railing in a wild attempt, he knew it was hopeless. Mr. Struthers signalled wildly to the overseers to stop the tractor, but the overseers were only human and it took time to act.

Robbie acted immediately and with precision.

With metal legs eating up the space between himself and his little mistress, he charged down from the opposite direction. Everything then happened at once. With one sweep of an arm, Robbie snatched up Gloria, slackening his speed not one iota, and consequently knocking every bit of breath out of her. Weston, not quite comprehending all that was happening, felt rather than saw Robbie brush past him, and he came to a sudden, bewildered halt. The tractor intersected Gloria's path half a second after Robbie, rolled on ten feet farther and came to a grinding, long-drawn-out halt.

Gloria finally regained her breath, submitted to a series of passionate hugs on the part of both parents, and turned eagerly toward Robbie. As far as she was concerned, nothing had happened except that she had found her robot.

Mrs. Weston regained her composure rather quickly, aided by a sudden suspicion that struck her. She turned to her husband, and, despite her disheveled and undignified appearance, managed to look quite formidable. "You engineered this, didn't you?"

George Weston swabbed at a hot, perspiring forehead with his handkerchief. His hand was none too steady, and his lips curved with a tremulous and exceedingly weak smile. "But Grace, I had no idea the reunion would be so violent."

Weston watched her keenly and ventured a further remark, "Anyway, you can't deny Robbie has saved her life. You can't send him away now."

His wife thought it over. It was a bit difficult to keep up her anger. She turned toward Gloria and Robbie and watched them abstractedly for a moment. Gloria had a grip about the robot's neck that would have asphyxiated any creature but one of metal, and was prattling nonsense in half-hysterical frenzy. Robbie's chrome-steel arms (capable of bending a bar of steel two inches in diameter into a pretzel) wound about the little girl gently and lovingly, and his eyes glowed a deep, deep red.

Mrs. Weston's anger faded still further and she became almost genial.

"Well," she breathed at last, smiling in spite of herself. "I guess Robbie can stay with us until he rusts, for all I care."

THE WARRIOR RACE

Astounding Science Fiction
October

by L. Sprague de Camp (1907-   )

L. Sprague de Camp was one of the first prolific science fiction and fantasy writers to branch out into nonfiction in a major way, one of his earliest efforts being Lost Continents *(1952). "The Warrior Race" appeared in* The Wheels of If, *one of the earliest collections of sf (most of the stories are fantasies) to be published by a major figure from within the genre (Shasta, 1949).*

(Since Sprague is my oldest friend in science fiction, it isn't surprising that in some cases I know the genesis of some of his stories. Sprague is the best amateur historian in science fiction. What he doesn't know about ancient engineering or ancient warfare, for instance, isn't known to anyone but professional specialists in the field.

It so happens that ancient Sparta had an extremely rigid war-centered society, with its aristocratic warriors held to an ascetic, incorruptible life. At the time of the Persian and, later, the Peloponnesian War, they came out of their shell and some of their leaders came to be in positions of authority. And what happened to them—Pausania, Lysander—was precisely what happened to the Centaurians in this story. Sprague was retelling history (my favorite trick, too).

Of course, Sprague points the moral at the end perhaps more explicitly than was necessary but that's not really Sprague. It was John Campbell, I'm certain.—I.A.)

They were serious these days, the young men who gathered in Prof. Tadeusz Lechon's room to drink his mighty tea and set up propositions for him to knock down. Between relief that the war was over without their having come to harm personally, and apprehension for the future, and some indignation at the prospect of foreign rule, there was not much room left for undergraduate exuberance and orneriness. Something was going to happen to them, they thought.

"Whatever it is," said Tadeusz Lechon, "it is not cowardice, I am sure." He moved his large bald head forward to a cup of tea the color of an old boot, his big gold-plated earrings bobbling. He sucked noisily, watching Frederick Merrian.

Fred Merrian, a sandy-haired sophomore with squirrel teeth, looked grateful but still defiant. He was in civilian clothes. Baldwin Dowling, the co-ed's dream, was in a very new U. S. Army uniform. The uniform was so new because, by the time Dowling had reached his unit in Los Angeles, the war was over, and he had been told to return home, free, on anything he liked. He had taken the next 'plane back to Philadelphia.

Lechon continued: "It is rather an example of the conviction of most thoughtful young men, that human problems *must* have a solution. Those problems being what they are, one cannot prove that any of them has *no* solution, the way Abel proved the problem of solving quintic equations algebraically impossible. So they try one idea after another, these young men; it may be Adrenalism or Anarcho-Communism or Neo-Paganism. In your case it was non-resistance. Perhaps it is well that they do—"

"But—" said Fred Merrian.

Lechon stopped the waiting flood of impassioned argument with a wave. "We have been over all this before. Some day you will tire of Centaurian rule, and join some other movement with equally impractical ideals. Our Centaurian is nosing around the campus. He may visit us. Suppose we let Baldwin tell us what he has learned about them."

"Yeah, what are they like?" asked Merrian.

"Much like other people," said Baldwin Dowling. "They're pretty big. I guess the original group of colonists that went to Proxima Centauri were a pretty tall bunch. They have a funny manner, though; sort of as if they ran by clockwork. You don't get palsy with a Bozo."

Arthur Hsi smiled his idiotic smile. His name was really Hsi A-tsz, and he was not at all idiotic. "I came halfway around the world so I could study away from the Bozos. Not far enough, it seems."

Dowling asked: "Heard anything from China?"

"Bozos are busy, trying to make everything sternly efficient and incorruptible, like themselves. May be the greatest fighters on earth, but don't know China. My father writes—"

"Shh!" hissed Lechon, his big red face alert. Then he relaxed. "I thought it was our Centaurian." There was an uncomfortable pause; nobody had much enthusiasm left for chatter, even if the superman failed to appear. Finally Lechon took it up: "Everybody I talk to says what an impossible thing it was, that war. But if you read your history, gentlemen, you will see that it was nothing new. In 1241 the Hungarians never dreamed the Mongols had things like divisional organization and wig-wig signals. So they were swamped. Our government never dreamed the Centaurians had an oxidizing ray, and airplanes with fifteen-centimeter armor. So we were swamped. You follow me? The tune is always different, but the notes stay much the same."

He broke off again, listening. A brisk step approached. Somebody knocked. The history professor said to come in. The Centaurian came.

"My name," he said in a metallic voice, "is Juggins." He was about thirty, with a lantern jaw, high cheekbones, and outstanding ears. He wore the odd plum-colored uniform of the Centaurians: descendants of those hardy souls who had colonized a planet of Proxima Centauri, had fought a three-generation battle against hostile environment and more hostile natives, and had finally swarmed back to earth fifty-odd years ago. Australia had been turned over to them, and their science had made this second most useless continent the world's most productive area. Their terrible stay on the other planet had made them something more and something less than men. Now they ruled the earth.

"Hello, Mr. Jug—" began Dowling. The Centaurian cut him off: "You will not use 'mister' in speaking to a Centaurian. I am Juggins."

"Will you sit down?" invited Lechon.

"I will." The Bozo folded his long legs, sat, and waited for somebody to say something.

Somebody finally did. Dowling asked: "How do you like Philly?"

"You mean Philadelphia?"

"Yeah, sure."

"Then kindly say so. I don't like it at all. It's dirty, corrupt, and inefficient. But we shall fix that. You will do well to cooperate with us. We shall give you a much healthier life than you have ever known." He got this out with some difficulty, as if saying more than one sentence at a time made him self-conscious.

Even Dowling, who, though a native, was not bothered by an excess of local pride, was taken aback by such candor. He murmured: "You guys don't pull any punches."

"I think I grasp the meaning of your slang expression. We are taught to tell the truth." He made telling the truth sound like a most unattractive occupation.

Hsi spoke up: "I hope you do something about the water system. This morning when I turned on the faucet, I got a live eel, a size twelve rubber, and about a cubic meter of chlorine gas before the water came through."

The Bozo stared at him coldly. "Young man, that is an unpardonable exaggeration. A rubber could not possibly pass through the waterpipes."

"He is juckink," said Lechon helplessly, the stress of conflicting emotions bringing out his Polish accent.

Juggins shifted his glare. "I understand. That's what you call a joke, is it? Very funny."

"Have a cigarette," suggested Dowling.

"We never use the filthy weed. It's unhealthy."

"Some tea, then," sighed Lechon.

"Hmm. It *is* a drug."

"Oh, I would not say that, Juggins. It does contain caffein, which is a stimulant, but most foods have one or more things like that in them."

"Very well, if you'll make it weak. And no sugar."

Hsi poured, and added some very hot water. The Bozo stirred it suspiciously. He looked up to say: "I want you, and everybody in the University, to look on me as a kind of father. There's no sense in your taking a hostile attitude, because you can't change conditions. If you will cooperate— Gaw!" He was staring popeyed at his spoon.

The lower half of the spoon had melted all at once and run down into a puddle of molten metal at the bottom of the cup.

"You stirred too hard," said Hsi.

"I—" said Juggins. He glared from face to face. Then he carefully put down his cup, laid the unmelted half of the spoon in the saucer, rose, and stalked out.

THE WARRIOR RACE

Lechon mopped his red forehead. "That was terrible, Arthur! You shouldn't play jokes on him. He might have us all shot."

Hsi let a long-suppressed giggle escape. "Maybe so. But I had that Wood's-metal spoon handy, and it was too good to miss."

"Is he real?" asked Merrian.

"Yeah," said Dowling. "A lot of people have wondered if the Bozos weren't robots or something. But they're real people; reproduced in the normal fashion and everything. They're a new kind of man, I guess."

"No," said Lechon. "Read your history, gentleman. The warrior race. The latest example of what can be done with men by intensive training and discipline. The Spartans and the Osmanli Turks did it in their time. Our Centaurian is more like a Spartan Peer than a Turkish Janissary. Lycurgus would know our father Juggins for a true Spartiate at once . . ."

He went on. The three undergraduates listened with one ear. Merrian was in the throes of a soul-search. Was force an evil when used against creatures like these?

Dowling and Hsi, not introspective idealists, were concerned with the recasting of their personal plans. Dowling guessed that there would still be local Philadelphia politics to get into when he finished his course, Bozos or no Bozos. There'd have to be go-betweens between the supermen and their subjects.

Hsi was thinking of the soft job in the Sino-American Transport Co. that his father would shoe-horn him into when he finished college. If he could, by hard work and family influence, worm his way to the Directorate, there were some big deals he had in mind . . . There would be the omnipresent and allegedly incorruptible Bozos. But that incorruptibility was, to his mind, still only alleged.

Class reunions, like weddings and funerals, bring together a lot of people who would not ordinarily cross the street to speak to one another. So when the class of '09 broke up after the formalities, Hsi and Dowling and Merrian drifted together and wandered off to a restaurant to compare biographies.

Baldwin Dowling had filled out a bit, though he still had the wavy black hair and flashing smile. He had acquired a wife and one child. Arthur Hsi looked much the same, but had acquired a wife and six children. Fred Merrian had lost most of his sandy hair, and had received in exchange two wives, two divorces, and a thin feverish look.

Hsi had just come from a trip to Australia, and was full of it. "It's a wonderful place. Everything goes just like clockwork. No tips, no bribes. No fun, either. Every Bozo is a soldier of some sort, even the ones who run elevators and sell dog-biscuit."

Fred Merrian showed signs of building up argumentative back-pressure. "You mean you approve of them?" he snapped.

Hsi looked stupidly amused. "I wouldn't say that, Fred. But we have to get along with them. The Sino-American Transport Company is a huge organization, with subsidiaries all over the Pacific: hotels and airlines and whale-hatcheries and things. So we must get along with them. What have you been doing the last ten years?"

Merrian looked bitter. "I'm trying to make a living as a writer. But I won't write the sort of trash the cheap magazines buy, so—" He shrugged.

"What about you, Baldwin? I seem to hear about you in politics."

Dowling said: "Yeah, maybe you have. I'm the official mediator for the city of Philadelphia. When one of my—ah—flock gets into trouble with the Bozos, I try to get him out."

"You look prosperous," said Hsi.

"I haven't done so badly." Dowling's smile had a trace of leer. "Sort of like a tribune of the people, as Professor Lechon explained it to me."

"Lechon?" said Hsi. "Is he still here?"

"Yep, and still dishing out the love-life of the ancient Parthians." He noted Merrian's expression, and said: "Fred no doubt thinks I'm a raw renegade. But as you said, the Bozos are here, and we've got to get along with them. By the way, I met a man who knows you; Cass Young. Said your Chinese business methods had nearly driven him crazy."

"What didn't he like?"

"Oh, the way you never mean exactly what you say, and act hurt when some sucker objects to it. And the—ah—dryness of the Oriental palm, as he expressed it. Oh, remember the Bozo Juggins? The first administrator of the University of Pennsylvania? He's still here; administrator for the whole metropolitan area."

"Really?" said Hsi. "By the way, did Mr. Young tell you what he had been seeing me about?"

"No."

"Well, I want to talk to you about it." Hsi looked questioningly at Fred Merrian. Merrian looked at his watch, and reluctantly took his leave.

"Too bad," said Dowling. "He's the most decent and upright guy I know. But he isn't practical." He lowered his voice. "I could swear he was mixed up in some anti-Bozo movement."

"That would account for the hungry-wolf look," said Hsi. "Do you know about such movements?"

"I know a lot of things I don't let on. But what's this deal you have in mind?"

"I say nothing about a deal." Hsi paused to giggle. "But I see I can't fool you, Baldwin. You know the Morehouse project?"

"The mailing-tube unification plan? Yeah."

"Well, Sino-American controls the Philadelphia-Baltimore tube, as perhaps you don't know. And the tubes from Boston to Miami can't be unified without the Philadephia-Baltimore link, obviously. But we don't want to sell our stock in the link outright."

"What, then?"

"If exchange of stock could be arranged—some good friends of ours already hold 45 per cent of the stock in the new Boston-Miami company—it would give us a strong voice in the affairs of the new company."

"In other words, majority control?"

"I would not say that. A strong voice."

Dowling grinned. "Don't try to kid me into thinking these 'good friends' aren't Sino-American dummies. How much stock of the new company do you want? Six per cent?"

"Seven and a fraction would look better."

"I get you. But you know how we do things here. The Bozos have their fingers in everything. If you make anything, they grab it; if you lose, that's your hard luck. All the disadvantages of socialism without the advantages. And it's as much as your life's worth to try to hush one of them up. Still, I *might* be able to handle Juggins."

Hsi giggled. "So they are still incorruptible here, eh? How much of that 'healthier life' they promised have you gotten?"

"Well," said Dowling dubiously, "they did clean things up somewhat."

"Have you a new water system yet?"

"No, though they've been talk—"

Boom! Far off across the Schuylkill, a yellow flash tore the night sky. Other explosions followed in quick succession. Broken glass tinkled. Hsi and Dowling gripped their table. Dowling muttered: "The fools!"

"A revolution?" asked Hsi.

"That's what *they* think." The faint tapping of gunfire became audible.

A pair of hard-looking men in uniform appeared in the doorway. Dowling murmured: "Watchdogs." He did not have to describe these police, whose list of virtues stopped after bravery and loyalty to their masters, the warrior race.

There was nothing to do but sit and listen. When the noise abated, Dowling went over to one of the watchdogs and spoke in a low voice.

The watchdog said: "Didn't recognize you, Mr. Dowling. I guess you can go home, and take your friend."

As the two men left the restaurant, Hsi was conscious of the hostile glares of the other customers. Outside, Dowling grinned wryly. "Nobody likes special privilege, except when he's the guy who's got it. We're walking."

"But your car—" wailed Hsi, a completely unathletic person.

"I'm leaving it here. If we tried to drive, the watchdogs would shoot first and ask questions afterwards. If we see anybody, we raise our hands and walk slowly."

Off to the northeast, the sky was red. A lot of houses in North Philadelphia had been set afire by the oxidizers ...

Hsi and Dowling spent the next day at the latter's home, without news of any kind. Edna Dowling tried to pump Hsi on the subject of ancient Chinese art. Arthur Hsi grinned foolishly, and spread his hands. "But Mrs. Dowling, I don't know anything about art. I'm a businessman!"

The next morning a newspaper did arrive over the ticker. It told of outbreaks, and their suppression, in Philadelphia, New York, Detroit, St. Louis ...

Baldwin Dowling was shown into Juggins' office. The Centaurian looked much the same, except that his hair was turning prematurely gray.

"Hello, Juggins," said Dowling. Then he sniffed. He sniffed again. There was an unmistakable smell of tobacco smoke.

Dowling looked accusingly at Juggins. Juggins looked back, at first blankly, then uncomfortably. "What is it?" he barked.

Dowling grinned easily. "Don't worry, Juggins. I won't—"

"You will kindly mind your own business!"

"What are you sore about? I didn't say anything. And I have every intention of minding my own business. That's what I came here about." He explained about the stock exchange proposed by Hsi. He put the most favorable interpretation on it. But Juggins was not fooled.

Juggins thoughtfully studied the ornate penholder that marred the Spartan simplicity of his office. He said: "Your plan may be sound. But if my superiors heard of it, they might take a—an excessively rigid view." Silence. "I try to be fair. Haven't I always been fair with the Philadelphians?"

"Of course, Juggins. And it's about time we showed our gratitude, don't you think?"

"Of course we Centaurians aren't swayed by material considerations."

"Sure. Utterly incorruptible. But it would make me happy if I could show my appreciation. I'm not one of you selfless supermen, you know."

"What had you in mind?"

Dowling told him. Juggins took a deep breath, pursed his lips, and nodded somberly. He kept his eyes on the penholder.

"By the way," said Dowling, "now that that's settled, there's another little favor you might do for me. I believe one of the people you captured in the recent uprising was an old classmate named Frederick Merrian."

"What about him?"

"What are the Centaurians' plans for disposing of the rebels?"

"The leaders will be shot, and the others blinded. I don't think your Merrian was a leader; I'd recognize his name if he were."

"For old times' sake, I wondered if you couldn't do something for Merrian."

"Is he an intimate friend of yours?" Juggins looked at Dowling keenly.

"No; I've seen him only occasionally since we finished college. He means well, but he goes off on crazy tangents."

"I don't know what I could do. I couldn't have him turned loose."

"You don't have to. Put in a death certificate for him. Say

he died of natural causes. Then substitute for him one of the regular prisoners in the Lancaster prison farm. They're dying all the time anyway."

"I'll see."

When Dowling picked up Arthur Hsi, his grin answered the Transport Director's question before it was asked.

"I offered him a hundred thousand, and he took it without argument."

Hsi whistled. "I was authorized to pay ten times that much! Our Bozo doesn't know his own value yet."

"Maybe it's the first real bribe he's taken."

"Really? Well, we don't put him wise to what he could have got, eh? He'll learn soon enough."

Fred Merrian shambled into the visitors' room, looking beaten but brightened a bit at the sight of Dowling, Hsi, and Dr. Lechon.

He sat down, then looked puzzled. "How come the guard went out? They don't do that ordinarily."

Dowling grinned. "He's not supposed to hear what we've got to say." He explained the plan for shifting Merrian to the Lancaster farm under a new name.

"Then—then I'm going to keep my eyes? Oh—"

"Now, now, don't break down, Fred."

They got the overwrought writer calmed. He said: "I still don't understand why the uprising failed. You have no idea how careful we were. We thought of *everything*."

Dowling said: "Guess you just didn't have the stuff. As long as the Bozos have a large and well-armed corps of watchdogs—" He shrugged.

"You mean it's hopeless?"

"Uh-huh. Knowing you, Fred, I know you'll find that a hard thing to reconcile yourself to."

"I'll never be reconciled to it. There must be *something*."

"I'm afraid not."

"I am not too sure," said Lechon. "Armed uprising, no. With the complicated weapons used nowadays, civilians can do little. It is like trying to stop a—a buzz-saw with your bare hands. But there are other possibilities."

"What?" asked the three younger men together.

"Read your history, gentlemen. Read your history." And that was all they could get out of him.

"I'm not worrying," said Juggins. "We can trust each other." He leaned back in his chair and sucked on a cigar. He coughed a bit, and said: "Damn, I keep forgetting that one doesn't inhale these things." He had taken to the American fashion of men's earrings.

Dowling smiled. "You mean, we'll *have* to."

"You might put it that way, yes. What's the proposal this time?"

Arthur Hsi explained: "You know the Atlantic City project Sino-American is trying to promote? Our subsidiary is all ready to set up."

"Yes."

"Well, first, there's a Society for Preservation of Ancient Monuments objecting. Say if we modernize Atlantic City we'll ruin it. Say Hotel Traymore has been there three hundred years and it would be sacrilege to tear it down."

Juggins waved his cigar. "I can shoot a few of this Society. That'll shut them up."

"Oh, no," said Hsi, shocked. "Cause all kinds of trouble. People would boycott the project."

"Well, what do you want me to do then?"

"If you could have some of these old ruins moved, as a government project—"

"Hmm. That would cost money."

"Perhaps my company could see its way to sharing the expense."

Juggins still frowned. "My superior, the Centaurian MacWhirtle, would have to approve. I think he's suspicious of me."

Dowling broke in: "Is MacWhirtle married?"

"Yes, but his wife's back in Australia. Why?"

"I just had an idea. Go on, Arthur."

Hsi continued: "Then there's the matter of financing improvement company. We thought we could have it issue some common stock, some non-cumulative preferred. Sino-American could buy most of former; public latter. You and MacWhirtle would have a chance at former also, before it was put on market."

Juggins frowned again. "I seem to remember some rule against non-cumulative preferred. Though I never knew why."

Hsi explained: "This wouldn't be called non-cumulative; some fancy name, but would mean same thing. You sell so much non-cumulative to public, and hold common. Then year comes along, you tell preferred stockholders, conditions are very bad, can't pay any dividends at all, on common *or* preferred. Then next year you say conditions are better. You pay preferred stockholders their regular seven percent—for that year only. You pay yourself regular dividend on common, plus the common stock dividend you didn't pay previous year, *plus* seven percent preferred stock dividend you didn't pay previous year also. It's wonderful."

"I see," said Juggins. "I see why there's a rule against it. But I suppose that sort of thing is necessary in modern finance."

"Oh, absolutely," said Dowling.

"I try to be fair," said Juggins. "Some of my fellow Centaurians lean over backward. I think they do more harm than good."

"Sure," said Dowling. "And do you suppose we could meet MacWhirtle? Socially, I mean."

Dowling dialed his wrist-phone. "Helen? This is Baldwin. . . . Yep, the old political wizard himself. Doing anything next weekend? . . . No, no. It's a party. . . . In New York. . . . Uh-huh, got a Bozo for you to waggle your alabaster torso at . . . Yep, a very big shot indeed. It's all very discreet, understand. . . . No, no, I will not! I've told you I'm very well satisfied with the woman I have. Love her, in fact. This is business. Right. See you Saturday."

The Centaurian MacWhirtle was a smaller and older edition of Juggins. Although his manner still retained most of the clockwork stiffness of the uncontaminated Bozo, it was evident he was under a strain of some kind.

"Sit down!" he barked.

Dowling sat.

MacWhirtle leaned forward. "I understand you're—you and that Chinaman Hsi are—are willing to let me have some common stock in the Atlantic City Improvement Company below the price it'll be offered the public at."

"Yep." Dowling grinned. "Reminds me, can my friend Osborn have his secretarial job back?"

"Why? What do you know about Osborn?"

"He was fired for using a preposition to end a sentence *with*. If we're offering the stock to the public *at*—"

The Bozo purpled. "I'll do what I—why you insolent—" The sentence died in sputters, while Dowling mentally kicked himself for breaking his long-standing rule never to joke with a Bozo.

MacWhirtle calmed himself enough to ask for more details about the stock. Dowling explained.

MacWhirtle looked intently at his fingernails. He said, barely audibly: "I could use force, but she'd hate me—" He realized that Dowling was listening to him, and yelled: "Get out! I won't have men spying on my private—"

Dowling, annoyed but not discouraged, got up to leave. MacWhirtle shouted: "Sit down, you silly ass! I didn't mean it seriously. I admit I've got to have money. You said. . . ."

Dowling walked from the hotel where he had met MacWhirtle to the Penn Station. It was after four, and the only time of day or night when New York's streets are almost deserted. MacWhirtle had shown a bargaining ability incongruous with the financial innocence expected of a true Bozo.

On West 35th he approached a group of men. He recognized the uniform of the watchdogs. One of the national police saw him, whipped out a pistol, and fired. Dowling dived down a set of basement steps. He yelled up: "What the hell's the matter with you?"

There were mutterings in the dark. A deep voice addressed the world at large: "The first open window gets a bullet through it. Go back to bed, all of you." Then the owner of the voice appeared, rocking a bulbous body along on huge flat feet.

The watchdog flashed a light at Dowling's face, and said: "Glory be, if it isn't Mr. Dowling, the Philadelphia mediator! Come out, Mr. Dowling. I'm sorry one of the boys got nervous and took a shot at you. You see—some of them Bozos was took sick, and we was helping them. Naturally we didn't want nobody to see them in that condition."

"You'd have been a hell of a lot sorrier if he'd hit me," grumbled Dowling. He followed the watchdog down to the knot. The three Bozos were sick, all right. The reek of regurgitated alcohol implied the nature of their sickness.

One of the other watchdogs was muttering: "So these are the supermen, who never have any fun, eh? Well, well. Well, well."

Weathered granite disintegrates, but it takes time. Dowling, as he helped Arthur Hsi to spin their web, reflected that he was getting a paunch. People might refer to him as a "rising young man" still, but without unduly stressing the "young." His daughter was in high school. He was not altogether pleased to observe that she was turning into a beauty. He'd have to keep her out of sight of the Bozos with whom he was in constant contact.

Hsi complained: "If we cut a few more Bozos in on this space-port deal, Sino-American might just as well sell out its American holdings and go back to China."

Dowling grinned. "We've got 'em where we want 'em, haven't we?"

"Oh, yes. They follow our—suggestions—like little lambs. But—"

Dowling's wrist-phone rang. Juggins' voice said hoarsely: "Dowling! A terrible thing has happened! MacWhirtle has just shot Solovyov!"

"Killed him?"

"Yes!"

Dowling whistled. Solovyov was Administrator for all of North America. Juggins continued: "It was a quarrel over— you remember that girl, that Miss Helen Kistler, whom you introduced to MacWhirtle last year? It was a quarrel over her!"

"What'll happen?"

"I don't know, but Australia will come down on us. They'll send investigators. God knows what they won't do."

"Well," soothed Dowling. "We'll just have to stick together. Pass the word along to the others."

Australia came down on them all right. In a week the Middle Atlantic States swarmed with Bozo investigators, stiff, grim, and arrogant. The plain citizens, whose hatred for their masters had become a bit dulled with familiarity, awoke to find their newspapers plastered with drastic new decrees—to "tighten up the incredibly lax moral standards prevailing in North America." "Absolute prohibition of intoxicating liquors." "No married women shall work for pay." "*No smoking in public places, the same to include public thoroughfares, hotels, restaurants. . . .*"

Baldwin Dowling entered Juggins' office—the Philadelphia Administrator now had a huge one with rugs in which one practically sank ankle-deep. Juggins and five other local Bozos were facing one of the investigators, a small waspish man.

"Get over there with the others," snarled the little man, evidently mistaking Dowling for another Centaurian. The investigator continued his tirade: "And here I find you fallen into the slime of corruption and depravity! Tea! Coffee! Tobacco! *Liquor! Women! Bribery!* Centaurians, eh? Rotten, filthy, weaklings! You're coming with me now. We're taking a special plane to Australia, where you shall stand trial for enough corruption and immorality to hang a continent. Don't worry about packing; you won't need anything but a coffin. Come on!"

He strode to the door and yanked it open. The six Bozos, looking dazed, started to file out. The frightful discipline of their childhood still told.

Dowling caught Juggins' eye. Juggins returned his look dully. Dowling muttered: "Going to let him get away with it?"

"What do you mean?"

"You're bigger'n he is."

Light slowly dawned. Juggins faced his small tormentor. The other Bozos stopped and faced him too.

"Well?" barked the little man. It did not seem to have occurred to him for an instant that his order might be disobeyed.

The six moved toward him. He looked puzzled, then incredulous, then furious, then alarmed. He reached for his pocket. The Bozos rolled over him in a wave. A gun went off, once. The Bozos untangled themselves. The investigator lay with half his face shot off.

"What now?" panted Juggins. "What'll they do when they hear of this? Where can we go? What's that?"

"That" was the noise of an angry mob, flowing along the street outside and smashing things for no reason other than that it was angry.

The Bozos raced downstairs, Dowling after them.

A dozen watchdogs lounged around the entrance of the building. The mob kept clear of them, though none of them had a weapon out.

"Why don't you shoot?" yelled one of the Bozos to the commander of the police.

The watchdog yawned ostentatiously. "Because, Jack, we don't like not being able to smoke in public no more'n they do." And he turned his back on the Centaurian.

That was all the encouragement the mob needed. But by the time they reached the portals, the six Bozos were not there. They had departed for the rear exit with an audible swish.

Baldwin Dowling, prudently keeping out of the mob's way, dialed his wrist-phone. "Hey, Arthur! Juggins and his friends killed the investigator, and skipped! It looks like maybe they've cracked. I'll try to raise New York, and see if I can start a rumpus there. They're a pushover! See if you can find out what's doing in China! I've got to organize an interim government for Philly. Boy, oh boy!"

A telephone call to New York informed Dowling that a mob had formed there—several mobs, in fact—and that the Centaurians had fled or been lynched. Their leader, the new New York Administrator, had been dead drunk, and had failed to give orders at the critical time....

The New York mob, like the Philadelphia mob, was not actuated by noble motives of daring all for freedom. They were rioting because they had been forbidden to smoke in public.

The same four men who had met in Professor Lechon's rooms in the University of Pennsylvania dormitories, so many years ago, met there again. Fred Merrian was tanned and husky, but subdued. The treatment at the Lancaster camp had almost killed him, but ended by hardening him.

He said: "The latest radio news is that the Second Garrison Corps is retreating through Russia."

"Uh-huh," said Dowling. "When they pulled them out of Europe to use against us, Europe went whoosh."

"Isn't it wonderful?" said Merrian. "It'll be a cleaner, finer world when we've gotten rid of them." He looked at his watch. "I've got to run. Everybody I ever knew wants to pinch me to see if I'm real."

When he had gone, Tadeusz Lechon (he was quite old now) said: "I didn't want to disillusion him again. You know how he is. It won't be a cleaner, finer world. It'll be the same old world, with rascals like you two running it."

"*If* we get rid of them," said Dowling. "They still hold Australia and most of southern Asia. It looks like years of war to me. And if we get rid of the Bozos, a lot of countries will be ruled by watchdogs, who won't be much improvement."

Arthur Hsi asked: "Why did they fold up so easily? One man with machine-gun could have dispersed that mob here last month."

Dowling said: "The Bozos didn't have the guts, and the watchdogs didn't want to. So there wasn't anybody to use the machine-gun. But it still seems goofy, Professor Lechon. Why could they beat us twenty years ago, and we beat them now, when they're at least as strong as they were then and we're very much weaker."

Lechon smiled: "Read your history, gentlemen. The same thing happened to the Spartans, remember, when Epaminondas beat them. Why? They were a warrior race, too. Being such, they were unfitted to live among civilized people. Civilized people are always more or less corrupt. The warrior race has a rigid discipline and an inhumanly high standard of conduct. As long as they keep to themselves they are invincible. When they mix with civilized people, they are corrupted by the contact.

"When a people that have never known a disease are exposed to it, it ravages them fearfully, because they have acquired no immunity to it. We, being slightly corrupt to begin with, have an immunity to corruption, just as if it were a bacterial disease. The Centaurians had no such protection. When exposed to temptation, from being much higher morally than we are, they fell much lower.

"The same thing happened to them as to the Spartans. When their government called on them to go to war to preserve its rule over the earth, most of them were too busy grafting off the civilized people to obey. So the Centaurian government found itself with the most powerful military machine on earth, but only a fraction of the men needed to man it. And many of those they did call home were rotten with dissipation, or were thoroughly unreliable watchdogs whose loyalty to their masters had turned to contempt.

"Aristotle said something on the subject a long time ago, in his *Politics*. If I remember the quotation rightly, it ran:

'Militaristic states are apt to survive only so long as they remain at war, while they go to ruin as soon as they have finished making their conquests. Peace causes their metal to decay; and the fault lies with a social system which does not teach its soldiers what to make of their lives when they are off duty.'

"All of which will not bring back the people the Centaurians killed, or give eyes back to those they blinded. Aristotle's statement, if true, is no ground for complacency. We have a grim time ahead of us yet.

"But to a historian like me it is interesting, from a long-range point of view. And it is somewhat comforting to know that my species' faults, however deplorable, do in fact afford it a certain protection.

"Read your history, gentlemen. The tune is always different, but the notes, as I once remarked, are always the same."

FAREWELL TO THE MASTER

Astounding Science Fiction
October

by Harry Bates (1900-)

> *Best known as the first editor of* Astounding Stories *(1930-33), Harry Bates was famous with science fiction readers as the author of the "Hawk Carse" series about the adventures of an interstellar adventurer that was published under the name "Anthony Gilmore." These stories, most of which Bates wrote with D. W. Hall, were quite popular and were later collected as* Space Hawk *(1952). Another exceptional story from this period was "A Matter of Size." (Astounding Stories, 1934).*
>
> *But Bates's real fame rests on this wonderful story, which provided the basis for the film* The Day the Earth Stood Still *(1951). The film version, which starred Michael Rennie and Patricia Neal, was one of the best of the Fifties attempts to bring science fiction to the screen, even though it did not faithfully follow the story. The story is also one of the first to portray mankind as inferior to aliens, especially in moral terms, and it anticipated similar messages from other, more famous writers, including Arthur C. Clarke's* Childhood's End *(1953).*

(It is always frustrating for an author, I imagine, to be known for a single story. And for the reader who yearns for other stories equally good. You have no idea how I feared that fate after "Nightfall" and how delighted I was when my "Foundation" stories caught on. Considering how much I loved this story, I was *so* frustrated when Lester del Rey and I were both commissioned to write memorial essays for John Campbell after his death and it was Lester, *not* I, who thought of entitling it "Farewell to the Master." I could have chewed nails.—I.A.)

I

From his perch high on the ladder above the museum floor, Cliff Sutherland studied carefully each line and shadow of the great robot, then turned and looked thoughtfully down at the rush of visitors come from all over the solar system to see Gnut and the traveler for themselves and to hear once again their amazing, tragic story.

He himself had come to feel an almost proprietary interest in the exhibit, and with some reason. He had been the only free-lance picture reporter on the Capitol grounds when the visitors from the Unknown had arrived, and had obtained the first professional shots of the ship. He had witnessed at close hand every event of the next mad few days. He had thereafter photographed many times the eight-foot robot, the ship, and the beautiful slain ambassador, Klaatu, and his imposing tomb out in the center of the Tidal Basin, and, such was the continuing news value of the event to the billions of persons throughout habitable space, he was there now once more to get still other shots and, if possible, a new "angle."

This time he was after a picture which showed Gnut as weird and menacing. The shots he had taken the day before had not given quite the effect he wanted, and he hoped to get it today; but the light was not yet right and he had to wait for the afternoon to wane a little.

The last of the crowd admitted in the present group hurried in, exclaiming at the great pure green curves of the mysterious time-space traveler, then completely forgetting the ship at sight of the awesome figure and great head of the giant Gnut. Hinged robots of crude man-like appearance were familiar enough, but never had Earthling eyes lain on one like this. For Gnut had almost exactly the shape of a man—a giant, but a man—with greenish metal for man's covering flesh, and greenish metal for man's bulging muscles. Except for a loin cloth, he was nude. He stood like the powerful god of the machine of some undreamed-of scientific civilization, on his face a look of sullen, brooding thought. Those who looked at him did not make jests or idle remarks, and those nearest him usually did not speak at all. His strange, internally illuminated red eyes were so set that every observer felt they were fixed on himself alone, and he engendered a feeling that he might at any moment step forward in anger and perform unimaginable deeds.

A slight rustling sound came from speakers hidden in the

ceiling above, and at once the noises of the crowd lessened. The recorded lecture was about to be given. Cliff sighed. He knew the thing by heart; had even been present when the recording was made, and met the speaker, a young chap named Stillwell.

"Ladies and gentlemen," began a clear and well-modulated voice—but Cliff was no longer attending. The shadows in the hollows of Gnut's face and figure were deeper; it was almost time for his shot. He picked up and examined the proofs of the pictures he had taken the day before and compared them critically with the subject.

As he looked a wrinkle came to his brow. He had not noticed it before, but now, suddenly, he had the feeling that since yesterday something about Gnut was changed. The pose before him was the identical one in the photographs, every detail on comparison seemed the same, but nevertheless the feeling persisted. He took up his viewing glass and more carefully compared subject and photographs, line by line. And then he saw that there was a difference.

With sudden excitement, Cliff snapped two pictures at different exposures. He knew he should wait a little and take others, but he was so sure he had stumbled on an important mystery that he had to get going, and quickly folding his accessory equipment he descended the ladder and made his way out. Twenty minutes later, consumed with curiosity, he was developing the new shots in his hotel bedroom.

What Cliff saw when he compared the negatives taken yesterday and today caused his scalp to tingle. Here was a slant indeed! And apparently no one but he knew! Still, what he had discovered, though it would have made the front page of every paper in the solar system, was after all only a lead. The story, what really had happened, he knew no better than anyone else. It must be his job to find out.

And that meant he would have to secrete himself in the building and stay there all night. That very night; there was still time for him to get back before closing. He would take a small, very fast infrared camera that could see in the dark, and he would get the real picture and the story.

He snatched up the little camera, grabbed an aircab and hurried back to the museum. The place was filled with another section of the ever-present queue, and the lecture was just ending. He thanked Heaven that his arrangement with the museum permitted him to go in and out at will.

He had already decided what to do. First he made his way to the "floating" guard and asked a single question, and anticipation broadened on his face as he heard the expected answer. The second thing was to find a spot where he would be safe from the eyes of the men who would close the floor for the night. There was only one possible place, the laboratory set up behind the ship. Boldly he showed his press credentials to the second guard, stationed at the partitioned passageway leading to it, stating that he had come to interview the scientists; and in a moment was at the laboratory door.

He had been there a number of times and knew the room well. It was a large area roughly partitioned off for the work of the scientists engaged in breaking their way into the ship, and full of a confusion of massive and heavy objects—electric and hot-air ovens, carboys of chemicals, asbestos sheeting, compressors, basins, ladles, a microscope, and a great deal of smaller equipment common to a metallurgical laboratory. Three white-smocked men were deeply engrossed in an experiment at the far end. Cliff, waiting a good moment, slipped inside and hid himself under a table half buried with supplies. He felt reasonably safe from detection there. Very soon now the scientists would be going home for the night.

From beyond the ship he could hear another section of the waiting queue filing in—the last, he hoped, of the day. He settled himself as comfortably as he could. In a moment the lecture would begin. He had to smile when he thought of one thing the recording would say.

Then there it was again—the clear, trained voice of the chap Stillwell. The foot scrapings and whispers of the crowd died away, and Cliff could hear every word in spite of the great bulk of the ship lying interposed.

"Ladies and gentlemen," began the familiar words, "the Smithsonian Institution welcomes you to its new Interplanetary Wing and to the marvelous exhibits at this moment before you."

A slight pause. "All of you must know by now something of what happened here three months ago, if indeed you did not see it for yourself in the telescreen," the voice went on. "The few facts are briefly told. A little after 5:00 p.m. on September 16th, visitors to Washington thronged the grounds outside this building in their usual numbers and no doubt with their usual thoughts. The day was warm and fair. A stream of people was leaving the main entrance of the museum just outside in the direction you are facing. This wing, of course, was not here at that time. Everyone was homeward bound, tired no doubt from hours on their feet, seeing the exhibits of the museum and visiting the many buildings on the grounds nearby. And then it happened.

"On the area just to your right, just as it is now, appeared the time-space traveler. It appeared in the blink of an eye. It did not come down from the sky; dozens of witnesses swear to that; it just appeared. One moment it was not here, the next it was. It appeared on the very spot it now rests on.

"The people nearest the ship were stricken with panic and ran back with cries and screams. Excitement spread out over Washington in a tidal wave. Radio, television, and newspapermen rushed here at once. Police formed a wide cordon around the ship, and army units appeared and trained guns and ray projectors on it. The direst calamity was feared.

"For it was recognized from the very beginning that this was no spaceship from anywhere in the solar system. Every child knew that only two spaceships had ever been built on Earth, and none at all on any of the other planets and satellites; and of those two, one had been destroyed when it was pulled into the sun, and the other had just been reported safely arrived on Mars. Then, the ones made here had a shell of a strong aluminum alloy, while this one, as you see, is of an unknown greenish metal.

"The ship appeared and just sat here. No one emerged, and there was no sign that it contained life of any kind. That, as much as any single thing, caused excitement to sky-rocket. Who, or what, was inside? Were the visitors hostile or friendly? Where did the ship come from? How did it arrive so suddenly right on this spot without dropping from the sky?

"For two days the ship rested here, just as you now see it, without motion or sign that it contained life. Long before the end of that time the scientists had explained that it was not so much a spaceship as a space-time traveler, because only such a ship could arrive as this one did—materialize. They pointed out that such a traveler, while theoretically understandable to us Earthmen, was far beyond attempt at our present state of knowledge, and that this one, activated by relativity principles, might well have come from the far corner of the Universe, from a distance which light itself would require millions of years to cross.

"When this opinion was disseminated, public tension grew until it was almost intolerable. Where had the traveler come from? Who were its occupants? Why had they come to Earth? Above all, why did they not show themselves? Were they perhaps preparing some terrible weapon of destruction?

"And where was the ship's entrance port? Men who dared go look reported that none could be found. No slightest break or crack marred the perfect smoothness of the ship's curving ovoid surface. And a delegation of high-ranking officials who visited the ship could not, by knocking, elicit from its occupants any sign that they had been heard.

"At last, after exactly two days, in full view of tens of thousands of persons assembled and standing well back, and under the muzzles of scores of the army's most powerful guns and ray projectors, an opening appeared in the wall of the ship, and a ramp slid down, and out stepped a man, godlike in appearance and human in form, closely followed by a giant robot. And when they touched the ground the ramp slid back and the entrance closed as before."

"It was immediately apparent to all the assembled thousands that the stranger was friendly. The first thing he did was to raise his right arm high in the universal gesture of peace; but it was not that which impressed those nearest so much as the expression on his face, which radiated kindness, wisdom, the purest nobility. In his delicately tinted robe he looked like a benign god.

"At once, waiting for this appearance, a large committee of high-ranking government officials and army officers advanced to greet the visitor. With graciousness and dignity the man pointed to himself, then to his robot companion, and said in perfect English with a peculiar accent, 'I am Klaatu,' or a name that sounded like that, 'and this is Gnut.' The names were not well understood at the time, but the sight-and-sound film of the television men caught them and they became known to everyone subsequently.

"And then occurred the thing which shall always be to the shame of the human race. From a treetop a hundred yards away came a wink of violet light and Klaatu fell. The assembled multitude stood for a moment stunned, not comprehending what had happened. Gnut, a little behind his master and to one side, slowly turned his body a little toward him, moved his head twice, and stood still, in exactly the position you now see him.

"Then followed pandemonium. The police pulled the slayer of Klaatu out of the tree. They found him mentally unbalanced; he kept crying that the devil had come to kill everyone on Earth. He was taken away, and Klaatu, although obviously dead, was rushed to the nearest hospital to see if anything could be done to revive him. Confused and frightened crowds milled about the Capitol grounds the rest of the afternoon and much of that night. The ship remained as silent and motionless as before. And Gnut, too, never moved from the position he had come to rest in.

"Gnut never moved again. He remained exactly as you see him all that night and for the ensuing days. When the mausoleum in the Tidal Basin was built, Klaatu's burial services took place where you are standing now, attended by the highest functionaries of all the great countries of the world. It was not only the most appropriate but the safest thing to do, for if there should be other living creatures in the traveler, as seemed possible at that time, they had to be impressed by the sincere sorrow of us Earthmen at what had happened. If Gnut was still alive, or perhaps I had better say functionable, there was no sign. He stood as you see him during the entire ceremony. He stood so while his master was floated out to the mausoleum and given to the centuries with the tragically short sight-and-sound record of his historic visit. And he stood so afterward, day after day, night after night, in fair weather and in rain, never moving or showing by any slightest sign that he was aware of what had gone on.

"After the interment, this wing was built out from the museum to cover the traveler and Gnut. Nothing else could very well have been done, it was learned, for both Gnut and the ship were far too heavy to be moved safely by any means at hand.

"You have heard about the efforts of our metallurgists since then to break into the ship, and of their complete failure. Behind the ship now, as you can see from either end, a partitioned workroom has been set up where the attempt still goes on. So far its wonderful greenish metal has proved inviolable. Not only are they unable to get in, but they cannot even find the exact place from which Klaatu and Gnut emerged. The chalk marks you see are the best approximation.

"Many people have feared that Gnut was only temporarily deranged, and that on return to function might be dangerous, so the scientists have completely destroyed all chance of that. The greenish metal of which he is made seemed to be the same as that of the ship and could no more be attacked, they found, nor could they find any way to penetrate to his internals; but they had other means. They sent electrical currents of tremendous voltages and amperages through him. They applied terrific heat to all parts of his metal shell. They immersed him for days in gases and acids and strongly corroding solutions, and they have bombarded him with every known kind of ray. You need have no fear of him now. He cannot possibly have retained the ability to function in any way.

"But—a word of caution. The officials of the government know that visitors will not show any disrespect in this building. It may be that the unknown and unthinkably powerful civilization from which Klaatu and Gnut came may send other emissaries to see what happened to them. Whether or not they do, not one of us must be found amiss in our attitude. None of us could very well anticipate what happened, and we all are immeasurably sorry, but we are still in a sense responsible, and must do what we can to avoid possible retaliations.

"You will be allowed to remain five minutes longer, and then, when the gong sounds, you will please leave promptly. The robot attendants along the wall will answer any questions you may have.

"Look well, for before you stand stark symbols of the achievement, mystery, and frailty of the human race."

The recorded voice ceased speaking. Cliff, carefully moving his cramped limbs, broke out in a wide smile. If they knew what he knew!

For his photographs told a slightly different story from that of the lecturer. In yesterday's a line of the figured floor showed clearly at the outer edge of the robot's near foot; in today's, *that line was covered*. Gnut had moved!

Or been moved, though this was very unlikely. Where were the derrick and other evidence of such activity? It could hardly have been done in one night, and all signs so quickly concealed. And why should it be done at all?

Still, to make sure, he had asked the guard. He could almost remember verbatim his answer:

"No, Gnut has neither moved nor been moved since the death of his master. A special point was made of keeping him in the position he assumed at Klaatu's death. The floor was built in under him, and the scientists who completed his derangement erected their apparatus around him, just as he stands. You need have no fears."

Cliff smiled again. He did not have any fears.

Not yet.

II

A moment later the big gong above the entrance doors rang the closing hour, and immediately following it a voice from the speakers called out, "Five o'clock, ladies and gentlemen. Closing time, ladies and gentlemen."

The three scientists, as if surprised it was so late, hurriedly washed their hands, changed to their street clothes and disappeared down the partitioned corridor, oblivious of the young picture man hidden under the table. The slide and scrape of the feet on the exhibition floor rapidly dwindled, until at last there were only the steps of the two guards walking from one point to another, making sure everything was all right for the night. For just a moment one of them glanced in the doorway of the laboratory, then he joined the other at the entrance. Then the great metal doors clanged to, and there was silence.

Cliff waited several minutes, then carefully poked his way out from under the table. As he straightened up, a faint tinkling crash sounded at the floor by his feet. Carefully stooping, he found the shattered remains of a thin glass pipette. He had knocked it off the table.

That caused him to realize something he had not thought of before: A Gnut who had moved might be a Gnut who could see and hear—and really be dangerous. He would have to be very careful.

He looked about him. The room was bounded at the ends by two fiber partitions which at the inner ends followed close under the curving bottom of the ship. The inner side of the room was the ship itself, and the outer was the southern wall of the wing. There were four large high windows. The only entrance was by way of the passage.

Without moving, from his knowledge of the building, he made his plan. The wing was connected with the western end of the museum by a doorway, never used, and extended westward toward the Washington Monument. The ship lay nearest the southern wall, and Gnut stood out in front of it, not far from the northeast corner and at the opposite end of the room from the entrance of the building and the passageway leading to the laboratory. By retracing his steps he would come out on the floor at the point farthest removed from the robot. This was just what he wanted, for on the other side of the entrance, on a low platform, stood a paneled table containing the lecture apparatus, and this table was the only object in the room which afforded a place for him to lie concealed while watching what might go on. The only other objects on the floor were the six manlike robot attendants in fixed stations along the northern wall, placed there to answer visitors' questions. He would have to gain the table.

He turned and began cautiously tiptoeing out of the laboratory and down the passageway. It was already dark there, for what light still entered the exhibition hall was shut off by the great bulk of the ship. He reached the end of the room without making a sound. Very carefully he edged forward and peered around the bottom of the ship at Gnut.

He had a momentary shock. The robot's eyes were right on him!—or so it seemed. Was that only the effect of the set of his eyes, he wondered, or was he already discovered? The position of Gnut's head did not seem to have changed, at any rate. Probably everything was all right, but he wished he did not have to cross that end of the room with the feeling that the robot's eyes were following him.

He drew back and sat down and waited. It would have to be totally dark before he essayed the trip to the table.

He waited a full hour, until the faint beams from the lamps on the grounds outside began to make the room seem to grow lighter; then he got up and peeped around the ship once more. The robot's eyes seemed to pierce right at him as before, only now, due no doubt to the darkness, the strange internal illumination seemed much brighter. This was a chilling thing. Did Gnut know he was there? What were the thoughts of the robot? What *could* be the thoughts of a man-made machine, even so wonderful a one as Gnut?

It was time for the cross, so Cliff slung his camera around on his back, went down on his hands and knees, and carefully moved to the edge of the entrance hall. There he fitted himself as closely as he could into the angle made by it with the floor and started inching ahead. Never pausing, not risking a glance at Gnut's unnerving red eyes, moving an inch at a time, he snaked along. He took ten minutes to cross the space of a hundred feet, and he was wet with perspiration when his fingers at last touched the one-foot rise of the platform on which the table stood. Still slowly, silently as a shadow, he made his way over the edge and melted behind the protection of the table. At last he was there.

He relaxed for a moment, then, anxious to know whether he had been seen, carefully turned and looked around the side of the table.

Gnut's eyes were now full on him! Or so it seemed. Against the general darkness, the robot loomed a mysterious and still darker shadow that, for all his being a hundred and fifty feet away, seemed to dominate the room. Cliff could not tell whether the position of his body was changed or not.

But if Gnut were looking at him, he at least did nothing else. Not by the slightest motion that Cliff could discern did he appear to move. His position was the one he had maintained these last three months, in the darkness, in the rain, and this last week in the museum.

Cliff made up his mind not to give away to fear. He became conscious of his own body. The cautious trip had taken something out of him—his knees and elbows burned and his trousers were no doubt ruined. But these were little things if what he hoped for came to pass. If Gnut so much as moved, and he could catch him with his infrared camera, he would have a story that would buy him fifty suits of clothes. And if on top of that he could learn the purpose of Gnut's moving—provided there was a purpose—that would be a story that would set the world on its ears.

He settled down to a period of waiting; there was no telling when Gnut would move, if indeed he would move that night. Cliff's eyes had long been adjusted to the dark and he could make out the larger objects well enough. From time to time he peered out at the robot—peered long and hard, till his outlines wavered and he seemed to move, and he had to blink and rest his eyes to be sure it was only his imagination.

Again the minute hand of his watch crept around the dial. The inactivity made Cliff careless, and for longer and longer periods he kept his head back out of sight behind the table. And so it was that when Gnut did move he was scared almost out of his wits. Dull and a little bored, he suddenly found the robot out on the floor, halfway in his direction.

But that was not the most frightening thing. It was that when he did see Gnut he did not catch him moving! He was stopped as still as a cat in the middle of stalking a mouse. His eyes were now much brighter, and there was no remaining doubt about their direction: he was looking right at Cliff!

Scarcely breathing, half hypnotized, Cliff looked back. His thoughts tumbled. What was the robot's intention? Why had he stopped so still? Was he being stalked? How could he move with such silence?

In the heavy darkness Gnut's eyes moved nearer. Slowly but in perfect rhythm the almost imperceptible sound of his footsteps beat on Cliff's ears. Cliff, usually resourceful enough, was this time caught flatfooted. Frozen with fear, utterly incapable of fleeing, he lay where he was while the metal monster with the fiery eyes came on.

For a moment Cliff all but fainted, and when he recovered, there was Gnut towering over him, legs almost within reach. He was bending slightly, burning his terrible eyes right into his own!

Too late to try to think of running now. Trembling like any cornered mouse, Cliff waited for the blow that would crush him. For an eternity, it seemed, Gnut scrutinized him without moving. For each second of that eternity Cliff expected annihilation, sudden, quick, complete. And then suddenly and unexpectedly it was over. Gnut's body straightened and he stepped back. He turned. And then, with the almost jerkless rhythm which only he among robots possessed, he started back toward the place from which he came.

Cliff could hardly believe he had been spared. Gnut could have crushed him like a worm—and he had only turned around and gone back. Why? It could not be supposed that a robot was capable of human considerations.

Gnut went straight to the other end of the traveler. At a certain place he stopped and made a curious succession of sounds. At once Cliff saw an opening, blacker than the gloom of the building, appear in the ship's side, and it was followed by a slight sliding sound as a ramp slid out and met the floor. Gnut walked up the ramp and, stooping a little, disappeared inside the ship.

Then, for the first time, Cliff remembered the picture he had come to get. Gnut had moved, but he had not caught him! But at least now, whatever opportunies there might be later, he could get the shot of the ramp connecting with the opened door; so he twisted his camera into position, set it for the proper exposure, and took a shot.

A long time passed and Gnut did not come out. What could he be doing inside? Cliff wondered. Some of his courage returned to him and he toyed with the idea of creeping forward and peeping through the port, but he found he had not the courage for that. Gnut had spared him, at least for the time, but there was no telling how far his tolerance would go.

An hour passed, then another, Gnut was doing something inside the ship, but what. Cliff could not imagine. If the robot had been a human being, he knew he would have sneaked a look, but as it was, he was too much of an unknown quantity. Even the simplest of Earth's robots under certain circumstances were inexplicable things; what, then, of this one, come from an unknown and even unthinkable civilization, by far the most wonderful construction ever seen—what superhuman powers might he not possess? All that the scientists of Earth could do had not served to derange him. Acid, heat, rays, terrific crushing blows—he had withstood them all; even his finish had been unmarred. He might be able to see perfectly in the dark. And right where he was, he might be able to hear or in some way sense the least change in Cliff's position.

More time passed, and then, some time after two o'clock in the morning, a simple homely thing happened, but a thing so unexpected that for a moment it quite destroyed Cliff's equilibrium. Suddenly, through the dark and silent building, there was a faint whir of wings, soon followed by the piercing, sweet voice of a bird. A mockingbird. Somewhere in the gloom above his head. Clear and full throated were its notes; a dozen little songs it sang, one after the other without pause between—short insistent calls, twirrings, coaxings, cooings—the spring love song of perhaps the finest singer in the world. Then, as suddenly as it began, the voice was silent.

If an invading army had poured out of the traveler, Cliff would have been less surprised. The month was December; even in Florida the mockingbirds had not yet begun their song. How had one gotten into that tight, gloomy museum? How and why was it singing there?

He waited, full of curiosity. Then suddenly he was aware of Gnut, standing just outside the port of the ship. He stood quite still, his glowing eyes turned squarely in Cliff's direction. For a moment the hush in the museum seemed to deepen; then it was broken by a soft thud on the floor near where Cliff was lying.

He wondered. The light in Gnut's eyes changed, and he started his almost jerkless walk in Cliff's direction. When only a little away, the robot stopped, bent over, and picked something from the floor. For some time he stood without motion and looked at a little object he held in his hand. Cliff knew, though he could not see, that it was the mockingbird. Its body, for he was sure that it had lost its song forever. Gnut then turned, and without a glance at Cliff, walked back to the ship and again went inside.

Hours passed while Cliff waited for some sequel to this surprising happening. Perhaps it was because of his curiosity that his fear of the robot began to lessen. Surely if the mechanism was unfriendly, if he intended him any harm, he would have finished him before, when he had such a perfect opportunity. Cliff began to nerve himself for a quick look inside the port. And a picture; he must remember the picture. He kept forgetting the very reason he was there.

It was in the deeper darkness of the false dawn when he got sufficient courage and made the start. He took off his shoes, and in his stockinged feet, his shoes tied together and slung over his shoulder, he moved stiffly but rapidly to a position behind the nearest of the six robot attendants stationed along the wall, then paused for some sign which might indicate that Gnut knew he had moved. Hearing none, he slipped along behind the next robot attendant and paused again. Bolder now, he made in one spurt all the distance to the farthest one, the sixth, fixed just opposite the port of the ship. There he met with a disappointment. No light that he could detect was visible within; there was only darkness and the all-permeating silence. Still, he had better get the picture. He raised his camera, focused it on the dark opening, and gave the film a comparatively long exposure. Then he stood there, at a loss what to do next.

As he paused, a peculiar series of muffled noises reached his ears, apparently from within the ship. Animal noises—first scrapings and pantings, punctuated by several sharp clicks, then deep, rough snarls, interrupted by more scrapings and pantings, as if a struggle of some kind were going on. Then suddenly, before Cliff could even decide to run back to the table, a low, wide, dark shape bounded out of the port and immediately turned and grew to the height of a man. A terrible fear swept over Cliff, even before he knew what the shape was.

In the next second Gnut appeared in the port and stepped unhesitatingly down the ramp toward the shape. As he advanced it backed slowly away for a few feet; but then it stood its ground, and thick arms rose from its sides and began a loud drumming on its chest, while from its throat came a deep roar of defiance. Only one creature in the world beat its chest and made a sound like that. The shape was a gorilla!

And a huge one!

Gnut kept advancing, and when close, charged forward and grappled with the beast. Cliff would not have guessed that Gnut could move so fast. In the darkness he could not see the details of what happened; all he knew was that the two great shapes, the titanic metal Gnut and the squat but terrifically strong gorilla, merged for a moment with silence on the robot's part and terrible, deep, indescribable roars on the other's; then the two separated, and it was as if the gorilla had been flung back and away.

The animal at once rose to its full height and roared deafeningly. Gnut advanced. They closed again, and the separation of before was repeated. The robot continued inexorably, and now the gorilla began to fall back down the building. Suddenly the beast darted at a manlike shape against the wall, and with one rapid side movement dashed the fifth robot attendant to the floor and decapitated it.

Tense with fear, Cliff crouched behind his own robot attendant. He thanked Heaven that Gnut was between him and the gorilla and was continuing his advance. The gorilla backed farther, darted suddenly at the next robot in the row, and with strength almost unbelievable picked it from its roots and hurled it at Gnut. With a sharp metallic clang, robot hit robot, and the one of Earth bounced off to one side and rolled to a stop.

Cliff cursed himself for it afterward, but again he completely forgot the picture. The gorilla kept falling back down the building, demolishing with terrific bursts of rage every robot attendant that he passed and throwing the pieces at the implacable Gnut. Soon they arrived opposite the table, and Cliff now thanked his stars he had come away. There followed a brief silence. Cliff could not make out what was going on, but he imagined that the gorilla had at last reached the corner of the wing and was trapped.

If he was, it was only for a moment. The silence was suddenly shattered by a terrific roar, and the thick, squat shape of the animal came bounding toward Cliff. He came all the way back and turned just between Cliff and the port of the ship. Cliff prayed frantically for Gnut to come back quickly, for there was now only the last remaining robot attendant between him and the madly dangerous brute. Out of the dimness Gnut did appear. The gorilla rose to its full height and again beat its chest and roared its challenge.

And then occurred a curious thing. It fell on all fours and slowly rolled over on its side, as if weak or hurt. Then panting, making frightening noises, it forced itself again to its feet and faced the oncoming Gnut. As it waited, its eye was caught by the last robot attendant and perhaps Cliff, shrunk close behind it. With a surge of terrible destructive rage, the gorilla waddled sideward toward Cliff, but this time, even through his panic, he saw that the animal moved with difficulty, again apparently sick or severely wounded. He jumped back just in time; the gorilla pulled out the last robot attendant and hurled it violently at Gnut, missing him narrowly.

That was its last effort. The weakness caught it again; it dropped heavily on one side, rocked back and forth a few times, and fell to twitching. Then it lay still and did not move again.

The first faint pale light of the dawn was seeping into the room. From the corner where he had taken refuge, Cliff watched closely the great robot. It seemed to him that he behaved very queerly. He stood over the dead gorilla, looking down at him with what in a human would be called sadness. Cliff saw this clearly; Gnut's heavy greenish features bore a thoughtful, grieving expression new to his experience. For some moments he stood so, then as might a father with his sick child, he leaned over, lifted the great animal in his metal arms and carried it tenderly within the ship.

Cliff flew back to the table, suddenly fearful of yet other dangerous and inexplicable happenings. It struck him that he might be safer in the laboratory, and with trembling knees he made his way there and hid in one of the big ovens. He prayed for full daylight. His thoughts were chaos. Rapidly, one after another, his mind churned up the amazing events of the night, but all was mystery; it seemed there could be no rational explanation for them. That mockingbird. The gorilla. Gnut's sad expression and his tenderness. What could account for a fantastic melange like that!

Gradually full daylight did come. A long time passed. At last he began to believe he might yet get out of that place of mystery and danger alive. At 8:30 there were noises at the entrance, and the good sound of human voices came to his ears. He stepped out of the oven and tiptoed to the passageway.

The noises stopped suddenly and there was a frightened exclamation and then the sound of running feet, and then silence. Stealthily Cliff sneaked down the narrow way and peeped fearfully around the ship.

There Gnut was in his accustomed place, in the identical pose he had taken at the death of his master, brooding sullenly and alone over a space traveler once again closed tight and a room that was a shambles. The entrance doors stood open and, heart in his mouth, Cliff ran out.

A few minutes later, safe in his hotel room, completely done in, he sat down for a second and almost at once fell asleep. Later, still in his clothes and still asleep, he staggered over to the bed. He did not wake up till midafternoon.

III

Cliff awoke slowly, at first not realizing that the images tumbling in his head were real memories and not a fantastic dream. It was recollection of the pictures which brought him to his feet. Hastily he set about developing the film in his camera.

Then in his hands were proof that the events of the night were real. Both shots turned out well. The first showed clearly the ramp leading up to the port as he had dimly discerned it from his position behind the table. The second, of the open port as snapped from in front, was a disappointment, for a blank wall just back of the opening cut off all view of the interior. That would account for the fact that no light had escaped from the ship while Gnut was inside. Assuming Gnut required light for whatever he did.

Cliff looked at the negatives and was ashamed of himself. What a rotten picture man he was to come back with two ridiculous shots like these! He had had a score of opportunities to get real ones—shots of Gnut in action—Gnut's fight with the gorilla—even Gnut holding the mockingbird—spine-chilling stuff!—and all he had brought back was two stills of a doorway. Oh, sure, they were valuable, but he was a grade A ass.

And to top this brilliant performance, he had fallen asleep!

Well, he'd better get out on the street and find out what was doing.

Quickly he showered, shaved, and changed his clothes, and

soon was entering a nearby restaurant patronized by other picture and newsmen. Sitting alone at the lunch bar, he spotted a friend and competitor.

"Well, what do you think?" asked his friend when he took the stool at his side.

"I don't think anything until I've had breakfast," Cliff answered.

"Then haven't you heard?"

"Heard what?" fended Cliff, who knew very well what was coming.

"You're a fine picture man," was the other's remark. "When something really big happens, you are asleep in bed." But then he told him what had been discovered that morning in the museum, and of the world-wide excitement at the news. Cliff did three things at once, successfully—gobbled a substantial breakfast, kept thanking his stars that nothing new had transpired, and showed continuous surprise. Still chewing he got up and hurried over to the building.

Outside, balked at the door, was a large crowd of the curious, but Cliff had no trouble gaining admittance when he showed his press credentials. Gnut and the ship stood just as he had left them, but the floor had been cleaned up and the pieces of the demolished robot attendants were lined up in one place along the wall. Several other competitor friends of his were there.

"I was away; missed the whole thing," he said to one of them—Gus. "What's supposed to be the explanation for what happened?"

"Ask something easy," was the answer. "Nobody knows. It's thought maybe something came out of the ship, maybe another robot like Gnut. Say—where have you been?"

"Asleep."

"Better catch up. Several billion bipeds are scared stiff. Revenge for the death of Klaatu. Earth about to be invaded."

"But that's—"

"Oh, I know it's all crazy, but that's the story they're being fed; it sells news. But there's a new angle just turned up, very surprising. Come here."

He led Cliff to the table where stood a knot of people looking with great interest at several objects guarded by a technician. Gus pointed to a long slide on which were mounted a number of short dark-brown hairs.

"Those hairs came off a large male gorilla," Gus said with

a certain hard-boiled casualness. "Most of them were found among the sweepings of the floor this morning. The rest were found on the robot attendants."

Cliff tried to look astounded. Gus pointed to a test tube partly filled with a light amber fluid.

"And that's blood, diluted—gorilla blood. It was found on Gnut's arms."

"Good Heaven!" Cliff managed to exclaim. "And there's no explanation?"

"Not even a theory. It's your big chance, wonder boy."

Cliff broke away from Gus, unable to maintain his act any longer. He couldn't decide what to do about his story. The press services would bid heavily for it—with all his pictures—but that would take further action out of his hands. In the back of his mind he wanted to stay in the wing again that night, but—well, he simply was afraid. He'd had a pretty stiff dose, and he wanted very much to remain alive.

He walked over and looked a long time at Gnut. No one would ever have guessed that he had moved, or that there had rested on his greenish metal face a look of sadness. Those weird eyes! Cliff wondered if they were really looking at him, as they seemed, recognizing him as the bold intruder of last night. Of what unknown stuff were they made—those materials placed in his eye sockets by one branch of the race of man which all the science of his own could not even serve to disfunction? What was Gnut thinking? What could be the thoughts of a robot—a mechanism of metal poured out of man's clay crucibles? Was he angry at him? Cliff thought not. Gnut had had him at his mercy—and had walked away.

Dared he stay again?

Cliff thought perhaps he did.

He walked about the room, thinking it over. He felt sure Gnut would move again. A Mikton ray gun would protect him from another gorilla—or fifty of them. He did not yet have the real story. He had come back with two miserable architectural stills!

He might have known from the first that he would stay. At dusk that night, armed with his camera and a small Mikton gun, he lay once more under the table of supplies in the laboratory and heard the metal doors of the wing clang to for the night.

This time he would get the story—and the pictures.

If only no guard was posted inside!

IV

Cliff listened hard for a long time for any sound which might tell him that a guard had been left, but the silence within the wing remained unbroken. He was thankful for that—but not quite completely. The gathering darkness and the realization that he was now irrevocably committed made the thought of a companion not altogether unpleasant.

About an hour after it reached maximum darkness he took off his shoes, tied them together and slung them around his neck, down his back, and stole quietly down the passageway to where it opened into the exhibition area. All seemed as it had been the preceding night. Gnut looked an ominous, indistinct shadow at the far end of the room, his glowing red eyes again seemingly right on the spot from which Cliff peeped out. As on the previous night, but even more carefully, Cliff went down on his stomach in the angle of the wall and slowly snaked across to the low platform on which stood the table. Once in its shelter, he fixed his shoes so that they straddled one shoulder, and brought his camera and gun holster around, ready on his breast. This time, he told himself, he would get pictures.

He settled down to wait, keeping Gnut in full sight every minute. His vision reached maximum adjustment to the darkness. Eventually he began to feel lonely and a little afraid. Gnut's red-glowing eyes were getting on his nerves; he had to keep assuring himself that the robot would not harm him. He had little doubt but that he himself was being watched.

Hours slowly passed. From time to time he heard slight noises at the entrance, on the outside—a guard, perhaps, or maybe curious visitors.

At about nine o'clock he saw Gnut move. First his head alone; it turned so that the eyes burned stronger in the direction where Cliff lay. For a moment that was all; then the dark metal form stirred slightly and began moving forward—straight toward himself. Cliff had thought he would not be afraid—much—but now his heart stood still. What would happen this time?

With amazing silence, Gnut drew nearer, until he towered an ominous shadow over the spot where Cliff lay. For a long time his red eyes burned down on the prone man. Cliff trembled all over; this was worse than the first time. Without having planned it, he found himself speaking to the creature.

"You would not hurt me," he pleaded. "I was only curious to see what's going on. It's my job. Can you understand me? I would not harm or bother you. I . . . I couldn't if I wanted to! Please!"

The robot never moved, and Cliff could not guess whether his words had been understood or even heard. When he felt he could not bear the suspense any longer, Gnut reached out and took something from a drawer of the table, or perhaps he put something back in; then he stepped back, turned, and retraced his steps. Cliff was safe! Again the robot had spared him!

Beginning then, Cliff lost much of his fear. He felt sure now that this Gnut would do him no harm. Twice he had had him in his power, and each time he had only looked and quietly moved away. Cliff could not imagine what Gnut had done in the drawer of the table. He watched with the greatest curiosity to see what would happen next.

As on the night before, the robot went straight to the end of the ship and made the peculiar sequence of sounds that opened the port, and when the ramp slid out he went inside. After that Cliff was alone in the darkness for a very long time, probably two hours. Not a sound came from the ship.

Cliff knew he should sneak up to the port and peep inside, but he could not quite bring himself to do it. With his gun he could handle another gorilla, but if Gnut caught him it might be the end. Momentarily he expected something fantastic to happen—he knew not what; maybe the mockingbird's sweet song again, maybe a gorilla, maybe—anything. What did at last happen once more caught him with complete surprise.

He heard a sudden muffled sound, then words—human words—every one familiar.

"Gentlemen," was the first, and then there was a very slight pause. "The Smithsonian Institution welcomes you to its new Interplanetary Wing and to the marvelous exhibits at this moment before you."

It was the recorded voice of Stillwell! But it was not coming through the speakers overhead, but much muted, from within the ship.

After a slight pause it went on:

"All of you must . . . must—" Here it stammered and came to a stop. Cliff's hair bristled. That stammering was not in the lecture!

For just a moment there was silence; then came a scream,

a hoarse man's scream, muffled, from somewhere within the heart of the ship; and it was followed by muted gasps and cries, as of a man in great fright or distress.

Every nerve tight, Cliff watched the port. He heard a thudding noise within the ship, then out the door flew the shadow of what was surely a human being. Gasping and half stumbling, he ran straight down the room in Cliff's direction. When twenty feet away, the great shadow of Gnut followed him out of the port.

Cliff watched, breathless. The man—it was Stillwell, he saw now—came straight for the table behind which Cliff himself lay, as if to get behind it, but when only a few feet away, his knees buckled and he fell to the floor. Suddenly Gnut was standing over him, but Stillwell did not seem to be aware of it. He appeared very ill, but kept making spasmodic futile efforts to creep on to the protection of the table.

Gnut did not move, so Cliff was emboldened to speak.

"What's the matter, Stillwell?" he asked. "Can I help? Don't be afraid. I'm Cliff Sutherland; you know, the picture man."

Without showing the least surprise at finding Cliff there, and clutching at his presence like a drowning man would a straw, Stillwell gasped out:

"Help me! Gnut . . . Gnut—" He seemed unable to go on.

"Gnut what?" asked Cliff. Very conscious of the fire-eyed robot looming above, and afraid even to move out to the man, Cliff added reassuringly: "Gnut won't hurt you. I'm sure he won't. He doesn't hurt me. What's the matter? What can I do?"

With a sudden accession of energy, Stillwell rose on his elbows.

"Where am I?" he asked.

"In the Interplanetary Wing," Cliff answered. "Don't you know?"

Only Stillwell's hard breathing was heard for a moment. Then hoarsely, weakly, he asked:

"How did I get here?"

"I don't know," said Cliff.

"I was making a lecture recording," Stillwell said, "when suddenly I found myself here . . . or I mean in there—"

He broke off and showed a return of his terror.

"Then what?" asked Cliff gently.

"I was in that box—and there, above me, was Gnut, the

robot. Gnut! But they made Gnut harmless! He's never moved!"

"Steady, now," said Cliff. "I don't think Gnut will hurt you."

Stillwell fell back on the floor.

"I'm very weak," he gasped. "Something—Will you get a doctor?"

He was utterly unaware that towering above him, eyes boring down at him through the darkness, was the robot he feared so greatly.

As Cliff hesitated, at a loss what to do, the man's breath began coming in short gasps, as regular as the ticking of a clock. Cliff dared to move out to him, but no act on his part could have helped the man now. His gasps weakened and became spasmodic, then suddenly he was completely silent and still. Cliff felt for his heart, then looked up to the eyes in the shadow above.

"He is dead," he whispered.

The robot seemed to understand, or at least to hear. He bent forward and regarded the still figure.

"What is it, Gnut?" Cliff asked the robot suddenly. "What are you doing? Can I help you in any way? Somehow I don't believe you are unfriendly, and I don't believe you killed this man. But what happened? Can you understand me? Can you speak? What is it you're trying to do?"

Gnut made no sound or motion, but only looked at the still figure at his feet. In the robot's face, now so close, Cliff saw the look of sad contemplation.

Gnut stood so several minutes; then he bent lower, took the limp form carefully—even gently, Cliff thought—in his mighty arms, and carried him to the place along the wall where lay the dismembered pieces of the robot attendants. Carefully he laid him by their side. Then he went back into the ship.

Without fear now, Cliff stole along the wall of the room. He had gotten almost as far as the shattered figures on the floor when he suddenly stopped motionless. Gnut was emerging again.

He was bearing a shape that looked like another body, a larger one. He held it in one arm and placed it carefully by the body of Stillwell. In the hand of his other arm he held something that Cliff could not make out, and this he placed at the side of the body he had just put down. Then he went to the ship and returned once more with a shape which he laid gently by the others; and when this last trip was over he looked down at them all for a moment, then turned slowly back to the ship and stood motionless, as if in deep thought, by the ramp.

Cliff restrained his curiosity as long as he could, then slipped forward and bent over the objects Gnut had placed there. First in the row was the body of Stillwell, as he expected, and next was the great shapeless furry mass of a dead gorilla—the one of last night. By the gorilla lay the object the robot had carried in his free hand—the little body of the mockingbird. These last two had remained in the ship all night, and Gnut, for all his surprising gentleness in handling them, was only cleaning house. But there was a fourth body whose history he did not know. He moved closer and bent very low to look.

What he saw made him catch his breath. Impossible!—he thought; there was some confusion in his directions; he brought his face back, close to the first body. Then his blood ran cold. The first body was that of Stillwell, but the last in the row was Stillwell, too; there were two bodies of Stillwell, both exactly alike, both dead.

Cliff backed away with a cry, and then panic took him and he ran down the room away from Gnut and yelled and beat wildly on the door. There was a noise on the outside.

"Let me out!" he yelled in terror. "Let me out! Let me out! Oh, hurry!"

A crack opened between the two doors and he forced his way through like a wild animal and ran far out on the lawn. A belated couple on a nearby path stared at him with amazement, and this brought some sense to his head and he slowed down and came to a stop. Back at the building, everything looked as usual, and in spite of his terror, Gnut was not chasing him.

He was still in his stockinged feet. Breathing heavily, he sat down on the wet grass and put on his shoes; then he stood and looked at the building, trying to pull himself together. What an incredible melange! The dead Stillwell, the dead gorilla, and the dead mockingbird—all dying before his eyes. And then that last frightening thing, the second dead Stillwell whom he had *not* seen die. And Gnut's strange gentleness, and the sad expression he had twice seen on his face.

As he looked, the grounds about the building came to life. Several people collected at the door of the wing, above sounded the siren of a police copter, then in the distance another, and from all sides people came running, a few at first, then more and more. The police planes landed on the lawn just outside the door of the wing, and he thought he could see the officers peeping inside. Then suddenly the lights of the wing flooded on. In control of himself now, Cliff went back.

He entered. He had left Gnut standing in thought at the side of the ramp, but now he was again in his old familiar pose in the usual place, as if he had never moved. The ship's door was closed, and the ramp gone. But the bodies, the four strangely assorted bodies, were still lying by the demolished robot attendants where he had left them in the dark.

He was startled by a cry behind his back. A uniformed museum guard was pointing at him.

"This is the man!" the guard shouted. "When I opened the door this man forced his way out and ran like the devil!"

The police officers converged on Cliff.

"Who are you? What is all this?" one of them asked him roughly.

"I'm Cliff Sutherland, picture reporter," Cliff answered calmly. "And I was the one who was inside here and ran away, as the guard says."

"What were you doing?" the officer asked, eyeing him. "And where did these bodies come from?"

"Gentlemen, I'd tell you gladly—only business first," Cliff answered. "There's been some fantastic goings on in this room, and I saw them and have the story, but"—he smiled—"I must decline to answer without advice of counsel until I've sold my story to one of the news syndicates. You know how it is. If you'd allow me the use of the radio in your plane—just for a moment, gentlemen—you'll have the whole story right afterward—say in half an hour, when the television men broadcast it. Meanwhile, believe me, there's nothing for you to do, and there'll be no loss by the delay."

The officer who had asked the questions blinked, and one of the others, quicker to react and certainly not a gentleman, stepped toward Cliff with clenched fists. Cliff disarmed him by handing him his press credentials. He glanced at them rapidly and put them in his pocket.

By now half a hundred people were there, and among them were two members of a syndicate crew whom he knew, arrived by copter. The police growled, but they let him whisper in their ear and then go out under escort to the crew's plane. There, by radio, in five minutes, Cliff made a deal which would bring him more money than he had ever before earned in a year. After that he turned over all his pictures and negatives to the crew and gave them the story, and they lost not one second in spinning back to their office with the flash.

More and more people arrived, and the police cleared the building. Ten minutes later a big crew of radio and television men forced their way in, sent there by the syndicate with which he had dealt. And then a few minutes later, under the glaring lights set up by the operators and standing close by the ship and not far from Gnut—he refused to stand underneath him—Cliff gave his story to the cameras and microphones, which in a fraction of a second shot it to every corner of the solar system.

Immediately afterward the police took him to jail. On general principles and because they were pretty blooming mad.

V

Cliff stayed in jail all that night—until eight o'clock the next morning, when the syndicate finally succeeded in digging up a lawyer and got him out. And then, when at last he was leaving, a Federal man caught him by the wrist.

"You're wanted for further questioning over at the Continental Bureau of Investigation," the agent told him. Cliff went along willingly.

Fully thirty-five high-ranking Federal officials and "big names" were waiting for him in an imposing conference room—one of the president's secretaries, the undersecretary of state, the underminister of defense, scientists, a colonel, excutives, department heads, and ranking "C" men. Old gray-mustached Sanders, chief of the CBI, was presiding.

They made him tell his story all over again, and then, in parts, all over once more—not because they did not believe him, but because they kept hoping to elicit some fact which would cast significant light on the mystery of Gnut's behavior and the happenings of the last three nights. Patiently Cliff racked his brains for every detail.

Chief Sanders asked most of the questions. After more than an hour, when Cliff thought they had finished, Sanders asked him several more, all involving his personal opinions of what had transpired.

"Do you think Gnut was deranged in any way by the

acids, rays, heat, and so forth applied to him by the scientists?"

"I saw no evidence of it."

"Do you think he can see?"

"I'm sure he can see, or else has other powers which are equivalent."

"Do you think he can hear?"

"Yes, sir. That time when I whispered to him that Stillwell was dead, he bent lower, as if to see for himself. I would not be surprised if he also understood what I said."

"At no time did he speak, except those sounds he made to open the ship?"

"Not one word, in English or any other language. Not one sound with his mouth."

"In your opinion, has his strength been impaired in any way by our treatment?" asked one of the scientists.

"I have told you how easily he handled the gorilla. He attacked the animal and threw it back, after which it retreated all the way down the building, afraid of him."

"How would you explain the fact that our autopsies disclosed no mortal wound, no cause of death, in any of the bodies—gorilla, mockingbird, or the two identical Stillwells?"—this from a medical officer.

"I can't."

"You think Gnut is dangerous?"—from Sanders.

"Potentially very dangerous."

"Yet you say you have the feeling he is not hostile."

"To me, I meant. I do have that feeling, and I'm afraid that I can't give any good reason for it, except the way he spared me twice when he had me in his power. I think maybe the gentle way he handled the bodies had something to do with it, and maybe the sad, thoughtful look I twice caught on his face."

"Would you risk staying in the building alone another night?"

"Not for anything." There were smiles.

"Did you get any pictures of what happened last night?"

"No, sir." Cliff, with an effort, held on to his composure, but he was swept by a wave of shame. A man hitherto silent rescued him by saying:

"A while ago you used the word 'purposive' in connection with Gnut's actions. Can you explain that a little?"

"Yes, that was one of the things that struck me: Gnut never seems to waste a motion. He can move with surprising speed when he wants to; I saw that when he attacked the gorilla; but most other times he walks around as if methodically completing some simple task. And that reminds me of a peculiar thing: at times he gets into one position, any position, maybe half bent over, and stays there for minutes at a time. It's as if his scale of time values was eccentric, compared to ours; some things he does surprisingly fast, and others surprisingly slow. This might account for his long periods of immobility."

"That's very interesting," said one of the scientists. "How would you account for the fact that he recently moves only at night?"

"I think he's doing something he wants no one to see, and the night is the only time he is alone."

"But he went ahead even after finding you there."

"I know. But I have no other explanation, unless he considered me harmless or unable to stop him—which was certainly the case."

"Before you arrived, we were considering encasing him in a large block of glasstex. Do you think he would permit it?"

"I don't know. Probably he would; he stood for the acids and rays and heat. But it had better be done in the daytime; night seems to be the time he moves."

"But he moved in the daytime when he emerged from the traveler with Klaatu."

"I know."

That seemed to be all they could think of to ask him. Sanders slapped his hand on the table.

"Well, I guess that's all Mr. Sutherland," he said. "Thank you for your help, and let me congratulate you for a very foolish, stubborn, brave young man—young businessman." He smiled very faintly. "You are free to go now, but it may be that I'll have to call you back later. We'll see."

"May I remain while you decide about that glasstex?" Cliff asked. "As long as I'm here I'd like to have the tip."

"The decision has already been made—the tip's yours. The pouring will be started at once."

"Thank you, sir," said Cliff—and calmly asked more: "And will you be so kind as to authorize me to be present outside the building tonight? Just outside. I've a feeling something's going to happen."

"You want still another scoop, I see," said Sanders not

unkindly, "then you'll let the police wait while you transact your business."

"Not again, sir. If anything happens, they'll get it at once."

The chief hesitated. "I don't know," he said. "I'll tell you what. All the news services will want men there, and we can't have that; but if you can arrange to represent them all yourself, it's a go. Nothing's going to happen, but your reports will help calm the hysterical ones. Let me know."

Cliff thanked him and hurried out and phoned his syndicate the tip—free—then told them Sanders' proposal. Ten minutes later they called him back, said all was arranged, and told him to catch some sleep. They would cover the pouring. With light heart, Cliff hurried over to the museum. The place was surrounded by thousands of the curious, held far back by a strong cordon of police. For once he could not get through; he was recognized, and the police were still sore. But he did not care much; he suddenly felt very tired and needed that nap. He went back to his hotel, left a call, and went to bed.

He had been asleep only a few minutes when his phone rang. Eyes shut, he answered it. It was one of the boys at the syndicate, with peculiar news. Stillwell had just reported, very much alive—the real Stillwell. The two dead ones were some kind of copies; he couldn't imagine how to explain them. He had no brothers.

For a moment Cliff came fully awake, then he went back to bed. Nothing was fantastic any more.

VI

At four o'clock, much refreshed and with an infrared viewing magnifier slung over his shoulder, Cliff passed through the cordon and entered the door of the wing. He had been expected and there was no trouble. As his eyes fell on Gnut, an odd feeling went through him, and for some obscure reason he was almost sorry for the giant robot.

Gnut stood exactly as he had always stood, the right foot advanced a little, and the same brooding expression on his face; but now there was something more. He was solidly encased in a huge block of transparent glasstex. From the floor on which he stood to the top of his full eight feet, and from there on up for an equal distance, and for about eight feet to the left, right, back, and front, he was immured in a water-clear prison which confined every inch of his surface and would prevent the slightest twitch of even his amazing muscles.

It was absurd, no doubt, to feel sorry for a robot, a man-made mechanism, but Cliff had come to think of him as being really alive, as a human is alive. He showed purpose and will; he performed complicated and resourceful acts; his face had twice clearly shown the emotion of sadness, and several times what appeared to be deep thought; he had been ruthless with the gorilla, and gentle with the mockingbird and the other two bodies, and he had twice refrained from crushing Cliff when there seemed every reason that he might. Cliff did not doubt for a minute that he was still alive, whatever that "alive" might mean.

But outside were waiting the radio and television men; he had work to do. He turned and went to them and all got busy.

An hour later Cliff sat alone about fifteen feet above the ground in a big tree which, located just across the walk from the building, commanded through a window a clear view of the upper part of Gnut's body. Strapped to the limbs about him were three instruments—his infrared viewing magnifier, a radio mike, and an infrared television eye with sound pickup. The first, the viewing magnifier, would allow him to see in the dark with his own eyes, as if by daylight, a magnified image of the robot, and the others would pick up any sights and sounds, including his own remarks, and transmit them to the several broadcast studios which would fling them millions of miles in all directions through space. Never before had a picture man had such an important assignment, probably—certainly not one who forgot to take pictures. But now that was forgotten, and Cliff was quite proud, and ready.

Far back in a great circle stood a multitude of the curious—and the fearful. Would the plastic glasstex hold Gnut? If it did not, would he come out thirsting for revenge? Would unimaginable beings come out of the traveler and release him, and perhaps exact revenge? Millions at their receivers were jittery; those in the distance hoped nothing awful would happen, yet they hoped something would, and they were prepared to run.

In carefully selected spots not far from Cliff on all sides were mobile ray batteries manned by army units, and in a hollow in back of him, well to his right, there was stationed a huge tank with a large gun. Every weapon was trained on the door of the wing. A row of smaller, faster tanks stood ready fifty yards directly north. Their ray projectors were aimed at the door, but not their guns. The grounds about the building contained only one spot—the hollow where the great tank was—where, by close calculation, a shell directed at the doorway would not cause damage and loss of life to some part of the sprawling capital.

Dusk fell; out streamed the last of the army officers, politicians, and other privileged ones; the great metal doors of the wing clanged to and were locked for the night. Soon Cliff was alone, except for the watchers at their weapons scattered around him.

Hours passed. The moon came out. From time to time Cliff reported to the studio crew that all was quiet. His unaided eyes could now see nothing of Gnut but the two faint red points of his eyes, but through the magnifier he stood out as clearly as if in daylight from an apparent distance of only ten feet. Except for his eyes, there was no evidence that he was anything but dead and unfunctionable metal.

Another hour passed. Now and again Cliff thumbed the levels of his tiny radio-television watch—only a few seconds at a time because of its limited battery. The air was full of Gnut and his own face and his own name, and once the tiny screen showed the tree in which he was then sitting and even, minutely, himself. Powerful infrared long-distance television pickups were even then focused on him from nearby points of vantage. It gave him a funny feeling.

Then, suddenly, Cliff saw something and quickly bent his eye to the viewing magnifier. Gnut's eyes were moving; at least the intensity of the light emanating from them varied. It was as if two tiny red flashlights were turned from side to side, their beams at each motion crossing Cliff's eyes.

Thrilling, Cliff signaled the studios, cut in his pickups, and described the phenomenon. Millions resonated to the excitement in his voice. Could Gnut conceivably break out of that terrible prison?

Minutes passed, the eye flashes continued, but Cliff could discern no movement or attempted movement of the robot's body. In brief snatches he described what he saw. Gnut was clearly alive; there could be no doubt he was straining against the transparent prison in which he had at last been locked fast; but unless he could crack it, no motion should show.

Cliff took his eye from the magnifier—and started. His

unaided eye, looking at Gnut shrouded in darkness, saw an astonishing thing not yet visible through his instrument. A faint red glow was spreading over the robot's body. With trembling fingers he readjusted the lens of the television eye, but even as he did so the glow grew in intensity. It looked as if Gnut's body were being heated to incandescence!

He described it in excited fragments, for it took most of his attention to keep correcting the lens. Gnut passed from a figure of dull red to one brighter and brighter, clearly glowing now even through the magnifier. And then he moved! Unmistakably he moved!

He had within himself somehow the means to raise his own body temperature, and was exploiting the one limitation of the plastic in which he was locked. For glasstex, Cliff now remembered, was a thermoplastic material, one that set by cooling and conversely would soften again with heat. Gnut was melting his way out!

In three-word snatches, Cliff described this. The robot became cherry-red, the sharp edges of the icelike block rounded, and the whole structure began to sag. The process accelerated. The robot's body moved more widely. The plastic lowered to the crown of his head, then to his neck, then his waist, which was as far as Cliff could see. His body was free! And then, still cherry-red, he moved forward out of sight!

Cliff strained eyes and ears, but caught nothing but the distant roar of the watchers beyond the police lines and a few low, sharp commands from the batteries posted around him. They, too, had heard, and perhaps seen by telescreen, and were waiting.

Several minutes passed. There was a sharp, ringing crack; the great metal doors of the wing flew open, and out stepped the metal giant, glowing no longer. He stood stockstill, and his red eyes pierced from side to side through the darkness.

Voices out in the dark barked orders and in a twinkling Gnut was bathed in narrow crisscrossing rays of sizzling, colored light. Behind him the metal doors began to melt, but his great green body showed no change at all. Then the world seemed to come to an end; there was a deafening roar, everything before Cliff seemed to explode in smoke and chaos, his tree whipped to one side so that he was nearly thrown out. Pieces of debris rained down. The tank gun had spoken, and Gnut, he was sure, had been hit.

Cliff held on tight and peered into the haze. As it cleared he made out a stirring among the debris at the door, and then dimly but unmistakably he saw the great form of Gnut rise to his feet. He got up slowly, turned toward the tank, and suddenly darted toward it in a wide arc. The big gun swung in an attempt to cover him, but the robot side-stepped and then was upon it. As the crew scattered, he destroyed its breech with one blow of his fist, and then he turned and looked right at Cliff.

He moved toward him, and in a moment was under the tree. Cliff climbed higher. Gnut put his two arms around the tree and gave a lifting push, and the tree tore out at the roots and fell crashing to its side. Before Cliff could scramble away, the robot had lifted him in his metal hands.

Cliff thought his time had come, but strange things were yet in store for him that night. Gnut did not hurt him. He looked at him from arm's length for a moment, then lifted him to a sitting position on his shoulders, legs straddling his neck. Then, holding one ankle, he turned and without hesitation started down the path which led westward away from the building.

Cliff rode helpless. Out over the lawns he saw the muzzles of the scattered field pieces move as he moved, Gnut—and himself—their one focus. But they did not fire. Gnut, by placing him on his shoulders, had secured himself against that—Cliff hoped.

The robot bore straight toward the Tidal Basin. Most of the field pieces throbbed slowly after. Far back, Cliff saw a dark tide of confusion roll into the cleared area—the police lines had broken. Ahead, the ring thinned rapidly off to the sides; then, from all directions but the front, the tide rolled in until individual shouts and cries could be made out. It came to a stop about fifty yards off, and few people ventured nearer.

Gnut paid them no attention, and he no more noticed his burden than he might a fly. His neck and shoulders made Cliff a seat hard as steel, but with the difference that their underlying muscles with each movement flexed, just as would those of a human being. To Cliff, this metal musculature became a vivid wonder.

Straight as the flight of a bee, over paths, across lawns and through thin rows of trees Gnut bore the young man, the roar of thousands of people following close. Above droned copters and darting planes, among them police cars with their nerve-shattering sirens. Just ahead lay the still waters of the Tidal Basin, and in its midst the simple marble tomb of the slain ambassador, Klaatu, gleaming black and cold in the light of the dozen searchlights always trained on it at night. Was this a rendezvous with the dead?

Without an instant's hesitation, Gnut strode down the bank and entered the water. It rose to his knees, then waist, until Cliff's feet were under. Straight through the dark waters for the tomb of Klaatu the robot made his inevitable way.

The dark square mass of gleaming marble rose higher as they neared it. Gnut's body began emerging from the water as the bottom shelved upward, until his dripping feet took the first of the rising pyramid of steps. In a moment they were at the top, on the narrow platform in the middle of which rested the simple oblong tomb.

Stark in the blinding searchlights, the giant robot walked once around it, then, bending, he braced himself and gave a mighty push against the top. The marble cracked; the thick cover slipped askew and broke with a loud noise on the far side. Gnut went to his knees and looked within, bringing Cliff well up over the edge.

Inside, in sharp shadow against the converging light beams, lay a transparent plastic coffin, thick walled and sealed against the centuries, and containing all that was mortal of Klaatu, unspoken visitor from the great Unknown. He lay as if asleep, on his face the look of godlike nobility that had caused some of the ignorant to believe him divine. He wore the robe he had arrived in. There were no faded flowers, no jewelry, no ornaments; they would have seemed profane. At the foot of the coffin lay the small sealed box, also of transparent plastic, which contained all of Earth's records of his visit—a description of the events attending his arrival, pictures of Gnut and the traveler, and the little roll of sight-and-sound film which had caught for all time his few brief motions and words.

Cliff sat very still, wishing he could see the face of the robot. Gnut, too, did not move from his position of reverent contemplation—not for a long time. There on the brilliantly lighted pyramid, under the eyes of a fearful, tumultuous multitude, Gnut paid final respect to his beautiful and adored master.

Suddenly, then, it was over. Gnut reached out and took the

little box of records, rose to his feet and started down the steps.

Back through the water, straight back to the building, across lawns and paths as before, he made his irresistible way. Before him the chaotic ring of people melted away, behind they followed as close as they dared, trampling each other in their efforts to keep him in sight. There are no television records of his return. Every pickup was damaged on the way to the tomb.

As they drew near the building, Cliff saw that the tank's projectile had made a hole twenty feet wide extending from the roof to the ground. The door still stood open, and Gnut, hardly varying his almost jerkless rhythm, made his way over the debris and went straight for the port end of the ship. Cliff wondered if he would be set free.

He was. The robot set him down and pointed toward the door; then, turning, he made the sounds that opened the ship. The ramp slid down and he entered.

Then Cliff did the mad, courageous thing which made him famous for a generation. Just as the ramp started sliding back in he skipped over it and himself entered the ship. The port closed.

VII

It was pitch dark, and the silence was absolute. Cliff did not move. He felt that Gnut was close, just ahead, and it was so.

His hard metal hand took him by the waist, pulled him against his cold side, and carried him somewhere ahead. Hidden lamps suddenly bathed the surroundings with bluish light.

He set Cliff down and stood looking at him. The young man already regretted his rash action, but the robot, except for his always unfathomable eyes, did not seem angry. He pointed to a stool in one corner of the room. Cliff quickly obeyed this time and sat meekly, for a while not even venturing to look around.

He saw he was in a small laboratory of some kind. Complicated metal and plastic apparatus lined the walls and filled several small tables; he could not recognize or guess the function of a single piece. Dominating the center of the room was a long metal table on whose top lay a large box, much like a coffin on the outside, connected by many wires to a complicated apparatus at the far end. From close above spread a cone of bright light from a many-tubed lamp.

One thing, half covered on a nearby table, did look familiar—and very much out of place. From where he sat it seemed to be a briefcase—an ordinary Earthman's briefcase. He wondered.

Gnut paid him no attention, but at once, with the narrow edge of a thick tool, sliced the lid off the little box of records. He lifted out the strip of sight-and-sound film and spent fully half an hour adjusting it within the apparatus at the end of the big table. Cliff watched, fascinated, wondering at the skill with which the robot used his tough metal fingers. This done, Gnut worked for a long time over some accessory apparatus on an adjoining table. Then he paused thoughtfully a moment and pushed inward a long rod.

A voice came out of the coffinlike box—the voice of the slain ambassador.

"I am Klaatu," it said, "and this is Gnut."

From the recording!—flashed through Cliff's mind. The first and only words the ambassador had spoken. But, then, in the very next second he saw that it was not so. There was a man in the box! The man stirred and sat up, and Cliff saw the living face of Klaatu!

Klaatu appeared somewhat surprised and spoke quickly in an unknown tongue to Gnut—and Gnut, for the first time in Cliff's experience, spoke himself in answer. The robot's syllables tumbled out as if born of human emotion, and the expression on Klaatu's face changed from surprise to wonder. They talked for several minutes. Klaatu, apparently fatigued, then began to lie down, but stopped midway, for he saw Cliff. Gnut spoke again, at length. Klaatu beckoned Cliff with his hand, and he went to him.

"Gnut has told me everything," he said in a low, gentle voice, then looked at Cliff for a moment in silence, on his face a faint, tired smile.

Cliff had a hundred questions to ask, but for a moment hardly dared open his mouth.

"But you," he began at last—very respectfully, but with an escaping excitement—"you are not the Klaatu that was in the tomb?"

The man's smile faded and he shook his head.

"No." He turned to the towering Gnut and said something in his own tongue, and at his words the metal features of the robot twisted as if with pain. Then he turned back to Cliff. "I am dying," he announced simply, as if repeating his words for the Earthman. Again to his face came the faint, tired smile.

Cliff's tongue was locked. He just stared, hoping for light. Klaatu seemed to read his mind.

"I see you don't understand," he said. "Although unlike us, Gnut has great powers. When the wing was built and the lectures began, there came to him a striking inspiration. Acting on it at once, in the night, he assembled this apparatus . . . and now he has made me again, from my voice, as recorded by your people. As you must know, a given body makes a characteristic sound. He constructed an apparatus which reversed the recording process, and from the given sound made the characteristic body."

Cliff gasped. So that was it!

"But you needn't die!" Cliff exclaimed suddenly, eagerly. "Your voice recording was taken when you stepped out of the ship, while you were well! You must let me take you to a hospital! Our doctors are very skillful!"

Hardly perceptibly, Klaatu shook his head.

"You still don't understand," he said slowly and more faintly. "Your recording had imperfections. Perhaps very slight ones, but they doom the product. All of Gnut's experiments died in a few minutes, he tells me . . . and so must I."

Suddenly, then, Cliff understood the origin of the "experiments." He remembered that on the day the wing was opened a Smithsonian official had lost a briefcase containing film strips recording the speech of various world fauna. There, on that table, was a briefcase! And the Stillwells must have been made from strips kept in the table drawer!

But his heart was heavy. He did not want this stranger to die. Slowly there dawned on him an important idea. He explained it with growing excitement.

"You say the recording was imperfect, and of course it was. But the cause of that lay in the use of an imperfect recording apparatus. So if Gnut, in his reversal of the process, had used exactly the same pieces of apparatus that your voice was recorded with, the imperfections could be studied, canceled out, and you'd live, and not die!"

As the last words left his lips, Gnut whipped around like a cat and gripped him tight. A truly human excitement was shining in the metal muscles of his face.

"Get me that apparatus!" he ordered—in clear and perfect

English! He started pushing Cliff toward the door, but Klaatu raised his hand.

"There is no hurry," Klaatu said gently; "it is too late for me. What is your name, young man?"

Cliff told him.

"Stay with me to the end," he asked. Klaatu closed his eyes and rested; then, smiling just a little, but not opening his eyes, he added: "And don't be sad, for I shall now perhaps live again . . . and it will be due to you. There is no pain—" His voice was rapidly growing weaker. Cliff, for all the questions he had, could only look on, dumb. Again Klaatu seemed to be aware of his thoughts.

"I know," he said feebly, "I know. We have so much to ask each other. About your civilization . . . and Gnut's—"

"And yours," said Cliff.

"And Gnut's," said the gentle voice again. "Perhaps . . . some day . . . perhaps I will be back—"

He lay without moving. He lay so for a long time, and at last Cliff knew that he was dead. Tears came to his eyes; in only these few minutes he had come to love this man. He looked at Gnut. The robot knew, too, that he was dead, but no tears filled his red-lighted eyes; they were fixed on Cliff, and for once the young man knew what was in his mind.

"Gnut," he announced earnestly, as if taking a sacred oath, "I'll get the original apparatus. I'll get it. Every piece of it, the exact same things."

Without a word, Gnut conducted him to the port. He made the sounds that unlocked it. As it opened, a noisy crowd of Earthmen outside trampled each other in a sudden scramble to get out of the building. The wing was lighted. Cliff stepped down the ramp.

The next two hours always in Cliff's memory had a dreamlike quality. It was as if that mysterious laboratory with the peacefully sleeping dead man was the real and central part of his life, and his scene with the noisy men with whom he talked a gross and barbaric interlude. He stood not far from the ramp. He told only part of his story. He was believed. He waited quietly while all the pressure which the highest officials in the land could exert was directed toward obtaining for him the appartus the robot had demanded.

When it arrived, he carried it to the floor of the little vestibule behind the port. Gnut was there, as if waiting. In his arms he held the slender body of the second Klaatu. Tenderly he passed him out to Cliff, who took him without a word, as if all this had been arranged. It seemed to be the parting.

Of all the things Cliff had wanted to say to Klaatu, one remained imperatively present in his mind. Now, as the green metal robot stood framed in the great green ship, he seized his chance.

"Gnut," he said earnestly, holding carefully the limp body in his arms, "you must do one thing for me. Listen carefully. I want you to tell your master—the master yet to come—that what happened to the first Klaatu was an accident, for which all Earth is immeasurably sorry. Will you do that?"

"I have known it," the robot answered gently.

"But will you promise to tell your master—just those words—as soon as he is arrived?"

"You misunderstand," said Gnut, still gently, and quietly spoke four more words. As Cliff heard them a mist passed over his eyes and his body went numb.

As he recovered and his eyes came back to focus he saw the great ship disappear. It just suddenly was not there any more. He fell back a step or two. In his ears, like great bells, rang Gnut's last words. Never, never was he to disclose them till the day he came to die.

"You misunderstand," the mighty robot had said. "I am the master."

BUTYL AND THE BREATHER

Astounding Science Fiction
October

by Theodore Sturgeon

> Sequels are almost invariably disappointing. The fire and drive that produced the first story is extremely difficult to replicate and the reader's expectations are usually too high to satisfy. This story, which is a sequel to Sturgeon's first published work ("Ether Breather"—see Volume One of this series), is one of the rare exceptions.

(I was still not old enough to vote in 1940—in those days voting age was 21. All the great writers whom I was envying and worshipping and trying to emulate were older than I was, and to my dazzled eyes *much* older. I suppose that was, in part, a bit of self-protection on my part. It excused their superiority to me and saved me from unbearable humiliation. And yet Ted Sturgeon, who was burning up the sf track in this year was only 22 years old in 1940. It's a lucky thing 22 seemed quite mature to me at the time, or I might have crawled into a hole and pulled it in after me. —I.A.)

I was still melancholic about chasing the Ether Breather out of the ken of man, the day I got that bright idea of bringing the Breather back. I should have let it stay in idea form. I should not have gone to see Berbelot about it. I also should have stayed in bed. I've got brains, but no sense. I went to see Berbelot.

He wasn't glad to see me, which he did through the televisor in his foyer. Quite a gadget, that foyer. I knew that it was an elevator to take guests up to his quarters in the mansion, the "House that Perfume Built." I hadn't known till now that it was also a highly efficient bouncing mechanism. I had no sooner passed my hand over the sensitized plate that served as a doorbell when his face appeared on the screen. He said "Hmph! Hamilton!" and next thing I knew the foyer's walls had extended and pinned me tight. I was turned upside down, shaken twice, and then dropped on my ear outside the house. I think he designed that bouncer just for me. He was a nice old boy, but, man, how he could hang on to a grouch. A whole year, this one had lasted. Just because I had been tactless with the Breather.

I got up and dusted myself off and swore I'd never bother the irascible old heel again. And then I hunted a drugstore to call him up. That's the way it was. Berbelot was a peculiar duck. His respect for me meant more than anger against him could make up for. He was the only man I ever met that ever made me sorry for anything.

I went into the visiphone booth and pressed my identification tab against the resilient panel on the phone. That made a record of the call so I could be billed for it. Then I dialed Berbelot. I got his bun-faced valet.

"I want to speak to Mr. Berbelot, Cogan."

"Mr. Berbelot is out, Mr. Hamilton."

"So!" I snapped, my voice rising. "You're the one who tossed me out just now with that salesman mangler on your doorstep! I'll macerate you, you subatomic idiot!"

"Oh . . . I . . . I didn't, Mr. Hamilton, really. I—"

"Then if you didn't Berbelot did. If he did, he's home. Incidentally, I saw him in the viewplate. Enough of the chit-chat, doughface. Tell him I want to speak to him."

"B-but he won't speak to you, Mr. Hamilton. He gave strict orders a year ago."

"Tell him I've thought of a way to get in touch with the Ether Breather again. Go on. He won't fire you, you crumb from the breadline. He'll kiss you on both cheeks. Snap into it!"

The screen went vacant as he moved away, and I heard Berbelot's voice—"I thought I told you"—and then the bumble of Cogan's, and then "WHAT!" from the old man, and another short bumble that was interrupted by Berbelot's sliding to a stop in front of the transmitter. "Hamilton," he said sternly into the visiplate, "if this is a joke of yours . . . if you think you can worm your way into my confidence with . . . if you dare to lead me on some wild-goose cha . . . if you—"

"If you'll give me a chance, King of Stink," I said, knowing that if I got him really mad he'd listen to me, being the type that got speechless with rage, "I'll give you the dope. I have an idea that I think will bring the Breather back, but it's up to you to carry it out. You have the apparatus."

"Come up," he whispered, his wattles quivering. "But I warn you, if you dare to take this liberty on a bluff, I shall most certainly have you pried loose from your esophagus."

"Comin' up!" I said. "By the way, when I get into that foyer again, please be sure which button you push."

"Don't worry," he growled, "I have a dingus up here that is quite as efficient. It throws people from the sixtieth floor. Do come up." The screen darkened. I sighed and started for the "House that Perfume Built."

The elevator glided to a stop that made my stomach feel puffy, and I stepped out. Berbelot was standing in front of it looking suspicious as a pawnbroker. I held out my hand with some remark about how swell it was to see him again, and he just stared at it. When I thought he was going to forego the honor of shaking it, he put his hand into mine, withdrew it quickly, looked at it, and wiped it carefully on his jacket. Without his saying a word I gathered that he wasn't glad to see me, that he thought I was an undesirable and unsanitary character, and that he didn't trust me.

"Did I ever tell you," I said as calmly as I could, "that I am terribly sorry about what happened?"

Berbelot said, "I knew a man who said that after he murdered somebody. They burned him anyway."

I thought that was very nice. "Do you want to find out about my idea or not?" I gritted. "I don't have to stay here to be insulted."

"I realize that. You're insulted everywhere, I imagine. Well, what's your idea?"

I saw Cogan hovering over the old man's shoulder and threw my hat at him. Since Berbelot apparently found it difficult to be hospitable, I saved him the trouble of inviting me to sit down by sitting down.

"Berbelot," I said, when I had one of his best cigarettes fuming as nicely as he was, "you're being unreasonable. But I have you interested, and as long as that lasts you'll be sociable. Sit down. I am about to be Socratic. It may take a little while."

"I suffer." He sat down. "I suffer exceedingly." He paused, and then added pensively, "I never thought I could be so irritated by anyone who bored me. Go ahead, Hamilton."

I closed my eyes and counted ten. Berbelot could manufacture more printable invective than anyone I ever met.

"Question one," I said. "What is the nature of the creature you dubbed Ether Breather?"

"Why, it's a ... well, apparently a combination of etheric forces, living in and around us. It's as if the air in this room were a thinking animal. What are you—"

"I'll ask questions. Now, will you grant it intelligence?"

"Of course. A peculiar kind, though. It seems to be motivated by a childish desire to have fun—mostly at some poor human's expense."

"But its reactions were reasonable, weren't they?"

"Yes, although exaggerated. It reached us through color television; that was its only medium of expression. And it raised particular hell with the programs—a cosmic practical joker, quite uninhibited, altogether unafraid of any consequences to itself. And then when you, you blockhead, told it that it had hurt someone's feelings and that it ought to get off the air, it apologized and was never heard from again. Again an exaggerated reaction. But what has that got to do with—"

"Everything. Look; you made it laugh easily. You made it ashamed of itself easily. It cried easily. If you really want to get in touch with it again, you just have to go on from there."

Berbelot pressed a concealed button and the lights took on a greenish cast. He always claimed a man thought more clearly under a green light. "I'll admit that that particular thought sequence has escaped me," he nodded, "since I do not have a mind which is led astray by illogical obscurities. But in all justice to you—not that you deserve anything approaching a compliment—I think you have something there. I suppose that is as far as you have gone, though. I've spent hours on the problem. I've called that creature for days on end on a directional polychrome wave. I've apologized to it and pleaded with it and begged it and told it funny stories and practically asked it to put its invisible feet out of my television receiver so I could kiss them. And never a whisper have I had. No, Hamilton; the Ether Breather is definitely miffed, peeved, and not at home. And it's all your fault."

"Once," I said dreamily, "I knew a woman whose husband went astray. She knew where he was, and sent him message after message. She begged and she pleaded and she wept into visiphones. It didn't get her anywhere. Then she got a bright idea. She sent him a tele-facsimile letter, written on her very best stationery. It described in great detail the nineteen different kinds of heel she thought he was."

"I don't know what this has to do with the Breather, but what happened?" asked Berbelot.

"Why, he got sore. He got so sore he dropped everything and ran home to take a poke at her!"

"Ah," said Berbelot. "And the Breather laughs easily, and you think it would—"

"It would," I nodded, "get angry easily, if we could find the right way to do it."

Berbelot rubbed his long hands together and beamed. "You're a hot-headed fool, Hamilton, and I'm convinced that your genius is a happy accident quite unattached to your hypothetical mind. But I must congratulate you for the idea. In other words, you think if we get the Breather sore enough, it will try to get even, and contact us some way or other? I'll be darned!"

"Thought you'd like it," I said.

"Well, come on," he said testily. "What are we waiting for? Let's go down to the laboratory!" Suddenly he stopped. "Er . . . Hamilton . . . this story of yours. Did that man poke his wife after he got home?"

"I dunno," I said blankly. "I just made up the story to illustrate my point. Could be."

"Hm-m-m. If the Breather decided to . . . I mean, it's a big creature, you know, and we have no idea—"

"Oh, never mind that," I laughed, "the Breather can't get past a television screen!"

Which only goes to show you how little I knew about the Ether Breather.

I was amazed by Berbelot's laboratory museum. Did you know that in the old days more than two hundred years ago, they used electrically powered sets with a ground glass, fluorescent screen built right into the end of huge cathode tubes? Imagine. And before that, they used a revolving disk with holes punctured spirally, as a scanning mechanism! They had the beginnings of frequency modulation, though. But their sets were so crude, incredible as it may seem, that atmospheric disturbances caused interference in reception! Berbelot had copies of all these old and laughable attempts at broadcasting and receiving devices.

"All right, all right," he snapped, elbow-deep in one of the first polychrome transmitters, "you've been here before. Come over here and give me a hand. You're gawking like a castor bean farmer."

I went over and followed his directions as he spot-welded, relayed, and wound a coil or two of hair-fine wire. "My gosh," I marveled, "how did you ever learn so much about television, Berbelot? I imagine it must have used up a little of your spare time to make a fortune in the perfume business."

He laughed. "I'll tell you, Hamilton," he said. "Television and perfumery are very much alike. You know yourself that no such lovely women ever walk the Earth as you see every day in the news broadcasts. For the last eighty years, since the Duval shade selector was introduced, television has given flawless complexions to all the ladies that come over the air, and bull-shoulders to all the men. It's all very phony, but it's nice to look at. Perfumery is the same proposition. A woman who smelled like a rose petal naturally would undoubtedly have something the matter with her. But science gets to work on what has been termed, through the ages, as 'B.O.' My interest in esthetically deluding the masses led me to both sciences."

"Very ingenious," I said, "but it isn't going to help you to make the Breather sore."

"My dear boy," he said, "don't be obtuse. Oh, turn down the nitrogen jets a trifle—that's it." He skillfully spotted seven leads into the video-circuit of the polychrome wave generator. "You see," he went on, running the leads over to a box control with five push buttons and a rheostat set into it, "the Breather requires very special handling. It knows us and how our minds work, or it could never have thought, for instance, of having our secretary of state recite risqué verse over the air, the first time that official used color television. Now, you are noteworthy for your spontaneity. How would you go about angering this puff of etheric wind?"

"Well, I'd . . . I'd tell it it was a dirty so-and-so. I'd insult it. I'd say it was a sissy and dare it to fight. I . . . I'd—"

"That's what I thought," said Berbelot unkindly. "You'd cuss it out in your own foul idiom, forgetting that it has no pride to take down, and, as far as we know, no colleagues, communities, enamoratae, or fellows to gossip to. No, Hamilton, we can't insult it. It can insult us because it knows what we are and how we think, but we know nothing of it."

"How else can you get a being sore, then, when you can't hold it up to ridicule or censure before itself or its fellow creatures?"

"By doing something to it personally that it won't like."

"Yeah—take a poke at it. Kick it in its vibrations. Stick a knife into its multiple personality."

Berbelot laughed. "To change the subject, for no apparent reason," he said, "have you ever run across my *Vierge Folle?*"

"A new perfume? Why, no."

Berbelot crossed the room and came back with a handful of tiny vials. "Here."

I sniffed. It was a marvelously delicate scent. It was subtle, smooth, calling up a mental picture of the veins in fine ivory. "Mmm. Nice."

"Try this one," he said. I did. It was fainter than the other; I had to draw in a lot of it before I detected the sweet, faint odor. "It's called *Casuiste*," said Berbelot. "Now try this one. It's much fainter, you'll have to really stretch to get it at all."

"Nice business," I grinned. "Making the poor unsuspecting male get inside the circle of the vixen's arms before he's under her spell." I'd been reading some of his ad proofs. He chuckled. "That's about the idea. Here."

Berbelot handed me the vial and I expelled all the air in my lungs, hung my nose over the lip of the tube and let the air in with a roar. Next thing I knew I was strangling, staggering, swearing and letting go murderous rights and lefts at empty air. I thought I was going to die and I wished I could. When I blinked the tears out of my eyes, Berbelot was nowhere to be seen. I raged around the laboratory and finally saw him whisk around behind a massive old photoelectric transmitter. With a shriek I rushed him. He got practically inside the machine and I began taking it apart, with the firm conviction that I would keep on taking things apart long after I reached him. Luckily for him there were four thick busbars between us. He crouched behind them giggling until I reached a red-eyed state of wheezing impotence.

"Come out!" I gasped. "You ape-faced arthritic, come out of there and I'll hit you so hard you'll throttle on your shoelaces!"

"That," he said instructively, "was a quadruple quintessence of musk." He grinned. "Skunk." He looked at me and laughed outright. "Super-skunk."

I wrenched ineffectually at the bars. "A poor thing, but your very own, I'll bet," I said. "I am going to stick your arm so far down your neck you'll digest your fingernails."

"Mad, aren't you?"

"Huh?"

"I said, you're sore. I didn't cuss you out, or hold you up to ridicule, or anything, and look how mad you are!"

I began to see the light. Make the Breather angry by—

"What are you gibbering about?"

He took out a white handkerchief and waved it as he unwrapped his own body from the viscera of the old-fashioned transmitter. I had to grin. What can you do with a man like that?

"O.K.," I said. "Peace, brother. But I'd suggest you treat the Breather better than you just treated me. And how in blazes you expect to get a smell like that through a polychrome transmitter is a little beyond me."

"It isn't simple," he said, "but I think it can be done. Do you know anything about the wave theory of perception?"

"Not a helluva lot," I said. "Something about a sort of spectrum arrangement of the vibrations of sensory perception, isn't it?"

"Mmm . . . yes. Thought waves are of high-frequency, and although ether-borne, not of an electromagnetic character. So also are the allied vibrations, taste and smell. Sound, too."

"Wait a minute! Sound is a purely physical vibration of air particles against our auditory apparatus."

"Of course—from the source of the sound *to* that apparatus. But from the inner ear to the hearing center in the brain, it is translated into a wave of the spectrum group I'm talking about. So with touch and sight."

"I begin to see what you're driving at. But how can you reach the Breather with these waves—providing you can produce and transmit them?"

"Oh, I can do that. Simply a matter of stepping up high-frequency emanations."

"You seem pretty confident that the Breather will be affected by the same waves that influence our senses."

"I wouldn't use the same waves. That's why I brought up the spectrum theory. Now look; we'll take thought waves of the purely internal psyche . . . the messages that relay brain impulses to different brain centers. Pure thought, with no action; pure imagery. These are of a certain wave length. We'll call it 1000. Now, take the frequencies of smell, touch and sight waves. They're 780, 850, and 960 respectively. Now, how did we contact the Ether Breather?"

"By the polychrome wave."

"That's right."

"And you mean that the ratio—"

Berbelot nodded. "The ratio between the Breather's thought waves and its sensory vibrations must be the same as that between ours."

"Why must it be?"

"Because its mental reactions are the same, as I told you before—only exaggerated. It reasons as we do, more or less. Its mental set-up corresponds with ours."

"Doggone," I said admiringly, "it's all so simple when you're told how to do it. You mean, then, to discover the ratio between what is to me a pain in the neck, and what it would be to the Breather."

"That's it. But it won't be a pain in the neck."

"Where will it be, then?"

"You're tuning in the wrong frequency," he chuckled. "I'm going to make him suffer the best way I know how, and—my business is perfumery."

"Ah," I breathed.

"Now, I'm going to cook up something really pretty. I'm going to turn out a stench that will make the Breather's illimitable edges curl!"

"From the smell of the essence of ancient egg you just gassed me with," I said, "it ought to be pretty."

"It will be. Let's see; for a base we'll use butyl mercaptan. Something sweet, and something sour—"

"—something borrowed and something blue."

"Don't be a silly romanticist." He was busy at his chemical bench. "I'll scorch a little pork fat and . . . ah. Attar of roses."

For a moment he was quiet, carefully measuring drops of liquid into a sealed exciter. Then he flipped the switch and came over to me. "It'll be ready in a jiffy. Let's rig up the transmitter."

We did as we had done before, a year ago. We maneuvered the transmitting cells of the polychrome transmitter over and above a receiver. It would send to Berbelot's country place eight hundred miles away by a directional beam, and return the signal by wire. If the Breather interfered, it would show up on the receiver. When we had done it before, we had had the odd experience of holding a conversation with our own images on the screen.

"Now I'll distill my *odeur d'ordure*," he said, "and when it's run through, you can be my guinea pig."

"Not on your life, Berbelot," I said, backing away. He grinned and went about fixing his still. It was a beautiful little glass affair, and he worked entirely under a huge bell jar in transferring it from the exciter. Butyl and burned meat and attar of roses. My gosh.

In half an hour it was ready—a dusty-brown colloid, just a few drops in the retort. "Come on, Hamilton," said Berbelot, "just a little sniff. I want to give you a preview."

"Uh-uh!" I snorted. "Here—wait."

I gave a buzz on the buzzer, and in a couple of seconds Cogan, Berbelot's valet, popped in. Cogan's face always reminded me, for some reason, of a smorgasbord tray.

"Did you bring your nose?" I asked, leading him over to the chemical bench.

"Yessir."

"Well"—I slid back the little panel in the neck of the retort, standing at arm's length—"stick it in there."

"Oh, but I—" He looked plaintively toward Berbelot, who smiled.

"Well . . . oh!" The "Well" was diffidence, and the "Oh" was when I grabbed him by the collar and stuck his face in the warm fumes.

Cogan went limp and stiffened so fast that he didn't move. He rose slowly, as if the power of that mighty stench was lifting him by the jawbone, turned around twice with his eyes streaming, and headed for the door. He walked lightly and slowly on the balls of his feet, with his arms bent and half raised, like a somnambulist. He walked smack into the doorpost, squeaked, said "oh . . . my . . . goodness—" faintly, and disappeared into the corridor.

"Well," said Berbelot pensively. "I really think that that stuff smells bad."

"Seems as though," I grinned. "I . . . oh, boy!" I ran to the retort and closed the slide. "Good gosh! Did we give him a concentrated shot of *that*?"

"*You* did."

It permeated the room, and of all malodorous effluvia, it was the most noisome. It was rotten celery, than which there is no more sickening smell in nature. It was rancid butter. It was bread-mold. It was garlic garnishing fermented Limburger. It was decay. It was things running around on six legs, mashed. It was awful.

"Berbelot," I gasped, "you don't want to kill the Breather."

"It won't kill him. He just won't like it."

"Check. *Whew!*" I mopped my face. "Now how are you going to get it up to the Ether Breather?"

"Well, we'll use the olfactometer on it," he said.

"What's that?"

"Trade gadget. I knocked it together years ago. Without it I wouldn't have made a cent in this business." He led me over to a stand on which was an enormously complicated machine, all glittering relays and electratomic bridges. "Good heavens!" I said. "What does it do—play music?"

"Maybe you wondered why I could reel off so much about the wave theory of sensory perception," he said. "Look—see these dials? And this sensitized knob?"

"Yeah?"

"That fist size, faceted knob has each of its twelve hundred and two sides coated with a different chemical reagent, very sensitive. I drop it into a smell—"

"You *what?*"

"You heard me. An odor is an emanation of gases from the smellable specimen, constituting a loss of mass of about one fifty-billionth in a year, more or less, depending on the strength of the odor and the consistency of the emanating body. Now, I expose this knob to our Cogan-crusher"—he walked over to the retort with the knob in his hand, trailing its cable, and slid the panel back a bit—"and the gas touches every surface. Each reacts if it can. The results are collected, returned to the olfactometer, translated into a number on the big dial."

"And that is—"

"The ratio I spoke to you about. See . . . the dial reads just 786. With the frequency of abstract thought set arbitrarily at one thousand, we have a ratio between this smell and thought."

"Take it easy, Berbelot. I'm a layman."

He smiled. "That gives us an equation to work with. 786 is to 1000 as x is to our polychrome wave."

"Isn't that a little like mixing liquor?" I said. "One set of figures is in thought vibrations, the other in radio waves."

"Ratios are like that," he reminded me. "I can have one-third as many apples as you have oranges, no matter how many or how few oranges you have."

"I consider myself stood in the corner," I said. "By golly, with that gadget, no wonder your perfumes are practically a monopoly nowadays. Would it be giving away a trade secret to tell me what went into that *Doux Rêves* of yours? How on earth did you figure out that odor? It'll make a ninety-year-old woman put on lipstick and a centenarian buy spats."

He laughed. "Sure, I'll tell you. *Doux Rêves* is 789.783 on that dial, which happens to be the smell of a rich juicy steak! But they don't associate it with steak when they buy it—at three hundred an ounce. It just smells like something desirable."

"Berbelot, you're chiseling the public."

"Mmmm-hm. That's why I pay half a billion in income tax every year. Get over on that bench."

"In front of the receiver? What are you going to do?"

"Oh, I'll have to be over here by the transmitter. I've got to adjust a carrier wave that will have the right ratio to the polychrome wave. Don't turn on the receiver yet."

I sat down. This amazing man was about to pull something unheard of. I didn't feel comfortable about it, either. How could he be so confident? He didn't know much about the Breather, any more than I did. He was acting like a man in perfect control of everything—which he was—who didn't have to worry about taking a rap for what he was about to do. Well, he built that smell, didn't he? I didn't. I could always blame him for it, even if I was the instigator. I remember wondering if I'd be able to convince the Ether Breather of that, in case the Breather got tough. Oh, well.

"O.K., Hamilton. Turn her on!"

I did so, and a few seconds later the transmitting floods clicked on. From the suspended bank of cells came a hum as soft as their soft glow. The screen flickered and cleared, and I saw myself in it, almost as if I were looking into a mirror, except that my image was not reversed. "O.K., Berbelot."

"Right. Here goes a shot of Berbelot's *Essence of Evil!*"

I heard a switch click and then the faint grate of a rheostat. I stared at my image and my image stared back, and Berbelot came and stood where he could see me. It was only later that I remembered noticing that he was careful to stand out of range of the transmitter. The image didn't change—each tiny movement was mine, each facial twist, each—

"Look!" snapped Berbelot, and faded back to his switchboard again.

For a moment I didn't notice anything in particular, and then I saw it, too. The smallest possible twitching of the nostrils. A sudden little movement of the head. And then a just audible sniffing through the speaker. As suddenly the movement stopped.

"You got something that time, Berbelot," I yelped, "but it seems to have gone away again. The image is true."

"Splendid!" said the old man. He clicked off the transmitter and the receiving screen glowed blankly. "Now listen. I only gave it about as much as we got a few minutes ago when you left the slide open. This time I'm going to give it what you gave poor Cogan!"

"My gosh! What am I supposed to do?"

"Sit tight! If and when the Breather starts kicking, give it right back to him. Don't admit that we did it to coax him back, or, being what he . . . it . . . is, he'll just get coy and disappear again."

"I think you're right. Want me to get him real mad, then?"

"For a while. Then we'll sign off and go to work on him tomorrow. After a bit we'll tell him the whole story; he'll think it's funny. Having fun seems to be his reason for living—if you can call that supercosmic existence living. Then he'll be appeased. Y'know Hamilton, if we get him running errands for us he might make us a nice piece of change. We could buy up an advertising agency and have him blank out all competition with his typically wise-guy sort of interference, for instance."

"You think of everything! All right, let's go!"

The floods and cells lit up again, and in a few seconds I was staring at myself in the screen. It made me feel a little queasy. There I was looking at myself, looking at myself, looking at myself, as it were. It dizzied me.

The rheostat twirled over, and an auxiliary somewhere deep in the complicated transmitter moaned quietly. For about five minutes I strained my eyes, but not by the slightest sign did my image show that it sensed anything off-color.

"Are you sure your gadgets are working all right?" I asked Berbelot.

"Absolutely. Nothing yet? I'll be darned. Wait. A little more juice here, and I think I can build that smell up a—"

"What goes on here?" roared the speaker.

I stared. I was still seated, but my image was rising slowly. One odd thing about it—when it had been my true image, it showed me from the waist up. As it rose from the bench in the picture, it had no legs. Apparently the Breather could only distort just those waves that were transmitted. A weird sight.

I'd never have known that as my face. It was twisted, and furious, and altogether unpleasant.

"Are you doing that, punk?" it asked me.

"Wh-what?"

"Don't be like that," whispered Berbelot. He was off to one side, staring entranced and exultant into the receiver. "Give'm hell, Ham!" I drew a deep breath. "Am I doing what, and who's a punk?" I asked the receiver pugnaciously.

"That stink, and you are."

"Yeah, I'm doing it, and who are you to call me one?"

"Well, cut it out, and who do I look like?"

"I wish you boys would have one conversation at a time," said Berbelot.

"None of your lip, pantywaist," I told the Breather, "or I'll come out there and plaster your shadow with substance."

"Wise guy, huh? Why, you insignificant nematode!"

"You etheric regurgitation!"

"You little quadridimensional stinkpot!"

"You faceless, formless, fightless phantasm!" I was beginning to enjoy this.

"Listen, mug, if you don't stop that business of smelling up my environment I'll strain you through a sheet of plate glass."

"Try it and I'll knock you so flat you'll call a plane a convex hemisphere."

"If you had the guts that God gave a goose, you'd come up here and fight me."

"If you weren't about as dangerous as a moth on a battle cruiser, you'd come down here and fight."

"Touché," said Berbelot.

"Oh, yeah?" said the Breather.

"Yeah."

"Cliché," said Berbelot.

"I don't like your face," said the Breather.

"Take it off then."

"Not as long as I can insult you by making you look at it."

"It's more of a face to brag about than you got."

"Why, you hair-mantled, flint-hurling, aboriginal anthropophagus!"

Berbelot clicked off both transmitter and receiver. It was only then that I realized the Breather had made me see red. I was in the laboratory, on my feet, all set to take a swing at a thousand-dollar television set.

"What'd you do that for?" I snapped, turning on Berbelot.

"Easy, lad, easy!" he laughed. "The Breather's had enough, in the first place. In the second place, he was quoting Carlyle, an ancient seventeenth or eighteenth century author. You ran him plumb out of originality. You did fine!"

"Thanks," I said, wiping my fevered brow. "Think he was sore?"

"I gathered as much. We'll work on him in the morning. I'm going to leave the smell on—just a suggestion of it, so he won't forget us."

"Don't you think he'll start messing up commercial programs again?"

"No. He knows where the trouble is coming from. He's too sore just now to think of anything but that source. He might think of the commercials later on, but if there's any danger of that we'll wise him up and laugh the whole thing off."

"Darned if you don't get me into the doggonedest things," I said wonderingly.

He chuckled, and slapped me on the back. "Go on upstairs and get Cogan to feed you. I'll be along soon; I have some work to do. You're spending the night here, my boy."

I thanked him and went upstairs. I should have gone home.

I was dog tired, but before I thought of going to bed I had some figuring to do. It had been a delicious meal, though from the way Cogan acted I thought dark thoughts about arsenic in the coffee and or a knife in the back. But the room he had shown me to was a beauty. Berbelot, as I should have expected, was as good at decorating as he was at anything else. The place was finished in chrome and gray and black, the whole thing centering around a huge mirror at one end. Building a room around a mirror is the most complimentary thing a host can do in a guest room.

It was a fascinating mirror, too. It wasn't exactly silvered—it was of a dull gray sheen, like rough-finished stainless steel. And whether it was metal or glass I couldn't tell. It gave a beautiful image—deep and true, and accentuating natural color. Probably something he "knocked together" himself.

I walked up and down absently, thinking about Berbelot and the Breather. They had a lot in common. No one could tell exactly what they were, or how great, or how powerful. Thinking about the Breather's series of cracks at me, I realized that he, or it, had spoken exactly in my idiom. Berbelot did that, too. And yet I knew that both of them could have completely swamped me with dialectical trickery.

My shadow caught my eye and I amused myself for a moment by making shadows on the wall opposite the mirror. A bird—a cat—a funny face. I'd done it ever since I was a kid and the thing fascinated me. I was pretty good at it. I wandered around the room making shadow pictures on the wall and thinking about the Breather and Berbelot, and then found myself looking into that deep mirror.

"Hi!" I said to my reflection.

It looked out at me placidly. Not a bad-looking guy, in a pair of Berbelot's cellusilk pajamas and that cocky expression. That was quite a mirror. What was it that made a guy look different? The color trick? Not entirely. Let's see. I stuck out my tongue and so did my reflection. I thumbed my nose, and turned cold inside. I knew now what it was.

The image was—not reversed.

I stood there with my right arm up, my right thumb to my nose. The reflection's right arm—the one toward my left, since it was facing me—was raised, and it thumbed its nose. I was white as a sheet.

Was I bats? Did I have a mental hangover from seeing that unreversed image in the television set downstairs?

"This is awful," I said.

It couldn't be a mirror. Not even Berbelot could build a— or was it a mirror? A—a television screen? Couldn't be—not with the depth it had. It was almost as if I were standing in front of a glass cabinet, looking at me inside. The image was three dimensional. I suddenly decided I had been thumbing my nose long enough. This must be some trick of that old devil's, I thought. No wonder he didn't have dinner with me. He was rigging up this gadget while I was eating. If it *was* a television screen—and I'd never heard of one like this—then that thing in there wasn't me—it was the Ether Breather. I listened carefully, and sure enough, heard the hum of transmitting cells. What a gag! There were cells somewhere hidden in this room sending my image away and returning it by wire! But that screen—

My reflection suddenly set its legs apart and put its hands on its hips. "What are you looking at?" it asked me.

"N-nothing," I said as sarcastically as I could while my teeth were chattering. "The Breather again, huh?"

"That's right. My, but you're ugly."

"Mind your tongue!" I said sharply. "I can switch you off, you know."

"Heh!" he jeered. "I don't have to be afraid of that any more, thanks to a trick you just showed me."

"Yeah? You can't kid me, bud. You're just some amoral cosmic ray's little accident."

"I warn you, don't get tough with me."

"I'll do what I please. You couldn't pull your finger out of a tub of lard," I euphemized.

He sighed. "O.K. You asked for it."

And then I had to live through the worst thing that any poor mortal in the history of the world ever experienced. It's one thing to have an argument with yourself in the mirror. It's something entirely different to have your reflection reach out a leg, kick down the mirror with a shattering crash, walk up to you and belt you in the mouth a couple of times before it smears you on the carpet with a terrific right hook. That's what happened to me. Just that, so help me, Hannah.

I lay there on the rug looking up at me, which had just socked I, and I said "Whooie!" and went to sleep.

I've no idea how long I lay there. When light glimmered into my jarred brain again, Berbelot was kneeling beside me chafing my wrists. The beautiful mirror—or whatever the devil it was—was in some thousand-odd pieces on the floor, and I had gone to about as many pieces psychically. I finally realized that Berbelot was saying something.

"Hamilton! What happened? What happened? Do you realize you just busted thirty thousand dollars' worth of apparatus? What's the matter with you . . . are you sick?"

I rolled over and sat up, then went hand over hand up Berbelot until I was standing beside him. My head felt like a fur-lined ball of fire and every time my heart beat it blinded me.

"What did you wreck that receiver for?" Berbelot said irascibly.

"Me wreck it? Me didn't wreck it . . . I wrecked it," I said groggily. "I was standing in front of the mirror when who should kick it down and poke me but myself"—I shook my head and let the pain of it shake my carcass—"Ow! *Whew.* I was just—"

"Stop it!" Berbelot snapped.

Almost suddenly I recovered. "Receiver . . . what do you mean receiver?"

Berbelot was hopping mad. "The new job," he shouted, pointing at the debris. "My first three-dimensional television receiver!"

"Three . . . what are you talking about, man?"

He calmed down the way he invariably did when he was

asked a question about television. "It's a box of tiny projectors," he said. "They're set . . . studded . . . inside that closet affair behind the screen you just broke. The combined beams from them give a three-dimensional, or stereoscopic, effect. And now you've gone and wrecked my screen," he wailed. "Why were you ever born? Why must I suffer so because of you? Why—"

"Wait a minute, Pop—hold on there. I didn't bust your precious screen."

"You just said you did."

"Mmm-mm. So help me. It was the Breather. I had a little argument with him and he kicked down the screen and came out and beat the stern off me."

"What?" Berbelot was really shocked this time. "You're a gibbering maniac! That was your own image! You were broadcast and your image reproduced there!"

"You're a muddy-headed old stink-merchant!" I bellowed. "I suppose I kicked down your mirror, put three teeth on hinges, and then knocked myself colder'n a cake of carbon-ice just for a chance to lie to you!"

"This is what comes of getting an overgrown cretin to help out in an experiment," moaned Berbelot. "Don't try my patience any more, Hamilton!"

"*Your* patience? What the hell was that new-fangled set doing in this room anyway?"

He grinned weakly. "Oh—that. Well, I just wanted to have some fun with you. After you left I tuned in on the Breather and told him to stand by; I'd put him in touch with . . . with the guy that was smelling up his world."

"You old crumb! Fun! You wanted me to argue with that misplaced gamma-particle all night, hey? Why, I ought to . . . I think I will at that!" And I grabbed him by the neck.

"Allow *me*," said a voice behind us, and we were seized, each by a shoulder. Then our heads were cracked violently together and we found ourselves groveling at the feet of my spittin' image. Berbelot looked up at my erstwhile reflection in silent awe.

"Where were you?" I growled.

"In the corner," he said, throwing a thumb over his shoulder. "You're a pretty-looking pair, I must say."

"Berbelot," I said, "meet your Ether Breather. Now I'm going to stand on your face until you eat the shoes off my feet, because you called me a liar."

Berbelot said, "Well, I'm damned!"

The Breather remarked quietly, "You two better explain yourselves in a hysterical hurry. Otherwise I shall most certainly take you apart and put you together again, alternating the pieces."

"Oh, we were just trying to get in contact with you again."

"What for?"

"We were interested in you. We talked to you a year or so ago and then you disappeared. We wanted to talk to you again." In spite of my anger at him I found something else to admire Berbelot for. He had remembered the Breather's peculiar childishness and was using it just when somebody had to do something, quickly.

"But you told me to stop interfering!" Presto—the creature was already plaintive, on the amicable defensive. Its mutability was amazing.

"He told you," Berbelot snorted, indicating me, where I rolled and moaned over my twice-bruised sconce. "I didn't."

"Don't you speak for each other, then? We do."

"You—singular and plural—are a homogeneous being. All humanity is not blessed with my particularly affable nature."

"Why you old narcissist!" I snorted, and lunged at him. For every inch of my lunge the Breather calmly kicked me back a foot. I did some more moaning.

"You mean you are my friend and he is not?" said the Breather, staring at me coldly as one does at a roach which is going to be stepped on if and when it moves out from the wall.

"Oh, I wouldn't go so far as to say that," said Berbelot kindly.

I had an inspiration which, for all I know, saved my life. "You said you learned from me how to come out of the television set!" I blurted.

"True. I should be grateful for that, I suppose. I shall not tear you in little pieces." He turned to Berbelot. "I heard your call, of course, but being told once was enough for me. I did not understand. When I say anything I generally mean it. Humans are not understandable, but they are very funny."

The scientist in Berbelot popped up. "What was that you said about Hamilton showing you how to come out of the set?"

"Oh, I was watching him from the screen over there. I am sorry I broke it. He was walking around the room making pictures on the walls with shadows. That's what I am doing now."

"Shadow pictures?"

"Certainly. I am a creature living in five dimensions and aware of four, just as you live in four dimensions and are aware of three. He made three-dimensional shadows that were projected on a two-dimensional surface. I am making four dimensional pictures that are being projected in three dimensions."

Berbelot frowned. "On what surface?"

"On that of your fourth dimension, of course."

"Our fourth. Hm-m-m . . . with what light source?"

"A five-dimensional one just as your sun, for instance, has four."

"How many dimensions are there altogether?"

"How high is up?" twinkled the Breather.

"Could I project myself into your world?"

"I don't know. Maybe . . . maybe not. Are you going to stop making that awful smell?" he said suddenly.

"Of course! We only made it to get you angry enough to come to us for a talk. We didn't mean anything by it."

"Oh!" squealed the Ether Breather delightedly. "A joke! Fun!"

"Told you he'd take it well," murmured Berbelot.

"Yeah . . . suppose he hadn't? You're a rat, Berbelot. You made darn sure that if someone had to take a rap for this aeration here, it wouldn't be you. Nice guy." There was a strained silence for a while, and then I grinned. "Aw, hell, you had it doped out, Berbelot. Shake. I'd have done the same if I had the brains."

"He isn't bad at all, is he?" asked the Breather in surprise, staring at me.

"Well, is everything all right now, Breather? Do you feel that you're welcome to come any time you wish?"

"Yes . . . yes, I think so. But I won't come this way again. I can only take form in that lovely new three-dimensional machine of yours, and I have to break a screen to get out. I am sorry. I'll talk to you any time, though. And may I do something for you sometime?"

"Why should you?" I piped up glumly.

"Oh, think of the *fun* we'll have!"

"Would you really like to do something for us?"

"Oh, yes. Please."

"Can you direct that interference of yours into any radio frequency at any time?"

"Sure."

"Now look. We are going to start a company to advertise certain products. There are other companies in the same business. Will you leave our programs strictly alone and have all the fun you want with our competitors?"

"I'd love that!"

"That will be splendid!"

"Berbelot, we're rich!"

"You're rich," he corrected gleefully, "I'm richer!"

THE EXALTED

Astounding Science Fiction
November

by L. Sprague de Camp (1907-   )

During his long and productive career, L. Sprague de Camp frequently worked within a series format. He has developed at least five series: the Viagens Interplanetarias stories, of which the best known is "The Queen of Zamba"; the Poseidonis stories, most of which have been collected as The Tritonian Ring; *the Harold Shea tales (written with the late Fletcher Pratt), two of which comprise* The Incomplete Enchanter; *the Gavagan's Bar stories, also written with Pratt and collected as* Tales From Gavagan's Bar; *and the least known—the Johnny Black stories about a bear too smart for his own good.*

"The Exalted" is the last (there were four) of these stories and the funniest.

(Next to John Campbell, L. Sprague de Camp was my father figure in science fiction. He was the first of the authors to accept me as a social equal and to invite me to his home—where I promptly fell in love, platonically, with his beautiful wife. We were at the Philadelphia Navy Yard together—along with Bob Heinlein—during World War II. We are now fellow-members of the Trap-Door Spiders—along with Lester del Rey. In all that time, his friendship has never wavered and he has always been kind and affectionate and I have admired and loved everything he has ever written—his nonfiction even more than his fiction. In fact, my nonfiction style began as a conscious imitation of his.—I.A.)

The storklike man with the gray goatee shuffled the twelve black billets about on the tabletop. "Try it again," he said.

The undergraduate sighed. "O. K., Professor Methuen." He looked apprehensively at Johnny Black, sitting across the table with one claw on the button of the stop clock. Johnny returned the look impassively through the spectacles perched on his yellowish muzzle.

"Go," said Ira Methuen.

Johnny depressed the button. The undergraduate started the second run of his wiggly-block test. The twelve billets formed a kind of three-dimensional jigsaw puzzle; when assembled they would make a cube. But the block had originally been sawn apart on wavy, irregular lines, so that the twelve billets had to be put together just so.

The undergraduate fiddled with the billets, trying this one and that one against one he held in his hand. The clock ticked round. In four minutes he had all but one in place. This one, a corner piece, simply would not fit. The undergraduate wiggled it and pushed it. He looked at it closely and tried again. But its maladjustment remained.

The undergraduate gave up. "What's the trick?" he asked.

Methuen reversed the billet end for end. It fitted.

"Oh, heck," said the undergraduate. "I could have gotten it if it hadn't been for Johnny."

Instead of being annoyed, Johnny Black twitched his mouth in a bear's equivalent of a grin. Methuen asked the student why.

"He distracts me somehow. I know he's friendly and all that, but . . . it's this way, sort of. Here I come to Yale to get to be a psychologist. I hear all about testing animals, chimps and bears and such. And when I get here I find a bear testing *me*. It's kind of upsetting."

"That's all right," said Methuen. "Just what we wanted. We're after, not your wiggly-block score by itself, but the effect of Johnny's presence on people taking the test. We're getting Johnny's distraction factor—his ability to distract people. We're also getting the distraction factor of a lot of other things, such as various sounds and smells. I didn't tell you sooner because the knowledge might have affected your performance."

"I see. Do I still get my five bucks?"

"Of course. Good day, Kitchell. Come on, Johnny; we've just got time to make Psychobiology 100. We'll clean up the stuff later."

On the way out of Methuen's office, Johnny asked: "Hey, boss! Do you feer any effec' yet?"

"Not a bit," said Methuen. "I think my original theory was right: that the electrical resistance of the gaps between human neurons is already as low as it can be, so the Methuen injections won't have any appreciable effect on a human being. Sorry, Johnny, but I'm afraid your boss won't become any great genius as a result of trying a dose of his own medicine."

The Methuen treatment had raised Johnny's intelligence from that of a normal black bear to that of—or more exactly to the equivalent of that of—a human being. It had enabled him to carry out those spectacular coups in the Virgin Islands and the Central Park Zoo. It had also worked on a number of other animals in the said zoo, with regrettable results.

Johnny grumbled in his urso-American accent: "Stirr, I don't sink it is smart to teach a crass when you are furr of zat stuff. You never know—"

But they had arrived. The class comprised a handful of grave graduate students, on whom Johnny's distraction factor had little effect.

Ira Methuen was not a good lecturer. He put in too many uh's and er's, and tended to mumble. Besides, Psychobiology 100 was an elementary survey, and Johnny was pretty well up in the field himself. So he settled himself to a view of the Grove Street Cemetery across the street, and to melancholy reflections on the short life span of his species compared with that of men.

"Ouch!"

R. H. Wimpus, B.S., '68, jerked his backbone from its normally nonchalant arc into a quivering reflex curve. His eyes were wide with mute indignation.

Methuen was saying: "—whereupon it was discovered that the . . . uh . . . paralysis of the pes resulting from excision of the corresponding motor area of the cortex was much more lasting among the Simiidae than among the other catarrhine primates; that it was more lasting among these than among the platyrrhines—Mr. Wimpus?"

"Nothing," said Wimpus. "I'm sorry."

"And that the platyrrhines, in turn, suffered more than the lemuroids and tarsioids. When—"

"Unh!" Another graduate student jerked upright. While

Methuen paused with his mouth open, a third man picked a small object off the floor and held it up.

"Really, gentlemen," said Methuen, "I thought you'd outgrown such amusements as shooting rubber bands at each other. As I was saying when—"

Wimpus gave another grunt and jerk. He glared about him. Methuen tried to get his lecture going again. But, as rubber bands from nowhere continued to sting the necks and ears of the listeners, the classroom organization visibly disintegrated like a lump of sugar in a cup of weak tea.

Johnny had put on his spectacles and was peering about the room. But he was no more successful than the others in locating the source of the bombardment.

He slid off his chair and shuffled over to the light switch. The daylight through the windows left the rear end of the classroom dark. As soon as the lights went on, the source of the elastics was obvious. A couple of the graduates pounced on a small wooden box on the shelf beside the projector.

The box gave out a faint whir, and spat rubber bands through a slit, one every few seconds. They brought it up and opened it on Methuen's lecture table. Inside was a mass of machinery apparently made of the parts of a couple of alarm clocks and a lot of hand-whittled wooden cams and things.

"My, my," said Methuen. "A most ingenious contraption, isn't it?"

The machine ran down with a click. While they were still examining it, the bell rang.

Methuen looked out the window. A September rain was coming up. Ira Methuen pulled on his topcoat and his rubbers and took his umbrella from the corner. He never wore a hat. He went out and headed down Prospect Street, Johnny padding behind.

"Hi!" said a young man, a fat young man in need of a haircut. "Got any news for us, Professor Methuen?"

"I'm afraid not, Bruce," replied Methuen. "Unless you call Ford's giant mouse news."

"What? What giant mouse?"

"Dr. Ford has produced a three-hundred-pound mouse by orthogonal mutation. He had to alter its morphological characteristics—"

"Its *what?*"

"Its shape, to you. He had to alter it to make it possible for it to live—"

"Where? Where is it?"

"Osborn Labs. If—" But Bruce Inglehart was gone up the hill toward the science buildings. Methuen continued: "With no war on, and New Haven as dead a town as it always has been, they have to come to us for news, I suppose. Come on, Johnny. Getting garrulous in my old age."

A passing dog went crazy at the sight of Johnny, snarling and yelping. Johnny ignored it. They entered Woodbridge Hall.

Dr. Wendell Cook, president of Yale University, had Methuen sent in at once. Johnny, excluded from the sanctum, went up to the president's secretary. He stood up and put his paws on her desk. He leered—you have to see a bear leer to know how it is done—and said: "How about it, kid?"

Miss Prescott, an unmistakable Boston spinster, smiled at him. "Suttinly, Johnny. Just a moment." She finished typing a letter, opened a drawer, and took out a copy of Hecht's "Fantazius Mallare." This she gave Johnny. He curled up on the floor, adjusted his glasses, and read.

After a while he looked up, saying: "Miss Prescott, I am halfway srough zis, and I stirr don't see why zey cawr it obscene. I sink it is just durr. Can't you get me a *rearry* dirty book?"

"Well, really, Johnny, I don't run a pornography shop, you know. Most people find that quite strong enough."

Johnny sighed. "Peopre get excited over ze funnies' sings."

Meanwhile, Methuen was closeted with Cook and Dalrymple, the prospective endower, in another of those interminable and indecisive conferences. R. Hanscom Dalrymple looked like a statue that the sculptor had never gotten around to finishing. The only expression the steel chairman ever allowed himself was a canny, secretive smile. Cook and Methuen had a feeling he was playing them on the end of a long and well-knit fish line made of U.S. Federal Reserve notes. It was not because he wasn't willing to part with the damned endowment, but because he enjoyed the sensation of power over these oh-so-educated men. And in the actual world, one doesn't lose one's temper and tell Croesus what to do with his loot. One says: "Yes, Mr. Dalrymple. My, my, that *is* a brilliant suggestion, Mr. Dalrymple! Why didn't we think of it ourselves?" Cook and Methuen were both old hands at this game. Methuen, though otherwise he considered Wendell Cook a pompous ass, admired the president's endowment-snagging ability. After all, wasn't Yale University named after a retired merchant on the basis of a gift of five hundred and sixty-two pounds twelve shillings?

"Say, Dr. Cook," said Dalrymple, "why don't you come over to the Taft and have lunch on me for a change? You, too, Professor Methuen."

The academics murmured their delight and pulled on their rubbers. On the way out Dalrymple paused to scratch Johnny behind the ears. Johnny put his book away, keeping the title on the cover out of sight, and restrained himself from snapping at the steel man's hand. Dalrymple meant well enough, but Johnny did not like people to take such liberties with his person.

So three men and a bear slopped down College Street. Cook paused now and then, ignoring the sprinkle, to make studied gestures toward one or another of the units of the great soufflé of Georgian and Collegiate Gothic architecture. He explained this and that. Dalrymple merely smiled his blank little smile.

Johnny, plodding behind, was the first to notice that passing undergraduates were pausing to stare at the president's feet. The word "feet" is meant literally. For Cook's rubbers were rapidly changing into a pair of enormous pink bare feet.

Cook himself was quite unconscious of it, until quite a group of undergraduates had collected. These gave forth the catarrhal snorts of men trying unsuccessfully not to laugh. By the time Cook had followed their stares and looked down, the metamorphosis was complete. That he should be startled was only natural. The feet were startling enough. His face gradually matched the feet in redness, making a cheerful note of color in the gray landscape.

R. Hanscom Dalrymple lost his reserve for once. His howls did nothing to save prexy's now-apoplectic face. Cook finally stooped and pulled off the rubbers. It transpired that the feet had been painted on the outside of the rubbers and covered over with lampblack. The rain had washed the lampblack off.

Wendell Cook resumed his walk to the Hotel Taft in gloomy silence. He held the offensive rubbers between thumb and finger as if they were something unclean and loathsome. He wondered who had done this dastardly deed. There hadn't been any undergraduates in his office for some days, but you never wanted to underestimate the ingenuity of undergraduates. He noticed that Ira Methuen was wearing rubbers of the same size and make as his own. But he put suspicion in that direction out of his mind before it had fully formed. Certainly Methuen wouldn't play practical jokes with Dalrymple around, when he'd be the head of the new Department of Biophysics when—if—Dalrymple came through with the endowment.

The next man to suspect that the Yale campus was undergoing a severe pixilation was John Dugan, the tall thin one of the two campus cops. He was passing Christ Church—which is so veddy high-church Episcopal that they refer to Charles I of England as St. Charles the Martyr—on his way to his lair in Phelps Tower. A still small voice spoke in his ear: "Beware, John Dugan! Your sins will find you out!"

Dugan jumped and looked around. The voice repeated its message. There was nobody within fifty feet of Dugan. Moreover, he could not think of any really serious sins he had committed lately. The only people in sight were a few undergraduates and Professor Methuen's educated black bear, trailing after his boss as usual. There was nothing for John Dugan to suspect but his own sanity.

R. Hanscom Dalrymple was a bit surprised at the grim earnestness of the professors in putting away their respective shares of the James Pierpont dinner. They were staying the eternal gnaw of hunger that afflicts those who depend on a college commissary for sustenance. Many of them suspected a conspiracy among college cooks to see that the razor edge wasn't taken off students' and instructors' intellects by overfeeding. They knew that conditions were much the same in most colleges.

Dalrymple sipped his coffee and looked at his notes. Presently Cook would get up and say a few pleasant nothings. Then he would announce Dalrymple's endowment, which was to be spent in building a Dalrymple Biophysical Laboratory and setting up a new department. Everybody would applaud and agree that biophysics had floated in the void between the domains of the departments of zoölogy, psychology, and the physiological sciences long enough. Then Dalrymple would get up and clear his throat and say— though in much more dignified language: "Shucks, fellas, it really isn't nothing."

Dr. Wendell Cook duly got up, beamed out over the ranked shirt fronts, and said his pleasant nothings. The professors exchanged nervous looks when he showed signs of going off into his favorite oration, there-is-no-conflict-between-science-and-religion. They had heard it before.

He was well launched into Version 3A of this homily, when he began to turn blue in the face. It was not the dark purplish-gray called loosely "blue" that appears on the faces of stranglees, but a bright, cheerful cobalt. Now, such a color is all very well in a painting of a ship sailing under a clear blue sky, or in the uniform of a movie-theater doorman. But it is distinctly out of place in the face of a college president. Or so felt the professors. They leaned this way and that, their boiled shirts bulging, popping and gaping as they did so, and whispered.

Cook frowned and continued. He was observed to sniff the air as if he smelled something. Those at the speakers' table detected a slight smell of acetone. But that seemed hardly an adequate explanation of the robin's-egg hue of their prexy's face. The color was now quite solid on the face proper. It ran up into the area where Cook's hair would have been if he had had some. His collar showed a trace of it, too.

Cook, on his part, had no idea of why the members of his audience were swaying in their seats like saplings in a gale and whispering. He thought it very rude of them. But his frowns had no effect. So presently he cut Version 3A short. He announced the endowment in concise, businesslike terms, and paused to the expected thunder of applause.

There was none. To be exact, there was a feeble patter that nobody in his right mind would call a thunder of anything.

Cook looked at R. Hanscom Dalrymple, hoping that the steel man would not be insulted. Dalrymple's face showed nothing. Cook assumed that this was part of his general reserve. The truth was that Dalrymple was too curious about the blue face to notice the lack of applause. When Cook introduced him to the audience, it took him some seconds to pull himself together.

He started rather lamely: "Gentlemen and members of the Yale faculty . . . uh . . . I mean, of course, you're *all* gentlemen . . . I am reminded of a story about the poultry farmer who got married—I mean, I'm not reminded of *that* story, but the one about the divinity student who died and went to—" Here Dalrymple caught the eye of the dean of the divinity school. He tacked again: "Maybe I'd . . . uh . . . better tell the one about the Scotchman who got lost on his way home and—"

It was not a bad story, as such things go. But it got practically no laughter. Instead, the professors began swaying, like a roomful of boiled-shirted Eastern ascetics at their prayers, and whispering again.

Dalrymple could put two and two together. He leaned over and hissed into Cook's ear: "Is there anything wrong with me?"

"Yes, your face has turned green."

"Green?"

"Bright green. Like grass. Nice young grass."

"Well, you might like to know that yours is blue."

Both men felt their faces. There was no doubt; they were masked with coatings of some sort of paint, still wet.

Dalrymple whispered: "What kind of gag is this?"

"I don't know. Better finish your speech."

Dalrymple tried. But his thoughts were scattered beyond recovery. He made a few remarks about how glad he was to be there amid the elms and ivy and traditions of old Eli, and sat down. His face looked rougher-hewn than ever. If a joke had been played on him—well, he hadn't signed any checks yet.

The lieutenant governor of the State of Connecticut was next on the list. Cook shot a question at him. He mumbled: "But if I'm going to turn a funny color when I get up—"

The question of whether his honor should speak was never satisfactorily settled. For at that moment a thing appeared on one end of the speakers' table. It was a beast the size of a St. Bernard. It looked rather the way a common bat would look if, instead of wings, it had arms with disk-shaped pads on the ends of the fingers. Its eyes were as big around as luncheon plates.

There was commotion. The speaker sitting nearest the thing fell over backward. The lieutenant governor crossed himself. An English zoölogist put on his glasses and said: "By Jove, a spectral tarsier! But a bit large, what?"

A natural-sized tarsier would fit in your hand comfortably, and is rather cute if a bit spooky. But a tarsier the size of this one is not the kind of thing one can glance at and then go on reading the adventures of Alley Oop. It breaks one's train of thought. It disconcerts one. It may give one the screaming meemies.

This tarsier walked gravely down the twenty feet of table. The diners were too busy going away from there to observe that it upset no tumblers and kicked no ashtrays about; that it was, in fact, slightly transparent. At the other end of the table it vanished.

Johnny Black's curiosity wrestled with his better judgment. His curiosity told him that all these odd happenings had taken place in the presence of Ira Methuen. Therefore, Ira Methuen was at least a promising suspect. "So what?" said his better judgment. "He's the only man you have a real affection for. If you learned that he was the pixie in the case, you wouldn't expose him, would you? Better keep your muzzle out of this."

But in the end his curiosity won, as usual. The wonder was that his better judgment kept on trying.

He got hold of Bruce Inglehart. The young reporter had a reputation for discretion.

Johnny explained: "He gave himserf ze Messuen treatment—you know, ze spinar injection—to see what it would do to a man. Zat was a week ago. Should have worked by now. But he says it had no effec'. Maybe not. But day after ze dose, awr zese sings start happening. Very eraborate jokes. Kind a crazy scientific genius would do. If it's him, I mus' stop him before he makes rear troubre. You wirr he'p me?"

"Sure, Johnny. Shake on it."

Johnny extended his paw.

It was two nights later that Durfee Hall caught fire. Yale had been discussing the erasure of this singularly ugly and useless building for forty years. It had been vacant for some time, except for the bursar's office in the basement.

About ten o'clock an undergraduate noticed little red tongues of flame crawling up the roof. He gave the alarm at once. The New Haven fire department was not to be blamed for the fact that the fire spread as fast as if the building had been soaked in kerosene. By the time they, and about a thousand spectators, had arrived, the whole center of the building was going up with a fine roar and crackle. The assistant bursar bravely dashed into the building and reappeared with an armful of papers, which later turned out to be a pile of quite useless examination forms. The fire department squirted enough water onto the burning section to put out Mount Vesuvius. Some of them climbed ladders at the ends of the building to chop holes in the roof.

The water seemed to have no effect. So the fire department called for some more apparatus, connected up more hoses, and squirted more water. The undergraduates yelled:

"Rah, rah, fire department! Rah, rah, fire! Go get 'em, department! Hold that line, fire!"

Johnny Black bumped into Bruce Inglehart, who was dodging about in the crowd with a pad and pencil, trying to get information for his New Haven *Courier*. Inglehart asked Johnny whether he knew anything.

Johnny, in his deliberate manner, said: "I know one sing. Zat is ze firs' hetress fire I have seen."

Inglehart looked at Johnny, then at the conflagration. "My gosh!" he said. "We ought to feel the radiation here, oughtn't we? Heatless fire is right. Another superscientific joke, you suppose?"

"We can rook around," said Johnny. Turning their backs on the conflagration, they began searching among the shrubbery and railings along Elm Street.

"Woof!" said Johnny. "Come here, Bruce!"

In a patch of shadow stood Professor Ira Methuen and a tripod whereon was mounted a motion-picture projector. It took Johnny a second to distinguish which was which.

Methuen seemed uneasily poised on the verge of flight. He said:

"Why, hello, Johnny, why aren't you asleep? I just found this ... uh ... this projector—"

Johnny, thinking fast, slapped the projector with his paw. Methuen caught it as it toppled. Its whir ceased. At the same instant the fire went out, vanished utterly. The roar and crackle still came from the place where the fire had been. But there was no fire. There was not even a burned place in the roof, off which gallons of water were still pouring. The fire department looked at one another foolishly.

While Johnny's and Inglehart's pupils were still expanding in the sudden darkness, Methuen and his projector vanished. They got a glimpse of him galloping around the College Street corner, lugging the tripod. They ran after him. A few undergraduates ran after Johnny and Inglehart, being moved by the instinct that makes dogs chase automobiles.

They caught sight of Methuen, lost him, and caught sight of him again. Inglehart was not built for running, and Johnny's eyesight was an affair of limited objectives. Johnny opened up when it became evident that Methuen was heading for the old Phelps mansion, where he, Johnny, and several unmarried instructors lived. Everybody in the house had gone to see the fire. Methuen dashed in the front door three jumps ahead of Johnny and slammed it in the bear's face.

Johnny padded around in the dark with the idea of attacking a window. But while he was making up his mind, something happened to the front steps under him. They became slicker than the smoothest ice. Down the steps went Johnny, *bump-bump-bump.*

Johnny picked himself up in no pleasant mood. So this was the sort of treatment he got from the one man— But then, he reflected, if Methuen was really crazy, you couldn't blame him.

Some of the undergraduates caught up with them. These crowded toward the mansion—until their feet went out from under them as if they were wearing invisible roller skates. They tried to get up, and fell again, sliding down the slight grade of the crown of the road into heaps in the gutter. They retired on hands and knees, their clothes showing large holes.

A police car drove up and tried to stop. Apparently neither brakes nor tires would hold. It skidded about, banged against the curb once, and finally stopped down the street beyond the slippery zone. The cop—he was a fairly important cop, a captain—got out and charged the mansion.

He fell down, too. He tried to keep going on hands and knees. But every time he applied a horizontal component of force to a hand or knee, the hand or knee simply slid backward. The sight reminded Johnny of the efforts of those garter snakes to crawl on the smooth concrete floor of the Central Park Zoo monkey house.

When the police captain gave up and tried to retreat, the laws of friction came back on. But when he stood up, all his clothes below the waist, except his shoes, disintegrated into a cloud of textile fibers.

"My word!" said the English zoölogist, who had just arrived. "Just like one of those Etruscan statues, don't you know!"

The police captain bawled at Bruce Inglehart: "Hey, you, for gossakes gimmie a handkerchief!"

"What's the matter; got a cold?" asked Inglehart innocently.

"No, you dope! You know what I want it for!"

Inglehart suggested that a better idea would be for the captain to use his coat as an apron. While the captain was knotting the sleeves behind his back, Inglehart and Johnny explained their version of the situation to him.

"Hm-m-m," said the captain. "We don't want nobody to get hurt, or the place to get damaged. But suppose he's got a death ray or sumpm?"

"I don't sink so," said Johnny. "He has not hurt anybody. Jus' prayed jokes."

The captain thought for a few seconds of ringing up headquarters and having them send an emergency truck. But the credit for overpowering a dangerous maniac singlehanded was too tempting. He said: "How'll we get into the place, if he can make everything so slippery?"

They thought. Johnny said: "Can you get one of zose sings wiss a wood stick and a rubber cup on end?"

The captain frowned. Johnny made motions. Inglehart said: "Oh, you mean the plumber's friend! Sure. You wait. I'll get one. See if you can find a key to the place."

The assault on Methuen's stronghold was made on all fours. The captain, in front, jammed the end of the plumber's friend against the rise of the lowest front step. If Methuen could abolish friction, he had not discovered how to get rid of barometric pressure. The rubber cup held, and the cop pulled himself, Inglehart, and Johnny after him. By using the instrument on successive steps, they mounted them. Then the captain anchored them to the front door and pulled them up to it. He hauled himself to his feet by the door handle, and opened the door with a key borrowed from Dr. Wendell Cook.

At one window, Methuen crouched behind a thing like a surveyor's transit. He swiveled the thing toward them, and made adjustments. The captain and Inglehart, feeling their shoes grip the floor, gathered themselves to jump. But Methuen got the contraption going, and their feet went out from under them.

Johnny used his head. He was standing next to the door. He lay down, braced his hind feet against the door frame, and kicked out. His body whizzed across the frictionless floor and bowled over Methuen and his contraption.

The professor offered no more resistance. He seemed more amused than anything, despite the lump that was growing on his forehead. He said: "My, my, you fellows *are* persistent. I suppose you're going to take me off to some asylum. I thought you and you"—he indicated Inglehart and Johnny— "were friends of mine. Oh, well, it doesn't matter."

The captain growled: "What did you do to my pants?"

"Simple. My telelubricator here neutralizes the interatomic bonds on the surface of any solid on which the beam falls. So the surface, to a depth of a few molecules, is put in the condition of a supercooled liquid as long as the beam is focused on it. Since the liquid form of any compound will wet the solid form, you have perfect lubrication."

"But my pants—"

"They were held together by friction between the fibers, weren't they? And I have a lot more inventions like that. My soft-speaker and my three-dimensional projector, for instance, are—"

Inglehart interrupted: "Is that how you made that phony fire, and that whatchamacallit that scared the people at the dinner? With a three-dimensional projector?"

"Yes, of course, though, to be exact, it took two projectors at right angles, and a phonograph and amplifier to give the sound effect. It was amusing, wasn't it?"

"But," wailed Johnny, "why do you *do* zese sings? You trying to ruin your career?"

Methuen shrugged. "It doesn't matter. Nothing matters. Johnny, as you'd know if you were in my . . . uh . . . condition. And now, gentlemen, where do you want me to go? Wherever it is, I'll find something amusing there."

Dr. Wendell Cook visited Ira Methuen on the first day of his incarceration in the New Haven Hospital. In ordinary conversation Methuen seemed sane enough, and quite agreeable. He readily admitted that he had been the one responsible for the jokes. He explained: "I painted your and Dalrymple's face with a high-powered needle sprayer I invented. It's a most amusing little thing. Fits in your hand and discharges through a ring on your finger. With your thumb you can regulate the amount of acetone mixed in with the water, which in turn controls the surface tension and therefore the point at which the needle spray breaks up into droplets. I made the spray break up just before it reached your face. You were a sight, Cook, especially when you found out what was wrong with you. You looked almost as funny as the day I painted those feet on my rubbers and substituted them for yours. You react so beautifully to having your dignity pricked. You always were a pompous ass, you know."

Cook puffed out his cheeks and controlled himself. After all, the poor man was mad. These absurd outbursts about Cook's pompousness proved it. He said sadly: "Dalrymple's leaving tomorrow night. He was most displeased about the face-painting episode, and when he found that you were under observation, he told me that no useful purpose would be served by his remaining here. I'm afraid that's the end of our endowment. Unless you can pull yourself together and tell us what's happened to you and how to cure it."

Ira Methuen laughed. "Pull myself togehter? I am all in one piece, I assure you. And I've told you what's the matter with me, as you put it. I gave myself my own treatment. As for curing it, I wouldn't tell you how even if I knew. I wouldn't give up my present condition for anything. I at last realize that nothing really matters, including endowments. I shall be taken care of, and I will devote myself to amusing myself as I see fit."

Johnny had been haunting Cook's office all day. He waylaid the president when the latter returned from the hospital.

Cook told Johnny what had happened. He said: "He seems to be completely irresponsible. We'll have to get in touch with his son, and have a guardian appointed. And we'll have to do something about you, Johnny."

Johnny didn't relish the prospect of the "something." He knew he had no legal status other than that of a tamed wild animal. The fact that Methuen technically owned him was his only protection if somebody took a notion to shoot him during bear-hunting season. And he was not enthusiastic about Ralph Methuen. Ralph was a very average young schoolteacher without his father's scientific acumen or whimsical humor. Finding Johnny on his hands, his reaction would be to give Johnny to a zoo or something.

He put his paws on Miss Prescott's desk and asked: "Hey, good-rooking, wirr you cawr up Bruce Ingrehart at ze *Courier?*"

"Johnny," said the president's secretary, "you get fresher every day."

"Ze bad infruence of ze undergraduates. Wirr you cawr Mr. Ingrehart, beautifur?" Miss Prescott, who was not, did so.

Bruce Inglehart arrived at the Phelps mansion to find Johnny taking a shower. Johnny was also making a horrible bawling noise. *"Waaaaa!"* he howled. *"Hoooooooo! Yrrrrrrr! Waaaaaaa!"*

"Whatcha doing?" yelled Inglehart.

"Taking a bass," replied Johnny. *"Wuuuuuuh!"*

"Are you sick?"

"No. Jus' singing in bass. People sing whire taking bass; why shouldn't I? *Yaaaaaaaaaa!"*

"Well, for Pete's sake don't. It sounds like you were having your throat cut. What's the idea of these bath towels spread all over the floor?"

"I show you." Johnny came out of the shower, lay down on the bath towels, and rolled. When he was more or less dry, he scooped the towels up in his forepaws and hove them into a corner. Neatness was not one of Johnny's strong points.

He told Inglehart about the Methuen situation. "Rook here, Bruce," he said, "I sink I can fix him, but you wirr have to he'p me."

"O. K. Count me in."

Pop!

The orderly looked up from his paper. But none of the buttons showed a light. So, presumably, none of the patients wanted attention. He went back to his reading.

Pop!

It sounded a little like a breaking light bulb. The orderly sighed, put away his paper, and began prowling. As he approached the room of the mad professor, No. 14, he noticed a smell of limburger.

Pop!

There was no doubt that the noise came from No. 14. The orderly stuck his head in.

At one side of the room sat Ira Methuen. He held a contraption made of a length of glass rod and assorted wires. At the other side of the room, on the floor, lay a number of crumbs of cheese. A cockroach scuttled out of the shadows and made for the crumbs. Methuen sighted along his glass rod and pressed a button. *Pop!* A flash, and there was no more cockroach.

Methuen swung the rod toward the orderly. "Stand back, sir! I'm Buck Rogers, and this is my disintegrator!"

"Hey," said the orderly feebly. The old goof might be crazy, but after what happened to the roach— He ducked out and summoned a squad of interns.

But the interns had no trouble with Methuen. He tossed the contraption on the bed, saying: "If I thought it mattered, I'd raise a hell of a stink about cockroaches in a supposedly sanitary hospital."

One of the interns protested: "But I'm sure there aren't any here."

"What do you call that?" asked Methuen dryly, pointing at the shattered remains of one of his victims.

"It must have been attracted in from the outside by the smell of that cheese. *Phew!* Judson, clean up the floor. What *is* this, professor?" He picked up the rod and the flashlight battery attached to it.

Methuen waved a deprecating hand. "Nothing important. Just a little gadget I thought up. By applying the right e.m.f. to pure crown glass, it's possible to raise its index of refraction to a remarkable degree. The result is that light striking the glass is so slowed up that it takes weeks to pass through it in the ordinary manner. The light that is thus trapped can be released by making a small spark near the glass. So I simply lay the rod on the window sill all afternoon to soak up sunlight, a part of which is released by making a spark with that button. Thus I can shoot an hour's accumulated light-energy out the front end of the rod in a very small fraction of a second. Natuarlly when this beam hits an opaque object, it raises its temperature. So I've been amusing myself by luring the roaches in here and exploding them. You may have the thing; its charge is about exhausted."

The intern was stern. "That's a dangerous weapon. We can't let you play with things like that."

"Oh, can't you? Not that it matters, but I'm only staying here because I'm taken care of. I can walk out any time I like."

"No you can't, professor. You're under a temporary commitment for observation."

"That's all right, son. I still say I can walk out whenever I feel like it. I just don't care much whether I do or not." With which Methuen began tuning the radio by his bed, ignoring the interns.

Exactly twelve hours later, at 10 A.M., Ira Methuen's room in the hospital was found to be vacant. A search of the hospital failed to locate him. The only clue to his disappearance was the fact that his radio had been disemboweled. Tubes, wires, and condensers lay in untidy heaps on the floor.

The New Haven police cars received instructions to look for a tall, thin man with gray hair and goatee, probably armed with death rays, disintegrators, and all the other advanced weapons of fact and fiction.

For hours they scoured the city with screaming sirens. They finally located the menacing madman, sitting placidly on a park bench three blocks from the hospital and reading a newspaper. Far from resisting, he grinned at them and looked at his watch. "Three hours and forty-eight minutes. Not bad, boys, not bad, considering how carefully I hid myself."

One of the cops pounced on a bulge in Methuen's pocket. The bulge was made by another wire contraption. Methuen shrugged. "My hyperbolic solenoid. Gives you a conical magnetic field, and enables you to manipulate ferrous objects at a distance. I picked the lock of the door to the elevators with it."

When Bruce Inglehart arrived at the hospital about four, he was told Methuen was asleep. That was amended to the statement that Methuen was getting up, and could see a visitor in a few minutes. He found Methuen in a dressing gown.

Methuen said: "Hello, Bruce. They had me wrapped up in a wet sheet, like a mummy. It's swell for naps; relaxes you. I told 'em they could do it whenever they liked. I think they were annoyed about my getting out."

Inglehart was slightly embarrassed.

Methuen said: "Don't worry; I'm not mad at you. I realize that nothing matters, including resentments. And I've had a most amusing time here. Just watch them fizz the next time I escape."

"But don't you care about your future?" said Inglehart. "They'll transfer you to a padded cell at Middletown—"

Methuen waved a hand. "That doesn't bother me. I'll have fun there, too."

"But how about Johnny Black, and Dalrymple's endowment?"

"I don't give a damn what happens to them."

Here the orderly stuck his head in the door briefly to check up on this unpredictable patient. The hospital, being short-handed, was unable to keep a continuous watch on him.

Methuen continued: "Not that I don't like Johnny. But when you get a real sense of proportion, like mine, you realize that humanity is nothing but a sort of skin disease on a ball of dirt, and that no effort beyond subsistence, shelter, and casual amusement is worthwhile. The State of Connecticut is willing to provide the first two for me, so I shall devote myself to the third. What's that you have there?"

Inglehart thought. *They're right; he's become a childishly irresponsible scientific genius.* Keeping his back to the door, the reporter brought out his family heirloom: a big silver pocket flask dating back to the fabulous prohibition period. His aunt Martha had left it to him, and he himself expected to will it to a museum.

"Apricot brandy," he murmured. Johnny had tipped him off to Methuen's tastes.

"Now, Bruce, that's something sensible. Why didn't you bring it out sooner, instead of making futile appeals to my sense of duty?"

The flask was empty. Ira Methuen sprawled in his chair. Now and then he passed a hand across his forehead. He said: "I can't believe it. I can't believe that I felt that way half an hour ago. O Lord, what have I done?"

"Plenty," said Inglehart.

Methuen was not acting at all drunk. He was full of sober remorse.

"I remember everything—those inventions that popped out of my mind, everything. But I didn't care. How did you know alcohol would counteract the Methuen injection?"

"Johnny figured it out. He looked up its effects, and discovered that in massive doses it coagulates the proteins in the nerve cells. He guessed it would lower their conductivity to counteract the increased conductivity through the gaps between them that your treatment causes."

"So," said Methuen, "when I'm sober I'm drunk, and when I'm drunk I'm sober. But what'll we do about the endowment—my new department and the laboratory and everything?"

"I don't know. Dalrymple's leaving tonight; he had to stay over a day on account of some trustee business. And they won't let you out for a while yet, even when they know about the alcohol counter-treatment. Better think of something quick, because the visiting period is pretty near up."

Methuen thought. He said: "I remember how all those inventions work, though I couldn't possibly invent any more of them unless I went back to the other condition." He shuddered. "There's the soft-speaker, for instance—"

"What's that?"

"It's like a loud-speaker, only it doesn't speak loudly. It throws a supersonic beam, modulated by the human voice to give the effect of audible sound-frequencies when it hits the human ear. Since you can throw a supersonic beam almost as accurately as you can throw a light beam, you can turn the soft-speaker on a person, who will then hear a still small voice in his ear apparently coming from nowhere. I tried it on Dugan one day. It worked. Could you do anything with that?"

"I don't know. Maybe."

"I hope you can. This is terrible. I thought I was perfectly sane and rational. Maybe I was— Maybe nothing *is* important. But I don't feel that way now, and I don't want to feel that way again—"

The omnipresent ivy, of which Yale is so proud, affords splendid handholds for climbing. Bruce Inglehart, keeping an eye peeled for campus cops, swarmed up the big tower at the corner of Bingham Hall. Below, in the dark, Johnny waited.

Presently the end of a clothesline came dangling down. Johnny inserted the hook in the end of the rope ladder into the loop in the end of the line. Inglehart hauled the ladder up and secured it, wishing that he and Johnny could change bodies for a while. That climb up the ivy had scared him and winded him badly. But he could climb ivy and Johnny couldn't.

The ladder creaked under Johnny's five hundred pounds. A few minutes later it slid slowly, jerkily up the wall, like a giant centipede. Then Inglehart, Johnny, ladder, and all were on top of the tower.

Inglehart got out the soft-speaker and trained the telescopic sight on the window of Dalrymple's room in the Taft, across the intersection of College and Chapel Streets. He found the yellow rectangle of light. He could see into about half the room. His heart skipped a few beats until a stocky figure moved into his field of vision. Dalrymple had not yet left. But he was packing a couple of suitcases.

Inglehart slipped the transmitter clip around his neck, so that the transmitter nestled against his larynx. The next time Dalrymple appeared, Inglehart focused the crosshairs on the steel man's head. He spoke: "Hanscom Dalrymple!" He saw the man stop suddenly. He repeated: "Hanscom Dalrymple!"

"Huh?" said Dalrymple. "Who the hell are you? Where the hell are you?" Inglehart could not hear him, of course, but he could guess.

Inglehart said, in a solemn tones: "I am your conscience."

By now Dalrymple's agitation was evident even at that distance. Inglehart continued: "Who squeezed out all the common stockholders of Hephaestus Steel in that phony reorganization?" Pause. "You did, Hanscom Dalrymple!

"Who bribed a United States senator to swing the vote for a higher steel tariff, with fifty thousand dollars and a promise of fifty thousand more, which was never paid?" Pause. "You did, Hanscom Dalrymple!

"Who promised Wendell Cook the money for a new biophysics building, and then let his greed get the better of him and backed out on the thin excuse that the man who was to have headed the new department had had a nervous breakdown?" Pause, while Inglehart reflected that "nervous breakdown" was merely a nice way of saying "gone nuts." "You did, Hanscom Dalrymple!

"Do you know what'll happen to you if you don't atone, Dalrymple? You'll be reincarnated as a spider, and probably caught by a wasp and used as live fodder for her larvæ. How will you like that, *heh-heh?*

"What can you do to atone? Don't be a sap. Call up Cook. Tell him you've changed your mind, and are renewing your offer!" Pause. "Well, what are you waiting for? Tell him you're not only renewing it, but doubling it!" Pause. "Tell him—"

But at this point Dalrymple moved swiftly to the telephone. Inglehart said, "Ah, that's better, Dalrymple," and shut off the machine.

Johnny asked: "How did you know awr zose sings about him?"

"I got his belief in reincarnation out of his obit down at the shop. And one of our rewrite men who used to work in Washington says everybody down there knows about the other things. Only you can't print a thing like that unless you have evidence to back it up."

They lowered the rope ladder and reversed the process by which they had come up. They gathered up their stuff and started for the Phelps mansion. But as they rounded the corner of Bingham they almost ran into a familiar storklike figure. Methuen was just setting up another contraption at the corner of Welch.

"Hello," he said.

Man and bear gaped at him. Inlgehart asked: "Did you escape again?"

"Uh-huh. When I sobered up and got my point of view back. It was easy, even though they'd taken my radio away. I invented a hypnotizer, using a light bulb and a rheostat made of wire from my mattress, and hypnotized the orderly into giving me his uniform and opening the doors for me. My, my, that *was* amusing."

"What are you doing now?" Inglehart became aware that Johnny's black pelt had melted off into the darkness.

"This? Oh, I dropped around home and knocked together an improved soft-speaker. This one'll work through masonry walls. I'm going to put all the undergraduates to sleep and tell 'em they're monkeys. When they wake up, it will be most amusing to see them running around on all fours and scratching and climbing the chandeliers. They're practically monkeys to begin with, so it shouldn't be difficult."

"But you can't, professor! Johnny and I just went to a lot of trouble getting Dalrymple to renew his offer. You don't want to let us down, do you?"

"What you and Johnny do doesn't matter to me in the slightest. Nothing matters. I'm going to have my fun. And don't try to interfere, Bruce." Methuen pointed another glass rod at Inglehart's middle. "You're a nice young fellow, and it would be too bad if I had to let you have three hours' accumulation of sun-ray energy all at once."

"But this afternoon you said—"

"I know what I said this afternoon. I was drunk and back in my old state of mind, full of responsibility and conscientiousness and such bunk. I'll never touch the stuff again if it has that effect on me. Only a man who has received the Methuen treatment can appreciate the futility of all human effort."

Methuen shrank back into the shadows as a couple of undergraduates passed. Then he resumed work on his contraption, using one hand and keeping Inglehart covered with the other. Inglehart, not knowing what else to do, asked him questions about the machine. Methuen responded with a string of technical jargon. Inglehart wondered desperately what to do. He was not an outstandingly brave young man, especially in the face of a gun or its equivalent. Methuen's bony hand never wavered. He made the adjustments on his machine mostly by feel.

"Now," he said, "that ought to be about right. This contains a tonic metronome that will send them a note of frequency of 349 cycles a second, with 68.4 pulses of sound a minute. This, for various technical reasons, has the maximum hypnotic effect. From here I can rake the colleges along College Street—" He made a final adjustment. "This will be the most amusing joke yet. And the cream of it is that, since Connecticut is determined to consider me insane, they can't do anything to me for it! Here goes, Bruce—*Phew*, has somebody started a still here, or what? I've been smelling and tasting alcohol for the last five minutes—*ouch!*"

The glass rod gave one dazzling flash, and then Johnny's hairy black body catapulted out of the darkness. Down went Ira Methuen, all the wind knocked out of him.

"Quick, Bruce!" barked Johnny. "Pick up zat needre sprayer I dropped. Unscrew ze container on ze bottom. Don't spirr it. Zen come here and pour it down his sroat!"

This was done, with Johnny holding Methuen's jaws apart with his claws, like Sampson slaying the lion, only conversely.

They waited a few minutes for the alcohol to take effect, listening for sounds that they had been discovered. But the colleges were silent save for the occasional tick of a typewriter.

Johnny explained: "I ran home and got ze needre sprayer from his room. Zen I got Webb, ze research assistant in biphysics, to ret me in ze raboratory for ze arcohor. Zen I try to sneak up and squirt a spray in his mouse whire he talks. I get some in, but I don't get ze sprayer adjusted right, and ze spray hit him before it breaks up, and stings him. I don't have fingers, you know. So we have to use what ze books cawr brute force."

Methuen began to show signs of normalcy. As without his glass rod he was just a harmless old professor, Johnny let him up. His words tumbled out: "I'm so glad you did, Johnny— you saved my reputation, maybe my life. Those fatheads at the hospital wouldn't believe I had to be kept full of alcohol, so, of course, I sobered up and went crazy again—maybe they'll believe now. Come on; let's get back there quickly. If they haven't discovered my absence, they might be willing to keep this last escape quiet. When they let me out, I'll work on a permanent cure for the Methuen treatment. I'll find it, if I don't die of stomach ulcers from all the alcohol I'll have to drink."

Johnny waddled up Temple Street to his home, feeling rather smug about his ability as a fixer. Maybe Methuen, sober, was right about the futility of it all. But if such a philosophy led to the upsetting of Johnny's pleasant existence, Johnny preferred Methuen drunk.

He was glad Methuen would soon be well and coming home. Methuen was the only man he had any sentimental regard for. But as long as Methuen was shut up, Johnny was going to take advantage of that fact. When he reached the

Phelps mansion, instead of going directly in, he thrust a foreleg around behind the hedge next to the wall. It came out with a huge slab of chewing tobacco. Johnny bit off about half the slab, thrust the rest back in its cache, and went in, drooling happily a little at each step. Why not?

OLD MAN MULLIGAN
Astounding Science Fiction
December

by P. Schuyler Miller (1912-1974)

Although he had a master's degree in chemistry, P. Schuyler Miller's first love was archaeology, a passion that found its way into several of his best sf stories. He began to publish in the 1930s, with stories like "The Chrysalis" (1936), the justly famous "The Sands of Time" (1937), and "Spawn" (1939). Best known as the long-time book reviewer (1951-1975) for Astounding/Analog, There his "The Reference Library" became an institution, he published only two books in the field: Genus Homo (1950, a revision of a 1941 story), a novel written in collaboration with L. Sprague de Camp; and an excellent collection, The Titan (1952). Please. Won't someone bring these two fine books back into print?

(I met Schuyler Miller now and then at science fiction conventions. He was gentle, rational, and a comer. So it seemed to me. He had begun writing in 1931 and one of his early stories "Tetrahedra of Space" transfixed me in my pre-teen days. He was a regular in John Campbell's stable in the first three or four years of that editor's incumbency and then, during World War II, Schuyler stopped writing. He spent the rest of his science fiction life as Campbell's book reviewer and the kindest and least impassioned reviewer there was. I was always sorry he had stopped writing though.

"Old Man Mulligan" was perhaps his most popular story and it's easy to see why. The rest may be cops and robbers but Mulligan is a work of genius. There's a Neanderthal that's a Neanderthal. "Old Man Mulligan" is at one end; Lester del Rey's "The Day Is Done" is at the other and L. Sprague de Camp's "The Gnarly Man" is somewhere in between. —I.A.)

Davis stopped under the glowlamp to light a cigarette. Ten feet away the mist clamped down, swallowing all but the pale cone of light in which he stood, the hulking shape of Top-Sergeant Gibbon casting its gorilla's shadow beside his own. The fishy reek of Venus's shallow sea and the stench of discarded garbage in Laxa's narrow alleys got in a man's throat and made his mouth taste like rotten cabbage. He'd be glad to breathe canned air again, and see the stars hanging like diamond spangles against space. There wasn't a planet in the System, outside of Earth, fit for a man to live on—and Venus was the worst of the lot.

Down the street a door swung open, silhouetting two wavering shapes against a blur of yellow lamplight. The yowl of maudlin voices spilled out after them, with one raucous bellow rising above the rest:

"I was bo-o-orn a hunnerd thousan' years ago-o-o,
An' there's nothin' in the world that I dunno-o-o;
I seen Peter, Paul an' Moses . . ."

The door slammed, shutting it off, but Davis was already grinding his cigarette under his heel and the sergeant's boots were scuffing restlessly on the cobbled street. They knew that voice of old. Mulligan! And when Mulligan sang that song there'd be hell to pay in a matter of minutes!

Gibbon's hairy fist smashed into the door. Gun in hand, Davis stepped after him into the barroom. Over the heads of the cutthroat crew that packed the place the patrolman's eyes went unerringly to the source of trouble. Mulligan was standing on the bar, spraddle-legged, his favorite oaken staff gripped threateningly in one huge fist and his beet-red face thrust forward like an angry ape's. His little red eyes peered furiously out from under massive eaves of bone and his bun-shaped skull shone like a china doorknob. His back was hunched, his shirt was open on a barrel chest, and an empty bottle swung at the end of his long left arm.

"Who called me that?" he bellowed.

There was a party of slummers in a wall booth—a blonde girl and three pale, sleek youths in faultless formal dress. One, with a smear of mustache and horn-rimmed spectacles, was pretty far gone. His face was as red as Mulligan's as he wavered to his feet.

"S'a lie!" he shouted. "S'a damn lie! He—nobody's that old!"

Davis's gun snapped up. The drunken fool! But he was too late. Mulligan's arms swung like striking snakes. The bottle smashed on the wall above the youngster's head. His legs slid out from under him and he sat down hard just as the oaken staff bored a hole through the flimsy partition beside his ear.

Things happened then. The girl was on her feet, slim, white-faced, scarlet-lipped, wound in a sheath of silver. Her escorts were struggling with their chairs. And from somewhere behind their booth came the *sput* of a silenced gun. A dripping red line slashed across Mulligan's receding jaw. And in the same instant Gibbon shouted, David spun instinctively, and the world went out in a splash of fire.

That same hoarse voice wormed its way into Davis's dreams and made him wince. It brought back memories that started chariots of fire careening around inside his skull:

"... I seen Peter, Paul an' Moses
Playing 'ring-around-the-roses
Aaaan' I'll lick the guy who claims that it ain't so!

"I'm the guy that got ol' Sampson's whiskers curled;
I helped Joe an' Adolf divvy up the world,
An' I led the gang to cover
When George Washington came over
With the A.E.F. to see their game was spoiled!

"I taught Solomon to say his A-B-C's;
I helped Brigham Young invent Limburger cheese;
An' I ran the plane for Lindy
On his trans-Atlantic shindy,
While Chris Columbus whistled for a breeze!"

It was all he could endure. He pulled himself up on his rubber legs and held his splitting head in both hands and yelled *"Shuddup!"* Then he opened his eyes.

He saw bare gray rock and gray sky, and a curtain of gray mist that blanketed it all. It was drizzling, and he was stark naked, with little dribbles of tipid water running down his spine and dripping off the end of his nose. He saw Mulligan, a hundred yards away at the edge of the gray sea that lapped and gurgled horridly against the wet, gray rocks. The old man was as bare and pink as a skinned monkey, hunkered down puzzling over a clam.

Mulligan's monkey-face twisted toward him. It grinned, and the old man brought his fist down with a whack on the rock in front of him. Clam juice spurted and Mulligan began painstakingly to slurp up the mess out of his cupped palm.

Behind him Davis heard the noises of someone being sick. It was the very drunk young man of the barroom. In nothing but spectacles and a mustache he looked even less impressive than he had in a boiled shirt and a red sash. He was a little knock-kneed and his belly bulged more than it should have at his age. Davis patted his own taut abdomen approvingly and strode masterfully to investigate.

They were on a lump of rock that stuck up out of the steaming, stinking waters of Venus's mud-hole of a sea. From the marks on the rock they'd have six or eight feet to themselves at high tide. And there'd be things that would want to eat them.

He counted noses. Six, with Mulligan. Gibbon was sitting up in a puddle, staring ruefully at his bare toes. There was a bullet hole through the biceps of his right arm and a bloody gash in the clipped hair of his round skull. The two kids who had been with Goggles and the girl were still out. And they were all as naked as the day they were born, if you excepted the fur on Gibbon's chest and the toothbrush under Goggles' nose.

Old Man Mulligan came paddling over the rocks toward them. He was sober now and looked as harmless as a kitten. Davis felt his official temper rising.

"You got us into this mess, Mulligan," he snarled. "Now get us out of it!"

Mulligan's long face wrinkled in a toothless grin. "You look pretty good without pants, Cap," he observed. "I remember one time down in Nubia we run into a tribe that didn't wear nothing at all—but could they fight! Pharaoh, he says to me, 'Mike' he says—that was short for whatever it was those Egyptians used to call me—'Mike, you train me a couple thousan' of them cannibals an' we'll wipe ol' Hubble-Bubble an' his damn' Hittites right off the map!" So I picked me a brigade of the biggest an' barest an' blackest bucks I could find an' put 'em through the ol' West Point stuff. Then we got over in there back of Carchemish, an' damn' if the lot of 'em didn't get homesick an' light out for Nubia! Left me with my pants down, so to speak, so I hopped a ship for Mycenae an' got mixed up in a war they was havin' over a babe called Helena. Redhead, she was." His little eyes had a faraway look. "Geez, Cap—them was the days!"

Davis found his shoulder muscles sagging. You couldn't

bawl Mulligan out. Tougher men than he had tried. "You damned old liar!" he snapped. "Can't you drop that phoney past of yours long enough to think about the mess we're in?"

The red glint came into Mulligan's eyes again and the chin he didn't have jammed forward and set. "They was too many of 'em," he complained. "I'd of handled 'em, only the barkeep took me from behind with a full bottle." He fingered the back of his hairless skull. "Look—I got a bump like a egg."

"Never mind your bump!" There was more in this than met the eye. Mulligan's ruckuses usually landed him in jail or the hospital, not on a rock in the middle of the ocean. "Who shot you—and why?"

"Oh—him? That was one of Slip Hanlan's boys. I got him with a chair while Slip an' the rest was busy with the girl."

"What about the girl? What happened to her? How did we get here?" It was the young man with the mustache. He had come up silently in his bare feet, and the others were with him. "What happened to the girl?" he repeated. "Where is she?"

"Her?" Mulligan seemed surprised that anyone should be interested. "Hanlan got her." He chuckled. "She's got guts, that babe! Blacked Slip's eye for him an' damn near took the ear off one of his monkeys with a bottle. They had to put a bag over her head an' tie her up like a bale of weeds. That was when the barkeep slugged me. You was already out, Cap—you an' the Sarge both."

Davis heard Gibbon's growl and intervened hastily. "Who is this girl?" he demanded. "What does Slip Hanlan want with her—and why did he dump us here?"

One of the pale young men answered. "She's my cousin—Anne Bradshaw. Her father's Regent, you know. I—I guess they just figured she'd be worth a lot of money, so they kidnapped her."

The Regent's daughter! The kid was right—she would bring anything Hanlan wanted to ask—but the System wouldn't hold the man who kidnapped her after she was back in her father's hands, nor the man who failed to return her after the ransom was paid. Every man in the Space Patrol would be personally pledged to blow the guts out of the man who laid hands on Anne Bradshaw—and Slip Hanlan was ordinarily a smart guy. Too smart to stick his neck out—unless he had an absolutely sure thing.

"What were you punks doing in that dump, anyway?" he

asked. "Haven't you got sense enough to keep a woman out of a dive like that? Hell—you might have run into some lug who didn't know who she is and was too hopped up to care!"

"Captain Davis." It was Goggles again. "Perhaps I can explain. I am at the University—professor of anthropology there—and these two young men are my students. There was a dance at the University Club and Miss Bradshaw herself insisted on our taking her to the place. We must find her, at once!"

He looked like the kind of daisy the government would import for their pet boarding school at Laxa. All on a very high plane—no rough competitive sports, no engineering, nothing practical: the young of Laxa's Brass Hats had to have culture, so the pedigreed cream of Earth's Ph.D.'s was shipped to Venus to teach them. What the planet needed, Davis reflected grimly, was a military academy with a major in pioneering. Because the first generation on Venus had had a tough time keeping alive, they wanted everything to be silk and sugar for their offspring. The only trouble with that was that human beings had a toehold on less than two percent of the planet's surface, and the days of pioneering had a couple of generations yet to run.

"Look, boss." Gibbon's face was glum and he seemed self-conscious in his nakedness. "The way I see it there's got to be politics mixed up in this business. Any other way Slip'd be drizzly to try it. It's been fixed at headquarters that the whole thing'll be hushed up when he brings the girl back. The Patrol won't even know she was missing—or the professor here, or these young punks. Only Mulligan mixed in and we showed up. So they ferried us out here where we'd be out of their way, and no questions asked. Somebody'll come past with a boat when it's all over and be very much surprised to find us here. Then we'll be told just what we're supposed to know and how unfortunate it'd be to have other ideas about things.

"Only we won't be alive. Not in winter, and without clothes. Slip Hanlan's foxy that way!"

The girl's cousin, young Bradshaw, pushed forward. His face was flushed. "I don't believe it!" he cried. "Uncle Arthur would never stoop to anything like that."

Davis patted his thin shoulder. "Take it easy," he advised. "Even if the Sergeant's right, that doesn't mean your uncle is mixed up in it. There are powers behind him, here and on Earth, with their own strings to pull and their own reasons for pulling them. It could be pretty smart to pick up his daughter and keep him worried about her instead of about other things that may be brewing. If nothing happens to her, he'll play along for the good of the colony. That's how politics works."

He turned to Mulligan. The old man was down on his hunkers again, pulling shellfish off the rocks and sucking them out of their shells with gusto. "Mike," he called, "come back here. You know more about Venus than any man on it. My father told me so. Where are we, and how do we get out of here?"

Mulligan's face wrinkled perplexedly. "I been here," he admitted. "There's a lot of these little islands off the coast where the main ridge of the Skyscrapers runs into the ocean. I was here once with Morgan, back in the old days, fishin' for sea serpents."

"Sea serpents?" It was the second boy. "You mean here, in these waters—around us?"

The old man nodded. "Yeah. It's pretty deep here. There's plenty room for 'em to get real big, like they used to be back on Earth. Why, I remember—"

"You forget it!" Davis told him. "Do you mean that we're stuck here?"

"I wouldn't say that," the old man protested. "You better leave me puzzle it over a bit. We got to wait for high tide, anyway."

They left him opening clams and sought shelter under a ledge where they could hug their knees and steam in a little less discomfort. Winter on Venus was predominantly wet and windy. It was hot, the air was soakingly humid, and the rain was like cold soup, but the rock-shelter made them feel a little more like men.

The Professor had given up trying to see through his glasses and was peering owlishly over them. "Can we trust this man?" he wanted to know. "What can he do?"

Davis shrugged. "He can do all anyone can," he replied. "Old Man Mulligan's the biggest puzzle on Venus. He's been around as long as anyone living can remember. He was here with Morgan on the first exploring trip, if you believe the records. He hasn't changed a bit in two men's lifetimes, and I seriously doubt that he'll change in mine or yours. He knows Venus better than any man in the system, and if he says he can get us off, he's got a way of doing it. Am I right, Gibbon?"

"Yeah!" The sergeant had been packing lichens over the

hole in his arm. "That song of his was the first thing I heard when I stepped out of the transport thirty years ago. He was drunk and whalin' the bejasus out of some dope that called him a liar, and I had to get three other cops to help me put him in a cell. Then I had to hear him tell about Moses and Pharaoh's daughter, and how he'd been a priest over in a place called Midian and this Moses married his daughter. He's got daughters all over the system, if you believe half he says."

"Fantastic!" The Professor was on the verge of exploding. "No man can have lived since the days of Moses. Four thousand years! It's absurd! I happen to be an anthropologist, and I know!"

"He lays claim to a hundred thousand, if I remember," Davis said dryly. "I know for a fact he was alive eighty years ago, when my father came out here, and the records give him nearly twice that. He knows a lot about history, too, if he does get it garbled up sometimes. There must be a hell of a lot in your head to get twisted if you've lived a hundred thousand years!"

The Professor stared at him accusingly over his glasses. "Be serious!" he snapped. "You're an educated man; you know as well as I do that no man can live a thousand years, let alone a hundred thousand. It's ridiculous! I'll admit there is something peculiar about the man—the shape of his head for one thing, and his posture, and that brow-ridge. He definitely represents a very primitive type. Almost Neanderthaloid, I would say. A throwback, I presume. Where is he now?"

The second boy, Wilson, was at the far end of the shelter. "He's been hammering at a big rock," he reported, "and now he's knocking little pieces off it with another stone. Look— about those clams. If we're marooned here, shouldn't we be doing something to conserve them? I mean, they're all we have to eat, and they won't last long if Mulligan goes on wolfing them down like that!"

It was growing colder as night drew on. Venus never got really cold, even now, near the Pole and in the dead of "winter," but night in the rainy season could be as dismal an affair as you'd ask for. Davis tried to remember how the tides were running. The shallow sea and submerged coastline made them freakish and irregular, even though Venus had only the sun to produce them. Getting to his feet he peered out to sea. There was a definite strong current setting past the end of the island and rocks he had seen well above water a half hour before were buried in phosphorescent spume. The tide was rising.

He scrambled painfully down over the ledges to where the old man squatted. In the open the rising wind caught him and he shivered with the sudden chill. He heard other feet padding behind him and saw that Gibbon and the Professor were following him.

Mulligan had found a vein of flint in the limestone of which the island was made. He had half a dozen big chunks of the stuff on the ground beside him and was knocking fist-sized spalls off them with a lump of waterworn quartzite. He had about a dozen of them, and as the men approached began to work them down to shape with deft, quick raps of his hammer-stone, flaking off smaller chips all round their edge. Pretty soon he had a spear-shaped blade, flat on one side and rounded on the other, with an uneven cutting edge and a rounded base. He laid it down and started on another. The Professor nudged Davis excitedly.

"The Mousterian technique," he whispered. "Indubitable! Extraordinary!"

Davis cleared his throat apologetically. He felt like an ass, standing here in the rain watching an old man play caveman, but he had a feeling that he was intruding on something important.

"Mulligan," he said, "the tide's rising. Hadn't we better do something pretty soon?"

The old man looked up at him. "I am," he answered. "I'm makin' knives an' spears for the lot of us. There's things comin' in with the tide that'd make one nip of the Sergeant or you an' use the Professor for a toothpick. If I was you, I'd get them punks out lookin' for somethin' I can use for handles. It ain't always convenient to get real close to critters like them."

"Do you claim that you are one hundred thousand years old?" The professor's voice nearly cracked.

Mulligan ducked his head sheepishly. "I guess mebbe that's a little strong," he admitted, "but it fits good in the song. Last time I figured it out for a feller that knew about things like that it came out about thirty thousand. Might be five or ten thousand off one way or the other, he thought. There was a long time there I didn't have no inclination to keep track of stuff like that, an' it was pretty hard to catch up. Even in Sumer they wasn't much good at big numbers, an' this was way before that—before they come down out of the hills, even."

Davis turned away as he saw the professor's jaw beginning to drop. The damned old liar! He rounded up Gibbon and the two boys, and they began to search for long, straight staves of driftwood which might serve as spear shafts. They found only three which were long enough and strong enough to be of any use. The continent must be fairly close, Davis reflected, to get any green wood out here at all. Maybe Mulligan knew what he was doing, after all.

They still had an hour's half-light left, Davis estimated. The dense Venusian atmosphere strung twilight out into what was practically a diurnal season. They found Mulligan up to his armpits in the surf, his enormous nose nearly in the water prodding and poking with a notched and pointed stick. As they reached the water's edge he jabbed viciously at the general neighborhood of his feet and plunged after the harpoon to come up coughing and spewing salt water, with something leggy and shapeless squirming on the end of his stick.

Davis watched with interest and the Professor with what bordered on despair as the old man planted his bare feet on the thing's lashing tectacles and proceeded to slice it up with his flint knife. Presently he had several long strips of tough leathery tissue with which he lashed his spearheads firmly into the cleft ends of the shafts they had found. Inasmuch as Gibbon's right arm was useless, Davis decided that he would have to be their reserve. To the tune of the sergeant's grumbling the five men returned to their shelter to watch and wait.

Mulligan did not join them. He was making a weapon for himself—a wicked-looking tooth of chipped flint half as long as his forearm, with the butt rounded for a grip. The professor called it a fist-axe and went into a profound sulk because evidence and science were growing more and more at odds with every moment.

It was fast growing darker. Mulligan's squat frame was barely visible against the pallid phosphorescence of the sea, perched on the end of a spine of rock that thrust out into deep water. Davis wondered how long it would be before the tide flooded them out and forced them to take refuge on the exposed crown of the island, at the mercy of winds and rain and every famished sea monster that came that way. Grimly he watched the glowing line of surf lap higher and higher. It was almost up to Mulligan's dangling legs when he let out a piercing yell and vanished.

They went pelting down the rocks, spears in hand, to the promontory where Mulligan had been. Waist deep in the rising water, the old man was jumping up and down like a maniac, waving his arms and hooting like a demented ape. Then a hundred feet beyond, Davis saw something rise sluggishly to the surface. The old man saw it too. He retreated toward shore, still yelling and waving his arms frantically. Then it rose again!

It was like Leviathan of the legends. It rose out of the sea like a billowing wave, washed over with creamy spume—a colossal turtle's carapace, studded and ribbed and grown over with barnacles and clinging weeds—an armored, vast-eyed head with sneering beak, set on a wrinkled neck—huge, curving flippers that hooked and scrabbled at the sloping rock. The black bubbles of its lidless eyes stared at the little bandy-legged creature who danced tauntingly before it. A wave broke over its back, hiding it, and then it appeared again, much closer, and began to move ponderously toward the shore, its snaking dragon's head thrust evilly forward.

Mulligan came scrambling over the rocks toward them, shouting at them in some unknown tongue. With a yell to the others Davis began the same insane dance, drawing the thing's attention, luring it ashore. The hooked beak and staring eyes rose out of the foam at their very feet. It lunged at the little group on the rock's summit, fell short, and before it could recover the old man leaped.

He twisted like a cat in midair and came down astride of the monster's wrinkled neck. Flat on his belly, legs locked around that barrel of muscle, he drove his fist-axe into the creature's throat. Blood spurted like black oil into the burning sea. His whole arm was buried in the gaping wound he had torn. The monster writhed and twisted, striving vainly to reach him. Its flippers churned the sea. It was turning—heading for deeper water!

Gibbon, empty-handed, went over the side of the rock. He came up flailing madly with his good arm, found footing and dashed at the thing's head, turning it. As it snapped at him he leaped back, and then Davis and the others were beside him. Young Bradshaw's spear glanced harmlessly off the monster's armored head and vanished into the sea. The professor's eyes were gleaming strangely behind his spectacles. He danced down the slippery ledge under the sea-thing's very beak, and rising on tiptoe planted his spear deep in the giant turtle's staring eye.

The thing recoiled, nearly hurling Mulligan from his perch, then lunged viciously. The edge of its carapace caught the professor, spinning him aside, and its beak gaped before Davis's startled eyes. Before it could close he drove his spear deep down that reeking gullet and flung himself out of its path. Its horny jaws closed on the shaft, clipping it like a twig, then the Wilson boy darted in and drove his weapon into its other eye and through into the brain beyond.

The gigantic jaws gaped wide. Black blood poured out of them. The scrabbling flippers sagged and the monster surged forward on the beach, its long neck writhing blindly. Then Mulligan's blade reached home and the life gushed out of the great beast in a steaming stream, leaving it inert on the rocks with the tide lapping against its vast, curving shell.

The old man clambered to his feet and stood looking them over. They were a bloody, draggled crew—but they had won! He grinned approvingly and waved an arm up the beach.

"Get the knives," he ordered. "We got work to do."

Thigh-deep in blood and foam the six men hacked and pried at the giant carcass, hewing away the muscles which held the bowl-shaped carapace, separating the ribs and cutting through the giant spinal column. The sea was red around them, and beyond the first line of breakers they could see black, misshapen forms rising and falling with the surge of the waves. Ghouls, drawn by the taste of death. And, Davis reflected, a living wall between them and the mainland.

The tide had nearly reached the high-water mark when they finally lifted the edge of the great shell and tipped it over into the sea. It floated low in the water, with a bloody soup slopping around inside it, and Davis's stomach turned over as he realized that this was to be their ferry to the mainland.

A rocky point, which had been a ridge when the day began, ran into the sea at the tip of the island. At Mulligan's direction they dragged the huge shell away from the carcass—and away from the ravening creatures of the deep that had scented its blood nad were waiting for the tide to float it out to them. Young Wilson had kept his spear, and the professor's had been dragged out of the ruin of the turtle's eye after it collapsed. Mulligan's fist-axe was their only other weapon. And the thrash and bellow of monstrous life out there in the darkness told them what they might expect before their crazy coracle reached shore.

While Mulligan busied himself with the sea-thing's tangled

entrails, cutting long strips of gut and twisting it into a kind of cord which he wrapped around his waist, the others bailed out what they could of the mess inside the shell and gingerly took their places on its slippery bottom. Davis and the old man were last. Slowly they edged the great bowl along the rocks and out into the current that swirled past the point. As the tide caught it, they tumbled in and crouched with the others in the bottom. It rocked drunkenly with the force of their shove, grated for a moment on a submerged rock, then swung ponderously around and was loose.

Every other wave, it seemed, broke into the sluggish craft. Gibbon and the boys bailed furiously with their hands. Davis took Wilson's spear and stationed himself at what had been the tail end of the oval shell. The professor, using his weapon as a staff, crouched unsteadily in the middle, and Mulligan, still gripping his spike of flint, squatted in the bow, his long toes gripping the slimy ladder made by the creature's ribs.

The old man's restless eyes sighted the first danger. At his grunt Davis raised himself as far as he dared. Ten yards away the thing broke water. It had a snout like a crocodile and a streamlined, glistening body that slipped effortlessly through the waves. It rolled over, showing a gleaming belly, and dove. Ten seconds slipped by—twenty—a minute, and Davis let himself drop back. Then at his very elbow the monster rose again. Two tiny red eyes, buried in slits in the glistening flesh, glared down at him. A snout edged with tiny, saw-edged teeth grinned at him. And with all his strength he drove his heavy spear into the soft, pouched throat beneath that narrow jaw.

The great thing rose like a breaching whale—up and up and up until it seemed to stand on its tail in midair. Then with a crash that nearly swamped the shell it fell back. Davis hung on grimly with both hands and watched the sea spin past. Off to the left the creature rose again. Its outline was barely visible against the pale phosphorescence of the water. Something stout and stubby, with bristling fins, had fastened itself savagely to its dangling lower jaw.

Suddenly the sea about them was alive. The taint of fresh blood was in the waves, and the death-watch gathered. A vast, scaly something rose almost under the shell, tipping it, and hurled Davis back into the human tangle in the bottom. Water poured over them, and out of the murk a spined and wattled head peered down at them. Mulligan yelled defiance, brandishing his fist-axe like a war club. Another wave caught

Davis in the face and bowled him over. Over the bellow of the sea beasts the sergeant's voice rose in a howl of anguish:

"Bail, damn you! We'll be under!"

They bailed—Gibbon with his one good arm, the others with both hands, splashing bloody water out a little faster than it vomited in. The professor's spear was somewhere underfoot, swashing back and forth in the reeking bilge, and Mulligan still clung like a limpet to his perch. Off in the night another of the sea monsters grumbled, and Davis's fingers closed on the floating spear.

He straightened up, straddling the knobby column of bone that ran from stem to stern of their drunken craft—the turtle's spine. His eyes fell on Mulligan, silhouetted against the pallid glow of the sea, and a tingling chill ran down his spine. The old man's head was drawn down between his scarred shoulders, his chinless face thrust out, tasting the wind. His broad back was curved like a crouching wolf's, his bandy legs drawn up under him, his long arms dangling. He was like a great, hairless ape of the night, carved out of ebony and set there for a figurehead to ward off demons. His great bald head swung suddenly toward the men, and Davis thought he caught a glint of greenish fire in the little eyes before it turned away.

The minutes passed by over them, and the hours. How long it was Davis could not tell. The wind had fallen and the sea was more quiet. There was an oily swell that rocked their cranky craft like a cradle, up and down, back and forth. The professor was sick and the two boys crouched miserably together in the bottom. Hour after hour passed, while Davis watched vainly for some glint of dawn in the sky and Old Man Mulligan squatted silent and inscrutable in the bow, peering ahead into the darkness.

They were the sea's toy, tossed where it willed, at the mercy of unknown, uncharted currents. If the tide had turned they might be drifting away from land, out into the unmapped, unfathomed, mist-wrapped waste that covered half of Venus. Five men, naked in the night with the cold rain slatting down across their backs and the slap and whisper of the phosphorescent waves the only sound in the world. Five men, Davis thought—and Mulligan.

He closed his eyes and listened. Very far away, he thought, he could hear a sullen roar as of surf against rocky ledges. Perhaps the tide was carrying them back to the island. It might be land. He strained his ears, but it was gone, and Mulligan had not stirred.

Suddenly the old man was on his feet, his legs braced, his head thrust forward like a scenting hound's. He was unwinding the rope of twisted gut from his waist and running it through his gnarled fingers, tightening it, forming a noose. Cautiously Davis got to his feet. It was lighter now. Past the old man's tense shape he saw the arch of a glistening dome—another of the great turtles. Mulligan crouched lower, and with a cry to Gibbon Davis hurled himself back into the stern as the old man's noose settled over the monster's head.

Their weight in the stern was all that saved the shell from going over. As the rope tightened the front of the carapace plowed deep into the waves. Davis was hanging to the rim with both hands; Gibbon had him around the waist, and the others were sprawled on the bottom. One by one they scrambled to join the two Patrolmen. Like five naked apes they perched on the edge of the great shell, balancing the pull of the runaway monster. Both feet planted against an arching rib, Old Man Mulligan was lying back with all his weight, the rope tight around his waist. The muscles stood out like oak roots on his arms and back. They were on their way at last, but where they were going only the Almighty—or the turtle—knew.

At a word from Davis, young Bradshaw slipped down from his perch and went to give Mulligan a hand. He was the lightest of them, and the old man could not stand the strain alone much longer. Side by side, like charioteers of old, they stood and rode the sea—the gnarled, brown body and the slim white one, outlined in the brightening day.

There was no doubt—ahead there came the roar of surf. Mulligan shouted back at them but his voice was whipped away in the wind. Then with a crash that hurled them headlong into the sea the shell struck. It split like a gourd and went down sucking them after it. Savagely Davis fought his way to the surface. Gibbon was clinging to a rock, just clear of the water. Wilson's head bobbed up between them, and the boy struck out vigorously to join the sergeant. But of Mulligan and young Bradshaw there was no trace.

The mist was lifting. There were rocks all around them, jagged and black, with the waves breaking angrily over them. Then out of the gloom came a hail:

"Ho-o-o o-o!"

A second voice joined the first "Ho-o o-o-o! Da-a-avis!"

Gibbon answered with a strangled bellow, and then Davis saw them. The cliffs were close, steep and frowning, with the sea smashing against them. Mulligan and the boy were clinging to a long, rocky spit that ran out from a little cove at their base. Davis took a long breath and let the sea carry him in.

Mulligan's hand closed over his wrist and dragged him to safety on the reef. Out in the welter of foam he saw Gibbon's clipped head and young Wilson's sleek one. The sergeant was forging ahead vigorously in spite of his wounded arm. A few minutes later they were all together—all but the Professor.

A step at a time, feeling their way through the surf that broke over the reef, they edged their way shoreward. It was Gibbon who saw the missing man, lying in the wash of the waves. His glasses were gone and there was a great bruise on his forehead, but when they dragged him up on the little beach he stirred feebly and opened his eyes.

Watching Gibbon drain the water out of the bedraggled teacher, Davis wondered what came next. They were naked, famished, marooned miles from the nearest settlement. There might be a way over the circle of cliffs, but beyond was the unexplored wilderness of the Skyscrapers, peaks that dwarfed many of Earth's proudest ranges, and beyond them the jungle. Venus was no Eden.

He studied Mulligan, busy over the professor. The old man was the only one of them who didn't seem out of place. Those cruel scars and massive muscles spoke of battles with nature more terrible than anything they had yet gone through. What was the truth about him?

Gibbon limped over, hugging his hurt arm. "The prof took quite a beating, Boss," he observed sourly. "We better stay here a while." He scowled. "We won't get any place barefoot, without anything in our bellies."

"You'd oughta have feet like mine." It was Mulligan. The old man's soles were like black horn. "I been goin' barefoot every chance I get, ever since I can remember. Shoes is crampin' if you was brought up free-footed like me."

"We weren't," Davis pointed out acidly. "We've got to get back and start on Hanlan's trail before he puts over whatever trick he has up his sleeve, but without shoes we won't make a mile a day over those mountains. What's more, we'll starve at that pace."

The old man chuckled. "You'll get shoes," he said. "Nor you won't starve. I been here before, remember, an' if I hadn't I could still keep goin' any place that'll grow worms. Tell those two punks they got to find a little pile of sand, up above high water. When they got it, yell."

In less then ten minutes Bradshaw let out a whoop. Almost simultaneously Wilson called from further down the beach. Each had a low mound about eight feet in diameter, heaped up in the sand. Mulligan went at the first like a terrier in a rat-hole. Sand flew for a minute; then he swung back on his heels and held up a dirty yellow object about a foot long.

"Turtle eggs," he explained. "There's a string of these little beaches along the coast where they come to lay. The one we rode in was likely headed for this one, but we scared her off."

There were twelve eggs in the nest Bradshaw had found, and ten in Wilson's. Mulligan made himself another crude stone knife with which he carefully cut a circle out of an egg, just short of the end, big enough to push a foot through. The leathery shell made a crude but effective moccasin, and the egg itself went a long way toward satisfying their hunger.

They spent the night huddled together under the cliffs, wet and miserable. What wood they could find was too waterlogged to burn, even if they had had any way of lighting a fire. As the first gray light began to filter through the clouds they gulped down a breakfast of raw turtle eggs, pulled on their clumsy shoes, and set out to explore the circuit of the cliffs. The professor seemed himself again, and Mulligan was as chipper as a youngster. Gibbon's arm was paining him, and Davis fashioned a sling out of strands of seaweed, but there was nothing more he could do.

Davis had been planning a conference in which every contingency would be brought up and disposed of, and a plan of action worked out. He never had the opportunity to suggest one. Before he could protest, Mulligan went at the cliffs like a squirrel, his seaweed basket of eggs bobbing merrily on his back. They could only follow.

The old man was thoroughly at home. He trotted along with the thin drizzle of rain cascading down his backbone, uncomplaining and sure-footed as a goat. The others were less fortunate. After struggling painfully up a precipitous slope, clinging to the rock with tooth and nail, they would reach the top and find him squatting on a hand's breadth of level ground, only to have him swing tirelessly to his feet and disappear into some chasm or up a steepling crag.

When at last they came down out of the mountains into the jungle it was worse. There was no trail. Mulligan seemed to flow through the underbrush where the others had to fight their way step by step through a wall of thorns and tangled vines. Nevertheless, it was Mulligan who kept them alive. The six-foot staff he had provided for himself was like a magic wand. With it he probed seemingly bottomless morasses or made a bridge from root to root where black ooze crawling with venomous life was the only floor to the jungle. With it he knocked down small animals which they learned to eat raw, and on it he strung poisonous looking fungi which nevertheless filled their stomachs. With it, once, he fought off a snarling, yellow cat-like thing which contested their way.

Once, even, the old man found a tree whose inner bark was dry and tindery, and all that night they crowded gratefully around the little fire he made by rubbing a stick of dry wood in a wooden groove. By morning the crude friction device was soaked and their fuel gone. They got stiffly to their feet and stumbled on, cold and empty, following the old man's great splayed footprints in the mud.

They had spent a night at sea in the shell and a night on the beach. They spent a night in the mountains and three more in the forest. A little light was still filtering down through the giant tree-ferns when they suddenly came upon Mulligan, flat on his face in the mud at the edge of a clearing.

Davis was bringing up the rear. He nearly fell over the professor, who was lying in the middle of the trail peering near-sightedly ahead. On hands and knees he made his way to where Mulligan and the sergeant were lying. Gibbon pointed wordlessly.

There was a house in the clearing. It was the familiar pillbox of the Venusian trader, a rambling affair of concrete without windows or any other unnecessary openings which would afford an entrance for the unpleasantly persistent fauna of the jungle.

"Hanlan!" the sergeant muttered through his teeth.

Hanlan? Then Mulligan had known all along where they were. He had brought them here deliberately, naked and unarmed, where they could only sit and fume at their helplessness. Red spots danced before Davis's eyes. He'd been playing second fiddle long enough!

"Sergeant Gibbon," he snapped, "we're taking over. I'll reconnoiter. Stay here until I signal you. If Hanlan is here, he won't be expecting us. We have the advantage of surprise, and we'll have to use it."

OLD MAN MULLIGAN

Beside them in the mud old Mulligan chuckled. "You ain't got a badge any more Cap'n," he pointed out slyly. "You ain't even got a uniform. Mebbe Slip won't reconnize you."

Davis ignored him. "Hanlan may not be here," he went on. "We have only Mulligan's word that it's his hideout. But if it is his, and I don't come back, you're in command. Understand?"

"Sure, Boss." Gibbon saluted awkwardly. "Only I don't see what we can do about it if he puts up an argument."

Well inside the forest, Davis made a circuit of the clearing. Someone was evidently in the place, for a good-sized launch was tied up inside a breakwater where the jungle met an arm of the sea. For safety's sake, he removed some of the engine's vitals and watched them disappear in a dozen feet of turgid water.

A series of terraces rose steeply behind the hut, and a quick examination showed him no easy road over them. The place was set in a sort of niche in the hillside and would probably be entirely invisible to patrol boats unless they ventured into the unknown waters of the fjord on which it faced. It was an ideal hideout.

If Hanlan had tele-cells set, there was no evidence of it. When he made sure that there were none of the scanning eyes in evidence anywhere on the hut's interior, Davis made bold to scurry up close to its walls. He located the radiation plate of the cooling system, at the end opposite the single door. It was hot, proving that there was someone inside.

There might be spying devices in the door frame, invisible from a distance, and he kept away from that. The rest of the walls he went over foot by foot. There was a ventilator on the roof, but it had a stout grating across it and in any case was barely big enough to admit a man's head, let alone his body. If Slip Hanlon wanted to stay inside till doomsday there was nothing Davis could do about it.

He went back to the radiation plate. If the hut was built on the usual plan, the conditioner would be in a booth in the little storeroom which was in the rear of most such shacks. The chances were good that nobody ever went into the place unless something went wrong. He studied the plate carefully. The metal grid of cooling fins was set flush with the wall, but the concrete was stained and crumbling around its edges, and in one place there was a good-sized crack. If only he had some sort of tool!

He remembered the launch. Fifteen minutes later he was

hard at work, chipping away at the concrete. It was soft and fell away easily. Soon he was able to get the end of a steel bar under the edge of the plate. He heaved with all his strength and the thing yielded a little. He heaved again. Inside the hut something spanged and the plate came out a good two inches.

Whoever had set the conditioner up had been careless. The bolts which held the plate were loose enough for Davis to get a wrench in through the slit and remove them completely. This gave him enough room to push an arm through and grope around for the couplings of the heat exhaust tubes. He found them at once because they were hot, and it took much poking and swearing before he had them loose from the radiation plate, and had lowered it gently to the ground.

He listened. Everything was dark and still inside except for the liquid chuckle of the refrigeration fluid in the pipes of the conditioner. Using wads of wet leaves to protect his hands, he bent the tubes aside as far as they would go. With a chisel from the yacht's tool kit he slid back the tongue of the lock on the cabinet door. It swung noiselessly open. With a wriggle he went through the hole, grazing the hot tubes painfully and scraping a patch of skin off his hip.

The storeroom was dark, but there was a crack of light under the door leading to the other part of the hut. He tiptoed toward it, one fist closed tightly around a man-sized wrench. Then something clipped him neatly behind the left ear and he went down with a thud.

His legs were hobbled and his arms tied behind his back when he came to. A wad of metallic tasting cloth was jammed into his mouth. He struggled and commented violently through the gag. A small hand slapped him smartly on the jaw.

"Shut up!" a woman's voice hissed.

Twenty years later in life Davis might have been in danger of apoplexy. "Gug ga gu!" he gargled. "Ge goe gow! Gu-gu!"

A small, cold circle pressed purposefully into his naked stomach. He knew the feeling. She had a gun.

"Be quiet!" she whispered. "They'll be in here any minute! Get under that bed at once or I'll knock you out again and put you there."

He submitted meekly to being rolled under a small iron cot that stood against one wall. She dropped a blanket over the side to hide him and switched on the lights. He twisted his wrists tentatively. She'd done a good job, but maybe not good enough. By dint of much writhing he was able to bring one eye close to a hole in the blanket. What he saw made his jaws clamp down hard on his gag.

It was the girl in the bar-room, Anne Bradshaw. It would be, he thought. Her silver gown was rumpled, and the skirt had been torn off knee-high, revealing a pair of entirely satisfactory legs. She was fiddling with her hair. With a glance toward the bed, she turned her back and rummaged for a moment under her skirt. Davis's eyes hardened when he saw the gun in her hand—small but businesslike. Chances were that it threw the new high-velocity slug that bowled a man over like a cannonball.

There was a brisk knock on the door. Stooping, the girl slid the little gun across the floor and under the bed. A key rattled in the lock and two men stepped into the room.

The smaller of the two was Slip Hanlan. Every man in the Patrol knew his face and record. He was sleek and dark, with a ratty little mustache. He had a long red scratch down one cheek which might have been made by an enameled fingernail. The man with him was the standard slugger: burly, empty faced, thoroughly overdressed in imitation of his leader.

At Hanlan's gesture the gun-lug closed the door and leaned against it. The gang leader looked the girl over coolly from head to toe and she stared calmly back at him, eye to eye. Straining furiously at his bonds, with the little gun lying under his very nose, Davis watched apprehensively.

"We have visitors." Hanlan was going to be silky about it. "Know anything about 'em? It wouldn't be nice to have 'em trying to bust in where they're not wanted."

The girl stared at him, blank faced. "What do you mean?" she inquired.

His smile was very like a snarl. "I mean that if any snooping sons of crump-worms interfere with our little conference it might be embarrassing for you. Regent's Daughter Surprised with Gang Boss. Debutante in Jungle Rendezvous. That stuff. It'll stink!"

She sat down on the bed and crossed her long legs calmly. "There were friends with me who know what really happened. The Patrol knows by now. Probably they're getting ready to give you the going over you deserve! They've wanted to get something on you for a long time. I'll enjoy watching them!"

Hanlan's little laugh was nasty. "Whoever it is out there is lying low," he told her. "The Patrol don't act like that. As for those monkeys you were with, they're keeping cool where nobody'll bother 'em until I say so."

The strands of twisted cloth with which Davis's hands were tied yielded so suddenly that he nearly rammed his elbow into the wall behind him. He pulled the gag out of his mouth and unfastened the hobbles on his legs, then cautiously picked up the little gun. It was loaded.

"Plug." Hanlan jerked a thumb at the lug by the door. "Get outside and tell the boys to keep an eye open. Old Bradshaw may have put a scout on the babe here, but it won't do him any good. I'm calling the play from here on."

"Are you really?" Anne Bradshaw's voice dripped icicles. "And what is the play, as you see it?"

Hanlan's nasty little smile vanished. "I'm sick of being kicked around by stuffed shirts," he snapped. "Twenty years ago every one of 'em was doing what I've done, an' getting rich on it. They were pioneers an' I'm a criminal. They're rich an' have fancy mansions, an' I have to hide out in a stinking shack. They've killed and thieved and cut the government's throat, and they're respected for it. Well—I'm joining 'em!"

"What do I have to do with that?" There was a satin-smooth note in the girl's voice that made Davis suspicious.

"You're my ticket," Hanlan sneered. "Right now there's a bill on the Regent's desk. It's had the vote of all the Council and all he's got to do is put his name to it. It leases the government development on the West Continent to the Dobermann Colonization Association for ninety-nine Earth years. The Association has to build roads and houses, and provide transportation for good, able-bodied, honest settlers who want to come out and be big shots in a new world. They're all members of the Association, and if they're still alive after ten years they can sell out or sign up for another ten. If a man don't stick out his time he pays cash for every day he's used the land and every mouthful of food he's put in his belly up to the time he quits. The government goes his bond when it picks him to come out here and sells the Association the idea he's a good risk. If he can't pay up, or won't, his holdings go to the Association outright, on account of the trouble and money it's put into him. It's legal and it's respectable. Only—if the regent should somehow get the idea that Felix Dobermann, the millionaire promoter, is also Slip Hanlan, he might let his own respectability run away with his common sense.

"That's where you come in. While he's reading that bill over an' reaching for his pen he'll be remembering where his daughter is, and how long you've been here, and the kind of stink the papers will make if they hear about it. He'll remember that Slip Hanlan never backtracks on his sayso and that you're okay unless something happens to that bill. If it was crooked he might hold out, but it's legal and it's got big men behind it. Bigger than he is, maybe. So he'll figure what he don't know is none of his business and maybe Felix Dobermann is just as good as any other man with the same money and the same friends. He'll sign—and ten minutes after he does you'll be on your way home. Simple, ain't it?"

Anne Bradshaw began to laugh. It was silvery, taunting laughter, but there was nothing hysterical about it. She was just very, very much amused about something, and from what Davis could see of Slip Hanlan's face the gangster didn't like it much.

"So that's it!" she gasped. "Slip Hanlan—a social climber. Trying to buy into the white coat circle. I suppose Felix Dobermann would be trying to buy himself a seat on the Council after a while. Maybe he'd like to be regent, after the big boys got to know what a square guy he is. It's funny!"

Davis saw Slip Hanlan's lips curl in a snarl of fury. No dame laughed at him! He slipped back the safety catch on the little gun. Then something crashed into the back of the shack with a shock that brought flakes of concrete rattling down from the ceiling.

It was a privilege to watch Hanlan draw. There were guns in both hands before he had turned. As he reached the door a second blow shook the hut. A long crack opened in the rear wall and more fragments of concrete dusted down.

The door burst open in his face. It was the slugger, Plug. The man's eyes were popping. "Gees, Slip," he cried, "they're rollin' rocks down on us! Whatta we do?"

There was no silk in Hanlan's snarl now. "Get out there with the Manton and cut their guts out! Use hot stuff on 'em. If they want to play, we'll play with 'em!"

As the door closed behind them Davis was crawling out from under the bed. The girl confronted him, face white, blue eyes blazing. "You meddling fool!" she snapped. "Can't you play detective somewhere else?"

Another boulder struck the rear of the hut with terrific

force. Davis remembered the steeply mounting ledges behind the clearing. Gibbon was using a potent weapon, but against a Manton rapid-fire gun with explosive bullets five naked men would be like babies. Why hadn't the fool stayed put!

What was left of the girl's skirt after she had bound him was on the bed. He twisted it around his middle in a kind of kilt and cautiously tested the door. It was unlocked. He eased it open.

There were three men with Hanlan in the outer room. A frantic pounding began on the outside door. One of the three pulled it open. A man crumpled on his face on the floor. Something whizzed past Davis's head and stuck singing in the wall behind him. It was a long sliver of wood, smeared with some black stuff that smelled like dead fish. As they rolled the man over he saw a second dart buried in his throat.

A man whimpered as another blow rocked the hut. "Whatta we do, Slip?" he wailed. "They got poison on them darts. They got Plug an' Benny too. Whatta we do?"

"We sit tight!" Hanlan snarled. "They can't get us by rollin' rocks. Blowguns won't shoot through concrete. We can wait as long as they can, an' when old Bradshaw gets wise to himself he'll call 'em off!"

"Will he?" Davis stepped out into the room, his gun ready. "Those are my men out there, Hanlan. The men you left sitting on a rock in the middle of the ocean. The regent has nothing to do with them. Open that door."

There was an ugly glint in Hanlan's eyes. It changed suddenly as something dropped over Davis's head, binding his arms to his side. A slim leg tangled with his and he went down with the girl on top of him.

Propped against the wall with his wrists wired together and his legs doubled behind him, Davis watched furiously as Hanlan and the girl faced it out across the little room. She had the gun now, and Hanlan seemed distinctly uncomfortable.

"You talk like a politician, Mr. Hanlan—or is it Dobermann?" she said coolly, "but you don't think like one. Who really planned your little deal for you? Who taught you the pretty speech you made just now? My father has been very curious about that ever since he heard that your precious association was lobbying for a land grant. He wants settlers on Venus, but he doesn't want them exploited, you see. And he's not interested in figureheads. He likes to get to the bottom of things, and so do I."

Hanlan eyed her sullenly. The nose of the little gun was

leveled at the fancy silver buckle on his belt. He said nothing.

"The naked gentleman was telling the truth," the girl told him. "I'm perfectly able to take care of myself without calling in the Boy Heroes. I came here of my own free will, to see just what your game was and how you were going to play it. I want to know who is playing it with you."

"What does it get me?" Hanlan demanded. "I been paid well to keep my mouth shut about that. Why should I spill it to you."

"That's a good question," the girl admitted. "You're really a businessman. You've lost two men, you know. You can't leave this place until someone calls off that blowgun squad." She lifted one slim foot and unfastened a silver rosette from her shoulder; tossed it to the gangster. "That little gadget has been buzzing over since you picked me up," she told him. "There's a Coast Patrol cruiser offshore now, listening to it and waiting for me to signal them in. There'll be a kidnapping charge against you. Our gallant hero here may want to add a charge of *lese majesté* unless you give him back his badge and uniform. Tell me what I want to know and we'll all walk out of here together like old friends."

An oily smile had crept over Hanlan's face. He flipped the little transmitter lightly in the air and caught it again. "Clever, ain't you?" he jeered. "The boat that brought you here was screened against gadgets like this. This shack is screened. Nobody's heard it, and nobody's going to."

Davis thought the gun wavered a little in the girl's hand. His own patience was exhausted. "Stop your crazy chatter and untie me," he growled. "I have men out there who can handle him if you haven't. The Patrol knows how to deal with lugs like him. Now we've got something we can prove on him, there'll be a hundred rats squealing about other things we've known for years but couldn't prove. That's what his kind is like. You won't have to worry about Mister Slip Hanlan Dobermann!"

Anne Bradshaw's eyes blazed. "I expected that of you!" she cried. "The way you blundered into this affair in the beginning was typical of you high and mighty tin horn policemen. You got what you deserved, and I'm glad of it! The Venus government is handling this business in its own way, and that happens to be my way. The Space Patrol will have nothing whatever to do with it!"

Davis wriggled into a sitting position. The maneuver brought his bound wrists against an angular bit of steel that had been digging into his shoulder for the past several minutes. It was apparently a bit of the skeleton of the shack, and it was firmly anchored where it would do the most good.

"When I do get out of here we'll see who handles this case how!" he retorted. "If you think the Patrol or the Triplanetary Commission is going to stand by and see a lot of fat-headed politicians exploit some poor half-starved imbeciles who'll sign anything for a chance at a decent living, you're mistaken. I know too much. My men know too much. Maybe Hanlan and his lugs won't be the only ones we lock up!"

The girl turned her back on him with a jerk. She was fairly quivering with anger. "Mr. Hanlan," she said. "You're looking for a chance to be respectable. All right, you can have it. For the information we want you can be Felix Dobermann. We want settlers here, and the people who can hurt them are the crooked politicians, not nobodies like you. Tell me who is back of this deal and we'll forget I ever left Laxa. We'll forget there ever was a Slip Hanlan. I think you can make sure that the news doesn't slip out in any other way."

Hanlan's jaw sagged. His beady eyes scanned the girl incredulously. "What are you drivin' at?" he demanded.

She never answered, because at that moment one of Hanlan's gunmen let out an anguished yelp and batted at his neck. A new sound impressed itself on Davis—a shrill, humming whine that grew louder every minute. Hanlan himself ducked violently and began to wave his arms like a madman. Then Davis saw them—a little cloud like a wisp of black smoke, streaming through the ventilator grille above his head. Midges!

He sawed furiously at the wires that bound him. Midges had made their life miserable in the jungle. Their bite was sheer torment, and men had been killed by them. Mulligan had found a plant whose odor kept them off, but the cure was about as bad as the complaint.

The room was full of the little demons. The four men were stamping, swatting, stumbling blindly around in what must have been an agony. Then the first of the midges found Davis. Its bite was like a hot needle, pouring vitriol into his veins. Through the tears that filled his eyes he saw Anne Bradshaw, backed against the door with an arm over her eyes, the gun pointed waveringly in front of her.

"Keep back!" she cried. "You'll stay here until you answer me—every one of you!"

The wire on Davis's wrists seemed looser. He hooked the

loop under the little point of steel and jerked on it with all his might. A stab of fire under his left ear and another in his thigh spurred him on. The wire broke. Tottering on his bound legs, he snatched the fragment of cloth from his waist and stuffed it into the ventilator, then dove for the safety of the floor just as Hanlan lunged at the girl.

She was blind with the pain of the midge bites. As Hanlan caught her around the waist her little gun went off with a wicked *spat*, bringing a howl of new pain from one of the three gunmen. She came spinning across the room, tripped over Davis's prone form, and fell. Then Hanlan yanked the door open and there was a rush for the open air.

Through half-closed eyes Davis saw Slip Hanlan go down like a rag doll under an enormous club wielded by a monster out of a nightmare. There were five of the things, black and shapeless, plastered from head to foot with dripping, stinking mud and swinging their clubs with a will. Clouds of midges swarmed like smoky haloes around their heads, and there were tufts of leaves growing out of their scalps and behind their ears as though they had taken root and were sprouting.

One of them was fumbling with the wire on his legs. Another was bending over the girl. The door was shut again and the midges were no longer pouring in through the air-intake. Painfully, through one good eye, Davis surveyed the besmeared, one-armed monstrosity which was presumably Top-Sergeant Gibbon.

"Account for yourself!" he barked. "You had orders to stay where you were until I signalled an attack. I gave no signal."

The mud-covered figure snapped to attention. "Yessir! It was Mulligan, sir. I saw 'em whisperin' and then the four of 'em jumped me. By the time I got loose Mulligan and the kids was rollin' rocks down on the shack and the professor was whittlin' himself a blowgun. When he poked a hole in the air filter and began pourin' in some stinkin' stuff as bait for the midges, I figured I might as well lend 'em a hand."

The girl was staring in bewilderment at the mud-covered figure bending over he. "It's Tomkins, Miss Bradshaw," it said apologetically. "Professor Tomkins, from the university. I was with you when—when it happened. Remember?"

That silvery laugh made Davis wince. He distrusted it. "If father could see you now!"

The professor undoubtedly blushed under the mud. "They took our clothes, you know," he told her owlishly. "All of them. But for Captain Davis and Mr. Mulligan we might not be here."

"Not *the* Captain Davis?" She was being acid-sweet. "I've heard so much about you, Captain. I hardly exepcted to meet you so—informally, shall we say?"

Someone had brought in a blanket. Davis draped it around him like a toga and drew himself up with what dignity a badly swollen face left him. She didn't look much better herself, he reflected with satisfaction.

"Bring them in here," he commanded. "All of 'em. We're going to have a showdown!"

They lined up across the end of the little room. Hanlan and his men were swollen and sullen, Gibbon looked sheepish, and the professor and the two boys had dried a little and were beginning to peel. They looked thoroughly embarrassed in spite of the clothes they had managed to find. Only Mulligan and the girl seemed calm.

The old man ambled in after the others, black gobs of mud still dripping from his broad body. "Too bad you got bit, Cap," he said solicitously. "It looked like the best way to smoke 'em out, when the rocks wouldn't fetch 'em." He giggled. "Last time I remember rollin' rocks on anyone was clean back when I was just a cub. The Horse-Eaters was tryin' to take over our caves an' we stood 'em off until our food give out. That was when I got hit on the head. They was a doctor once claimed that might be why I'm so old. I heal quick, like a lizard when you pull his tail off. I dunno how many sets of teeth I had. They just keep on pushin' out an' comin' in again."

"The blowguns were the professor's idea," Gibbon volunteered. "They found some kind of big red snail with poison in it that keeps a man paralyzed for two-three days. Mulligan knew about it. Then the two of 'em kept the door covered while the boys rolled rocks."

Tomkins blushed under his mud. His face, with a disreputable stubble bristling on the chin, was almost clean. "As an anthropologist I have had the opportunity to observe primitive man and study his methods of assault and defense," he explained pedantically.

"Just a moment!" The girl's voice was very quiet but it held a sting. "As representative of the Venus government I happen to be in authority here. These gentlemen will bear me out. And I intend to find out before we leave this room who is really behind the land-grab to which Mr. Hanlan is so naively hitching his wagon. When Mr. Mulligan—interfered—I had made an offer. It is still good."

Davis stared at her aghast. "You'll let that crawling worm get away with this?" he demanded.

She eyed him calmly. "That was my offer," she said. "The government has enough information about Mr. Hanlan to make a very good executive out of him if he chooses to turn his talents and his money to such a worthy project as colonization of the West Continent. I'm sure he will cooperate. If he agrees we will forget about what may have happened in the past few days—all of us. That is an order too. You understand orders, of course, Captain Davis."

A grin spread over Mulligan's long face, cracking its crust of mud. "I got a few scars here some place 'at Slip Hanlan give me onetime," he observed hopefully. "That was quite a while back, when he was just a punk. I'd be willin' to persuade him for you, ma'am."

"Forget it!" Hanlan's swollen face was dark. "It'll be a pleasure to see the slob get it in the neck. Cookson is the one who's behind it. I put up the scrip and he put it through the Council—for half the profits. Only half wasn't enough. If I didn't cut him a bigger piece he was going to let the Regent know about me and get the whole deal turned over to his Department of Immigration, to be handled at government expense until the Council could be sure everything was over the table. That's why I grabbed you—so the Regent would think twice about listening to what he might have to say. You gimme a chance and there won't be any more Slip Hanlan. You have Slip Hanlan's say-so for that!"

Stuffed into pants that were too small for him, Davis sat gloomily in the stern of the Coast Patrol launch that had come at Anne Bradshaw's signal to pick them up. Dimly, through his gloom, he heard Old Man Mulligan's hoarse voice making highly mythical replies to Professor Tomkins' persistent questions. Maybe he was a Neanderthal hangover who had lived out the whole span of human history. Maybe he was Moses' father-in-law and Abraham's bodyguard and Julius Caesar's blacksmith. Maybe he had won the American War and the battle of the Drylands. What difference did it make?

What it boiled down to was that the Space Patrol had been given a going-over by a cocky girl and a doddering old man. It had lost its pants, not to mention its shirt, and it was being ferried back to Laxa by those damned mud-bound landsmen of the Coast Patrol to be the laughing stock of every needle-headed nincompoop in the system!

He'd show 'em yet what the Patrol was! If any living being so much as breathed a word of what had happened he'd blow their pretty little deal wide open! He'd give Slip Hanlan a going-over that would last him as long as he could remember. He'd make old Bradshaw bow and scrape and back water like a crab. He'd get Old Man Mulligan roaring drunk and put him in the Patrol where he'd learn what discipline was like, if he had to drink the old liar silly himself to do it. And as for that girl!

He colored at the flashing smile she threw him. Maybe she could read minds. He hoped so!

He sucked in a long breath of fishy, clammy fog. He'd be glad to smell the tang of canned air again. He'd be glad to get off this hog-wallow of a world and feel peace under him again. He'd be glad to see the stars. Damn glad!

But before he went he'd give that blonde hell-cat something to worry about!

- [ ] **THE 1979 ANNUAL WORLD'S BEST SF.** The latest "World's Best" with David Lake, C. J. Cherryh, Ursula K. Le Guin, and more. (#UE1459—$2.25)

- [ ] **THE 1978 ANNUAL WORLD'S BEST SF.** Leading off with Varley, Haldeman, Bryant, Ellison, Bishop, etc. (#UJ1376—$1.95)

- [ ] **THE 1977 ANNUAL WORLD'S BEST SF.** Featuring Asimov, Tiptree, Aldiss, Coney, and a galaxy of great ones. An SFBC Selection. (#UE1297—$1.75)

- [ ] **THE 1976 ANNUAL WORLD'S BEST SF.** A winner with Fritz Leiber, Brunner, Cowper, Vinge, and more. An SFBC Selection. (#UW1232—$1.50)

- [ ] **THE 1975 ANNUAL WORLD'S BEST SF.** The authentic "World's Best" featuring Bester, Dickson, Martin, Asimov, etc. (#UW1170—$1.50)

- [ ] **THE DAW SCIENCE FICTION READER.** The unique anthology with a full novel by Andre Norton and tales by Akers, Dickson, Bradley, Stableford, and Tanith Lee. (#UW1242—$1.50)

- [ ] **THE BEST FROM THE REST OF THE WORLD.** Great stories by the master of sf writers of Western Europe. (#UE1343—$1.75)

- [ ] **THE YEAR'S BEST FANTASY STORIES: 3.** Edited by Lin Carter, the 1977 volume includes C. J. Cherryh, Karl Edward Wagner, G.R.R. Martin, etc. (#UW1338—$1.50)

If you wish to order these titles,

please see the coupon in

the back of this book.

If you *really* want to read the best . . .

- ☐ **WYST: ALASTOR 1716** by Jack Vance. What was going wrong in this self-advertised Utopian metropolis? A new novel by a Hugo-winning author. (#UJ1413—$1.95)
- ☐ **Z-STING** by Ian Wallace. After a hundred years, the peace system began to promote war! And they had to cross the Solar System to get at the answer. (#UJ1408—$1.95)
- ☐ **PURSUIT OF THE SCREAMER** by Ansen Dibell. When the Deathless One awakes, the alarm goes out across a frightened world. (#UJ1386—$1.95)
- ☐ **CAMELOT IN ORBIT** by Arthur H. Landis. Magic and superscience do not mix, except near Betelguise—and the cause of this has to be solved. (#UE1417—$1.75)
- ☐ **EARTH FACTOR X** by A. E. van Vogt. The invaders knew all about Earth—except for the little matter of half the human race. (#UW1412—$1.50)
- ☐ **TOTAL ECLIPSE** by John Brunner. Sigma Draconis—was it a warning of things to come for Sol III? (#UW1398—$1.50)
- ☐ **THE SURVIVORS** by M. Z. Bradley and P. Zimmer. The companions of the Red Moon brave the terrors of a world invaded by phantom monsters. (#UJ1435—$1.95)
- ☐ **KIOGA OF THE UNKNOWN LAND** by William L. Chester. The epic novel of an American "Tarzan" in a lost land of the farthest north. (#UJ1378—$1.95)

DAW BOOKS are represented by the publishers of Signet and Mentor Books, **THE NEW AMERICAN LIBRARY, INC.**

THE NEW AMERICAN LIBRARY, INC.,
P.O. Box 999, Bergenfield, New Jersey 07621

Please send me the DAW BOOKS I have checked above. I am enclosing
$_____ (check or money order—no currency or C.O.D.'s).
Please include the list price plus 35¢ a copy to cover mailing costs.

Name _____

Address _____

City _____ State _____ Zip Code _____
Please allow at least 4 weeks for delivery